River Rats and Salty Dogs

A Novel by Leon Reed Bloodworth

Published by:
Leon R. Bloodworth
PO Box 760
Apalachicola, FL 32329

All rights reserved. No part of this publication may be reproduced, stored in a retrieval system, or transmitted in any form or by any means, electronic, mechanical, photocopying, recording, scanning or otherwise, without the prior written permission of the Publisher. For permission or further information contact Leon R. Bloodworth, PO Box 760, Apalachicola, FL 32329.

This is a work of fiction. Names, characters, places and events that occur either are the products of the author's imagination or are used fictitiously. Any resemblance to actual persons, places, or events is purely coincidental, with the exception of the character of James Bloodworth, who is based on the author's father of that name, who played professional baseball from 1935 to 1951.

The Hunting and Fishing Map was originally published in the 1930's and is part of the author's personal memorabilia. The original publisher is unknown.
The photograph of Chapman School is from a postcard and is part of the author's personal memorabilia. The original publisher is unknown.
All other photographs are the personal property of the author.

ISBN-13: 978-0-578-72931-2

Copyright © 2020 by Leon R. Bloodworth
Front Cover Design: Leon R. Bloodworth
Illustrations: Leon R. Bloodworth

Printed in the United States of America
First Edition
July 2020

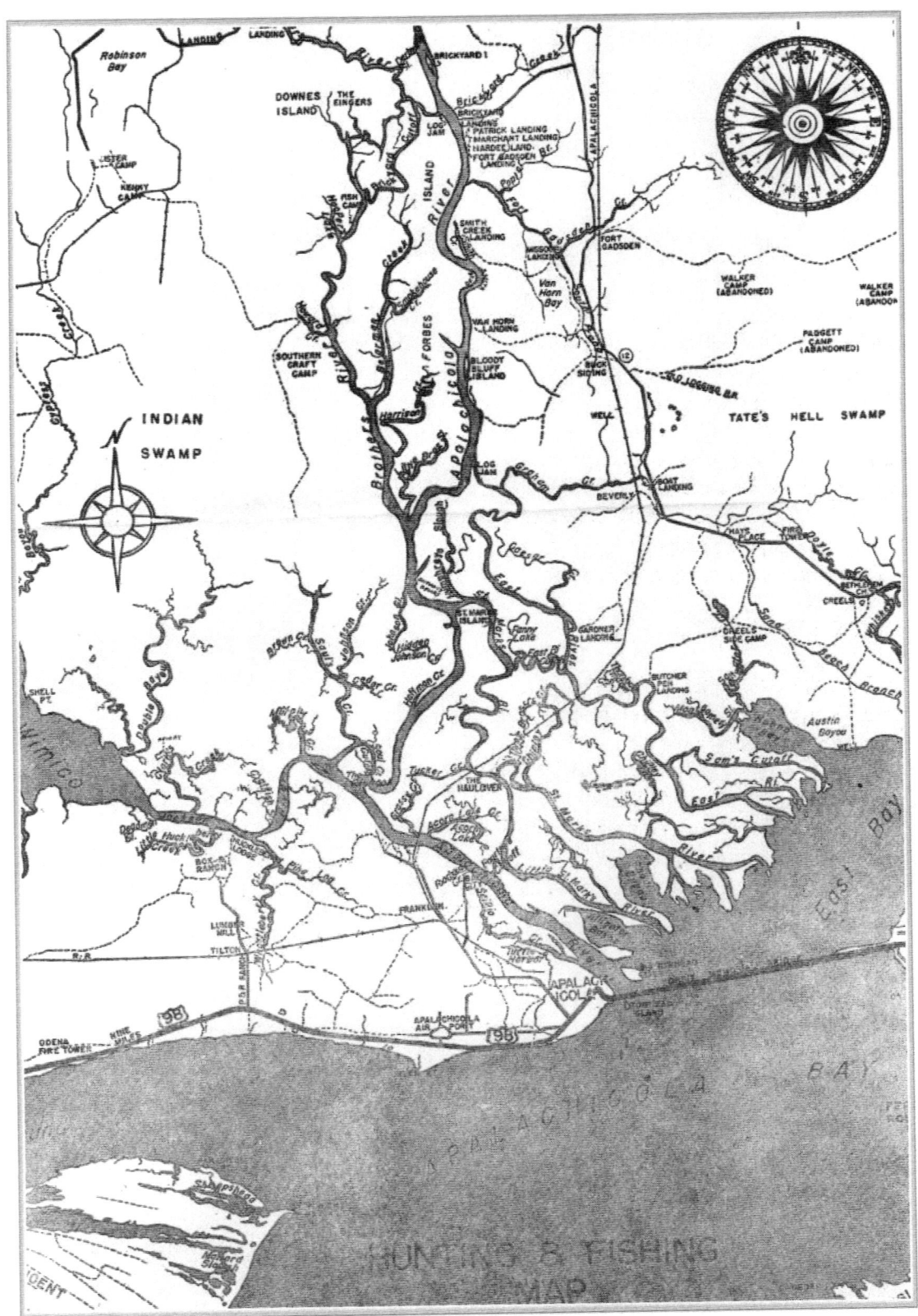

Table of Contents

1. Sh*t Happens — page 5
2. Salty Dog — page 13
3. River Rat — page 35
4. Owl Creek — page 48
5. Summer Baseball — page 57
6. The Invisible Sands — page 73
7. It's an Inside Game — page 87
8. Little Pearls of Desire — page 98
9. Chapman High — page 111
10. Harvest Time — page 134
11. Festival — page 144
12. Columbus — page 153
13. The Report — page 165
14. The Knowing — page 172
15. The Best Christmas Ever — page 185
16. Celebration — page 193
17. Remarkable Coincidences — page 200
18. The Glue — page 207
19. Ashwanna — page 214
20. The Big Leaguer — page 224
21. Yellow Bird — page 213
22. The Ties that Bind Us — page 238
23. Epilogue — page 242

Chapter 1: Sh*t Happens

Oh my God, I've killed him.

I looked down at Shuler's body, laid out on the ground, his face white, completely drained of blood. It didn't look like he was breathing. I know I liked to win, but what had I just done?

Mom and Dad were there in the stands, behind the first base dugout, with a few hundred other parents and high school students. It was the last Friday in May, 1958, and we were playing against Port St. Joe High for the conference championship. They were wearing their white uniforms with the purple pinstripes, and even though the game was being played in Apalachicola, they drew the call to be home team. We were wearing our grey pinstripes with blue caps, and we had the crowd with us.

It was the bottom of the ninth, one out, we were up 3 to 2. They had men on first and second and their cleanup hitter was at the plate. Coach called a time out and we gathered at the pitcher's mound. Rod Morris was our senior pitcher, a strong right hander, and this would be his last game. He could throw some heat, but that's all he had.

"All right guys," Coach began, "make sure we get the lead runner, but play for a double play. Drugar, you've got the bag" nodding at me. He looked at Morris, "Drugar's got the bag." Billy Smith was our junior third baseman; Coach turned his attention to him. "Smitty, play back, don't crowd the grass. Remember, we've got to get the lead runner." Bud Carlson was our first baseman, a tall, lanky kid with clumsy movements and an awkward throwing motion, but he always made plays. "Carlson!" Coach barked, "Act like you're holding that runner on, but get off that bag when Morris goes into the pitch, and if you have a play, get the lead runner." Coach turned his attention to Bob Riley, short stop, "Riley, you and Drugar get it together! Just a routine double play and we'll send the crying towel to Port St. Joe." Coach, looked at each one of us, sweat was running down his temples, his cap was cocked to his right side, but there was a little smile on his lips like he was watching a movie, seeing the future, and playing a role at the same time. His chewing tobacco was stuffed into his right jaw, brown tobacco stains showed at the corners of his mouth. He had taken the ball from Morris when he got to the mound, and now he rubbed it over and over again in his hands. He turned to the catcher, Rob Gant, put the ball into Rob's mitt and hollered "Let's do this!" and jogged off the field.

We took our positions and the umpire called "Play ball!" I moved in toward the infield, closer to the bag. You have to cheat a little to quicken up the double play. I glanced at the runner on first base, Joe Shuler, a junior and a good athlete. We had played against each other since junior high. Shuler was a good three inches taller than me, and I expected him to play college ball one day. He was also fast, so any double play had to be quick.

The crowd came to their feet as Morris went into his stretch, the cheers and rumbles got louder; Morris fired a high fast ball for a ball. The crowd got louder still, Morris back into the stretch, a low fast ball for a strike. Riley kept jockeying back and forth behind the runner at second, motioning to me and yelling "Take two!" I joined the cry, "Come on Morris, let's take this goon, give us a play." Morris was back in his stretch, inside fast ball, ball two.

The crowd started chanting, "Blue! Blue! Blue! Blue!" just like they do at football games, especially when we wear the all blue uniforms, instead of the blue and gold. Morris into the stretch, fast ball down the middle, the crack of the bat; Riley broke to his left as the ball exploded off the bat, to the left side of the pitcher's mound. As he reached for the ball I was already at the bag. I planted my left foot and drug my right foot along the bag toward first as he flipped the ball into my outstretched glove. Weight shifted back to my right foot as I made the shuffle, planting my footing and cut it loose as hard as I could throw to first base.

With the double play there's one rule: never throw around a runner. You throw to first base, you throw through the runner, never, ever, around him. As the ball left my hand, the runner, Shuler, was in full stride toward second; his head was coming up sprinter style as if breaking from the blocks. My focus fixed on the ball, it was headed directly toward Shuler's face. For a brief moment, a partial second in time, our minds were tied together with the speeding white light of a baseball thrown at over 70 miles an hour. I was sure I'd killed him, and he was sure he was dead. Luckily, Shuler's mind must have screamed "Oh shit, duck!" because his legs collapsed, his head flew backward, and the baseball barely nicked the bill of his cap, knocking it from his head, and then there was the sweet sound of slapping leather as the baseball hit the first baseman's mitt. GAME OVER!

Carlson hollered, jumped up and down off first base like a jack in the box, and galloped toward the pitcher's mound. My teammates burst from the dugout, yelling at the top of their lungs and ran toward the pitcher's mound. Fans rushed onto the field, slapping hands, high fives, and hugged every player available. I glanced over at Shuler, he was just sitting up. His face was as white as his uniform. He looked at me, I looked at him, and he knew. I knew. I turned and ran toward the mass of players piling on each other at the pitcher's mound.

After Coach finally calmed us down we had to line up and march toward the St. Joe players' line for the obligatory hand shake. As we slapped gloves and said "Good game." I came face to face with Shuler. "I'll get my shot at you this summer, Drugar." It's good to be cocky, so I replied,

"Be careful Shuler, I might get another shot at you, and next time you might not be so lucky." The ride home from the field with my folks was great; we were in our new, pale blue '58 Chevy. By the end of the summer I would have my driver's license. Excitement boiled through my veins. Summer lay out in front of me, calling me for the adventure.

Mom made our usual Friday night dinner, hamburgers and fries. Dad always said that the hamburger was the perfect meal: meat, bread, and salad all in a single serving. Mom asked if I was going out this evening. "Just to the Canteen. Most of the team will be there."

Dad jumped into the conversation, "You boys looked really good out there today, and that final double play made the game. Has Coach scheduled the summer baseball games yet?"

"I think summer practice will begin the second week of June, games start the next week. Coach said that we are going to try to play at least two to four games a week through July or early August."

"That's great" he replied. "It will keep all of you boys in shape for fall football. Also, I think Coach has some money to hire a couple of guys for the summer maintenance program. Ask around and see who might be interested."

I finished my meal, went to change and then told Mom I'd be home by eleven. Heading to the Canteen I walked toward the bay to Bay Avenue only a couple of blocks from our house at the corner of 12th and Ave C. The sun was already setting, a mild breeze was blowing off the bay out of the south. I could smell the scent of jasmine, blooming on the fence across the street. St. George Island lay to the South across the bay, a purple- gray ribbon separating the bay from the Gulf.

The Canteen is the City run recreation spot for the teenagers and the building also serves as a community center. It's right across the street from the boat basin and docks. We call the boat basin the 10 foot hole simply because when it was constructed it was dug out to 10 feet deep. The Canteen is only about 8 blocks from our house on 12th street. Along Bay Avenue there are several grand old houses that date back to the turn of the century. Most are large two story homes, with porches, gables, and upstairs balconies that look out over the bay with nothing to obstruct the view. The breeze off the bay was cool as the summer heat not yet arrived and I was feeling good. We had won our conference in football the previous fall, and now we were conference champs in baseball as well. We only had three more days of school, I would be able to drive by fall and my upcoming junior year was already promising. Hopefully, Jill would be at the Canteen tonight. Jill is a year older than me, but the guys in her class are the ones I've played ball with since elementary school. Jill is really cute, with dark hair and big green eyes. She's been a cheerleader since junior high. I'm hoping we will start dating as soon as I can drive. Excitement had me picking up my steps. There was lots to do.

Within a couple of blocks of the Canteen, out on the street between the Canteen and 10 foot hole, three guys were standing in the middle of the street. I could see it was Bud Carlson, Bob Riley, and Billy Fields. Bud is easy to pick out, he's six feet one, about 210 pounds with a big frame. Bob and I are almost identical in size, we're both pushing five ten, around 170 pounds. Bob has light, sandy brown hair and a fair complexion. My complexion tends to be darker because I tan easily and I'm outside a lot. My hair is dark. Most of the girls in our class think Bob is the most handsome guy in school. Now Billy is in a class of his own. He's pushing six feet tall, and plays basketball. He jumps and shoots well, but he has narrow shoulders, long legs and curly red hair that leans toward orange. He has enough freckles to notice. Now most of the guys wear jeans and either a plain pull-over shirt or a plain button up shirt. Not Billy! He wears jeans, but his shirts are loud, loud, loud. His selection of colors are bright yellow, bright orange, bright red, or like today, bright lime green. Seeing him in the middle of the road made me think of the channel buoys down the bay. As soon as they saw me the chant began: "Droo". "Gar". Bob repeated "Droo", and Bud repeated "Gar" over and over and over again. This was their usual chant at me anytime I was approaching, leaving, or if called upon to do anything. Then, of course, came the laughter. Billy laughed at anything. He was probably the funniest guy I've ever known. His sense of humor is crazy, he laughs at anything and anybody, and at almost any time. Teachers don't appreciate him very much.

We stood in the street for probably 30 minutes joking and laughing until Bob saw Gooch headed our way down Bay Avenue. Now Gooch is a year younger than us but always seems to be around when we do anything. He's only about 5 foot 4, but weighs around 170 pounds. He must be 40 inches in the waist. His Mom has to alter his pants by cutting off the legs, and when hemmed, there's usually no taper to the pant legs, they're just wide, straight legged pants. Billy calls them Gooch's old man pants. He was wearing them today. He's always either eating something or saying he's hungry. Today he was carrying a brown paper bag and was continually sticking his hands into the bag and then stuffing something in his mouth. He approached with cheeks bulging. "What you eating Gooch?" from Bob.

"Plums"

"What kind of plums?"

"Yellow ones."

"Let me see!"

"You can have some."

"Those are Japanese plums" said Bob. "Where did you get'em?"

"From that tree next to the alley behind Dr. Blackwell's house. The tree is full of 'em."

"Well hell, let's go get some!!" someone said, and the next thing I knew we were all running back up Bay Ave in the direction I had just come from. I don't know why we were running, but after about a block Gooch stopped running, and started picking up the plums that were falling from his bag. So, we all stopped but let Gooch do the picking up. "Does Dr. Blackwell know you were getting those plums?" I asked.

"Nope, but he's said I could have some before."

"Do you think we should ask him before we take some?" I asked, looking at Gooch, but hoping the others would respond. Gooch just shrugged his shoulders.

Dr. Blackwell's house is across the street from Lafayette Park just past 13th street on the north side of Ave. B. We still had some daylight left when we got to the plum tree and started climbing and picking plums. Gooch stayed on the ground. The tree was large for a plum tree but four guys was a bit much. Within a few seconds it dawned on us that we didn't have anything to put the plums in so we started dropping the plums to Gooch. Bob was further up the tree than me, and I told him I didn't think plum trees were particularly strong and we shouldn't try to get up high. By the time I finished my sentence Bob's limb began to crack, and slowly bent toward the ground. It was all slow motion, at first Bob's legs dangling in front of me, then his flailing arms passing me. He was grasping at limbs too small to support him, looking to me for help, and as he passed me he reached toward me with his outstretched hand. My free hand held plums, the other the tree, so I handed him my plums. "Shiiiiittttttt" is all I heard as he crashed to the ground.

Gooch was already laughing before Bob hit the ground. He was laughing so hard and had a mouth full of plums which immediately spewed from his mouth all over Bob. We were all laughing and hollering so loud that Dr. Blackwell must have heard us because someone from his house yelled out to us, "Who's out there? What are you doing?"

We took off running away from Avenue B up the alley toward Avenue C, and then on to Avenue D. By the time we stopped running we could hardly breathe; we were spitting plums and laughing so hard at Bob that our sides hurt. Billy had tears running down his cheeks. He continued to laugh and was trying to talk but his laughter kept him sounding like coughing which made him laugh even more.

After a bit we finally stopped laughing at each other and headed back toward downtown but on Avenue D; at Tenth Street we turned back toward the bay and went to Bay Ave. It was getting dark and I thought we would go on to the Canteen, but at Bay Avenue Gooch starts stammering. "I've gotta take a dump!" Billy started laughing again.

"Come on Gooch, you can use the bathroom at the Canteen," Bob offered.

"It can't wait" Gooch hollered and he darted across the street to the bay side. Trousers dropped, awful sounds and Billy's laughter got louder! "I need some paper" cried Gooch. Pockets checked, no paper.

"Gooch" I offered, "I don't have any paper but I do have a handkerchief."

"Anything" Gooch pleaded. We stood there, not too close, giggling at Gooch. I really wanted to get on to the Canteen in case Jill got there early.

"Hey Guys," Billy started, "y'all wanna have some fun?"

"Like what?" from Bud.

"I heard about this joke, where you light a bag full of shit on somebody's door step and then holler fire! When they come out to stomp the fire out, they get shit all over their legs." We all looked at Billy, then at each other. Gooch, glad to have the attention off himself, joined in,

"That sounds great, let's do it!" Bud said that it sounded like fun but where do we get the bag, the shit, and whose house gets the honor? We turned around to face the houses along Bay Avenue. Billy suggested the big one on the corner. I told them it was Judge Olsen's house and I suggested that he might not think it was a funny joke. But Billy persisted,

"Come on, we can do this! Anyway, that Judge took my cousin's driver's license away."

"Which cousin?" asked Bud.

"Doesn't matter." Billy shrugged.

"Where can we get the bag? And the shit?" Bob asked. Gooch lived on 7th street, so he said he could get the bag. He also offered the shit, but Billy, being the expert, decided we needed more. There was a family that lived on 5th street that kept a horse on their adjoining lot. Twenty minutes later found us back on Bay Avenue across the street from Judge Olsen's house. Billy had taken charge, he held the bag with a sizeable sample of horse shit, and of course he wanted to pick up Gooch's mess. He managed that with a palm frond.

Judge Olsen's house was one of the stately houses on Bay Avenue. It was two stories, painted white, and had a large portico extending out toward Bay Avenue which served as a screened porch and the entrance to the house. The house was built on piers about three feet off the ground. Four steps reached from the brick walkway to the door of the portico.

We slipped into the yard, trying our best to keep Billy from laughing. The yard was well landscaped, with large trees, shrubs, and a large weeping willow tree near the end of the brick walkway. The lights were on in the Judge's house and we could see movement through the windows on the first floor room that was adjacent to the portico. Bud and Billy led the way, crouching stealthily, carrying the bag which was becoming very soggy. Bob and I followed, but Gooch stayed back on the side of the road. Bob and I crawled the last several feet to the house and crouched below the window. Bud and Billy put the bag on the second step of the entrance. Billy was about to bust a gut to keep from laughing. Bob and I eased up to the lower edge of the window and peaked inside.

The Judge was sitting in a large, very comfortable looking chair, book in hand, and reading by the light of a standing floor lamp. He wore what appeared to be pajamas with a light weight robe. The pajamas and the robe were light blue. Bob called them baby blue. A wine glass half full of red liquid sat on an end table next to the chair. Billy was vibrating, trying to keep from exploding with laughter. Bud's hand held a pack of matches; he was visibly shaking. Bob reached over and grabbed my shoulder so hard I nearly yelled.

We watched Bud strike a match and light the bag, and before we could stand to run Billy was banging on the side of the house and yelling fire, fire, fire!! We took off running. Bud was in front of Billy and I was following Bob. Billy took a dive under the weeping willow tree and spun around to watch the Judge put out the fire. Bud was already in the street with Gooch. As Bob and I passed the weeping willow tree I called for Billy to come on, but he didn't move. I dove in after him like I was saving someone from drowning. Billy was pointing and laughing so hard no sounds were coming from his mouth. He started gagging, trying to breath, but he was in such a state of excitement he couldn't move. He just kept pointing toward the house. I looked, and oh my, the Judge was on the steps hollering for his wife to call the firemen, the police, and bring water. He was stamping out the fire with his bedroom slippers, and each time he stomped his foot brown speckles splashed up on his baby blue pajamas.

Billy had lost his breath, he gagged and pointed, and try as he did, nothing would come out of his mouth. His mouth was opened, tears were running down his cheeks, and with one hand he kept grabbing his side. I kept telling him we had to run. We have to go! We have to run! And then, the big hand of the law grabbed the back of my shirt and drug me out from under the weeping willow tree. I never even heard a car, never saw any lights, just Billy convulsing, tears running down his cheeks, and pointing at the Judge with the baby blue pajamas with brown specks up above his knees.

Billy and I were sitting in a cell while the deputy sheriff called our folks. The cell was all concrete, walls and floor, the off-gray colored paint was peeling from the walls and ceiling, and the only thing to sit on was a single iron bed with an uncovered mattress. The other three guys evidently had gotten away. Billy and I just sat there, not saying anything, but before our parents arrived the police brought in the other guys. They had gone to the Canteen; it took less than a couple of minutes for some of the girls to rat out the guys when the police arrived. I knew we were in trouble, and the look on the other three guy's faces convinced me they knew as well. Billy couldn't stop laughing. He even laughed at the grass stains, the dirt, and the splattered drool on the front of his lime green shirt. "Damn it Billy!" Bud started. "Look what you got us into. I ought to bust your butt!"

Billy looked stunned, started to apologize, but when he opened his mouth, nothing but laughter exploded. "Did you see his pants? Every time he stomped!" He sat down on the floor, tears running down his cheeks, and he made this statement, "Even if they send me to jail, that's the funniest damn thing I have ever seen in my life." And then our parents walked in!

It stopped being funny when we saw the look on our parent's faces. The judge showed up shortly after our parents arrived. He had changed clothes, no brown specks on his new pants. The Chief of Police said we could spend the night in jail, but with pleas from our parents, the judge said we could go home, but that we all had to be in his office Monday morning at 9:00, parents included. My parents didn't say a word to me on the way home. When we walked into the house my Dad said I should go to my room and not come out unless I had to use the bathroom. Later that night I started into the kitchen to get a snack, but Mom met me at the kitchen door and sent me back to my room. I told her I only wanted a snack. She suggested I think about it for a while. I spent all day in my room on Saturday; Mom brought me a bowl of cereal for breakfast, a sandwich for lunch, and a plate of something for dinner. There was no conversation. The expression on Mom's face hurt me just to see it, tears were in her eyes, her normal bright smile was gone, and stress lines shown around her eyes and the corners of her mouth. It was obvious she had been crying. By nightfall on Saturday I figured out that I was in serious trouble.

Now I'm not a bad kid. I don't cuss much, I play football and baseball, I make decent grades, and I usually have a summer job to make spending money. I help out around the house, I mow the grass, rake the yard, and I go to church with my folks every Sunday. The teachers don't complain about me; I guess that's because my Dad's the Principal. Maybe most of the teachers expect more from me because he is the Principal. But Bud, Bob, Billy and even Gooch could say the same things. We were just having fun. We weren't going to burn down a house or hurt anyone. Just play a joke. I had never been to a jail before. I don't think I want to go back to another one. School will be over in 3 days. I'll get a summer job, play baseball all summer, and be in good shape and ready for fall football. Certainly everyone will see it was just a joke.

Sunday morning around 8:00 AM I started to the bathroom. I didn't know if Mom or Dad were up so I was being quiet. As I eased out of my room I could hear them talking in their bedroom. It was past the bathroom I used. Their bathroom adjoined their bedroom. As I approached the bathroom I could make out what they were saying. Mom was asking what Dad thought the Judge would do. Dad said he didn't know but the Judge told the truant officer to be there. Mom sounded confused, she said, "But Matt hasn't missed any school. Why would the truant officer be needed?" After a long silence Dad said that the truant officer was also the one that recommend kids for reform school. "Reform School?" Mom questioned, her voice rising. Dad said he didn't know but he would talk with the other fathers. By the time I got back to my room my mind was visioning Reform School, the only kid I'd ever known that actually went to Reform School was a guy that was crazy as hell. He got caught when he stole a car and ran it into someone's house. He had dropped out of school a couple of times and always stayed in trouble. Certainly they, or the truant officer, didn't compare me and my friends to him? We didn't steal anything, or hurt anyone, it was just a joke! Sunday was a long day!

Monday morning Dad woke me at 6:30; he told me to dress like I was going to church. "Wear a white shirt and tie; a coat won't be needed. But clean up good." He left for work at 7:15 and told Mom he would be back to pick us up at 8:30. Mom was a nervous wreck; she kept talking to herself, repeating things I could not understand. She changes clothes three times. At 8:30 Dad walked into the house. Mom and I were sitting at the breakfast room table. All Dad said was "Let's go."

The Court House is located at the foot of the bridge downtown. To get to the Judge's chamber we had to go to the second floor. Besides the Clerk of Court office, the Tax Collector's office, the Court Room is also on the second floor. The Judge's Chamber is in the back, behind the Court Room. Bob and Bud, with their folks, showed up about the same time we did, we all walked up to the second floor together. No one spoke. We gathered in the Court Room to wait for the other folks. Within a couple of minutes, Billy and his family walked in, as did Gooch and his family. Coach Waller walked in within a minute. Mr. Tom McLeod, a local attorney, who is a good friend of my Dad's walked in behind Coach. Mr. McLeod knocked on the Judge's Chamber, was told to come in and he disappeared behind the dark wooden door. We all sat there for several minutes. No one spoke. After what seemed forever Mr. McLeod came out and said that we would be meeting with the Judge in the court room because his office wasn't big enough for all of us. There was a long table between the seats where we were sitting and the podium where the Judge normally sat. It was at that table that the Judge sat when he came into the room. The Truant Officer came in with the Judge and sat at the table with him. Mr. McLeod sat at the end of the long table.

The Judge took a long look at all of us, but especially the four hooligans! There wasn't a single sound to be heard in that court room. He began, "It bothers me that we are here today to address some actions from these four boys that I would have never believed they would have committed. You come from good families, you are active in school and I'm told you make good grades and play sports. To commit a crime of arson is beyond understanding. Your actions could have caused me and my wife to lose our home, maybe our lives. How can kids from such good families do such a dreadful thing? Now, I have some recommendations from our Truant Officer, but before I make any decision I want to hear from you boys. Who wants to go first? How about you Mr. Drugar?"

My tongue swelled up in my mouth and I could hardly speak. I expected I might pass out. Finally I stood, swallowed hard, and said, "Sir, we thought it was just a joke. We would never have done anything that would hurt you or your wife. We are very sorry." And I sat down. The Judge looked at Bud Carlson,

"How about you Mr. Carlson?" Bud stood up, cleared his throat, shifted his weight from one leg to the other, and finally said,
"Sir, it's just like what Matt said. We never thought we'd hurt anyone. I'm very sorry too."

The Judge was getting antsy; it didn't appear we were making a very good impression. He turned his attention to Billy, "Mr. Fields, would you like to speak?" As Billy stood up to speak, a few of the clerks from the Clerk of the Court's office slipped in the back of the Court Room. They stood near the door, were quiet. There were three of them, all female.
Billy began, "Sir, someone told me about the joke and it was my idea to play a joke on someone. It sounded like a lot of fun. We didn't mean any harm, and the reason we picked your house is because you were close to where we were talking and we could see that you were home."

The Judge interrupted, "So, you thought starting a fire on my steps would be a joke?"

"No sir!" exclaimed Billy. "We weren't starting a fire, we were just lighting up some sh- I mean crap! You did just what the joke was supposed to be about. When you started stomping that bag, and the sh—crap started flying" and then Billy started laughing, his eyes started watering, and he lost his breath.

One of the women in the back spoke up and said, "Oh, come on Stinky, a little shit on the shoe won't hurt you!" and then they ran from the Court Room and you could hear them laughing all the way back to the Clerk's Office.

When Billy started laughing, I couldn't help it. That picture in my mind of the Judge stomping that bag of shit, and his baby blue pajamas turning brown was more than I could take. Tears started running down my face, I bit my lip trying not to laugh. Bud and Bob both started giggling, and Gooch actually slid down to the floor. The Judge turned so red he was almost purple. He got up and started to say something, changed his mind and walked out of the Court Room back to his Chamber. The Truant Office followed him. Immediately my Dad, Coach, Mr. McLeod, and Bud's and Bob's dads got up and headed to the Judge's Chamber. I think Coach probably considered it a 25 yard dash!

After some serious pinching from our mothers, we all calmed down and stopped laughing. Sitting there I began to take notice. Bud's dad was the local bank's president; Bob's dad owned a title company, and Gooch's dad owned the A&P store. I didn't know what Billy's dad did. But I knew that my dad was the principal of the high school and I was in trouble. Before the men came out of the Judge's Chamber I got to thinking, if we, the hooligans, are kicked out of school then the sports program was going to suffer some. I was the quarterback on the football team, Bud was tight end, both defense and offense, and Bob was our best running back. Billy didn't play football but he did play basketball and started. Gooch wasn't playing yet, but everyone knew that within a year or two he would be a starting lineman. As for baseball, Bud, Bob, and I had been playing infield together since we were in elementary school. There weren't enough guys that could play to make up a team without us. It appeared to me that the Judge's decision was going to affect more than just us four hooligans.

Dad came out of the Judge's Chamber first, he didn't hesitate, he just pointed to me and Mom to come and we left the Court Room in a hurry. Later I would learn that Bud and Bob's family did the same. Billy and his folks took off when they saw us leave, as did Gooch and his family. No words were said before we got home. Dad told me to go to my room and stay there until he was ready to talk to me. Mom fed me later in the day, but no one said anything. But, I figured I had two more days of school and things would get back to normal after we finished school.

The next morning, Tuesday, I woke early and started to the bathroom when I heard Mom and Dad talking in the dining room. Our house is a ranch style home, when you walk in through the front door there's a small entry area, if you take a left you go into the kitchen and breakfast area; if you go straight you enter the living room, the dining room is on the far left side of the living room. If you take a right at the entrance you go down a short hall to two bedrooms on the right, the bathroom almost dead ahead. Mom and Dad's bedroom and bath are to the left. But hearing them I silently eased down the hall toward the living room to where I could hear them. Mom was saying "But James, you can't send him off with those two."

Dad replied, "Now Maurice, you know that I'm here today because of those two. They kept me straight and gave me an opportunity."

"I know," Mom said, "but they are just, they're just, a couple ole river rats and salty dogs."

Dad chuckled, "I can't argue with you there, but Matt needs to get out of town for a while. It will be good for him. I'll tell him to get ready." I slipped off to the bathroom. When I came out and headed to my room Dad came in and told me to pack some clothes. He said I'd need a few pair of shorts, a couple of long work pants, several t-shirts and a couple of long sleeve shirts. He also said I should pack a light jacket. I would need two pair of tennis shoes, one to work in and the other I could wade in. He said a couple old friends of his needed some help and he volunteered me. Thought it might be a few weeks' worth of work. As he was leaving he said he would be back to pick me up around 10:00 AM. I walked out to talk to mom, she was sitting at the dining room table, her bible in front of her. Her head was down, I don't know if she was praying or crying but I decided not to interrupt. I went to start packing. It looked like I was going to miss the last two days of school. I never could have seen what lay ahead.

Chapter 2: Salty Dog

When Dad got back there wasn't much conversation, he just said to load up. I grabbed my duffel bag and headed to the car. Mom came outside, tears were running down her cheeks, her lips were trembling. She came over to the car and kissed me on the cheek and said to be careful. I really hadn't thought about what I was expecting, but right then it dawned on me that another jail maybe waiting on me. Dad said let's go and we drove away. We headed back to Bay Avenue and turned left toward the boat basin; at the boat basin we turned right and went around the curve, under the bridge, to Water Street which parallels the river past downtown all the way to the BP bulk plant. Within a hundred yards or so Dad pulled over to the right in front of a small fish house. I had been with him there before to buy shrimp and fish.

The owner of the fish house was Gitano Siglio, an old Italian fisherman. He looked to only be about 5 foot 6 inches tall, but he was wiry. His hair was graying, but his hand shake was strong, and he was always smiling. He was several years older than Dad but they had been friends for years. Dad said "Bring your gear and let's go." From bright sunshine we entered the fish house, it was dark in there. We stopped to let our eyes adjust. The building was no more than 30 feet wide, maybe 50 feet long. There were no lights on but the doors on the river side were opened to the docks showing part of the bridge and the marsh reeds of Big and Little Towhead Islands. Fish tables were lined up end to end in the middle of the room where workers could clean fish or work shrimp. On the left hand side of the room there was a table, three men were sitting there drinking coffee.

Mr. Siglio stood up and spoke to my dad "Paisan, it's been a while." We approached the table and the other two men stood up. My Dad shook hands with the men and then turned to me.

"Matt, this is Walter Taylor, and his brother, Elzie." We shook hands, I said hello, and they immediately turned their attention back to my Dad. Walter was the taller of the two, maybe six feet tall; he had short graying hair, thick eyebrows, and high, stark cheek bones. He was slim and had an athletic look. I had seen him before. A couple of years before Dad had taken me on a dove hunt to Little St. George Island with some other fathers and sons from my class. He had been there and Dad said he invited us on the hunt. Elzie was just the opposite; he was shorter, maybe five feet nine inches, close to my height, but he was built like a tank. He had broad shoulders, a thick chest, and short dark hair. His arms looked like he worked out on weights. His face surprised me, he was not smiling but he looked as if he were getting ready to. Watching his expression while talking to my Dad made me think he was about to tell a joke or break out laughing.

Dad told me to find a place to sit and relax a bit. The men started talking, laughing and reminiscing. I moved over, dropped my duffel and sat on it. The fish house had concrete floors, no ceiling, just the rafters that supported the tin roof. The walls were cypress boards, rough cut, and many of them were pecky cypress with holes where knots may have been. In almost all of the holes were cobwebs. The cypress had not been painted but aging had turned the wood a dark grey. On the right hand side of the room upon entering from the street side there was an enclosed room which I suspected was the freezer/cold storage room. It must have been fifteen feet wide, maybe fifteen feet deep. What lights that were in the room ran in a single line above the fish tables. On the bay side of the fishing tables, toward the end closest to the street, large metal tubes angled from the table toward the floor where shrimp boxes awaited their product. These were the processing tubes where shrimp are separated by size and count. Large shrimp maybe 16/20s, meaning 16 to 20 shrimp to the pound; much smaller shrimp maybe 31/35. I had seen the black women working in the shrimp houses, singing as they worked, heading and separating the shrimp by count. In Franklin County, and especially in Apalachicola, shrimp meant money, sometimes lots of money. I was hoping that where ever I was headed some shrimp might be joining us.

Minutes passed and I was about to doze off when Dad said "OK, it's time to go!" I got up, grabbed my duffel and started for the door. "Whoa!" Dad exclaimed. "You're headed the wrong way, son. This way to the boat!" I followed Dad and Walter to the docks on the riverside. The boat was about 21 or 22 feet long, with a wide beam, and had a small covered cabin with a covered pilot station covering the first third of the boat. The steering wheel was on the right hand side. A large open deck ran to the stern of the boat, and hanging off the stern was the largest outboard I'd ever seen. It was a 100 horsepower Evinrude. Dad was standing next to me, he put his hand on my shoulder and said, "Walter needs you to help him some. So, be good and work hard." My mind was running in circles, I didn't know where I was going or how long I was to be there.

"Dad, summer baseball practice starts next week!" I was pleading.

"They can do without you for a while," he said. "I'll see you soon." And he turned and walked away.

Walter had climbed into the boat and was starting the motor. He told me to climb aboard, so I threw my duffel into the boat and started to get in, but he stopped me and told me to get the bow line. I untied the bow line, threw the line onto the boat, and returned to the stern, untied that line and jumped aboard. We pulled away from the dock and headed toward the bridge. Walter piloted the boat under the bridge and then accelerated to bring the boat onto plane.

Sitting on the left side gunnel I watched the bridge stretch out before me; Apalachicola was growing smaller, becoming only a skyline of trees, red brick buildings, and the water tank which supplied the town. I thought I was headed off to work, but watching my town sink into the horizon made me realize that somehow my life was changing and I wasn't sure it was for the best.

I always liked being on the water, and it didn't take but a little while before I began enjoying the ride. St. George Island was growing bigger, the white sand glowing at Bob Sike's Cut. The Cut was an Army Corp of Engineers project, orchestrated by Senator Bob Sikes of NW Florida, to help the shrimp fleet of Apalachicola get to the Gulf quicker and easier. It split St. George Island into Big St. George and Little St. George. Big St. George is approximately 20 miles long; Little St. George is approximately 10 miles long. The Intracoastal Waterway comes from the west, through Lake Wimico into Jackson River to the Apalachicola River and into the bay. Within two miles of St. George, north of the Cut, it turns east and exits into the Gulf at East Pass on the eastern tip of Big St. George Island. At that turn north of the Cut, we turned west and headed to Walter Taylors house. Later that day I learned that Walter was the unofficial light house keeper for Little St. George Island. Approaching Walter's house we passed the Government Dock, a 500 foot pier build by the Corp and maintained by the State of Florida, light house division, but the Coast Guard was known to supply the batteries to power the light house. The water along there was fairly shallow so the long dock allowed the Coast Guard, with their larger boats, to dock and unload the batteries. Within several hundred yards there was a smaller dock extending out into the bay and at the shore an enclosed boat house was built.

Walter slowed the boat, trimmed the motor up for shallow water and motored up under the boat house. As we approached the boat house I remembered being here before when we came for the dove hunt. I hardly remembered anything about Walter's house. Looking at it now made me think of the sawmill houses built in the early 1920s up on the Hill in Apalachicola. The home site was set in the middle of an oak grove, maybe 12 to 14 feet above water level. Tall pine trees sprinkled to the back and sides of the oaks. The house was lapboard siding, made of cypress and had turned gray with aging, but blended with the oaks to the point of almost becoming invisible except for the tin roof. It was only a couple hundred feet from the boat house.

We unloaded, making several trips to the house, carrying not only my gear but several bags of groceries, various tools, three ice chests full of frozen stuff, and twelve 5 gallon cans of fuel (gas I presumed). The front screen porch stretching across the house facing the bay was welcoming. We entered from the west side directly into the kitchen. There was an L shaped counter top on the right housing a sink and a window looking out over the rear of the house. Cabinets were above the counter. They were made from streaked cypress and apparently sealed with a clear satin varnish, none had grayed. A refrigerator and gas stove were on the left side. A small table and 3 chairs finished the kitchen, none had ever been painted.

In the middle of the house was a large brick wall with a fireplace opened to the kitchen and the living area. As you entered the living area a single door opened to the screen porch that looked out over the bay. The living area was not large but toward the eastern side of the house there were two bedrooms. It appeared that the bedroom on the right was unused, I assumed that would be my bedroom. There was a window in the room, but not very large and I was thinking that the room might be a bit warm, especially without any air conditioning. It also smelled like it hadn't been used in some time. There was a couch, and a few chairs in the living area. There were pictures scattered around the rooms on walls. There were ceiling fans with a single light on the ceilings of the kitchen area, the living area and in both bedrooms. Lantern type oil lights were attached to the walls on all sides, spaced approximately six feet apart.

A door leading out to the back of the house opened onto a small covered porch; on the left hand side a door opened to a bathroom with only a toilet and a sink with a hand pump. On the right hand side of the porch was a room with a shower. The room's walls started approximately one foot above the floor, and stopped about 6 ½ feet high. There was a tin building behind the house but back toward the east. It looked to be approximately 15 feet wide, maybe 30 feet deep. It certainly appeared to have been there for some time, rusted areas on the sides and roof offered proof of the salt environment. It was at ground level, with two swinging tin doors facing the house. They were closed. Behind the house but toward the west was an unfinished structure; it looked like a pole barn with a roof. The ground was level under the structure but the outline of a floor, cut into squares covered the entire floor area. It appeared that was my job site.

Walter suggested that I get one of the gas cans and fill up the generator located just to the right of the kitchen door we had entered. He started putting groceries away. Within half an hour the generator was running, lights and ceiling fans were on, and he suggested we take a ride. "On what, I replied?"

"The jeep, unless you would rather walk!"

"What jeep?"

"The one in the tin barn out back." Like several things I was seeing, it was Army surplus. It had a windshield but no top. The frame for the top was there but no top. The windshield could be lowered onto the hood, it had supports and latches if the windshield was lowered. It had front and rear seats, and a short flatbed out the back. It looked like it had been through World War one and two. But, I guess it beat walking.

So, after filling the jeep with gas, we took off. We first drove along the bay to where the Government Dock reached the Island. Walter explained that every few months the Coast Guard delivered new batteries to the Light House.

"The light for the light house changed from fuel oil to electric back in 1949, so there's really no need for a full time light house keeper, but batteries have to be delivered to the light house every few months and it's a haul from the Government dock to the light house, so the Government pays me a stipend to haul the Coast Guard boys around, and check on the light house regularly. The Coast Guard boys do the work, we just have to haul them to the light house. If ever I'm not here, make sure you help them. Keeping the light house operational is important work."

"But I'm not going to be here that long!" I exclaimed. Walter just smiled and turned the jeep toward the Gulf. The roads were sand of course, but some were packed pretty good and easy to travel. Others not so much. Four wheel drive was a necessity. The Light House stood a couple hundred yards back from the surf, 77 feet high. Walter suggested we climb to the top so I could get a bird's eye view of his paradise. The structure was tapered and inside the spiraling stair case took us to the top of the masonry portion. From there we had to climb a ladder to the lantern room, a 12 foot high metal enclosure with windows facing in all directions. Walter gave me a little history of how the light house use to work, the fuel used and the type of lens and reflectors it took to be effective. Since electric lights were put into use around 1949, and batteries used for power, daily maintenance was no longer necessary, but replacement batteries were delivered every few months. The view was breath taking! To the east I could see The Cut, and big St.George's beaches. The surf's wave actions created ribbons of white froth that stretched out like decorations between the sand dunes and the blue of the gulf. Back to the west the beaches ran beyond my sight, dunes, sea oats, pine and oak trees created a tapestry of colors unlike any painting I'd ever seen. "Wow!" Was the only thing I said.

"Yep, that's what I first said. And after all these years, I still say it." Walter added, then said we needed to go, we still have lots to see and do. Back on the sand an adjoining building used to house the light house keeper back in the late 1800s and early 1900s. The middle of the house had a huge fireplace with four sides, each side having a hearth. They provided the heat for each of the four rooms for the home. The windows were gone and three of the four doors were gone, but it made me think about the past and what life must have been like living on a barrier island. After the visit to the light house we headed back to the house. It was getting later in the afternoon and I was wondering about supper. As we pulled the jeep next to the back door, Walter asked "What would you like for supper tonight?" Of course shrimp jumped into my mind, but I hadn't seen him put any shrimp in the boat, so I told him I'd be happy with anything. "Well, why don't we catch us some fresh mullet for supper?" I thought it had been a question but before I could answer Walter was out of the jeep and walking toward the tin shed. He emerged with a castnet and a fish sack. "Grab that washtub over there and put it in the jeep." I followed orders and minutes later we were headed back to the Government Dock in the jeep.

"Ever thrown a castnet before?' Walter asked.

"No sir, but I'm pretty good with my hands. I don't think it would be hard to learn."

"Good! Let's catch enough for supper and then we'll give you a lesson." Walter handed me the sack and took the castnet and started to the dock. We walked 20 or 30 yards out onto the dock before Walter stopped and started preparing the net. I notice that the water was 3 or 4 feet deep, clear enough to see bottom. As if he was obligated Walter turned to me and started with instructions.

"Matt, there are two different types of castnets, this one is called a long brail net which means that the brails are attached to the handline. Notice that they run from the lead line through this circular ring to the hand line at the top of the circular net. When the net is drawn by the handline, the whole net becomes a bag. It's the best type of net to use when throwing off of a dock. A short brail net is where the brails are attached from the lead line to approximately two feet up inside the webbing and drawn up about half the length of the brail to form a sack. It's the best type of net to fish when wading."

Walter set the net down on the dock, took the end of the hand line, which had a loop, and attached the loop to his left wrist, and then started picking up the line in cowboy rope fashion and collecting all of the hand line in his left hand. When he got to the top of the net he continued collecting the webbing in circles just like the hand line until he had approximately two thirds of the net in his left hand. He held up the net with his left hand, reached down and took the lead line closest to his body with his right hand and put the lead line in his teeth; with his right hand he slid his hand and arm between the webbing until he had collected about half of the webbing of the circular net. At that time he lowered both hands and allowed the webbing to stretch out until both hands were about even. The lead line was still in his teeth. We proceeded down the dock slowly until Walter stopped and whispered, "There's some." I stayed back, out of his way. I couldn't see the fish, but Walter was frozen in place. And then with what I could only describe as grace he raised the net, arms outward, he rotated his body to his left bringing the net in motion until he hit a pivot point and then rotated his body back to the right, pulling the net in a throwing motion and releasing the net toward the bay and fish. The net's uncoiling motion spread out in saucer fashion and splashed several feet from the dock.

At first I didn't see any fish in the net but as Walter began retrieving the net fish began splashing in the net and hitting the webbing. With just a few short pulls the net had collapsed into a large bag, and with ease Walter brought the net onto the dock. Four big silver mullet kicked and flounced on the dock. We put the fish in the sack; Walter straightened out the net, took the hand line off his left wrist and handed it to me. "OK, let me get you started and I'll go clean the fish."

Within a few minutes Walter had me handling the net, prepping for throwing, and instructing while I made a few attempts. "It will take some practice," he offered. "Keep practicing. I'll call you when I'm ready to cook." And off he went. For the next hour I kept practicing what he instructed. For what seemed so easy and simple I just couldn't get the net to open all the way as it had done with Walter. After 20 or 30 cast I was getting tired and frustrated. My hands were beginning to hurt, my shoulders were hurting, sweat was burning my eyes, and my lips even tasted like salt. I just wished I was back home. Tomorrow is the last day of school. I really don't want to be here. And then Walter drove back to the dock to collect me. It was time to cook.

After washing and hanging the net per Walter's instructions, I washed my hands and rinsed off the sand from my feet and went inside. Walter was at the stove, grease was getting hot, and he was battering the fish filets with what looked like a flour cornmeal batter. He asked that I get out the plates and diner ware. As I set the table there in the kitchen, he mixed up a small batch of hushpuppies, put on some grits to boil, and cut up some lettuce and tomatoes and splashed something on them as a dressing. I had really gotten hungry and forgot my manners when plates were served. The light crust on the fish was seasoned with a lemon pepper flavor which made my mouth immediately water, but the meat of the filet was moist and delicate. I had eaten mullet many times before but nothing like this. The grits had cheese in them, and the hushpuppies were laced with diced onions. The salad had hints of vinegar, and the tanginess blended the meal to perfection. After stuffing my mouth as fast as I could I realized I was making a fool of myself, so I complimented Walter on the good meal. His only response was "Do you know what the secret ingredient is?" I guess I looked confused. "Fresh!" he followed. "With fish, fresh is always the secret ingredient!"

I washed the dishes, put everything away, and then went to join him on the front porch. He was reading a book but the light was getting low, the sun had already set.

"What work am I to help with?" I wondered aloud.

"We'll be doing some concrete work for the next few days. I need to get the floor poured under the pole barn." We set there in silence for several minutes. There was a west wind blowing, a light chop in the bay; with the breeze it actually felt cool on the porch. "You'll be much more comfortable sleeping on the porch," Walter began. "There's sheets and a blanket on the bed in the bedroom on the right. Why don't you get those and settle in out here for tonight."

"It's kinda hot for a blanket, isn't it?" I said as I headed toward the bedroom.

"Maybe, but you might be surprised before morning. Have it just in case." Walter offered, and he got up and went inside to make his own preparations.

I got my bed ready for the night; it was what Mom called a daybed. Walter had disappeared into his room, so I sat on the porch staring at the bay. Darkness came on quickly and soon I could see stars everywhere. The lights of Apalachicola could barely be seen, but right now, they seemed a million miles away. I wish I was home! I wish I could see Jill. I wish I hadn't listened to Billy! I knew better than that. I wish, I wish! I lay back on the bed and thought that I should pray. In my mind I said, "Lord, please help me to be strong." The cool night breeze off the bay felt good. At some point during the night I remember reaching for the blanket.

It was just beginning to get light when I awoke. I could smell coffee from the kitchen, and Walter was active with what sounded to be cooking. The bay looked like glass, there was no breeze but yet it was cool. Morning birds were beginning to sing, the seagulls were already calling to each other. I slipped on some shorts and a T-shirt and went to the kitchen.

"Coffee?" was the first word from Walter. He was already dressed and appeared to be happy and rested.

"No thanks," I replied.

"How about juice?" he offered. I accepted and sat at the table to begin with orange juice. Walter was busy at the stove. Within minutes he served me scrambled eggs, bacon, and toast that was actually buttered and seared in a cast iron frying pan.

"This must be fresh," I said, "because it sure is good!"

"Good breakfast makes for good work. We'll get started soon as it gets good light. We can get in a few good hours before it gets too hot." And then Walter took his coffee and went outside toward the bay.

After breakfast I cleaned my dishes, put on my tennis shoes and went looking for Walter. He was standing out in the front yard, near the highest point looking out over the bay. It was a clear spot but for a few sea oats. It was a great spot, you could see both east and west directions along the shore line, and even see Apalachicola across the bay. As I approached Walter was looking for something on the ground. I thought he had dropped something, but before I could ask, he picked up a forked stick about 2 feet long and pushed it into the ground so that it could stand up. "What's that for?" I asked.

"Come on and I'll show you," he replied and started for the pole barn. At the pole barn he handed me a pair of work gloves. There was a cement mixer under a tarp, which he removed. Under another tarp were a rather large number of bags of cement mix, and close by was a pile of rocks about 4 to 5 feet wide and 3 to 4 feet high, and maybe 10 to 12 feet long. Next to the rocks was a pile of sand about the size of the rock pile.

"Before we start work," Walter began, "I want you to get the wheel barrow out of the tin shed, fill it with these rocks and take it out and dump it where I planted that stick in the front yard. Then we'll get to making some cement."

"Why do you want the rock in the front?" I wondered out loud.

"I'll show you later." And he walked off toward the house.

By the time I had loaded the rock in the wheel barrow and dumped it in the front yard, Walter had an electric line run from the generator to the cement mixer. He also had a water hose pulled over next to the mixer. For five hours we mixed and spread cement into the squares that were installed under the pole barn. The squares were formed by 2 by 4's, 3 feet wide by 5 feet long, and four inches thick. Into the mixture we poured one part cement, 2 parts sand, and 4 parts gravel. Walter added water to the mixture until it combined into a workable mix and then we poured it into the wheel barrow and then into the squares. Once we completed one square and started on the second Walter would remove the dividing 2 by 4 and we would add additional mixture to fill the void and level the mix. For the leveling process we used a 2 by 4 as a screed. The pole barn was 20 feet wide by 36 feet long. There were 48 squares under the barn; the first morning we mixed, filled, leveled, and Walter rough finished 8 squares. By lunch time I was tired, hungry, and hot. I think Walter was ready for a break as well.

We had ham sandwiches, chips, and lots of cold water for lunch. Walter suggested we nap after lunch. He got no complaint from me. About 2 pm I awoke, did not see Walter anywhere so I looked around in the living room where there were a few books and picked one to read; it was *Something of Value* by Robert Ruark. Within several minutes my mind was far from Little St. George Island, on the plains of Africa filled with wild animals, native tribes, and conflict between races. I didn't even hear Walter when he entered the porch.

"That'll keep you up all night if you aren't careful!"

"I think you're right," I answered and put the book down.

"I'll be right with you," Walter said. "Meet me out front at the rock pile."

I was staring out over the bay watching some seagulls fight over something floating in the water when Walter appeared beside me. He was holding what looked like a fungo bat except the barrel of the bat wasn't as big as a regular fungo bat. It was 35 inches long, light but very hard. He handed to me. It felt like a regular fungo bat which I had used many time when hitting ground balls to infielders; it had a nice handle, but much lighter.

"What's this for?" I asked.

"Practice" he replied.

"For what?" I asked.

"Your hand and eyes! Let's see if you can hit one of those rocks." I picked up a rock, about the size of a marble, tossed it into the air and took a good swing with the bat. Nothing but air! "Try again," Walter said. "And again and again and again." I've hit fly balls to guys for years; I know how to throw a ball up and hit it to the outfield or the infield. Why I wasn't hitting the rocks was beyond me. Walter just smiled and said to pay a little more attention to where the rock was going to be instead of where I thought it was, and he walked away. I just stood there watching him walk away, thinking what the hell am I doing trying to hit a bunch of rocks.

I turned back toward the bay, Apalachicola was just a speck on the horizon, I should be home. I wonder what Mom and Dad are doing? I wonder if they even miss me? I wish I could call Jill even if just for a few minutes. Damn Billy! I picked up a large rock, pitched it into the air and slammed it like it was the last play of the game. My confidence came back. Thirty minutes later Walter returned. I had settled in and with every rock I was slamming it out into the bay. Walter watched for a few minutes and then suggested I try tossing the rocks a little higher into the air in front of me and then try striding into the swing. Again, nothing but air. Walter left me to my new challenge, but returned a while later. I wasn't a hundred percent but I was consistently hitting the rocks when striding into the swing.

"Looking good," Walter smiled. "Let's talk about it for a bit? Why do you think it was harder to hit the rocks when you had to stride into the swing?"

"I guess because my whole body was moving instead of just my arms swinging."

"Well, that makes sense. But doesn't your whole body move when you are swinging at a baseball?"

"Sure, but a baseball is a lot bigger than one of those rocks."

"True, but aren't the baseballs traveling a lot faster than a falling rock?"

"Sure, but as you see the baseball coming you know where to swing."

Walter smiled and then said, "So why don't you swing the bat where you know the rock is going to be instead of where you see it?" and he left me to think about it some more. Shortly thereafter he could hear my bat making contact. I started picking out spots on the Government dock and hitting toward that direction; I picked out floating objects in the water and tried to hit rocks to the objects. I focused on my stride, my weight on each foot. I decided to hit a rock to

Apalachicola. The sun was setting when I decided to stop for the day; Walter called me for supper shortly thereafter. It was barely nightfall when my head hit the pillow.

The next day was a repeat of the day before. We knocked out eight more squares, ate some lunch, and I went back to reading while Walter took a nap. By four o'clock I was back at my pile of rocks. I was just beginning to hit when Walter walked up.

"I read an article about Ted Williams one time," he began. I held onto the fungo bat and turned to listen. "The article spoke of how Ted Williams shifts his weight depending on where the pitch is pitched. For an inside pitch he takes his normal hitting stride but keeps his weight back and pulls the ball. For an outside pitch he shifts his weight forward to hit the ball to the opposite field. Now I'm not a ball player but if it's good enough for Ted Williams then I think it would be good enough for me. I do know that being able to hit to the opposite field will win you some ball games. During your practice sessions doesn't your coach put you in situations for different plays?"

"Sure," I replied, while trying to imagine where my weight should be when hitting to the opposite field.

"Well, why don't you do the same while hitting your rocks? Call a play, pitch the rocks where you would pull the ball, or hit to the opposite field. It should at least help with the fundamentals." And he walked away.

Pitching rocks to pull was easy; I had more control and strength when pulling, but when I pitched the rocks to the outside to hit to the opposite field I found that shifting balance was not so easy. By the time I pitched the third rock into the air I started reminiscing about some plays from last year's ball games, pitches I didn't hit, pitches I should have hit. Hitting rocks sounded silly, it probably was, but right there, looking out over the Apalachicola Bay, with Apalachicola way into the distance, I decided that those rocks, those little clinks against the fungo bat, were going to take me to college ball. I may be in a paradise for a jail, but my penance was a thousand rocks, to different fields, different plays, and a different attitude. For the next couple of hours I thought about plays and hitting to move runners. Hitting to the opposite field was going to take some practice. I found that sliding my front foot in toward the outside pitch and having less weight on my back foot allowed my swing to be more controlled. But I also found that my balance had to be more controlled. Stepping in toward the outside pitch put more weight on the front foot but I lost a lot of power. It became obvious that not only did I have to step into the outside pitch, I had to keep plenty weight on my back foot for power. Funny how hitting rocks was not so easy even if I was calling the plays.

Walter had cooked hamburgers and some French fries for supper. I didn't realize I was so hungry until Walter suggested I slow down and not choke myself shoving food in my mouth.

"But it's really good!" I exclaimed.

"There's plenty more where that come from. Take your time and enjoy." I sat back, drank some water, and tried not to be too hungry. Walter smiled and began some conversation. "How's the book coming?"

I thought about it for a moment and asked, "Have you read the book?"

"Yes, I've read most all of Ruark's books."

"Africa is so big, with lots of animals, lots of resources. But the Masai and the Kikuyu are always fighting? Why are the white people always afraid that the tribes will kill them?"

"I would expect for the same reason that the American Indians fought each other, and the new white people that came to this country were always afraid the Indians would kill them."

I sat there for a few minutes not responding, thinking that maybe it was all the same; Africa, America, the rest of the world. People fighting, people dying. What's it for? Walter sensed my despair and suggested we finish supper and go for a ride. Dishes done, we headed toward the Light House. The sun had set, the evening glow had settled over Little St. George Island. As we rounded a curve toward the beach the Southeast wind hit us directly. It was cool, and you could feel the salt in the air. The Light House stood glowing against the dark skies of the southeast. The temperature dropped a few degrees as we approached the beach. A light surf splashed on to the beach, and as the waves receded sparkles of light glistened from the shells sprinkled along the beach. A full moon was cresting to the east. For the last couple of days I had gone to bed before dark and was up at day break. I didn't even know that the moon was full. Walter stopped the jeep at the base of the light house and cut the motor.

"It's a beautiful time now," he said, not directing his statement to me. We sat there for several minutes, listening to the waves rumble along the shore. The sun's last rays lighting up the western skies, the moon's rays lighting up the gulf in front of us. For once in my life I sensed that I was in a place between two worlds, the last of sun, the beginning of moon. We sat there for several minutes, not saying anything, just soaking in the moment, the sounds, the smells, the changing light. Walter finally broke the silence,

"Matt, it's nesting season for sea turtles. Let's go find one." And, he turned the jeep toward the west, put it in low gear, and we started toward the last light of the day. Walter turned on the head lights after it became too dark to see and we eased along at a walking pace headed toward west pass. Certainly I had been on a beach before at night, but never one where the only inhabitants, besides us, were the sea turtles we were waiting for. We poked along for 15 or 20 minutes before Walter hit the brakes and said,

"There's an old girl's tracks." He turned off the jeep, pulled out a flash light and said come on. The tracks were wide, and straight. Fins digging into the sand, pulling the heavy body forward, making the tracks toward her nest at the base of the sand dunes. We approached slowly and quietly. The sea turtle was huge, maybe 200 pounds or more. She was digging with her fins, flipping the sand back behind her. Her shell glowed from flakes of fluorescence borne by the sea. We sat quietly watching her dig the nest. Each fin digging into the sand, depositing the sand behind her until her head was deep into the soil. After what seemed a long time she stopped digging and turned her body around and backed over the hole she prepared for her eggs. Silently she delivered her eggs into the nest. Over a hundred eggs, with tears in her eyes, she fulfilled her life's mission. We watched silently, consumed by the moment, the spectacle, and the solitude of a single turtle. After a long and silent act she began filling the nest with sand. It seemed she took forever. She packed it well, then headed to the sea. We walked beside her until she reached the water's edge. I knelt down beside her, patted her shell and wished her good journeys. I walked into the water with her as the waves washed onto the shore, slowly she made her way to the depths, and she disappeared into the gulf. I stood there for a long time, wondering where she came from, where she would go. I hoped I'd get to meet her offspring. Walter came out and got me, said we had to go.

Back at the house Walter began his teachings. He had seen many events like tonight, and he had read a great deal about sea turtles. He began, "Matt, I've read that sea turtles always return to the same beach to lay their eggs. They live a long live, similar to humans, living 60 to 100 years old. They are also known to travel. To distant seas, to distant lands, all around the world. Scientist have tagged sea turtles here in Florida and found them in the Caribbean, the Northeast Atlantic, and even the coast of Mexico. But when it's time to mate and deliver the eggs to the sand, they return home. That old girl tonight must have been here many times. Did you notice the barnacles on her back?"

"I did. Did you see the tears in her eyes?"

"Yes, they do cry. I've often wondered if they cry from happiness or sadness. Or if it's pain."

"As great as tonight was, it's got to be happiness."

"Maybe so! But let's get some rest. There's much to do tomorrow."

Day four, I had to think for a few minutes as I sat up in my bed, I believe it's Friday. The sun had not yet risen, but the gulls were calling, a light wind from the west was cool, and the lightening sky was cloudless. Friday! A week ago we won the conference baseball championship. It seemed like it was months ago. I wondered if Jill would be at the Canteen tonight. I wondered if Mom and Dad were missing me. I wished I was home. I wondered what Bob, Bud, and Billy were doing; I wondered if their parents had sent them off somewhere as punishment. I sure wish I could go downtown and get a milk shake at Buzzett's drug store and fountain. I wish! And then Walter called, "Let's go, we've got lots to do today."

After a quick bowl of cereal I headed out back to help with the concrete, except Walter wasn't at the pole barn. He was gathering stakes and putting them in the back of the jeep. I noticed that the stakes were approximately three feet long and painted red on the top six or eight inches. "Grab that ballpeen hammer over there and let's go."

"Where?"

"We've got to mark turtle nests." And we were off toward the beach. When we reached the light house we turned toward the east and drove along at a pretty good pace. Before we reached Bob Sikes' Cut we found another turtle crawl. Walter pulled the jeep up to where the turtle had made her nest and we stopped and got out. Walter grabbed the hammer and a stake and drove the stake into the sand near the nesting site.

"What's that for?" I asked.

"We need to mark all the nests, and then we'll come back and place some wire mesh over the nest to keep the hogs from digging them up. We have lots of wild hogs on the island and they are deadly on the turtle nest."

We continued on to Bob Sikes' Cut but found no more, so we turned around and headed west. We found no others until we reached the nest from last night; we marked it and continued toward West Pass. Over the next few miles we found three other nests. After reaching West Pass we turned around and hurried back to the house. In the back of the tin shed Walter had stacked squares of wire mesh, each square was approximately five feet by five feet. The wire mesh was heavy gage, the type used in fencing. After stacking them in the back of the jeep Walter dug out some stakes used to secure the mesh to the sand. Those stakes were like the ones we used to mark the nest. Back to the beach and at each nesting site we placed the mesh over the exact location where the eggs were laid. Walter secured the mess to the sand with the long stakes.

"Won't the mesh hinder the baby turtles from getting to the water?" I asked. Walter smiled at me, as if he had been asked that question hundreds of times,

"No, the spacing in the mesh is large enough for the baby sea turtles to escape, but small enough that the hogs can't dig through it. Hopefully you'll get to see the babies emerge from the sand and head home to the sea."

"How long before the eggs hatch?"

"Normally between 55 to 65 days." My face must have been revealing because Walter immediately said, "I hope you'll get to come back when they are hatching. It really is something to see."

When we finished with all five sites Walter suggested that I drive us back to the house. "But I can't drive yet!"

"There's no one over here to arrest you. Why can't you drive?"

"I don't have a license."

"You don't need a license to drive."

"But I've never driven a stick shift."

"Well, it's about time you learn. What if I can't drive for some reason? You've got to be able to take care of me!" And for the next several minutes Walter gave me instructions and had me take over the wheel. We jumped along for a bit until I finally figured out the relationship between the clutch and the gas pedal. "One other thing," Walter began, "if I catch you speeding on the sand, hot-rodding, I'll ban you from driving. This sand gets soft and it's easy to turn the jeep over if you're speeding and trying to make turns. I just want you to be safe."

I got pretty comfortable driving the jeep on the way back to the house. Walter acted pleased. I thought we were headed back to work on the concrete flooring but when we reached the house Walter suggested that we should put out some crab traps. Within minutes we had loaded up six crab traps and the castnet in the jeep and were headed to the government dock.

"Why don't you catch us some mullet for bait while I haul these traps out toward the end of the dock?" So, while Walter made three trips to the end of the dock hauling crab traps, I worked my way along the dock searching for mullet. After several attempts I finally got the net over some mullet and onto the dock. I had five in one throw. I was really excited but when I took the mullet from the net the first two kicked out of my hand and back over board. Walter was grinning as he approached me; he had seen the mullet kick out of my hand.

"They are tricky like that," he started. "If you don't have a sack or a tub to put them in you have to kill them quickly to keep them from getting away." And, in teaching fashion as if talking to a kindergartener, he showed me how to hold the mullet, put my finger in the mullet's mouth, pull backward, and break the fish's neck. "Also," he continued, "when castnet fishing from a dock, always try to have the fish swimming away from you when you throw the net. When they are swimming toward you they can see you and the net's shadow. Makes it hard to catch them. The mullet often swim under the dock, so if they are coming toward you from one side, try to catch them when they come out on the other side and swimming away from you." Within a few minutes we had a few more mullet. Walter had his pocket knife and shortly they were cut in large chunks and placed in the crab traps. Traps dropped under the dock and tied by lines to the dock. "We'll have crabs tomorrow!" Walter smiled.

The rest of the day was lazy; Walter piddled around the house and the tin shed, but had no request of me. By 4:00 PM I was back at the rock pile hitting rocks into the bay. Making the opposite field hit was getting easier. The sun was setting by the time I stopped hitting rocks. Gulls were settling in and gathering on the long dock. The wind was down and the bay was becoming glass-like. It was Friday night. I wondered if Mom and Dad would be having hamburgers. I wondered if Jill would be at the canteen tonight. I'm glad I don't have to go to jail tonight. What a week!

Walter woke me just as it was getting light in the east, "Wake up Matt! There's much to do." Within a few minutes he had breakfast on the table and while I ate he went outside and I could hear him filling the jeep with gas. I finished breakfast quickly and went out to see where we were going. "Matt, I want you to make the turtle run this morning, same as we did yesterday. Go to Bob Sike's Cut and work your way back to West Pass. Mark each nest with a stake and we'll take the mesh mats back together if you find any new nest."

Within a few minutes I was off toward the beach, driving the jeep I had just learned how to drive the day before. It felt like an adventure. There was very little wind, the gulf was calm, and the skies were clear. The beach was warming as I turned toward Bob Sikes' Cut. It's about four miles to the cut. I searched the beach as I drove along slowly, looking for signs of a crawl. Sand crabs were scurrying all over the beach and into the water. Gulls were calling and sailing along the shoreline searching for bait and breakfast. About a mile and a half later I found a new crawl. I pulled the jeep up closer to where the turtle would have made her nest, but there was no sign of a nest. It appeared the turtle had crawled to the base of the dunes and then turned around and made her way back to the gulf. I put a stake there just so I could show it to Walter later, and continued on toward the cut. alf a mile further I found another crawl. The old girl had made her nest, so I staked it and continued to the cut. Turning around at the cut I made good time back to the light house. From there I slowed down some and continued to West Pass. I found two more crawls with nests, and staked them. I was really beginning to enjoy this. My turtle mission! I bet Bud and Bob would love this. I can't wait to tell them about my experience. I had never heard them even mention sea turtles and how they crawl out to lay their eggs.

Back at the house I told Walter about the three nests I found and marked and also about the crawl where it appeared the turtle hadn't made a nest. He seemed pleased. Within a few minutes we had loaded the mesh squares and were headed back to the beach. He let me drive.
At the first site where the turtle appeared not to have made a nest we stopped. I showed Walter where I placed the stake and how the tracks appeared to reach the dunes but turned around and crawled back into the gulf. "Good call, Matt," Walter began, "you're right. The old girl evidently didn't like this spot and changed her mind. You said that there was another crawl a little beyond here?"

"Yes, sir. Maybe a half mile further."

"Well, there's no way to really tell, but often times when a turtle doesn't nest in one spot she will move down the beach and nest in another. When they come out and crawl it means they are ready. And if they're ready they've got to find the right spot. Let's go fix that nest."
We took care of the three new nests and headed back to the house. At the house Walter grabbed a wash tub and put it in the jeep. "Let's go collect our crabs!"

At the end of the dock where we had placed the crab traps Walter slipped on a pair of oyster gloves and pulled the first trap. A dozen nice big blue crabs were still picking at the bait. One end of the trap has a tie, which we released and shook the crabs from the trap into the tub. After all six traps were checked we had at least four dozen crabs.

"A fine feast this is!" Walter said. "Let's go prepare them."
We threw the remains of the bait into the bay and left the traps to dry on the dock. Back at the house Walter poured water over the crabs until they were barely covered and put them over an open fire he built in a pit behind the house. It didn't take long to bring the water to a boil and within just a few minutes the crabs were bright red.

"That will do it," Walter offered, and he handed me a pair of tongs and said put them in this other tub. Crabs transferred, Walter instructed me to grab the other handle of the tub and together we took the crabs back to the edge of the bay. "We"ll cool them with bay water." Minutes later we had cooled the crabs and, while sitting on a couple of oyster crates, we backed and cleaned the crabs, washing them in the bay water, and stacked them in the tub. Back at the house Walter got out a pair of paring knives and showed me how to cut and pick out the crab meat. He left me in the kitchen cleaning crabs and went outside. A couple of hours later he came in to fix lunch. I was still cleaning crabs.

"You're looking good," he complimented me. "Keep it up and we'll have crabs for dinner."
I was beginning to think I didn't want crabs quite that badly. Back at home Mom normally had me pick small shells and cartilage from a pint of crab meat. After lunch Walter went back outside and worked on the concrete flooring for a while. I think he only finished one square. I finished the crabs before 2:00 PM. Walter declared nap time and I went back to the porch and Something of Value. I got sleepy really quickly and before dozing off I remember thinking that all that crab meat ought to be Something of Value.

About 4:30 I was back at the rock pile. I noticed that the pile was beginning to shrink. My rock hitting experience was getting better; I was calling plays and hitting accordingly. If only I could be so successful when actually playing baseball. Certainly I'll get to play some summer ball?
That thought got me depressed in a hurry. Gosh, I sure hope I get to go home soon.

Walter called me for supper right at dark. Crab casserole! It was the best crab I've ever eaten. I ate so much my stomach hurt. Walter considered it a compliment. After cleaning dishes I went back to the porch. Stars were everywhere, and I could see the lights of Apalachicola. A good west wind picked up and the night began cooling. I was about ready for bed when Walter came out onto the porch.

"Matt," he began, "the moon will be pretty full for another three or four nights. The turtles should continue to nest for another several days. I'd like you to make the turtle run for the next few mornings. Is that ok with you?"

"Sure, it's really fun. But what about the concrete flooring?" I was beginning to add up the days before I could go home, and if completing the flooring was the goal, I needed to hurry with the flooring.

"I'll keep working on the flooring and you can help after your turtle run each day. Sound okay?"

"Yes sir! I was just thinking about when I could go home." Walter smiled and said we'd stay after it.

The next morning it was raining well before daylight. I stayed tucked under the covers until it lightened up enough for me to see. Clouds were hanging low over the bay, a southeast wind had chopped up the bay. What seagulls I could see were bunched together along the shoreline. Walter came out onto the porch an offered breakfast. While I was eating Walter began, "Matt, you still need to make the turtle run this morning. The turtles don't mind the rain! And, I have a top for the jeep."

Minutes later we were out in the tin shed, Walter pulled out an old canvas top for the jeep and we strung it over the roof frame and tied it at the four corners plus two ties in the middle. I was about to get into the jeep to head out when Walter told me to hold on a minute. He produced from an old army locker a rain poncho which I assumed was army issue as well. I figured I would be wet from sweat wearing that thing, but as I took off for the beach it sure was nice not having the rain soak me from the sides. The beach sand was packed from the rain which made driving much easier and faster.

In less than an hour I had surveyed the beach from the Cut to West Pass. Not a single sign of a turtle crawl. The rain had stopped by the time I returned to the house. Walter was already working with the concrete flooring so I joined him. We had completed two more squares before the rain started again. It looked as if it was settling in for the afternoon. Walter asked me to clean up the tools and cover the equipment and he went inside. It didn't take long to wash the tools and cover the mixer, but I did unplug the electric line from the generator before going inside.

I could hear Walter talking to someone from his bedroom, but I had not seen anyone come to the Island. As I walked toward his bedroom I could hear him saying, "Yes, we're making good progress on the flooring. Matt is a real help. Yes, maybe Thursday. I'll confirm. Talk later."

Walter was turning off what appeared to be a radio as I stuck my head into his room.

"Were you talking to someone?" I asked. "Yes, that was Elzie. He was just checking on our progress."

"What is that?" I questioned."

"A short-wave radio. You can communicate with others who have short-wave radios. It's helped me and Elzie stay in touch for the past few years. Damn shame we didn't have these many years ago." I had heard of short-wave radios but never seen one.

"Can I call my folks on that one?"

"No, the only person I know of in the Apalachicola area to have another is Elzie, and he's up the river. Come on, let's have some lunch and we'll make some plans."

Lunch was light, just sandwiches and some chips, lots of cold water. After lunch Walter headed for his nap and at Walter's request, I went to collect the crab traps from the dock. After returning the crab traps to the tin shed I went back to the porch. Reading my book was just not going to happen this afternoon. Walter's call to Elzie had me thinking about home. I kept wondering how long I had to be here. Summer baseball begins this coming week. I need to be there. I paced back and forth on the porch for a bit and finally went into the living room for what I don't know.

I was walking around looking at the different books and also some pictures on the walls. There was one of the lighthouse, a black and white that looked like it must have been really old. A man and a woman stood at the base of the ligh house, evidently they were the lighthouse keepers back then. There was another picture of what I guess was the Corps of Engineers when they were digging out Bob Sikes' Cut. A large dredge boat was pumping sand onto the shore. Several men were on the back of the dredge boat waving at whomever was taking the picture. And there was a black and white picture of two young men on each side of a young woman. The woman looked older than the two men. I kept staring at the picture for some time. The men looked familiar, then it dawned on me, it was Walter and Elzie, much younger. I wondered if the woman was their mother or sister. The woman was attractive; she had dark hair, dark eyes, and high cheekbones. She was smiling. Walter was lean and tall. Elzie was shorter and not near as stocky as he was when I met him at the fish house last week. Also in the room on a shelf there was a large fish hook. I'd never seen a fish hook that large. It must have been a foot long; next to it was a fishing reel, larger than any I'd seen before. Certainly Walter would have a story about them. I went back to the porch to try reading again, but the rain stopped. I couldn't relax, so I picked up the fungo bat and went back to my rock pile. Sometime before darkness settled in Walter called me for supper. He had made a gumbo with fish and crab meat, and some sausage of some sort. It was really good. At supper I asked him about the picture.

"Walter, the picture in the living room, the one with the two guys and a woman, is that you and Elzie?"

"Yes it is. It was a long time ago."

"Who's the woman? Is it your mom?"

"No, that was our sister. She was older than us."

"Where is she?"

"She died many years ago."

"What happened?"

"She got sick. It was a sad time."

I sat picking at my gumbo, wondering how they came to be friends with my Dad. Walter finished his meal and started cleaning up. I continued, "How did you become friends with my Dad?" My question hung there like a flickering light bulb. Walter stopped washing his dishes, didn't turn to look at me for a bit, but slowly dried his hands on a dish towel, turned and came back to the table. With a caution that seemed calculated he began,

"Matt, has your Dad ever told you about his Dad?"

"No sir, just that he and my grandma had been killed in an accident when Dad was 9 or 10 years old."

"That's correct. Your Granddad, we called him Captain Mac, was in the timber business. He cut cypress timber out of the river swamps, floated the logs to mills down the river. Elzie and I worked for Captain Mac from the time we could handle an ax until his death. I was twenty-four when he died, Elzie was twenty-one. Captain Mac and his wife didn't have any other family that we could find. No one even knew where she came from. We were working up on the Chattahoochee River near Columbus when it happened. Elzie and I were the closest thing your Dad had to family, so we took him in."

"How did it happen? The accident?"

"From what we could tell the Captain's car stalled on a railroad crossing and a train hit their car." My mind started racing with imagines, sounds, questions. I sat there for a long time just thinking. Walter didn't continue. He sat there in silence also.

After a while I asked, "Where did y'all live?"

"Captain Mac owned a home in Apalachicola, so we moved in there. Elzie and I had to work to support us, so we would each stay in Apalachicola a week at a time so your Dad could go to school, while the other worked. All we'd ever known was timbering the river swamps, so we kept at it. Within a couple of years we were able to buy a small mill and started cutting the cypress we timbered from the swamps. It was enough to keep us afloat, and when your Dad graduated from high school, we were able to help him with college. He also worked his way through college, but your Dad's smart, and he didn't mind working. He went straight through, no summer vacations for him."

"Where did you live in Apalach?"

"There's a house at the corner of Ave B and 7th street. It was built in Port St. Joe in the middle 1800s, and moved to Apalachicola at the turn of the century when St. Joe just about got wiped out from yellow fever. Captain Mac bought that house several years before Elzie and I even started working for him. He used to say that he would retire there one day."

"So Dad grew up there?"

"Yep!"

"Did Dad play ball in high school?"

"Yes, he did. He was a pretty good player too. Played baseball and football, just like you."

"How did you know I played baseball and football?"

"Oh, your Dad keeps us posted on your accomplishments."

We sat there in silence for quite a while. My thoughts were all over the place, I had more questions than I could put in order. I didn't know any of what Walter had told me. If he and Elzie took care of my Dad, why hadn't they been around most of my life? Why am I just now finding this out? Why hasn't Dad told me?

Walter got up and went back to cleaning the kitchen. After a few minutes he turned to me and began, "Matt, your parents are very proud of you. They expect you to be an excellent student. They want only the best for you. It's easy to get side tracked when you're 15 or 16. Sometimes a young man needs to see different sides of life; maybe get a little closer to nature. Take time to watch the clouds, smell the sea, even watch a turtle build her nest. There's some good things in store, try to appreciate it along the way." And he walked out of the kitchen. I sat there for a long time, trying to take it all in. Finally, I got up and went to the porch. The sky was beginning to clear, I could see stars sprinkled around the darkness. A light northeast wind had sprung up, it was getting cooler on the porch. I was glad I had a blanket, sleep came eventually.

Monday morning I awoke with energy. I was ready to get on with it. I had turtle runs to make but I was determined to get back quickly so Walter and I could finish the concrete flooring under the pole barn. Sometime during the night, in fits between sleep, I made up my mind that I needed to get home. I needed Dad to tell me about the past. I needed to know our family history. And, I was ready to play summer baseball.

Walter wasn't even up when I poured myself a bowl of cereal. I was headed out the door, just at daylight, when Walter headed to the kitchen. "I'll be back shortly," I hollered as I ran out the back door. Within an hour or so I was back at the house. I had found two new nests, staked them, and was ready to begin the flooring work. Walter sensed my enthusiasm and we started mixing concrete even before taking the mesh squares back to cover the turtle nest. Just before lunch Walter called it quits.

"Enough concrete work for today! Let's get a sandwich and then we'll go cover the turtle nests."

By early afternoon our chores were done. Walter said he was going for a nap. Reluctantly, I reached for my book. By 4:00 PM I was headed to the rock pile when Walter called me to come help him.

He was out by the tin shed and apparently looking for something. As I approached he walked out carrying a ball of twine and a large fishing weight. It was the largest fishing weight I had ever seen. He explained that it was used when fishing well off shore in very deep waters. I followed him back behind the pole barn, to the southwest approximately 50 yards. There were some large pine trees back there and there was a sand dune that ran from east to west for approximately 100 yards. One of the large pine trees, located at the base of the sand dune, had a large and long branch that grew at an angle parallel to the sand dune. Walter walked around looking at the tree branch, the sand dune, and what grew around the site. There wasn't much brush under the pine trees, just some island grass, and lots of sand dune.

After a few minutes Walter called me over to him and, after tying the twine to the heavy weight, he stripped off lots of twine from the ball and suggested that I throw the weight over the long pine branch. He picked out a spot on the branch which was well away from the trunk of the tree and told me to give it a try. I moved toward the sand dune, going under the branch, where I could throw the weight over the branch and it would fall onto the open ground away from the sand dune. He held onto the ball of twine with extra line gathered around me. Without much ado I threw the weight over the branch and it landed in the open maybe 20 feet from me. Walter smiled, said it was a good throw and then got both strings of the twine hanging down from the pine limb, cut the twine from the ball and tied the two ends together. "That will do for now," he said and walked back toward the tin shed.

"What's that for?" as always.

"I'll show you later." As always!

From the tin shed Walter brought out a coil of rope, maybe a quarter or 3/8th inch size. It appeared to be a long rope. Back at the pine tree Walter cut the string and tied one end of the string to one end of the rope. He handed me the other end of the string and told me to pull the string and the rope over the limb. I pulled until I had the end of the rope in my hand. Walter came over, cut the string loose from the rope, and then tied a loop into the end of the rope. There was still a lot of rope on the other end but Walter had me hold the loop end until he uncoiled the rest of the rope and passed the other end through the looped end and started pulling the rope on his end. In short order the rope was pulled taught against the branch. Walter pulled the rope tight, pulled the remaining rope down to ground level and then cut the rope.

"What are we doing? Making a swing?" I asked.

"Sort of," he replied. "Now go over to the back of the tin shed, the outside, behind the shed. There's an old tire there; bring it here." A few minutes later he was tying the rope to the tire. He had me hold it up until the top of the tire was just over head high to me.

"Are we going to swing on that tire?" I asked.

"Not exactly," he replied. After attaching the tire to the rope he told me to wait there and he walked back to the house. I decided to give the tire a try and while holding onto the rope at the top of the tire I made a dash toward the sand dune and jumped into the tire for a swing. My hands immediately slipped from the rope and before sliding out of the tire I grabbed the tire sides and hung on. One swing, that's all it took. I slid out of the tire onto the ground, a bit embarrassed and hoping Walter had not seen my swinging attempt. I was still brushing sand out of my hair and off my clothes when Walter returned.

"I hear you're a pretty good quarterback?" he began. "Let's see how well you throw the ball," and he handed me a football.

"Where'd that come from?" I asked.

"Oh, I found it on the beach one day. Back up over there and let's see you throw through the circle." I backed up about 15 yards and easily threw the football through the tire. "Very good!" Walter began. "Now, let's see how you do with a moving target?" He grabbed the tire while I retrieved the ball; I backed up to my 15 yard spot and Walter gave the tire a big push. I went into quarterback mode, shifted my weight to my right foot and shot a spiral toward the swinging tire. The ball hit the side of the tire. "That's still pretty good," from Walter, "but you need to work on your control. Think of the circle as your target." For the next several minutes Walter kept swinging the tire while I threw passes at the tire. It wasn't long before I was hitting the circle consistently. "You're looking good,' Walter complimented me, "now let's make it real. Come over here, stand about 15 yards directly behind me. When I push the tire I want you to break to your right, running and throw through the circle."

It was just like football practice, it was a down and out pass play. I'd thrown those passes for years. I was feeling confident. A few minutes later Walter switched sides, pulling the tire as far to the right as he could. I followed and as he pushed the tire in the opposite direction I ran to my left and threw to the tire. Not quite as easy, but we practice those plays all the time during football season. The trick is how you rotate your body while running. While running to my left I have to rotate my body to where I face the line when I throw. It's tough at first, but after a while you get used to it. "Why don't you work on those pass plays for a little while and I'll go find out what we can have for supper," Walter offered and he walked off. For the next hour I pushed the tire in one direction and immediately rolled in that direction for the throw. After several passes in one direction I changed and went back to throwing from the other direction.

Walter finally called me to dinner. It was getting dark by the time we finished our meal and as I was working on the dishes Walter sat at the table and began talking. "You throw those roll out passes very well. Do you have some good receivers?"

"Yes sir. Our tight end, Bud Carlson, has good hands, and we've got a couple of good running backs that can catch too."

"Football's a great game! I always enjoyed watching good running backs, but when you have a quarterback that can throw, it sure opens up the playing field. I've noticed that most defenses flow in the direction of the run or pass. Have you ever run pass plays where you throw to a receiver who's actually running in the opposite direction of the play?" I wasn't quite sure what Walter was describing.

"What do you mean?" I questioned.

"Well, let's talk about the tire. When you push it and roll out in the same direction the play moves all in one motion. Let's say you push the tire and roll out in that direction but instead of throwing immediately you wait until the tire starts back in the other direction and then you pass. Think you could do that?"

"Sure, I'll work on that tomorrow." I started dreaming of plays as I headed off to bed. At some point the thought occurred to me that Walter was coaching, not just working me. I wondered if he had ever played any ball. Sleep came shortly. I was kicking cover by daylight.

The eastern sky was just beginning to lighten when Walter called me. A light wind from the north was cool, but the bay was quiet. I dressed quickly, just shorts, a t-shirt, and my tennis shoes. Walter had boiled some eggs and fried some bacon. He made me some more fried toast with butter. I told him it wouldn't take long for the turtle run and I'd be back to help with the concrete. He agreed and I was out the door. The light north wind had the gulf slick as glass. The skies were clear, and the gulls were again working the beach shoreline. Occasionally I could see schools of fish striking bait at the surface. Dolphin were working in close to shore this morning. It appeared that some were mothers of babies and the babies were getting fishing lessons. They rolled, they jumped, and often I could see them attacking schools of bait.

I was almost to the cut when I found my first crawl of the morning. From the size of the crawl tracks it appeared to be a very large turtle. I staked the nest and headed back toward the west. I was almost to west pass when I found the second crawl. It was much smaller but there was a nest. I staked it quickly and headed back toward the house. The west end of the Island is pretty low, not many sand dunes, but about a mile eastward large sand dunes spring from the salt grasses making hill-like dunes. Pine tree growth starts behind the large dunes and runs for a few miles before dropping off again to low salt grass flats.

I needed to get back to the house and help Walter with the concrete, but as I neared the large sand dunes I had some crazy desire to ride up on top of the largest. The grade was not real steep, but it was high. I put the jeep into four wheel drive and slowly crawled to the peak. After turning off the jeep I got out and stood there just staring at the gulf. The water was bluer than I had seen all week; I could see the lighter colors of the reef that ran perpendicular to the shore just 40 or more yards off the beach. Schools of fish were striking just outside the reefs, dolphin were numerous. Back toward the west I could see St. Vincent Island, its dune line similar to what I was standing on. West pass was dark blue, and palms stood along the shore line of St Vincent. Several miles off shore of west pass I could see three shrimp boats. They appeared to be at anchor. I assumed they were dragging nets at night. It dawned on me that I had never been on a large shrimp boat. A couple of my friends' fathers owned small shrimp boats only used in the bay, I had been on them, but never had I been on one of the large boats that traveled all over the gulf to shrimp. I would ask dad or maybe Walter if they could arrange for us to board one of the big boats. It was all so beautiful, and remote. I wanted to experience it all, yet I wanted to be home. I stood there for a few minutes not thinking, just feeling, and as if once again awake, I headed back to the house. Walter was already working on the concrete when I returned, so I joined him.
"I found 2 more nests today," I began. "Do you want to go put out the mesh now or later?" I questioned.

"Later," Walter replied. 'We can't stop this concrete from setting up. Let's finish another couple of squares and then we'll take care of the turtles." We waited until after lunch to cover the nest with the mesh. On the way back to the house Walter suggested we pick up some oysters this afternoon. "Tide will be low around 4:30 or 5 today. Let's pick up some oysters for supper."

Around 4, after Walter's nap, he started gathering oyster gloves, culling irons, and a couple of oyster crates. Putting them in the jeep he hollered for me to put on my wading shoes. Minutes later we were heading toward the light house. At the light house we turned toward the east and within half a mile Walter turned onto an overgrown trail leading to the bay. We stopped about 40 yards from the shoreline of the bay and Walter began his teachings,

"This is pilot's cove. There is a very large oyster bar that runs well into the bay here," he pointed. "See how it dog legs to the left, the west? Between here and there the water is deep enough where larger boats can moor. Many of the bigger shrimpers moor here overnight when they are shrimping the bay in the fall. There are lots of oysters next to the shore here."

I could see the oyster bar as it spread out into the bay. The water color was much darker in the area where Walter said the larger shrimp boats anchored. Flats were showing along the shoreline headed north into the bay. We picked our way through the marsh until we reached the water line. We were just west of the long point Walter had just pointed out to me. Oysters were everywhere, some out of the water due to the low tide, and others still under water but in the shallows. I had picked up oysters many times with my dad so I knew how to choose which oysters and how to cull the smaller oysters and barnacles off the larger oysters. It didn't take very long before we both had more than half a crate full of oysters, so Walter called it quits and we headed back to the house.

"Matt, I'll wash off these oysters. Why don't you dry off and change and maybe hit some rocks for a while. I'll prepare a fine feast for us." It really wasn't a question or an offer so I went to change. Within a few minutes I was calling for hits to right field.

It was well before dark, I was still hitting rocks, when I smelled the smoke. I stopped the rock hitting and went to see what was happening. Just a few yards off the back entrance to the kitchen Walter had a fire going in the same pit we used to boil the crabs. Fat lighter pieces of wood were burning as a base and Walter had begun putting oak pieces on top for a cooking fire. He had driven two U-shaped metal sakes on each side of the fire to create supports for racks. He had put a couple of concrete blocks to one side and placed a wide board between them to create a work table for his cooking. On the make shift table he had two wire racks that looked to be about 16 to 18 inches wide and a couple of feet long. Each rack held what looked to be a couple of dozen oysters. They had already been shucked and were on the half shell. Also on the table was a bowl with crumbled cheese in it; also another bowl with a sauce mixture. I had no idea what was in the sauce mixture. He also had a pair of gloves next to him the likes of what I had never seen. "What type of gloves are those?" I asked.

"Those, my lad, are firemen's gloves. Heat resistant. It's the only gloves you should use when handling hot oyster racks." We sat there for several minutes just starring at the fire until Walter decided it was time to cook. He put both racks of oyster onto the grates, and carefully spooned onto the oysters the mixture he had in one of the bowls. The aroma filled the air immediately. My mouth began to water. I hadn't realized I was hungry until I could smell those oysters cooking, but my, how they smelled. It didn't take very long before the oysters, stewing in the sauce, began to shrink in size. At that time he sprinkled the crumbled cheese over the oysters. They were approximately half their original size when Walter put the hot gloves back on and told me to open the back door. He took each rack into the kitchen and placed them on a wooden board he had placed on the kitchen counter. After removing his gloves he squeezed fresh lime juice onto the oysters from slices of limes.

At the kitchen table he had two small bowls of what he called his oyster sauce. He had a plate set ready for each of us. As I sat down he went to the refrigerator and retrieved two bowls of salad he had prepared. Saltine crackers were on the table. "How would you like a coke to have with your oysters?"

"Yes sir!" He retrieved it from the refrigerator, put it on the table and then put 8 or 9 oysters on my plate, still on the half shell. I put a small amount of the oyster sauce on one oyster and tried it. I wasn't sure I wanted any additional sauce, but after one bite, I went back for more. We sat there in silence, except for smacking and sighing as to how good they were. I finished my entire rack of oysters, as well as the salad, and my coke. Darkness had covered us by the time I finished with the dishes. I took my full belly to the porch and fell asleep within minutes.

Wednesday morning was cool. I dressed quickly and went to the kitchen for some breakfast. Walter was drinking coffee and offered to cook me some eggs. I decided on cereal and was out the door before the sun hit the horizon. I made the turtle run in less than an hour; I found no nest that morning. Walter was already working the concrete when I returned so I jumped right in to help. "We're about to whip this job," Walter began. "A couple of more days should finish it up."

"Yes sir," I replied. "Will you be able to take me home when we're finished?"

"You sure are in a hurry to get home. Got a girlfriend you're missing?" Walter cut his eyes over toward me, a little smile crossed his lips.

"Well, she's not official yet, but maybe."

"Girls been interfering with work as long as men been working!"

"Were you ever married Walter?" I asked.

"No, I never really had enough money or time for a wife. From what I understand it takes both." I thought about that for a few minutes. We went to screeding the concrete about that time; the conversation stopped. When we finished work there were only four more squares left to complete the floor.

"Looks like tomorrow will be the day," I offered.

"Sure does," Walter offered. "Why don't you clean up the tools while I go take care of some paper work. I've also got to put my shopping list together. We're running a little low on gas for the generator. Don't want to forget that!" And Walter left me to my chores. After lunch Walter suggested we take another ride around the Island. I expected it to be another turtle run but before we reached the beach Walter turned westward onto an old road that ran through the timber. I had not been on that road, so I asked where we were going.

"Remember a few years ago when your Dad and you, along with some other fathers and sons, came for a dove shoot?
I told Walter I remembered it, but didn't remember where we actually had the shoot. "Well, we're headed to the field to check it out." We traveled through the timber until it thinned out onto flats covered with island grasses and palmettos. I realized we were behind the tall sand dune I had been on the morning before. The field ran all the way to the small grove of pines just before west pass. I learned from Walter that the area where the pines were just before west pass was called Sand Island. There was also a small fresh water pond near the pines. It was surrounded by sawgrass. Walter said that he usually had a couple of duck hunts there each year. We slowed to a walking pace and picked our way along the field. Some areas were dry, others low and wet. About 100 yards past the tree line we stopped and got out of the jeep. As usual Walter began his teachings,

"Matt, see this grass right here?" It was more of a clump of grass with round needle type spikes. "It's called spartina grass. It's a type of cordgrass. And it stabilizes these flats. It's tough. It can be covered in saltwater or fresh water and still survive. We don't want to destroy this grass so when we put in a field for doves always be careful not to plant in these areas."

I noticed that from the short sand dunes facing the gulf it was three or four hundred yards to the bay. Most of the spartina grass grew within a couple hundred yards of the bay. We walked toward the sand dunes. Walter kept looking at the ground, checking different plants. He found a long stick which looked to be from a small tree, picked it up and used it as a walking stick. He poked at clumps of grasses, palmettos, and even trash that had floated there from high water. After 20 or 30 minutes he called me to him. "Matt, see this little bush? I don't know the proper name for it but we call it dove weed. In the fall it blooms; it has small flowers and it puts out small seeds that the doves love. See how the soil is much dryer here? It's not sandy like the dunes or the beach, but it's dryer and fertile. Along here is where we'll plant some millet."

"How will we do that?" I couldn't imagine raking or hoeing or any way to plant seeds here.

"With a tractor." Walter said, looking at me like I was simple.

"What tractor?" I questioned.

"Don't know yet. Depends on who has one we can borrow."

"And how does the tractor get here?" I asked. Walter looked at me, gave me that little smile when he starts playing me along, "Well, they don't fly. They can't swim. I've never been able to drive one across the bay. How about we put it on a barge and bring it over here?"

"Whose barge?"

"Don't know. We'll have to see who has one we can borrow!" I decided it best not to reply. "We'll need to plant the seed in early August to have feed for the doves in early October," Walter said, as much to himself as to me. "Come on and let's see if the pond is holding any water."
And we headed to Sand Island. Minutes later we were standing on a sand dune, peering at the saw grass surrounded pond lying within a hundred yards of the bay and the pine grove. "We'll have our

first bunch of teal visit here in early September. Blue wing teal. Very tasty," Walter spoke without looking at me. Sometimes I thought that maybe he wasn't talking to me at all, just voicing his opinions. Like releasing butterflies into the wind.

There had been little wind that day, but while Walter and I studied the pond a light breeze picked up out of the west. A light chop grew in the bay. Gulls called to each other from the bay side and the gulf. Feathery clouds floated in the western sky. I recalled the big shrimp boats from the morning before. "Walter, do you know any shrimpers that own a big boat? That shrimp the gulf? That travel?"

"Well, of course I do. Why do you ask?"

"I saw some yesterday and realized I'd never been on one of the big boats. Do you think we could go aboard one someday?"

"Certainly. Matter of fact we might just go shrimping with them one day."

"That would be great! When should we go?" I really wanted to experience that.

"The big boats will be working the gulf off here for the next few months. I'll work on arranging a trip. I bet your dad would enjoy it as well." My mind kicked into gear, I knew Dad would enjoy a day on a big shrimp boat. Maybe Bud or Bob could go as well. Wait until I tell them about that.

"Why don't you drive us home?" Walter interrupted my day dream. "And let's take the beach route." It was just past 4 PM when we reached the house. Walter suggested that I split my time between rocks and tire targets this afternoon while he hunted up something for supper. I started with the football and roll out passes, but my heart just wasn't in it today. After only 30 minutes or so I headed to the rock pile. The west wind felt really good. It had cooled off a lot since morning. My hitting was consistent; it helped that no one was throwing the rocks toward me, and no one there to catch them when I hit for my play calling. Gulls were back on the long dock. Apalachicola lay across the bay. It seemed like weeks since I was home. I really wished I could see Mom and Dad.

Walter called me for supper before the sun set. He had some type of stew. It was okay. Not nearly as good as the oysters the night before. There was no conversation. My mind was all over the place. Walter seemed distracted as well. By dark I was on the porch. The lights of Apalachicola twinkled across the bay, surrounded by darkness. I lay there in the bed wondering how much longer before I could go home. Sleep finally closed in.

Before daylight Walter had me up. He fixed scrambled eggs and toast. Before sunup I was on my turtle run. Like the day before, I found no nest. As I pulled into the back yard Walter was not to be seen. I thought he'd be working on the flooring, but not even the mixer was uncovered. I went into the house and called his name. Nothing. Back out in the back yard he wasn't there. Not in the tin shed. I headed toward the boat house. Before I even got out of the yard Walter appeared, walking toward the house. "Go pack your clothes," is all he said.

"Why? We haven't finished the flooring."

"Don't worry about the flooring. We can finish it later. I need to make a supply run."

"Am I going home?"

"Yep!" It took just a few minutes to stuff my clothes into my duffle. I was headed to the boat when Walter called, "After you drop your duffle in the boat, start getting those gas cans loaded into the boat." Within 20 minutes Walter had secured the house and we were easing out the narrow channel to deeper water in the bay. I sat back on the gunnel as I had come to the island and watched its colors blend into the horizon. At the intra-coastal waterway we turned north and headed home. A beautiful day! The sky was blue, the water was calm, I was deep down happy. I had learned a lot and I was really looking forward to telling Mom and Dad about my experiences. Maybe I could see Bud and Bob this afternoon. Hey, maybe I could go to baseball practice. I had worked hard. But I was going home. I sure hoped Mom and Dad are happy to see me. I hoped my time on the island earned my forgiveness. I hoped Dad will meet us at the fish house. Today would be a new beginning! Turns out, Dad was there to meet us, and there was a new beginning. Just not the one I expected.

Chapter 3: River Rat

Walter took us off plane before we reached the bridge. He idled the boat under the bridge and up to the fish house. Another boat built just like Walter's was there except it did not have a covered bow or wheel house. Walter eased the boat up to the dock and told me to get the bowline and tie it off to a piling. I threw my duffle onto the dock, jumped onto the dock, tied off the bow, and then Walter threw me a stern line which I tied off to a piling as well. Walter cut off the motor and was stepping onto the dock when Dad walked out of the fish house

"Dad!" I yelled, and ran to him. He gave me a big hug and asked how I was doing. "I've got lots to tell you Dad."

"I'm sure you do but let's go inside for a bit."

Walter shook Dad's hand and the three of us walked into the fish house.

"Paisan" was the first word I heard as we entered the fish house. Mr. Siglio came over and shook Walter's hand. "Come, come, have a seat," Mr. Siglio continued, "how are things on the island?" The men began talking. It was deja vu all over again. Besides me, Dad, Walter, and Mr. Siglio, Elzie was there as well. I dropped my duffle and sat on it. Mr. Siglio produced some coffee cups, and each poured a cup from an old percolator. Weather, the heat, local politics, and of course, shrimp season dominated the conversation. I tried paying attention at first, but after 10 or 15 minutes I was ready for a nap. Nothing had been said about my stay on the Island, but just before dozing off I heard Walter ask Mr. Siglio if he could arrange a shrimping trip on one of the big boats in a few weeks. Mr. Siglio acted excited and said he would like to join the gang. Dad even acted excited.

A nice breeze had picked up and was blowing through the opened doors on the river side. The door toward the street was also opened. The shrimp house was dark compared to the sunny outside and a little later Dad woke me and told me to come to the car with him. I grabbed my duffle and followed him. At the car Dad said to empty my duffle. That confused me a bit, but as I started dumping my dirty clothes on the back seat Dad produced another laundry bag and started taking out clean clothes. "You'll need these this week. You'll also need both pair of tennis shoes and your light jacket."

"But Dad, can't I go home?" I must have sounded pretty pathetic because Dad stopped issuing orders and gave me a sincere look.

"Not today son. You need to spend some time with Elzie up the river. It will be good for you, and there's lots to learn."

"But Dad, I want to play summer baseball. I've been practicing, and" Dad cut me off. "I know son, but things really need to settle down around town first. Baseball will be there when you get back." And that was that! I filled my duffle with clean clothes, went back inside. Dad told Elzie to make me behave. Elzie said he didn't think I'd have time to misbehave. With that we were out the back door, onto Elzie's boat, and headed up the river.

I found a place to sit and watched Apalachicola fade into the distance. The boat, like Walter's, was filled with grocery bags, ice chest, and lots of gas cans. I sure hope we don't have to pour concrete for a week. Another week of work wasn't going to bother me. I just wanted to be home. After a week working for Walter on the Island, I thought this would be more of the same. It wasn't the same!

I always enjoyed being on the river. The water was generally calm, cool, and fresh. Fresh meant a whole lot more after a week on salt water. The cypress and tupelo trees were already deep shades of green. Around each bend the ancient cypress and hickory trees cast deep, mysterious shadows against the shoreline. White swamp lilies sprinkled along the banks splashed brightness against the dark shaded swamp. River lily pads concentrated along the shallows, perfect for bream fishing. Dad had taught me that, we'd spent many summer days along these same banks fishing for bream, and in the fall we had hunted squirrels. Those were always special times. At home Dad was the principal, up here it was him and me. We have had some great times, I sure hope we'll have more.

We stayed on the big river, past the railroad trestle, and took the big river around pin-hook. Heading north the river was wide, no chop and the spray from the boat created miniature rainbows on both sides of the stern. At Mark's Point we turned south. I should tell you about the Apalachicola River, at least the portion that I know. As the big river gets closer to the bay it fingers off into smaller rivers. First there are the Brothers Rivers, big brother and little brother. They finger on the western side of the big river maybe 20 miles up the river. Their mouth, or entrance, empties back into the big river just a couple of miles above Mark's Point. Below the upper limits of the Brothers, there is another river, East River. It's located on the eastern side of the big river. East River flows all the way to the bay. Next is at Mark's Point. Big St. Marks travels to the bay, but about a mile south from the point there is a cut-off, East River Cut Off, that connects Big St. Marks to East River. Further down on Big St. Marks the river splits in to Big St. Marks and Little St. Marks. Both flow into the bay.

After turning at Mark's Point we ran down to just above East River Cut Off. On the eastern side of the Big St Marks there was a long house boat. The house boat appeared to be approximately 60 feet long, maybe 25 feet wide. On the northern end was a screened room, I guessed at 15 feet long. On the south end was another screened room, maybe 10 feet long. Not all of it appeared to have screen. The house boat was made from a large metal barge; it had a tin roof and the exterior was lap-board cypress. It had turned gray from weathering. The deck appeared to be three or more feet above the water line. Also, there was a two and a half foot walking deck around the entire barge. Cleats were spread every 5or 6 feet for attaching lines to boats or docks. Elzie throttled back on the engine and eased over to the barge. He swung the bow of the boat to where it was facing north. He held the boat steady against the barge and I stepped out onto the deck and tied the bow line to a cleat and then the stern line to another cleat.

"Welcome home," Elzie offered as he stepped onto the barge. There was a large screen door on our side; Elzie propped it open and we started shuttling the packages and gas cans from the boat to the screen porch. I noticed that there was a daybed on the porch just like at Walter's. Within a few minutes all was aboard and we entered the house portion of the boat. The first 20 feet served as a living and dining area. There were windows on both sides, as well as windows facing the front screen porch. The walls were made of streaked cypress. It appeared they were treated because none showed signs of graying. A small gas stove, and a refrigerator backed against the land side of the room and as far as they could go until merging with another dividing wall. That wall was about 10 feet wide and cornered toward the back. A hallway led to the back. Another wall river side of the hall formed another room. The main room had a table and four chairs on the land side of the room, and there was another chair and a couch on the riverside of the room. A few pictures were on the walls and a two rack shelf held a few books. Elzie motioned for me to follow him, "This is where we live," swinging his hand around the main room. "This is the bathroom," pointing to the room on the left hand side of the hall. "This area is for storage. There's shelves for groceries and stuff. You'll figure it out. Back here is my bedroom, closet, and where I keep my guns. Don't get a gun without asking first."

"Why would I need a gun?"

"In case you need to shoot something."

"Like what?"

"Anything! An alligator, a bear, maybe someone."

"Someone? Like who?"

"I guess you'd have to determine that."

"Have you ever shot anyone?"

"Not recently. But come on, we've got to catch some supper."

It wasn't even time for lunch, but I followed Elzie back out onto the large screened porch. Between the barge and the bank, about 8 or 10 feet from the bank there were seven large poles that were driven into the water. They served as stable pillars to tie the barge to. A walk way was constructed from the barge to the bank. It appeared to be about 6 feet wide, a hand rail on the south side. Nestled there between the barge and the bank, partly under the walk way was another boat. It looked to be about 14 feet long and had a 25 horse power Evinrude for power. We walked across the walk way to the bank. It had been cleared of any underbrush and there was a fire pit made from large stones within a few steps from the walk way. Metal stakes were driven on both sides of the pit and a wire mesh rack covered half of the fire pit. Off to the side was a deck about 5 feet wide and 8 feet long. It stood on post about 4 feet high. A large tarp covered it. I asked what it was and Elzie pulled the tarp off. It was another army issue generator like the one Walter had on the island.

"I know how to operate that," I offered.

"Good that you do." Elzie said with a slight smile. Some fat lighter and oak was stacked nearby the fire pit. Two beat up old chairs lay close to the pit. "One of your chores will be to help keep the brush cut and fire wood stacked," Elzie began. "There's an ax, a shovel, and a sling on the back porch. Come on, let's fish off the back porch."

The back porch was partially screened, but 6 or 7 feet from the end was opened but had a covered top. A table was constructed toward the bank side. It stood about waist high, had a sink and a hand pump, and a few feet which appeared to be a fish cleaning area. The remaining area toward the river side was open. Two chairs were there. Elzie retrieved a coffee can from inside the screened area, put it on the table and then went back around to the land side and retrieved a couple of cane poles. "Worms are in the can," he offered as he handed me a cane pole. "You know how to fish don't you?"

"Sure." I pulled a chair closer to the stern where I could fish, put on some bait and dropped a line into the river. A cork held the bait about 4 feet below the surface. Elzie went into the house and within a couple of minutes was back out with me. He was drinking a beer and mumbling something about how many bream we needed for supper. We sat there not saying much of anything for more than an hour. No fish. Finally Elzie said,

"I thought you said you knew how to fish?"

"What about you? You haven't caught any either."

"I didn't say I knew how to fish!" that smile creeping back to his face. "Well, how about a little lunch?" Lunch was a can of sardines and crackers. He did have some cokes; I washed my sardines down with one of those. Elzie decided he needed to rest a bit; I went back to fishing. Later in the day, before the sun dropped below the tree line, Elzie came back out onto the porch. "Any luck?" he asked.

"Nothing," I replied.

"Well, what are we going to do about supper?" Elzie questioned me.

"Maybe some more sardines?"

"Boy, you have lots to learn. Come on and help me. And bring that bucket with you," as he pointed to a five gallon bucket under the table. I took the bait off my fishing pole, put the pole against the wall, grabbed the five gallon bucket and followed Elzie around to the walk way. He eased into the smaller boat, turned to me for the five gallon bucket, and started, "In the river swamp always have a back-up plan!" He reached under the boat's walking deck and untied a rope that was unseen from up on the walk way. Slowly he pulled a wire basket to the surface and put it into the smaller boat. Bream and catfish kicked and flounced in the basket. I was shocked and confused.

"Why did we fish all afternoon if you knew you had those fish in the basket?"

"Did you mind fishing?"

"No."

"Then what's your point?" I didn't have an answer. As Elzie shook six large bream into the five gallon bucket he directed his attention to me again, "Matt, it's not lawful to use wire for fish baskets. Don't ever pull this trap when anyone is around. Hear me, anyone!" I was confused,

"Then why are you using a wire trap?"

"Because I have an obligation to feed you and me!" as if that made it all right. He put the wire trap back into the water, still with more fish in it, and handed me the five gallon bucket with the six bream in it. Back at the fish cleaning table I started to scale the fish when Elzie took over. "We're not going to fry these fish. Let me teach you how to prepare fish when you don't have grease and a frying pan." He took each bream and cut from their butt hole up through the under belly to the fish's mouth. He cleaned the insides very good, even raking his knife blade along the back bone to remove the blood vein that ran the length of the body. He then cut out the gills leaving the gill plates in place. "Let's go put these beauties on ice and then we'll get the fire pit ready." He laid the fire pit the same as Walter had done with the fat lighter on the bottom and the oak stacked on top. He then went and got another beer and we sat by the fire pit waiting for inspiration, I guess, because he didn't light the fire. The sun was below the tree line when inspiration finally took over. He lit the fire and told me to come help in the kitchen. There he brought out a ball of twine, cut several lengths of 10 to 12 inches each and then brought out the bream and a couple of limes. In each bream he shook salt, pepper and some garlic, and then placed a slice of lime in the cavity. Each bream was then tied with the string about a couple of inches apart. It took three strings for each bream to close the body cavity. He trimmed the extra string above the knot and put the bream on a platter and returned them to the refrigerator. He then brought out a frying pan and a pot and placed both on the stove. He added water and grits to the pot, put grease in the frying pan. Hush puppies were mixed and prepared to fry. "Go check the fire for us, Matt. It may need another piece of oak or two. We want a bed of coals, not a big fire for these bream."

I tended the fire with a few pieces of oak and returned to the kitchen. Elzie had started the grits, and was beginning to heat the grease for the hushpuppies. He also turned on the oven but set the temperature for its lowest setting. Grits came to a boil, the heat was reduced and the hushpuppies browned to a golden color before going into the oven to keep warm. At that point we took the bream to the fire. Elzie produced a pair of the hot gloves just like the ones Walter used, and he brought a pair of tongs for handling the bream. I noticed that the metal support post for the wire rack had stubs along the post so the wire rack's height could be adjusted. Elzie placed the wire rack approximately 8 inches above the bed of coals and spread the bream evenly across the rack.

"Won't the fire burn the twine?" I wondered.

"Nope," Elzie replied, "the string is butcher's twine. Heat resistant. You can buy it most grocery stores." It took just a few minutes before you could hear the sizzling of the bream cooking. Elzie turned the fish over and minutes later he started tapping the bream's sides with the tongs. "When they're done they'll sound hollow when you tap them like that." Within a couple of minutes he put them on a platter and we went back to the kitchen. He cut all the strings on the bream and put them on the table. A plate for each of us had grits, with butter, and hushpuppies. Elzie showed me how to remove the skin and scales to expose the meat. The scales and skin actually peel off together very easily. Starting near the head and pulling toward the tail the skin and scales peel off together in a single sheet. Elzie squeezed another slice of lime over the meat and said "Amen!" and we dug in. I had never eaten bream cooked like that, the meat was tender and moist, the seasonings and the lime married together with each bite. Fried bream tend to be tough and the grease dominates the flavor, not these! After supper I told Elzie that the bream were much better than the sardines. He didn't even think I was funny.

It was getting dark by the time I cleaned up the kitchen. I headed out to the front porch and my daybed when Elzie asked, "Where you going?"

"To bed, I guess."

"To bed? You've been around Walter too long. You've still got work to do."

"What kind of work?" I couldn't imagine what I would be doing after dark.

"Frog gigging! We've got to get supper for tomorrow night. You might want to wear long sleeves, bugs get bad sometimes." Frog gigging! I had never been frog gigging. Certainly I had heard about people gigging frogs, but never had I gigged a frog, or eaten one. Outlawing bream, now gigging frogs. What will we do tomorrow? Bronco riding alligators?

Elzie produced some head lights and a couple of gigs with small three pronged metal heads, and a large, heavy gig with a large three prong heavy gage steel head.

"What's the big gig for?" I asked.

"Gators!"

"Gators? You gig gators?"

"Yep!"

We turned on our headlights, eased into the smaller boat and headed up river. Within a few hundred yards we entered a creek on the right side of the river.

"Humphreys Slough! That's the name of this creek," Elzie instructed. "Good fishing in here. Frogs and gators too!"

The night was dark and the moisture in the air made the evening really cool. I was glad I had long sleeves on. The outline of the woods shone like a shadow against the evening sky. Our head lights didn't seem particularly bright, outside of their narrow beam darkness prevailed. Elzie cut the motor to an idle; it was very quiet and we eased along without speaking, swinging our lights along the shore line. Within a few minutes I heard Elzie whisper, "There's one." I followed his light to the bank and, with my light, picked up the shining eyes of a large bull frog. I was sitting in the bow of the boat. Elzie instructed me in a low voice, "As I get closer, stand up and brace yourself against the bow rail, keep your light aimed directly at the frog, and then as soon as you can reach him, pop him in the head." I followed his instructions. As soon as I gigged the frog Elzie said to swing the gig and frog around toward him. As instructed, I turned and brought the gig and frog around toward Elzie. He had a wooded box in front of him and was opening the lid. "Put him in here and when I close the lid turn your gig to where you can pull the gig out and the frog will remain in the box." Nothing to it. I was now an official frog gigger!

We backed away from the bank and returned to the hunting. Over the next hour I gigged 14 more bull frogs. My confidence was growing; this is fun! We were well back into the creek and were about to start working our way back when Elzie whispered again. "Wow! There's a good-un!"

"Where?" I followed his light again. It was a good ways off, but there were two frogs it appeared. "Is that two frogs?"

"Nope, a nice gator." He took the motor out of gear and while still keeping his light on the gator instructed me to get the heavy gig. I put my gig down and picked up the big one. He continued with instructions, "Matt, we'll ease up to him just like the frogs, but when you hit him, hit him hard. Very Hard. But listen, when you hit him he will begin to spin. You have to keep a good hold on to the gig, but you have to let the gig spin in your hand. If it doesn't spin and you're off balance it will flip you over board. Now, get braced up in the bow and I'll ease over to him. He's not on the bank, he's in the water. If you can't get a good shot at his head, just leave him. But if you can, hit him hard right above the eyes."

With the motor back in gear, very slowly we headed for the gator. Both lights were fixed on his eyes. With less than 8 to 10 feet from him I could see that he was pretty big. Maybe 6 or 7 feet long. Elzie cut the engine about that time and silently we coasted toward him. The bow was almost on top of him when I slammed him with the heavy gig. Just above the eyes. All hell broke loose. He spun just like Elzie said he would. Water was splashing everywhere. I kept a good grip on the gig, but also let it spin as the gator spun at the surface. Immediately Elzie was at my side, "Just keep a good grip, we've got him now. Ok, ease back toward the middle of the boat. I'll get on the other side of you. He'll stop spinning in a minute and then I can get a hold of his tail."

"What are you going to do?" I was excited, maybe a bit scared.

"If I can get a hold of his tail, I'll cut it off!" and Elzie showed me the machete he was holding.

"Do I try pulling him into the boat?" It sounded dumb, but I didn't know.

"Hell no! HELL NO!" He made that very clear. "When I get a hold of his tail I'll cut it off with this machete. Then we can knock him off the gig." Just like we did this every day, the gator quit spinning, Elzie got a hold of his tail, and with me pulling the gator to the surface, Elzie made two quick swings with the machete and voila, we had about three to four feet of gator tail in the boat. Elzie quickly grabbed an oar and while I held the gig, he knocked the gator from the barbs of the gig head. "I think I need a beer," and without any other comments Elzie headed us back to the house boat.

Back at the houseboat we unloaded our catch, tied off the smaller skiff, and Elzie went to crank up the generator. Once the lights were on we cleaned the frogs and the gator tail at the fish cleaning table. The frog remains we threw overboard; the gator remains, the tip of the tail and the skin, Elzie took back in the woods and discarded them. I stoked the fire a bit, added some more wood and was sitting in a chair when Elzie returned from the woods. "Best not to leave any evidence," he suggested. "I'll be right back to join you. I'll have that beer now. You want a coke?"

"Yes sir, that would be great! We sat by the fire until very late. We rehashed the frog gigging and the gator episode. I was really feeling excited. "By the way, what work am I supposed to do?" I asked.

"Work? Wasn't that enough work for you for today?"

"If that classifies as work, I guess so!"

"Well, let's sleep on it and we'll figure out what other work we can do tomorrow." And we headed to bed.

As I lay on the day bed on the front porch, I remembered what I heard my Mom tell Dad the morning Dad sent me with Walter to Little St. George Island, "They're just a couple of River Rats and Salty Dogs." As sleep approached I thought that I might be both.

When I woke the sun was already up and the tree line on the western bank was light and bright. Our side of the river was still in shadows but birds were singing and I could smell coffee from the kitchen area. Elzie was sitting at the table just starring out at the woods. He barely moved when I entered the room. "Everything okay?" I asked as I sat down at the table.

"Good, just trying to wake up. You sleep alright?"

"Yes sir. Like a baby." He made no efforts or said anything about breakfast so I got up and went looking for some cereal. Cheerios were in the storage room in the hall and milk was in the refrigerator. I found a bowl in the cabinets and a spoon in a drawer. I expected him to outline my chores for the day, but Elzie just sat there staring at the woods. Didn't say a thing for a long while. I had washed my dishes and was sitting on the couch when he finally spoke. "You know how to use a fly rod?"

"No sir." I knew what a fly rod was but never used one. We usually used the cane poles with worms when fresh water fishing.

"Then you need to learn," and he got up and went back into his bedroom. A minute later he was back in the room with several pieces of rod and a couple of reels. The pieces connected produced two rods and he attached a reel to each. He fed the fly line through the ferrules and then tied monofilament leaders to the fly line. After both rods were ready he went back to his room and came back with a fairly small plastic box. Opening it, he spread several flies onto the table. They were different colors, yellow, green, white, and all had bodies made from cork. Feather looking material covered the hook; rubber legs dangled to each side. "What's your color?" he asked me.

"I'll take the yellow one!" He picked it up and, like Walter had done, started educating me as to how to tie the fly with monofilament. He picked up the green fly and had me tie it onto the other fly line.

Once completed he said "Let's go." And we were out the door. He grabbed a dip net from the porch wall and we loaded into the small boat. There were still blood stains from the night before, marks of the outlaw I thought. Or maybe marks of the River Rat? Just as we entered Humphreys Slough he cut the engine and said I should practice first. As instructed, I moved to the bow of the boat with my fly rod; he stayed in the stern. "Now watch how I handle the rod." He held the rod out over the water and stripped line from the reel onto the bottom of the boat. Then, while lifting the rod, he began a throwing motion using only his wrist to control the rod tip, and fed line out toward the bank. "If the rod tip is straight up, call it twelve o'clock, your motion brings the rod tip back to about two o'clock, give the fly line time to react, and then with pressure shoot the rod tip, and the line, down to about nine o'clock. The control is in the wrist. Now you practice that for a few minutes before I get you within tree range."

For several minutes we sat in the middle of the creek, me casting in all directions, Elzie giving instructions and encouragement. Finally he said we should give it a try. He had a sculling lock on the stern of the boat, and with an oar he guided the boat nearer to the bank. As I began casting he moved us along at a slow but steady pace, keeping us back from the overhanging limbs, but close enough to place the fly close to the bank. "Now notice the branches and the growth along the bank. If a branch is hanging low over the water and you want to cast under it, you can't use an overhead cast. You'll have to roll the line under the branch. Watch and I'll show you." And without any effort at all he side armed a cast causing the fly line to roll under the branch and plop the fly next to the bank. Immediately a big bream slammed the fly. Elzie aimed the fly rod away from the bank and branches, and stripped the fly line into the boat bringing the bream to the net. As I lifted the bream I noticed that almost smile from Elzie I had seen at the shrimp house. "OK, your turn!"

For the next couple of hours he instructed, I cast. Of course I caught limbs several times, but Elzie didn't mind. We kept at it and after plenty of instructions I started catching a few fish. It was getting late in the morning, the sun was high, and heating up when we called it quits and headed back to the house boat.

Elzie put me in charge of cleaning the fish, we had an even dozen, and he went to find us some lunch. After lunch Elzie said he needed a nap, so I looked over the books on the two shelves. Another Ruark book was there, The Old Man and the Boy, so I picked it up and started to the front porch to read when I noticed the picture on the wall. It was the same picture as I found at Walter's. It was Walter and Elzie and their sister. There was something about the woman's look, like when I first saw the picture at Walter's, she just looked familiar. I don't know what it was, maybe her hair, her eyes, or the shape of her face. I just kept staring at her for several minutes. I settled in on the porch and started reading. Within an hour I was thinking that the Old Man was a combination of Walter and Elzie, maybe with the exception of appreciation for rules and laws. I dozed off after a bit. It was just after four o'clock when I awoke. I could hear Elzie doing something back in his room. I decided not to bother him and was about to start reading again when I noticed a person in a canoe, just south of Humphreys Slough, headed our way.

"Elzie, there's someone headed our way in a canoe."

"Shit! I forgot, I was supposed to call her yesterday."

"Who?"

"Cloud."

"Who's she?"

"You'll meet her in a few minutes." And out the door he went. I followed. The woman could certainly handle a canoe; it didn't take her very long before Elzie was tying her bow line to a cleat. Elzie offered her a hand and she stepped onto the barge. She looked to be about my Dad's age. She was pretty, maybe 5'5", dark hair, long and pulled back into a pony tail. Her eyes were dark, thick eye brows, high cheek bones, full lips, and a square jaw.

She kissed Elzie quickly on the mouth, then turned toward me and said, "Hi Matthew, I'm Cloud."

"How do you know my name?" I blurted.

"Oh, I know lots of things about you."

"How?"

"Well, for starters, I've watched you play ball for several years. And Elzie keeps me posted on your accomplishments."

"Watched me play ball? Are you from Apalach?"

"Oh no, I teach at Bristol."

Elzie broke in, "Let's at least get out of this sun. Let's sit on the porch." As the woman and I took our seats Elzie went into the kitchen and returned shortly with a pitcher of ice water and three glasses. I sat in silence as Elzie and Cloud talked. He apologized for not calling her the day before, she said she expected we were having too much fun. He asked why she came in the canoe instead of the skiff, she said she just decided a canoe trip would be more enjoyable.

After several minutes she turned to me, "I hear you've been having a good time?"

"I guess so." I didn't know what I should say. I had never even heard of this woman, who evidently, knew a lot about me, and was Elzie's girl friend?

"So, what did you boys do yesterday and last night?" Elzie said we did usual stuff. She turned to me, "what about you?"

"I learned how to grill bream, and I gigged some frogs and a gator!"

"Elzie, for god's sake, you shouldn't be teaching this boy to gig gators."

I thought I saw Elzie blush.

"The boy has lots to learn."

"Maybe so, but he doesn't need to end up in jail from your teachings."

Jail! My mind started into a panic. I was up here so that I wouldn't have to go to jail. Is this some prank? Am I going to end up in trouble again? My expressions must have been obvious because Cloud turned to me and said, "Well, maybe it was just a back-up plan!" This woman sure seemed to know a lot. I was afraid to say anything, but she turned to Elzie and said that she and I should visit a bit. So, Elzie excused himself and went into the main room and then disappeared into his bedroom. Cloud turned to me and began, "I know this seems strange, me showing up here and all, but maybe I can share some information that will make all this make sense? OK?"

"Yes ma'am!"

"First, Elzie and I have been a couple for longer than you've been alive. I teach at Bristol High School. I know your Dad. And, I've watched you play football and baseball since you were in elementary school. I heard about you and your buddies little joke with the Judge. Boy, I wish I could have been in that court room when he tried to break bad on y'all. Don't worry, the judge has a history too." I was beginning to relax. She seemed very nice. I still had a hundred questions, but thought I might want to keep them to myself for now. She wouldn't have it,

"So, young man, what would you like to know about me?" She sure was to the point. It was easy to see how she would be a teacher.

"Your name is Cloud? What kind of name is that?"

"My given name is White Cloud of the Apalachicola Indians, a sub-tribe of the Creek Indians. However, for my people to survive they had to assimilate. So, we took on white people's names. Our family are Taylors."

"Like Walter and Elzie? Are you related?"

"Yes, like Walter and Elzie, and no, we are not related. My name in Bristol is Anne Taylor."

"What do you teach?"

"History."

"How do you know my Dad?"

"As I said, Elzie and I have been a couple for a very long time. I met your Dad when he was still in college; Walter and Elzie still supported him. I also watched your Dad play ball. He was a good athlete like you."

This was beginning to be too much. It was like my whole life was a mystery. Until a couple of weeks ago I had never heard of these folks, and now they were telling me about my life, my Dad's life, and Indians living in Bristol. Again, my expressions must have given me away because Cloud excused herself and went in to find Elzie. I stayed on the porch and tried to read The Old Man and the Boy but I couldn't concentrate. Several minutes later Elzie appeared and said Cloud was going to fix us supper. The sun was setting, the heat had eased off a bit, and the river returned to glass like conditions. I was wondering what Mom and Dad were doing when Cloud called us to supper. We had fried frog legs, fried gator tail, hushpuppies, grits and a big salad. The salad had a zesty lemony flavored dressing that was really good. I ate so much my belly was hurting. I excused myself and went to lie down on the porch. It was late and very dark when I woke up. I thought I felt the barge rocking, but I sat up for a minute, decided I was dreaming and went back to sleep. The sun was already up when I woke. I heard two large splashes on the river side and got up and went to see what was happening. Elzie and Cloud were in the river back by the stern. It looked as if neither of them had on any clothes or bathing suits. I went back to bed. I acted like I was just waking up when Elzie came out to the porch to get me up.

"Breakfast will be ready shortly. Rise and shine." He appeared to be in a good mood. Cloud served an excellent breakfast of scrambled eggs, bacon, toast, and grits. Elzie produced a carton of orange juice. We ate in silence. They just smiled at each other. I was afraid to talk. After breakfast and the dishes cleaned, Elzie told me that we were going to take Cloud back to her home.

"In Bristol?" I asked.

"No, she doesn't live in Bristol, only works there. She lives a couple of miles south of Sumatra, on Owl Creek. Come help me load her canoe." Within minutes we had loaded the canoe into the larger boat, strapped it down, and headed up river. Cloud sat next to Elzie, I was in the stern. The river was calm, glassy, and the tree line was reflected in the water on both sides of the river. White fluffy clouds sprinkled the southern sky as we headed north.

It took about an hour until Elzie slowed as we approached Owl Creek on the eastern side of the river. Entering the creek it appeared narrow. The northern bank was filled with large cypress trees, but the southern bank was deceptive; the actual bank was not easily seen for between the creek and the southern bank there were small islands of miniature cypress. There were many islands, of different sizes, but none of the trees and vegetation growing on the islands was tall. Those islands continued for several hundred yards before merging back into the southern bank. At that point a high ridge developed on the southern shore. We had not gone much further when I noticed a couple of boats tied to the southern bank. A canoe and a bateau. As we idled to the landing site I noticed that the creek forked there; going forward the creek became narrower, but the fork to the left opened up lake-like and took a dog leg to the right. I couldn't see beyond that point, but I found myself thinking that I'd really like to fly fish that area one day soon.

We tied the boat at the landing site and unloaded Cloud's canoe. There was a well developed trail up the side of the hill, and someone had strung a rope through the adjoining trees to create a hand hold for climbing the hill. At the hill top was a large clearing with huge live oak trees spread over the area. There were five houses, spaced in a semi-circle fashion, behind the field and the live oak trees. Behind the houses were very tall white oak trees, the ones that produce the large acorns; they were in full foliage. The houses were very similar in size and design. They each had tin roofs, lap board cypress siding, which had greyed and each house had a chimney. There was a front stoop as the entrance, but each house had a screened back porch. Three of the houses had barns in their back yards. There were three vehicles there, a 1955 Chevy, and two pick-up trucks, one a Ford, the other a Chevy.

In the middle of the cleared area there was a fairly large building, all of it screened. To one side of the building there was a large fire pit with metal racks and supports. A few chairs were scattered in the yard. Off to the side was a swing set made from large poles; it had three swings. As we entered the cleared area we heard a young girl call out, "Cloud's home!"

From the houses women, children, and a few men came out to welcome us. They all had dark hair and looked suntanned. The men wore jeans, the women wore light colored day dresses, and the small children all wore shorts. The young girls immediately swarmed Cloud. Between the children laughing, the men shaking hands, and the women trying to get the children's attention, somehow, as if by habit, we all ended up in the screened-in building. It was one big open room. Ceiling fans were running, creating a breeze that was comfortable, and table and chairs were organized to feed and socialize. Along one end of the room counters provided a couple of sinks and lots of prep room for serving. Someone produced a couple of pitchers of sweet tea and we all dropped onto a chair, sweet tea in hand. I was introduced all around but I could not remember anyone's name. The children didn't last long in the room and were soon out at the swing set yelling and playing. Elzie talked to the men about timber cost, and of course fishing. The women were gathered around Cloud and teasing about something.

We had been there less than 15 or 20 minutes when a girl appeared at the screened room door. As she entered the room I think I bit my lip. She was beautiful! She looked like a younger version of Cloud. She had the same dark hair, which was long and pulled back into a pony tail, her eyes were dark and she had the same high cheek bones and square jaw. Her skin looked like light tan velvet, her lips were full, and she smiled showing the whitest teeth I'd ever seen. She wore cut-off jeans and a simple light blue knit blouse. She was barefoot. I couldn't take my eyes off her. Finally, Elzie leaned over and told me not to drool. She came over to introduce herself to me. I stood up, almost kicking my chair over, and stuttered a hello. She smiled and sat down next to me. "Matt, my name's Tess." Why was it everyone knew my name but I didn't even know these people existed?

"And how do you know my name?" I began.

"Well, of course from Cloud and Elzie, but I've been watching you play baseball and football since we were in junior high."

"We?" I asked.

"We're the same age. I'll be a junior next year too. Also, I'm a cheerleader at Bristol." That made sense. Well, I think it made sense. It made me feel like I had a fan club, except they were for the other team. I just sat there, I didn't know what else I should say. I wasn't about to tell her I gigged frogs and a gator. She'd think I was a river rat! Maybe I am. That thought was beginning to stick in my brain when she took over the conversation. "Are you playing baseball this summer?"

"I thought I was going to, but right now I don't know when I'll be going home."

"Why don't you know when you're going home?" A really good question.

"I didn't even know I was coming up here. Dad, evidently, has turned me over to Walter and Elzie."

"That can't be all bad?" She smiled, showing off those pearly whites. "So, will you be staying on the river for a while?"

"Like I said, I didn't even know I was coming up here. I have no idea when I'll be going home. I really want to play baseball this summer."

"I'm sure you'll get your chance. And maybe I'll get to spend some time with you." It wasn't a question. Maybe she was just being nice. Boy, I sure hope she's right. I needed to not act stupid. I need to be part of the conversation. Act like you've got some sense. I finally spoke,

"How long have you lived here?"

"All of my life."

"Is Cloud your mother?"

"No silly, she's my aunt. She's my mother's sister."

"Does your mother teach in Bristol too?"

"No, she works at a dentist office." That could explain those pearly whites, I thought.

"Are you a Taylor?"

"No, my mom's a Taylor; my dad was a Crawford."

"Was?"

"He was killed in a logging accident five years ago."

"Oh, I'm really sorry." This could be a lot easier if someone had forewarned me. "Do you have brothers or sisters?"

"Yes, a sister. See her over there by the swings. She's the one with the red scarf in her hair."

"Wow, she's a cutie. How old is she?"

"She'll be 12 in October."

"What's her name?"

"Sage, like the herb." I thought about that for a minute. At first I thought it sounded strange, but everything so far had been strange. Maybe an Indian name?

"Is that an Indian name, like Cloud?"

"No, like an herb." She laughed. She had a nice laugh. I realized I was acting stupid again, so I laughed with her. "Let's go for a walk." and she reached down and took my hand and led me out of the screened room into the sun light. We walked toward the creek, along the high ridge, until we could see the water. Large hickory, pines and oak trees cast long shadows across a well used trail. There was a bench between two trees so we stopped there; the view over the creek was picture worthy.

"This is a beautiful area," I offered. "I bet this spot gets used a lot?"

"It is beautiful. I've spent lots of evenings here. When times aren't good, it gives you hope. It keeps me in balance." She had a glow about her, a maturity I wasn't use to. I was really feeling out of my league. She smiled at me and then began talking. "Our family has always been close. Losing Dad is the hardest thing we've ever gone through. I am so thankful for Cloud. She has a spirit about her that seems to transcend hardships. At some of our worst times she gathers us around her and she tells us about our ancestors, their lives, their hardships, their love of the land, the rivers, the family. We come from good blood. Sometimes we just have to be reminded of that." She reached out and took my hand again and squeezed it. Her grip was strong. I sensed her spirit was strong too.

"Let's go back before Elzie comes barking at us. I think he likes putting on a show for Cloud." The walk back to the family and the big room was way too fast for me.

As we dropped back into some chairs conversations were going in several directions at once. Cloud appeared to be teaching some of the children; other women were laughing about something, and Elzie and a couple of the men were carrying on about Liberty County politics.

Our family is small, just me, mom and dad. I was becoming envious of these people. They seemed to get along so well; they acted happy. They acted like family. Tess and I listened to the adults for a while, then talked some more about school, sports, and even where we hoped to go to college.

I was at my dream of playing college sports stage when a couple of the women started bring food into the room for lunch. There were three or four types of sliced bread, platters of vegetables, platters of sliced meats, and a few bowls of fruit. Paper plates, plastic knives, forks, and spoons, and more glasses of sweet tea covered the tables. The children were served first, and not like back at school, they were actually behaved. Everyone settled at a table. Elzie, Cloud, Tess and I had a table to ourselves. The conversation soon got around to when Elzie and I would be back up to visit, maybe even stay overnight. That got my attention in a hurry. I was beginning to think that baseball could wait a little longer. Finally, Elzie promised he would call Cloud tomorrow to set a date. He had to check in with Walter, which I later found out meant Dad, and he would call Cloud before dark.

Elzie and Cloud went back to her house leaving Tess and me alone. We talked for a long time it seemed. She asked how I ended up here. I told her about the shit stomping joke and the meeting with the Judge. When I got to the part in the Court Room and Billy explaining everything, and the women from the Clerk's office, Tess started laughing so hard that I started laughing. At one point every time I started to move forward with my story Tess would start laughing again, and then I would start laughing again until we both had to stop to catch our breath. I told her about how Dad sent me off to work for Walter for a while. I told her about the turtle laying her eggs, how I ran the turtle patrol every morning. I told her how I learned to throw a castnet, and I told her about the rock pile and the tire swing where I threw passes every afternoon. The rest of the afternoon flew by so fast I was shocked when Elzie said we had to go. We said our goodbyes to the family; Cloud and Tess escorted Elzie and me back to the boat. Cloud kissed Elzie goodbye, Tess gave me a hug. I was happy and sad at the same time. I stared back at the high ridge, where Tess and I sat together on the bench, and watched the colors change against a setting sun. The run back to the house boat was filled with dreams.

By daylight the next morning Elzie had me up and eating breakfast. "We've got to run some fish traps this morning and take some catfish to Bay City Lodge," he began as I cleaned up the dishes.

"What traps?" I questioned.

"I've got several spread around. Try to run'em every few days. Bay City is always begging for fresh cat fish." We loaded the boat quickly. Elzie grabbed a wooden fish box from the back porch and threw it into the big boat. He reached under the wheel housing, retrieved 2 pair of rubber gloves and gave a pair to me. "You'll need those when pulling the traps."

We started south toward East River Cut Off but about 50 yards from its entrance he pulled over next to the bank. A submerged log angled away from the bank and only showed a few feet above the waterline. He handed me a short hand line and told me to loop it over the log and hold us in place until he got the trap. From underneath the side gunnel he retrieved a long handled gaff, and while I held the boat close to the log, he reached down into the water and hooked a line that was attached to the log. Lifting the line to where he could handle it by hand, he slid the gaff back onto the floor boards, then pulled the fish trap out of the water and into the boat. It was another wire mesh fish basket. It held more than a dozen nice fresh water cat fish. They were transferred to the fish box quickly, the basket repositioned on the river bottom, and we slowly motored around and into East River Cut Off.

We stopped three more times at submerged logs, retrieved lines not seen from above water, and collected at least three dozen more cat fish. All the baskets were made from wire mesh.
The run to Bay City Lodge only took about 25 minutes. Bay City Lodge is located about five miles up the river from the bridge at Apalachicola. It's an old fishing lodge that's been around since the 1920s. Dad takes Mom and me there often for supper. Lots of people come to stay and fish. Guides are available, the restaurant is excellent and the cooks will prepare anything you catch any way you want. Fresh water catfish are a favorite on the menu.

While Elzie unloaded the catfish and got credit to his ticket, I called home. Mom answered the phone. She sounded like she was about to cry when she heard my voice. She asked me questions faster than I could answer. I told her yes I was alright, yes I was eating well, yes I was getting plenty of rest, and yes I was having fun. I didn't tell her about a beautiful girl who lived on Owl Creek. I told her I didn't know when I would be home but I was sure it wouldn't be much longer. Dad wasn't home, he was at work. I told her we were delivering fresh water catfish to Bay City Lodge, but we were about to leave to head back up the river. I promised I'd be careful. I did NOT tell her I gigged a gator.

I had a coke while Elzie made a phone call. Shortly we were headed out of the creek, into the big river, headed home!

Chapter 4: Owl Creek

I woke the next morning before daylight; Elzie was still in his room. I could hear bull frogs croaking, the occasional fish strike, and the river owls were talking loudly, a sure sign that it was feeding time. There's no hooting with river owls, they're loud, sounding like people hollering back and forth. I know some folks back in Apalach that sound about the same way. Maybe they're part owl. I laid there listening to the night sounds, smelling the sweetness from the sweetgum flowers, not thinking about home, not thinking about baseball. I could not get Tess off my mind.

Back home I thought that Jill and I would start dating this fall. I should have my driver's license by then, and Dad had said I would be able to use the car. But I hadn't seen Jill in over a couple of weeks. I wonder if she had been at the Canteen the night of the shit-stomping. Somehow, right now, it really didn't matter. Tess was beautiful, but she also seemed kind. There was a maturity about her that I had not seen in any of the girls I knew in high school. She loved her family and she showed it. She was comfortable with adults, but also with the children too. I really hope Elzie and I get to go for an overnight visit soon. Baseball could wait. I think Dad was right, there is a lot to learn.

Elzie coughed, spit, cussed and then walked into the kitchen area, turned on coffee and then went back into his room. I figured I might as well get up, there wouldn't be any more sleeping when he started moving about. I dressed quickly and went in to have breakfast. Elzie hardly ever ate breakfast, except when someone else fixed it, so I found the cereal and milk and was already eating when he came back for coffee. The coffee pot was smoking, the aroma was strong but inviting. He fixed a cup and, without saying anything, walked out onto the front porch and sat down. I figured he wasn't ready for conversation so I stayed put. The sun had lightened up the western shoreline when he came back inside. I stayed quiet. After a little bit he started talking, "What kind of work do we need to do today?" I had no idea why he was asking me that, I was supposed to be there to help him, not make up work.

"How about we go back up and visit with Cloud's family?" I said with a straight face.

"I don't think it's Cloud you want to go see."

I had to play this out, "Why would you say that? I think Cloud is really nice."

"You sound like a city boy! You meet a girl one day and can't think of anything else for a week."

"It hasn't been a week!"

"No, you're right there. And I don't think I could put up with you for a week waiting to go for a visit!" He emphasized "go for a visit."

"Well, maybe we should go gig another gator?"

"Boy, you sure can be a smart ass. Wait until I tell your dad about that one." He sipped his coffee, rolled his eyes around as a way of making fun of me, and then said, "Well maybe we should make a run up there today!"

"Really? Are we going to stay over?"

"Your Dad said it would be okay."

"When did you talk to Dad?"

"Yesterday, while you had your coke-o-cola."

"When do we leave?"

"Calm down boy, there ain't no hurry. We need to clean up this place before we go make a mess at somebody else's." So, we cleaned, or at least I cleaned up our mess. I washed the dishes, cleaned out the coffee pot, fixed my daybed on the front porch, and even washed out the blood stains from the small boat left over from frog gigging. I fixed a smaller bag of clean clothes to take with me; I didn't think showing up with a duffle would be proper. We were going for a visit, not moving in. Elzie was about ready to start loading the big boat when I got to thinking about Owl Creek and maybe some fly fishing.

"Any chance we might be able to do some fly fishing on Owl Creek?" It stopped him like he had been hit.

"That sounds like a good idea. I haven't fly fished that creek in a very long time. It's got some whoppers in it. Hold on, I'll get the fly rods." And shortly thereafter, we were on an adventure.

I really thought we were going to surprise everyone but Cloud and four kids were waiting for us at the landing when we got there. I found out soon enough that Cloud also had a short wave radio. They were all waving and yelling as we eased the boat into the landing. I jumped out and secured the boat. Elzie started unloading, handing me our clothes bags and another bag that was cold. "What's this?" I asked.

"A present for Cloud's family." He didn't offer more, so I didn't ask. The kids all wanted to help so Cloud started issuing orders to them and giving them small bags and stuff to haul to the house. Elzie slid out of the boat, gave Cloud a kiss, and put his arm around her shoulders. As we all started up the hill I asked Cloud about Tess.

"She had to make a run to town, she'll be back soon." Thank goodness! I felt like a lost puppy. As we entered the big clearing more children and a few of the women came out to meet us. A much older woman came over and gave Elzie a hug. He presented her with the cold bag and said "Just for you!"

She scoffed back at him and said, "Just for me to cook something for you!" They laughed together. I didn't know who she was but it was obvious that they were close. We continued to the middle house in the semi-circle.

At the stoop the kids dropped the packages onto the porch and headed to the swings. Elzie, Cloud and I entered the house carrying the packages. The entrance was into a living area, it covered just over half the width of the building. On the left hand side doors opened to two bedrooms and a bath. As you passed the living area there was a dining area with an oak table and four chairs. An impressive ceiling light hung over the dining table. It was brass. It had a center pole hanging from the ceiling approximately two feet long and attached to a half moon vase. From the vase five arms extended out about a foot each. Each had a glass light receptacle hanging from the arms. From the dining area we entered the kitchen. It wasn't large, but had plenty of counters, built in U shape fashion which contained the sink. Cabinets were located above the counters. There was a refrigerator and a gas stove. To the left of the kitchen was a larger room, a combination of a bathroom and bedroom, I presumed it was Cloud and Elzie's. Past the kitchen on the right was a large closet/pantry. A screened-in porch the whole width of the house completed the structure. Cloud directed her attention to me, "Matthew, this is my house. Make yourself comfortable. The front bedroom is yours." I took my bag into the bedroom; it wasn't large but it had a ceiling fan and light, a window, and the bed was a full size bed. The head board was made from a solid piece of cypress and on one end was carved the shape of a turtle, it made me think of the sea turtle from the Island. This was the perfect room for me. I dropped my bag onto the bed and went back to the living area. All the rooms had ceiling fans. Most were large and had lights as well. In the dining area there were two small ceiling fans located on either side of the dining room light but closer to the adjoining walls.

As I took a seat in the living area, Elzie and Cloud went back to the bedroom and took his baggage. They returned shortly and suggested we go out onto the back porch. Several chairs and a couple of chaise lounges were spread over the porch. The chaise lounges had adjustable backs, and they were made from heavy cedar wood. Two large ceiling fans created a great breeze. After sleeping on porches for the last couple of weeks I was thinking that this would be a great porch for me. Cloud brought out some fresh made lemonade and glasses with ice in them. Elzie and I settled in like we belonged there. It didn't take long before Cloud started making fun of us, "You boys look like you could take a nap! You didn't go chase another gator last night did you?" She took a sharp look in my direction; I guess she expected I would tell the truth.

"No ma'am! I've sworn off gator gigging." At that she just had to laugh.

Elzie broke in, I think to change the subject and take the attention away from me, "What's the plan for tonight?"

"Why, it's a party. We don't often get such distinguished gentlemen come a calling." That almost smile came back across Elzie's face,

"Does that mean I'm cooking something?"

"What do you think?" She smiled back at him. About that time I realized Elzie had heard that line before.

"Well, if I'm cooking, what's it going to be?" Cloud smiled, reached over and pushed his hair from his forehead, and said,

"How about a venison ham and some gator tail?"

"Umm! Guess me and my partner gonna have to get to work pretty quickly."

"It isn't even lunch yet, you just relax for a bit. I'll go put some things away." And she disappeared. Elzie gave me a quick look and said something about women always being in charge. I decided not to participate in that conversation and kept sipping on my lemonade.

It wasn't long before Cloud was back. "Would either of you like a ham sandwich?" Of course I said yes, the cereal had not satisfied my appetite. Elzie said he needed to start putting the rubs together, but Cloud quickly informed him that she had put the rub on the venison last night. It was in the refrigerator. Elzie's almost smile gave him away.

"And how do you know you it's the right rub?

"Because it's the same rub you used last time!" Watching Elzie getting played by Cloud was entertaining. It was obvious that Elzie had been cooking for these folks for many years. He showed me how to grill bream, but I really didn't think of him as a cook. My education continued. By the time I finished my ham sandwich Elzie was pacing the floor. Cloud's patience ran out and she shoved us out the door.

At the fire pit Elzie began with instructions, "Matt: take those concrete blocks over there and stack them in two rows right here, three blocks high." He was pointing to the blocks and waving his hands like I was backing up a truck. As I started hauling blocks, he started laying the fire. There was plenty of fat lighter and oak. Within a few minutes he adjusted the blocks, adjusted the rack holders, and sent me to wash the racks at a water spigot. As I returned with the racks he was lighting the fire. "Put the racks over there, and see this metal sheet, go wash it as well. Make sure one side is very clean, we don't want dirt and trash falling on the meat."

"Why are we starting the fire now when suppers five or more hours away?" I thought it was a good question.

"Because it will take a good hour and a half to build the bed of coals I want. You keep an eye on the fire, I've got to go check on the meat and tend to the gator tail." And off he went. I was adding more wood and poking at the fire when Tess drove up. I literally felt my heart jump. She was driving a dark blue 56 Chevy. She saw me at the fire, gave a wave, and headed my way. Her long hair was around her shoulders, she wore blue jeans and a button up light blue blouse. She looked happy. My heart jumped again! I just got happy! She walked right up to me and gave me a hug.

Standing there with a fire poker in my hand, I'm sure with a dumb look on my face, I wanted to holler "You finally came back", but instead I mumbled "Whose car?" Get a grip, I know I can do better than that. "I mean, I'm glad you're back. What have you been doing? I really mean I'm glad you're back!" She smiled, then laughed, and then she hugged me again. That time I dropped the fire poker and hugged her back.

"The car's Cloud's. I had to go to the high school to meet with our Junior sponsor. I'm president of our class and she, the sponsor, was giving me some chores to do over the summer in preparation for next fall. It looks like Elzie has you working?"

"Not really, I think he's trying to keep me out of the way."

"Hardly, I've had that chore many times before."

"I didn't know he was a cook?"

"He is when you get him out of the house. You'll see. It'll be fun. I've got to take some things to the house. I'll be right back." And she turned and walked to the house on the right of Cloud's house. I starred at her butt so long I embarrassed myself. I glanced around hoping that no one was watching me, but of course, Elzie was headed back to check on me.

"Don't strain those eyes son. If you're not careful you'll be cross-eyed." What do you say? I said nothing. After checking the fire he required my help to bring a table from the screened-in room. We positioned it where the smoke would drift away from us. He sent me to Cloud's to retrieve his hot gloves, tongs, a very long fork, a large roll of paper towels, a roll of wax paper, and a roll of tinfoil. Cloud brought out the remains of the pitcher of lemonade, so of course, we had to get chairs to relax in. It's a requirement when there's lemonade.

Tess returned, I tended the fire, life was wonderful. It was well past an hour when Elzie brought out the venison ham. He spread the wax paper in overlapping pieces and then put the venison on the paper. The ham also included the upper part of the leg. It looked large. There was seasoning rubbed all over the ham, and small pieces of garlic and cloves were inserted into small slices in the meat. Elzie opened a package of bacon and strung individual slices on one side of the ham, attaching them to the meat with short tooth pics. When he finished one side he turned the ham over and repeated the process. The fire was down to a bed of coals; the racks were adjusted to about a foot above the coals, and when in place, Elzie brushed some cooking oil on the grates. The venison was placed on the rack! A cheer from his admirers. Of course I had to ask, "How long does it take to cook?"

"Until it's done!" from Elzie. Laughter from the girls. Maybe I'll learn. We settled in to chairs around the pit, it didn't take long before other members of the family started showing up. The older woman that Elzie had given the cold bag to joined us. Cloud introduced me to her, it was her mother.

"Matthew, this is my mother, Sol of the Apalachicola Indian tribe. Most of us just call her Mama. Others call her Mama Sol." I rose when the introduction started; she offered her hand, I shook it. She had a strong grip. I told her I was very honored to meet her.

She smiled at me, looked at some of the others while still holding my hand, and said, "You're cute like your papa!" I smiled back. What do you say to that? So, she knows my Dad too. Why am I almost 16 and I've never heard of these folks? She turned my hand loose and moved to a chair. I kept staring at her until Tess punched me in the arm with her elbow.

"Stop staring!" she whispered. Children were beginning to show up in numbers. They ran by each of us, played tag, and giggled with each other. A younger man joined us a little later. He was introduced as Cloud's cousin, his name was Mark. He didn't look like the rest of the family, but when his wife joined us a little later it was obvious who the family member was. Her name was Chloe. Dark hair, but cut short. Her shoulders were wide, she was shapely and very athletic looking. When she smiled her whole face smiled. She held that same happiness that I saw in Cloud. Three of the children, I was told, were hers and Mark's. A boy and two girls; ages 3, 5 and 8. They gathered up their kids and said they had to make them bathe before supper.

Elzie kept turning the ham about every 15 minutes. After just over an hour he motioned for my help. He had me pull out some long strips of tinfoil and overlap just like he did with the wax paper. When ready he took the venison ham and placed in onto the foil.
"Take some foil and fold it and place over the ham to where it covers the tooth picks, we don't want the tooth pics punching holds through the tin foil." The tooth picks weren't sticking up much, so after I covered them Elzie wrapped the entire ham with additional foil and folded it where it was sealed tightly. He raised the rack for the ham another 6 or 8 inches, put the ham back over the heat, and then had me help him put the metal sheet over the entire cooking area. "We needed to turn it about every 45 minutes." He instructed.

"How long will it cook?" I just couldn't help myself. Elzie looked at me, then the others, and in unison they offered in a loud voice,

"Until it's done!"

It must have been just past 5:30 when Elzie took the ham off the fire. He moved it to the table then put a few more oak pieces on the bed of coals. The women disappeared, including Tess. Mark left with Chloe and gathered their children. Elzie and I sat there for a short while; I didn't know what to expect and asked if I needed to do anything. He asked that I go to Sol's house and retrieve the gator tail. I knocked on her front door and she hollered for me to come in. As I walked into the house it appeared it had the same floor plan as Cloud's. As I moved toward the kitchen I could hear her preparing things for the evening. I stuck my head into the kitchen and said, "Mama Sol, Elzie sent me to retrieve the gator tail."

She smiled, and reached and patted my cheek. "You're a fine young man!" She handed me a tray with a rather large piece of gator tail. I had eaten Cloud's fried gator tail, but this one was rubbed with spices and herbs. It smelled wonderful. I could see bits and pieces of garlic and lemon and lime peel. My mouth started watering so I excused myself and headed back to Elzie. By the time he checked it over and got the fire to his liking the women were bringing food to the great room. I saw another car pull up behind the houses, and when Tess reappeared she had another adult with her. I assumed it was her mother. Tess had changed her top, she was now wearing a short sleeve sweatshirt. Tess and the woman came over to me and Tess introduced her to me. Her name was Alida. She was shorter than Tess, but commanding. She had broad shoulders, like the other women of the family, her hair, of course, dark and pulled into a French twist. Her eyes were dark and big, and her smile made me feel welcomed.

"You've been the center of attention around here lately," she began. "I was wondering if you rode in on a great white horse?"

"No Ma'am! Just Elzie's big river boat." That seemed to please her and Tess. I was beginning to believe that Elzie was some sort of big wig in these parts. I guess outlawing gators and catfish had its place. Within minutes we were all gathered in the great room. I don't think I'd ever seen such a feast. Fresh baked bread, salads, fresh green beans, baked potatoes, squash, and that didn't even include desert. There were cakes, pies, fancy jams and several bottles of tupelo honey. Besides the venison ham and gator tail, Mama Sol had fried up the remaining frog legs from the other night. I now knew what was in the cold bag. We each filled our plates and found a table. The mothers prepared the kid's plates. Iced tea in pitchers were on each table.

As we all settled at a table, Cloud stood and asked that we all bow our heads. She raised her arms, hands facing upward, and began, "Great Spirit, creator of all land and water, we give thanks this day for the bounty you have provided us. We give thanks to the animals and fish that sacrificed for our good. We give thanks for our family, for our history, for the legacies that brought us here. Help us never to forget those who sacrificed for our people, and thank you for sending us new friends. May the sun bless our crops, may the rain serve our soil, and may our love give us continued strength."

Mama Sol and the other women whispered, "Amen!" The evening was festive, there was much laughter, everyone was full. The food was outstanding. At some point the mothers took the children home for bed. Others, including the men, cleaned up the tables, washed the dishes, and stacked them on dish racks that had been stored under the counters. The left-over food was placed on plates and put into container and divided between the families. By ten o'clock everyone was headed to their respective homes. Tess suggested we go for a walk around the big cleared area to relieve the stuffiness. I thought that was a great idea. I told her it was either that or I was going to have to lie down in the yard. We walked from one end to the other and then back again. We held hands. We talked about school, sports, but mostly held on to each other and planned to get together often during the summer.

When we headed home we went around to the back of the houses and went inside to Cloud's porch. There were street type lights behind the houses so that they would light up the whole area. One light was located between the first and second house, and the other was between the fourth and fifth house. It took a few minutes for our eyes to adjust but the street lights helped. It was still pretty dark on the porch. Elzie and Cloud were already in bed. We couldn't hear any sound from the house. I settled on one of the chaise lounges, Tess took a chair right next to me. We sat in the darkness and held hands.

We whispered instead of talking. We didn't whisper much. After a few minutes Tess reached over and kissed me. Her lips were hot and wet, and she slid her tongue into my mouth. I had kissed a girl before but nothing like that. We kissed for a long time. I was afraid I wouldn't be able to breathe. I was so excited I didn't even care. After a few minutes Tess got out of her chair and sat on the chaise lounge in front of me. She had her back to me and I pulled her up close and held her around her waist. She leaned back against me on my right shoulder and turned her body to her left so that our mouths could touch. We kissed again, and again. I didn't ever want to stop kissing this beautiful girl. She moaned softly, her hand touched my face. I held her tight, pulling her toward me. Seconds later she turned her body back away from me. I still held her around her waist. She reached for my hands, took them in each of her hands and slid them up and under her sweat shirt. My God! She did not have on a bra. Her breasts were full and firm, and the nipples were hard. I held her breast, with the nipples between my fingers I rubbed softly and slowly. She moaned again, leaning back against me. Within just a few seconds I realized I needed to stop or I was really going to embarrass myself. I was losing control over my body and I had no idea what I should do. I pushed Tess upright, she turned toward me, her questioning look shook me. "Tess, I've never done anything like this before."

She giggled, "Neither have I silly."

"But you seem much more experienced than I am?"

"That's because I read a lot, and I have a couple of girl friends in Bristol who have been sexually active since they were 14."

"Fourteen!" I almost blurted out loud enough for the neighbors to hear. "At fourteen I doubt I knew which end of the donkey I was supposed to pin the tail." She started laughing, I started feeling stupid. "Tess, I've never felt this way before in my entire life. I want you more than anything I could ever have imagined. But Tess, I don't want to mess this up. I like being here, I love being with you. I don't want to do something to get myself uninvited!" She started giggling again,

"You are not going to get uninvited!"

"Well, let's not test the theory." So we got up and went for a walk. The sky was dark but clear, stars were everywhere, a light mist was forming along the ground, and within a few yards our feet were feeling wet. We went into the large screened-in room and sat down. Tess reached over and took my hand, raised it up to her face and kissed my palm. I was really feeling out of my league. I wanted her so much, but I didn't want to get shot or runoff by her family. I'm not even 16 yet, I can't even drive. "Tess, what do we do?'

"What do you mean?"

"I mean, how do we handle this? I can't even drive yet. How do we handle loving each other?"

"Do you love me?"

"I think I do?"

"Well, thank goodness, I'd hate to be in this alone." Somehow she could take my confusion, my ineptness, my fear and excitement, and make me feel silly and stupid all at the same time.

"I don't want to disappoint you Tess."

"You are not disappointing me. You are right not to rush this. This isn't the place or the time. But Matt, remember this, it's just the beginning. We have lots to look forward to." And then she kissed me again. I felt ready, I wanted the future, I wanted to grow up.

I walked her back to her home, then went back to Cloud's porch and laid back on the chaise lounge trying to get my mind around what just happened. I was excited! I was scared! I was happy. I worried. I fell asleep right there, never even made it to my bedroom.

The skies were just beginning to lighten when Elzie shook me awake. "Damn son! You try to stay up all night?" I sat up, looked him square in the eyes and said,

"I thought I did."

Just before sun-up Elzie slid one of the canoes into the water. I positioned myself in the bow and he did the paddling from the stern. I caught my first big bream on a yellow fly that morning before the sun hit the horizon. By eleven o'clock I had twenty-two bream in the boat. Elzie seemed pleased. I felt like a professional. I felt like a man! We cleaned the bream on the creek bank and when we returned to Cloud's house Elzie divided the bream into batches in plastic bags and said I should share with neighbors. About that time Tess walked in and said she would join me. We went to Mama Sol's first. She acted pleased. After taking the bream from me she put them in her refrigerator, then turned and patted my face again. She just smiled. She never did say anything. Tess and I went to the other houses, delivered bream to each. I thought it was a big deal, but evidently, it was a common occurrence for these folks. I felt like I was beginning to fit in, accepted. It felt good. We returned to Cloud's house and she fed us sandwiches and chips, and more of that great lemonade.

During lunch Tess suggested we go canoeing in the afternoon. Before two o'clock we were on the creek; Tess took the bow and I took the stern. She suggested we head out toward the river and within minutes she guided me through the mini-islands. The water was much shallower there but still deep enough for paddling. Each little collection of small cypress trees included water lilies, wild flowers, and bird nest. Elaborate spider webbing draped over limbs and small bushes. Each island was like its own universe. In the shallow water you could see small bream and other fish swimming around the cypress roots, occasionally striking bugs at the surface. It was enchanting. This whole place was enchanting. Tess was enchanting. We talked, we laughed, we teased each other, and then Tess made a mistake, she splashed water on me with her paddle. To defend my masculinity I splashed her back. She started to splash me again, but being the smarter one, I surrendered! We laughed all the way back to the landing. We were still giggling when we walked into Cloud's house. "You two look mighty happy," from Cloud. Tess responded,

"We sure are. Can I keep him?" and laughed again.

Cloud's smile shone approval, "Ok, but you have to feed him."

"In that case maybe I should just come and visit." From Tess. We all laughed at that, but I had to have a come-back,

"What if I promise not to eat too much?"

Cloud was too quick for us, "Now there he goes and starts lying!" That got a laugh from all of us. While we were still laughing, Elzie appeared from the bedroom, evidently we woke him from his nap.

"If y'all are going to carry on like that I'm going to have to find new sleeping quarters." Cloud shot a look at him and said,

"Be careful what you speak. It's lonely out there." Elzie even laughed with us.

Cloud asked Tess if she would join us for dinner and also said she should ask her mother if she would join us as well. Tess ran next door to talk with her mom; she returned shortly and said her mom said thanks but she couldn't join us tonight. There were some things she was working on. I noticed that Tess had changed her shorts and put on another short sleeve sweatshirt. But Tess said she could join us. It was almost dark when Cloud presented us with a single dish in a very large platter. The platter contained strips of the venison ham, sliced vegetables, a mixture of greens, and homemade bread. She had prepared a sauce for the dish; I had never had anything that tasted so good. She wouldn't tell me what it was or how to make it. I threatened to have her arrested if she didn't. Elzie said he would pay to see that. The evening was great; I felt like I was with family. After dinner Tess and I cleaned the dishes and then we all went to the back porch to enjoy the evening breeze. By ten o'clock Elzie and Cloud retired to the bedroom.

Tess joined me on the chaise lounge, facing away from me. I pulled her back closer to me and she swiveled around and kissed me long and with passion. I had the feeling as if I was in a dream. Tess leaned back against me, resting her head on my right shoulder. I slid my hands under her sweat shirt and up to her breast. She didn't resist at all. I started rubbing her as I had done last night. She moaned softly and snugged back against me. We kissed and groped and groped and kissed, but after several minutes we were back walking around the field.

All I could think about was how much I wanted her. I turned her around to face me "I really want to make love to you!" She smiled, reached up and caressed my face.

"We will soon." And then she kissed me again. We stood there for a little longer, but it was getting late so I walked her back to her house and kissed her good night. Back at Cloud's I figured I'd better not sleep on the porch again so I quietly slipped through the house to the front bedroom. I stripped to my shorts and climbed in bed. Before I fell into a deep sleep I remember reaching for my shirt, lifting it to my nose and smelling the sweet fragrance of passion. My last thoughts were that I was in love.

Noises in the house woke me early. I lay there in bed trying to figure out what day it was. After a few minutes counting on my fingers I decided it was Wednesday. I got up and dressed. Went to the bathroom to brush my teeth, but before I started I reached for my shirt again just to make sure I hadn't been dreaming. Yes, it was real. Yes, I am in love. After brushing my teeth and combing my hair I headed to the kitchen. Cloud was already working on breakfast. She smiled and told me to have a seat, it would be ready in a minute. Elzie walked in and sat down. "What's the plan for today?" I asked.

"We've got to go shortly."

"Where?"

"Home."

"Why?"

"Because I have obligations, things to do." I didn't respond but that just kicked me in the stomach. What is there to do at the house boat? Maybe I could stay and help Cloud around here. I can't leave now, I just fell in love!

"Eat your breakfast, we've got to go." Elzie made it clear. I finished my breakfast, packed my small bag of clothes and went to check on Cloud and Elzie. They were in the kitchen talking.

"How long before we leave?" I asked.

"Shortly!" from Elzie.

"Do I have time to go see Tess?"

"You'd better or you'll be in a heap of trouble." I went out the back door. It was still early. Tess's mom answered the back door. I asked if Tess was up. She said that she was and for me to have a seat on the back porch. She would be with me in just a minute. I barely got in a chair before Tess came out. She gave me a big smile and asked what's happening. "Elzie says we have to go!" I felt as if I might break down and cry. I had a lump in my throat.

"It's okay, you'll be back soon." Tess was trying to console me. I didn't see tears in her eyes. It occurred to me that I always seemed to be way over my head.

"But I don't want to go. I don't even know what we're going to do. I can't" and Tess said,

"Wait right here." And she went back into the house. In less than a minute she was back and handed me a slip of paper. There was a telephone number on it. I didn't understand. I'm sure I looked dumb-founded. "This is our telephone number. It's a local call from Apalachicola. Please call me when you get home."

"But I don't even know when I'll be going home!"

"Well, when you do get there call me." And she lifted up and kissed me. My balloon had popped. My strength was gone. My head ached. I mumbled okay and went back to Cloud's. Minutes later Elzie and I went to the boat. No one followed us. Watching the big ridge blend into the scenery made my heart sink. The mini islands slipped by, the boat's small wake intruding on the river lilies. When we reached the big river Elzie accelerated, bringing the boat to plane. Wind was in my face, the happiness I had found fading into the long shadows along the river's edge.

Chapter 5: Summer Baseball

As we approached the house boat Elzie took us off plane and idled to the barge. I got the bow line and stepped onto the deck, tied it to a cleat, then did the same with the stern line. Back in the boat I picked up my bag and headed to the porch. Elzie was bringing in his bag when he said, "Pack all your clothes. We're headed to town."

"Am I going home?"

"Yep!"

"Why? I thought I was suppose to help you?"

"You did."

"Then why can't I stay longer?"

"Because I don't think I can afford the gas to keep running back and forth to Owl Creek!" and he chuckled. "And anyway, I think your coach needs a second baseman today."

"What? How would you know that? Did you talk to my Dad?"

"No, a little bird swooped in and dropped me a note! Anyway, grab your stuff. I've got to check in with Bay City Lodge in a little while." And within minutes we were back on the big river headed to Apalachicola. When we got to Bay City Lodge Dad was there waiting on me. It was good to see him, but down inside I knew I really didn't want to be home right now. He gave me a hug, then shook Elzie's hand. Elzie told him about the fly fishing and suggested he and I visit him soon for a fishing trip. As Elzie went in to check with the management Dad and I headed home. Neither of us said anything for a bit but finally Dad began, "Well, did you have a good time?"

"I sure did."

"What all did you do?" It was obvious I wasn't going to tell him ALL that I had done, and I was sure Elzie wouldn't want me to disclose some of our adventures, so I answered,

"Elzie said that if I told you all that we did, he'd have to shoot me." That did it, Dad started laughing.

In a bit he said, "Well, I see that you've learned a lot." He seemed satisfied and happy. I still didn't think it was time for me to go home. Before we reached the house Dad said that I had a ball game this afternoon starting at five o'clock. At home Mom hugged me so hard I had to get her to turn me loose. She almost started crying when she saw me.

"You're so dark, your hair needs cutting. Have you been eating enough? Thank goodness you're home." I felt really tired. It wasn't even lunch and I felt really tired. I took my stuff to my bedroom, dropped it to the floor and lay down on my bed. It was almost two o'clock when Dad woke me and told me to get my uniform on get ready to go to the field. I hadn't even had lunch.

At the field most of the guys were there and the first thing I heard when I got out of the car was "Droo! Gar! Droo! Gar!" Bud and Bobby were already warming up. I joined them and started throwing the baseball between us. They started asking where had I been, what had I been doing? Did I ever hear what the Judge did? That got my attention.

"No, what did he do?"

"Nothing! Your Dad and Coach met with him separately and promised that Coach would work us all summer. Promised that if we started any more trouble they would personally bring us to him, I guess to hang!"

"Well, I don't see any rope burns on either of you, I guess you've been behaving."

About that time Coach called us together and started batting practice. When I had my swings I got their attention. I hit two out from inside pitches. I hit another off right field fence from an outside pitch. My confidence was back. I had rocks in my head! Infield practice was good, we all settled back into the rhythm from a few weeks ago. We played Carrabelle; we won eight to nothing. I went three for four, hitting one home run. In the 4th inning I came to the plate, we had men on first and second, one out. The count went to three and one, coach signaled for a double steal, hit and run. I knew the pitcher had to throw a strike or load the bases. I had stepped out of the hitter's box, shook a little sand on my hands, signed that I received Coach's signal, and stepped back into the batter's box. The pitch was a strike, on the outside of the plate. I was back at the rock pile, step in toward the plate, keep most of my weight on my back foot, and hit behind the runner to the opposite field. It bounced off the right center field fence. Both runs scored, I had a stand up double. From the dugout, "Droo! Gar! Droo! Gar!"

Dad and I got home around eight. Mom had steak and baked potatoes ready. I was starving. After dinner Dad and I went in to watch TV, Mom cleaned up the dishes and then joined us. It was just after nine o'clock when I went into my room and found the phone number Tess had given me. The phone was in the kitchen, so speaking softly when Tess answered the phone, I told her I was home. I told her about the baseball game and my hits and the home run. I think she was as pleased as I was. I told her I would call her tomorrow when we could talk more. Before we hung up Tess told me that she loved me. I said, "And I you!" My heart was at flight again.

As I started to bed I stopped to think about how long it had been since I slept in my own bed. I pulled out a calendar. May 30th had been the shit stomping night, June 2nd was the Judge, June 3rd was my first day on Little St. George. We met Elzie on the 12th, the night of the gator. Cloud showed up on the 13th and we went to Owl Creek on the 14th. Sunday the 15th we outlawed catfish, and returned to Owl Creek on the 16th and stayed through the 17th. Today, the 18th, home run day. It had been 15 days since I last slept in my own bed. I didn't know if I was happy to be home or not. Tess was on my mind and I didn't want her off of it. Before falling asleep I prayed I'd see her soon. The next morning I was awake before Mom and Dad began stirring. I had finished a bowl of cereal before Dad appeared and turned on the coffee.

"You're up mighty early," Dad began.

"Walter and Elzie think that if you get up after the sun comes up you've missed the best part of the day," I replied.

"They may be right, but I sure like a good night's sleep." And Dad went back to get started preparing for work. The last two weeks had changed my entire perspective of my parents, my life, our lives. Mom and Dad were the least exciting people anywhere.

Dad worked, it seemed he was always working. It was important to him that he always presented himself as a professional, the way he dressed, the way he walked, the way he shook your hand. He often told me that people judge you by how you look, how you act, and what you stand for. Present yourself well, be accepted well. Mom stayed home, she kept the house, she shopped for food, she paid the bills, everything, all bills were written down. Dad often said she should have been a CPA. With every bill, every mortgage payment, she broke down the interest from the principle, recorded every statement. All books were made to balance. Down inside I think Mom was even more controlling than Dad. She was only about 5'2", but she demanded respect. She dressed well, never went outside the house without makeup, and her hair was always perfect.

There was never any real excitement at our house, with the exception of Christmas. Mom really liked Christmas; she always wanted the house decorated, a perfect tree, lots of homemade candy, and certainly a party at the house during the Christmas season. I don't think Dad liked excitement. He wanted a routine, a daily schedule, a paycheck that came in the same time each month. He wanted a good home, a good wife, a good family, as long as they weren't too exciting. Dad believed in order, rules, and goals. Even the few hunting and fishing trips we went on he wanted certain times, certain baits, certain guns or fishing rods. He even required we fish on certain tides. I doubt that he had ever gigged a gator. Cloud said Dad was a good athlete. I'm sure he liked practice. Lots of practice. Routine, that was Dad. Good at the routine, good at your job. How could my Dad be so controlling when Walter and Elzie helped raise him. Well, Walter's influence? Certainly not Elzie's!

About then Mom walked into the kitchen, "You're up early. Would you like me to fix you some breakfast?"

"No Ma'am, I've already eaten."

"Well, you sure did get up early. Do you have a plan for today? Are you playing ball today?"

"I think we're just having practice this afternoon."

"Okay, I've got to run some errands this morning and go grocery shopping. Would you like to join me?"

"No thanks, I think I'll just hang around home for a while." Dad left for work shortly after that, and Mom left for grocery shopping before nine o'clock.

It was 9:20 when I called Tess. She answered the phone. "How are you?" she recognized my voice.

"I'm good, just looking after my little sister today. Mom's at work. How are you?"

"Lonely! I've been thinking of you constantly. I'm not handling this very well."

"I miss you too. Maybe you can come back soon?"

" I don't know. I haven't heard anything from Elzie. I can't drive; even if I could I don't have a car."

"Listen, it will come. It'll be all right."

"But I want to see you. I don't want to lose you." There was a long pause.

"Matthew, listen to me. You are not going to lose me. I will be here."

"But you're so beautiful and sexy, and I'm so far away.."

"Matthew, Owl Creek isn't far away. We can talk every day. And I'm not interested in anyone else. I will never be unless you dump me!"

"Why would you even say that?"

"Because you need to know who I am. You need to know our family. I'm, we, are not like most people. Cloud's been with Elzie for over 20 years, they don't even see each other every week. Lots of men have chased after her. She would never even give them the time of the day. I'm the same. That's who we are. When we find the right person, there's no turning back."

"I love you so much!"

"And I love you. It will work out. Please call me every day. We'll see each other soon. I promise."

"God, I hope so."

"Don't hope, know!" We said our good-byes and hung up. I thought about what she said, I felt better. But, how do you know? How can this girl, who I've only just met days before, know? How can I go from thinking I would begin dating this coming fall to being in love…with a girl who lives on Owl Creek? My head was cloudy. Thunder and lightning started pounding around in my skull. Maybe I should go lay back down.

I woke up a little later when Mom came in carrying groceries. "Matt, please come help with the groceries!" She had ice cream, chocolate ice cream! Well, maybe things weren't so bad after all. Chocolate Ice Cream!

Baseball practice was routine. Routine practice, routine game. I bet Dad loved practice. Mom fixed hamburgers for dinner. And it was Thursday, not Friday. "What gives?" I asked Mom.

"What do you mean? About what?" She looked confused.

"It's not Friday?" Maybe my tone wasn't what it should be. "How could you break the routine?"

"It doesn't have to be Friday to have hamburgers!" She explained. "What's wrong with hamburgers on Thursday nights?"

"Nothing, except in my entire life you've always fixed hamburgers on Friday nights!" Something must be wrong, "Are y'all sending me away again?"

"No, silly. I just thought you'd enjoy some hamburgers and French fries." Maybe something was wrong with me? Or, maybe they WERE going to send me away. If it's up the river with Elzie I can live with that. Maybe I've lost my mind. Why am I complaining?

I went into the living room and turned on TV. It was the first TV I'd seen in over two weeks. I wonder why no one watched TV up on Owl Creek? Maybe they don't have service. Maybe they do. Maybe I was just too interested in Tess to notice. OK, that satisfied me. Dad walked in shortly after the five o'clock news came on. At dinner Dad didn't even mention that we were having hamburgers on Thursday night. So much for the routine. After dinner Mom went to visit some lady about something to do with the Philaco Club. Dad and I sat watching TV. My mind was racing, I didn't want to watch TV.

"Dad," I began.

"Yes, Son?" and he turned the TV off.

"Could we talk a bit?"

"Sure, what's on your mind?"

"Dad, Walter told me that after Grandmama and Granddaddy died that you lived with him and Elzie. Why didn't you ever tell me?"

"Well, Son, I didn't think it would matter to you. I was more concerned about giving you a good home and a stable life. By the time you came along Walter was living on Little St. George and Elzie was living on his house boat up the river."

"Did you stay in touch with them?"

"Sure I did, but it wasn't like I could pick up the phone and call them. We would see each other a few times a year when they were in town."

"What about Cloud? How long have you known her?" I knew the answer to that question, but I wanted to know what he thought of her.

"I was in college when I met Cloud. I had come home on a break. Elzie and Cloud had started dating, and Cloud was in Apalachicola visiting Elzie when I met her."

"Do you like her?"

"Certainly! She's been very good for Elzie. And, she's a very good history teacher from what I've heard. We also serve on an education board together that covers the panhandle. I see her at meetings about once a year. Why the questions about Cloud?"

"She says she's an American Indian. Part of the Apalachicola Tribe. Is that so? Do you believe her?"

"I have no reason not to believe her. I've never researched the Indian history for our area."

"But you call her Cloud?"

"That's what she prefers when around friends and family. At school she's Anne."

"I know that, but why would someone change their name? Or use a different name one place and another somewhere else?"

"I'm sure she has her reasons. That is something you need to talk to her about. I can't answer that question."

"Are you sending me back to stay with Walter or Elzie anymore this summer?"

"No, I just thought it would be a good idea to get you out of town until the Judge incident calmed down. And, I figured it would be a good time to introduce you to them."

"Bud and Bobby said the Judge didn't do anything about our prank?"

"The Judge just needed to be reminded of some of his past experiences. We shared a few experiences that neither of us are proud of. However, I hope you're smart enough to not ever do anything like that again?"

"Don't worry, it's straight and narrow for me for now on." I thought it best not to tell him about the gator gigging. "But Dad, while on Little St. George I got to see a turtle crawl and lay her eggs. Walter said the babies should be hatching by early August, and that in early August we should be planting a dove field. Can I go back then?"

"That depends on Walter. If he invites you, you can certainly go."

"When can I go back and stay with Elzie again?"

"I guess you'd better ask Elzie that." It was way into the night before I fell asleep. I started making plans in my head. I had to talk to Tess the next day. We can make this happen. Owl Creek isn't that far away.

Friday morning was almost gone by the time I could have some privacy to call Tess. Dad was at work, Mom running errands. Tess answered on the second ring. I blurted out, "I'm making a plan!"

She laughed, then said "Good morning. So, what's the plan?"

"First, last night I had a good talk with my Dad. I'll tell you all about that later. But he said I could go back and stay with Elzie if Elzie asked me to." Tess was giggling,

"I think we can make that happen." She said.

"Exactly!" I agreed. "Now, the fourth of July is week after next, on Friday. We play Bristol at Bristol on Thursday the third. What if Elzie asks my Dad if it's alright for me to stay with him over the long weekend? We could be together from Thursday to Sunday or even Monday morning." Tess starting giggling again.

"What's so funny?" I asked.

"Yesterday you were in the dumps, said you couldn't do anything. Today you're planning everyone's lives, and they don't even know it yet. You are funny!"

"Don't you think it's a good plan?"

"Why of course I do. I'll talk to Cloud and see if she can make this happen for us. And, we usually have a big party on the fourth."

"Like we did on Monday?"

"Yes, but generally with more family members showing up. Elzie usually cooks."

"Great! Please talk to Cloud and see if we can get this set up. I don't know what I'll do if I can't see you."

"You will. Call me tomorrow. I love you." I sat there for several minutes, my mind was running wild. I was happy, I was nervous. I was scared to death that something might interfere. It has to happen. Maybe I should call Elzie. I can't call Elzie, he doesn't have a phone!

After a bit I wrote Mom a note and told her I was going downtown to Buzzett's drug store and soda fountain for a milk shake. There was hardly any activity in downtown, just a few folks leaving from lunch at the Grill. I walked into Buzzett's and there was Gooch, sitting at the counter, milk shake in one hand and eating ice cream with the other. He tried to say hello, but milk dribbled from his mouth. I sat next to him and order a chocolate shake. He finally swallowed and turned to me, "Where have you been? We thought they had sent you to reform school."

"Well, I guess you could say I went to a type of reform school!"

"Where?"

"Oh, just a couple of places. Had to stay with some of my Dad's friends. They worked me pretty hard." Gooch was classic. He never dresses well, his clothes were never well kept, he was always eating something, but he was always concerned about others. He really didn't care what anyone that wasn't his friend cared about him. "How about you? Did you get in any trouble?" I asked.

"No, I just told my folks that I was just following along. I didn't even know what was going on. They believed me. Good thing they don't know I help supply the shi—crap." We both laughed until we were spitting milk shake. Gooch asked about summer baseball, I told him we were playing a couple of games a week. He said he was going out for football this fall. I told him I was glad and looked forward to him being on the team. I decided to head back home, and as I headed out I told Gooch that he had better start working out. Practice would be hard. He just grinned and kept after the ice cream.

Back at home I turned on the TV. Friday afternoon cartoons came on, within a few minutes I turned it off. I decided I wanted to get back to reading the Ruark books again so I took off for the Library. They had Something of Value, so I checked it out and returned home. I was deep into Kikuyu history and African hunting when Mom and Dad got home. They were surprised to find me home. They both asked what I had been doing and if I was going to the Canteen tonight. I told them that I thought I should stay away from temptation for a while and that I was going to read. They were both impressed.

The weekend passed like thick molasses poured over ice cubes. I thought it would never end. I couldn't reach Tess on Saturday, but late afternoon on Sunday she answered the phone. We talked only for a short while. She said that Elzie had not been there this weekend but Cloud expected him on Monday or Tuesday. She assured me that Cloud would try to make our plans work. We played Carrabelle again on Tuesday, the game was in Carrabelle. We didn't get home until almost ten o'clock. I called Tess on Wednesday morning. She knew it had to be me calling, her voice was cheerful. "You must have played extra innings last night?"

"The pitchers didn't know I had an important phone call to make!" She laughed, said I was silly, but she had good news. She said Elzie would call my Dad later in the week or over the weekend. She said that if all went well she would pick me up after the game on the third. My heart leaped. Visions flashed across my brain. I love Cloud!

We played Crawfordville on Thursday afternoon late, in Crawfordville. They always had good ball players. It was always good games. They had a strong left handed pitcher; he would be a senior this coming year. We squeaked by 2 to 1. I was one for three, but it was a shot off the left center field wall for a double. We were pretty late getting home that evening. I slept late for the first time in forever, not getting up until almost ten o'clock on Friday morning. I read most of the afternoon, but around 4:30 I got to talk with Tess for a few minutes. As always, she seemed cheerful. She made me feel cheerful. I was ready for the next week. Another weekend. I read most of the weekend. Mom and Dad kept checking on me. I think they thought I must be sick. Mom offered to cook me anything I wanted. I told her it didn't matter. Dad asked about the ball games. I just told him about my hitting and the scores. But Sunday evening during supper Dad said that Elzie had called and invited me to stay with him over the 4th weekend. I asked if it was okay. Dad said it was. My appetite picked up considerably. I think they noticed.

We played Port St. Joe on Monday night in Port St. Joe. They have a great baseball park; it's lighted, a well- groomed infield, and covered stands. During warm ups Joe Shuler came over to me and shook my hand. Then he smiled at me and told me to look out, I had a payback coming. I smiled back and said, "Just remember a few weeks ago, Shuler; you might want to look out yourself. To my way of thinking it was a great ball game. I never liked blow out games, and I've always appreciated good competition. The score went back and forth for seven innings. We were at bat, top of the eighth. The score was three to three. Bud led off with a single to right field. Bobby followed with single to left field. I came up to bat with two on, no outs. The pitcher's first pitch was a knock down pitch. I hit the deck. The umpires cautioned everyone and I stepped back to the plate.

Now what I've always heard was a knock down pitch was designed to shake the batter. The next expected pitch should be a hard curve ball, started at the batter's head and then break over the plate. It was classic, just like the big boys tell you how to do it, he threw a hard curve ball that began about eye level, I could see the spin of the threads. It broke over the plate to the outside back corner. Back at the rock pile, I stepped into the pitch, weight on my back foot and slammed a shot to right center field. It barely topped the fence, but it did top the fence. Shuler gave me a high five as I rounded first. We shut them down the last two innings; we walked away from that one six to three.

I could hardly wait until Thursday. Our game was to start in Bristol at four o'clock. I had my duffle packed before eight-thirty that morning. I waited to eat until later in the morning because I don't like eating much before a ball game. Mom fixed me grill cheese sandwiches and a bowl of tomato soup. We dressed in our uniforms before leaving town. I had my duffle with me. Several of the guys asked what I was doing, I just told them I was meeting some friends in Bristol and would be staying with them for a few days. Coach drove the school bus, we arrived at the field about two-thirty.

The Bristol team was already on the field. We warmed up while they took their batting practice and infield routine. It was pushing four o'clock by the time we finished. The umpires started the game right at four. Tess hadn't shown up yet. I was hitting third and before the second batter was out Tess showed up. Elzie and Cloud were also there, and Tess had her little sister with her. I assumed her Mom was working. The pitcher for Bristol wasn't strong, he could throw pretty hard but didn't have much, if anything, of a breaking ball. I took a couple of pitches just to get a feel of what he was throwing. The third pitch he threw me was right down the middle; I slammed a rope to left field. The left fielder didn't even have to move. Not even a step. He just raised his glove and we had to take the field. I got back up again in the fourth inning, neither team had scored. We had a runner on second, two outs. Same story with the pitcher. Same story with my hitting. I slammed another shot to dead center. I'm surprised the ball didn't hit the pitcher. The center fielder didn't move a step. And we took the field again. I may be looking good but I sure wasn't getting the job done.

Bristol scored in the fifth inning on a walk and a double that their center fielder hit off left field wall. It was the eighth inning before I got to the plate again. We had a man on second and two outs. Bristol brought in a left handed pitcher. I stood off to the side while he took his warm up pitches watching his movement. He was smooth, but not much power. He did seem to have a breaking ball. The ump said play ball and I dug in at the plate. The first pitch was a curve ball that hung there like a basketball. I was shocked, I started to swing and then didn't swing. Then thought I should swing. I could punch it to right field. I swung. I don't even think I came close. I was totally embarrassed. I stepped out of the batter's box, dropped my head and pretended to dust up my hands; I would not even look toward the dugout. I could hear Bud and Bobby laughing.

I stepped back into the batter's box. I was thinking the pitcher ought to be showing me his fast ball next. Note, you're never supposed to try to out-think the pitcher. He threw me the exact same pitch as before. I was surprised, but I kept my weight back. If we could have taken the flight of the first pitch and then placed the flight of the second pitch over it, I doubt you could tell there were two pitches. The ball broke over the plate to the inside, large as a soft ball, and I snatched it to left field. I thought it was a home run, but it hit the fence about a foot inbounds. The run scored, I ended up on second. We had a new kid playing with us named Robby, he was our left fielder. He hadn't done much in the last couple of games, but our dugout became cheerleaders and yelled out encouragements. With a count of two and one, he hit an outside pitch that I thought the first baseman would catch. The balled cleared the first baseman and landed in the grass in right field, then because of the spin on the ball, squirted out of bounds to the right field fence line. A single from Robby and I scored. We ended that game two to one. And I was headed to Owl Creek!

We did the usual glove slapping, hand shaking the opposing team, and headed to the bus. Tess met me near the bus. I said to give me a minute and it took less than that for me to retrieve my duffle. I took off my cleats, slipped on some tennis shoes, and we headed off to meet up with Cloud, Elzie, and Sage. As we left the team at the bus I could hear some cat calls and whistles. I didn't even look back. Elzie and Cloud were in a good mood, they complemented me on my play, and Sage said she thought I was the best player there. Tess said I was the most handsome! Aw shucks, it's just a normal day for a hero! I could hardly control myself; I felt like soaring with the eagles. I felt like I was headed home! But I had never felt that way about my real home. Owl Creek! The mysterious land of love and legends. I reached and took Tess's hand and squeezed it. We were back together. It took just over 30 minutes to get home.

As we drove up behind Cloud's house Alida appeared at the back steps next door. She waved and said that she had supper ready for us and to come on. I grabbed my duffle and ran in to Clouds and dropped it on my bed. I was almost out the back door when I realize what I had just done, My Bed. It felt like my bed. It really did feel like home. Alida had three large pizzas already prepared and a huge bowl of salad. Two pitchers of ice tea were on the table. We gathered around the table, family style, and talked our way through supper. After Tess finished bragging about me the conversation turned to the event for the next day. Elzie informed me that we had to get up early because we were roasting half a pig, and a large bed of coals would be needed. Cloud and Alida talked about everyone who would be there, and all the fixings they needed to work on. It was pushing ten o'clock when someone suggested we call it a night. Cloud and Elzie headed home, I told them I'd be along shortly. Elzie reminded me, with a smile, that we would be getting up early. Alida went to put Sage to bed; Tess and I went to the back porch.

When we were alone the first thing Tess did was to grab me and kiss me passionately. We just stood there holding each other. It felt like I had been away for months. We finally took a seat and while holding hands we kissed and whispered and just stared into each other's eyes. By 10:45 Tess said she had to go in. A good night kiss and I headed home to bed.

I was already awake when Elzie came to get me up at six-thirty. Cloud fixed some pancakes for me while Elzie had coffee. We were lighting the fire by seven-thirty. Elzie said we had to modify the fire blocks a bit for cooking the half pig, completely inclosing the fire with block, but leaving openings for the fire to breath and making the oven-like pit taller. I retrieved the metal plate that was to cover the pit, and Elzie and I brought out another long table to work from.

It was pushing ten o'clock when Mark drove his pickup over to the fire pit. The truck bed held a large box with a cover; it looked to be about three feet wide and maybe seven feet long. He explained to me that he had made a cooler just for these occasions. A peek into the box showed half a pig, pearly white with the skin still on the outside, all hair had been scraped off, bedded in ice. Mark produced a large roll of butcher's paper, and Elzie sent me to Cloud's for the hot gloves, paper towels, long fork and a long butcher knife. Cloud followed me back to the fire pit carrying a large bowl of seasoning. She said Elzie put the rub together last night when they got home. The butcher's paper was spread over the table like we had done with the waxed paper and, once in place, Elzie and Mark laid the half pig on the table. Elzie actually put on white rubber gloves before applying the rub. I really think he did that just to impress Mark and anyone else who might be watching. I'd seen him barehanded clean gator tail; I didn't think pork would faze him. Within minutes the half pig was on the grates and the metal sheet covered the pit.

"Six hours," exclaimed Elzie. "We'll turn the meat in four hours." It was 10:30 and I realized I hadn't seen Tess all morning. I told Elzie I was going to check on her, but he said I should slow down a bit, that the women are cooking and making preparations. I'd just be in the way. "She's all right, and she'll be along in a little while." A little while turned out to be four hours. But around twelve-thirty an old dark gray pick up drove into the yard and slowly made its way around to us. It parked well back from the fire pit and who stepped out? Walter! I couldn't believe it. I didn't even know he was coming. I got excited and ran over to welcome him. He actually gave me a hug and then told me to get that fish he'd brought, it's in a cooler in the back.

That fish was a 10 pound red snapper. It was huge. I wrestled the fish to the table, plopped it down and waited instructions. I knew this wasn't a first for these folks so I'd better take note. Elzie and Mark shook Walter's hand, bragged on the fish. Elzie sent me to get the butcher's twine. Cloud came back with me to see Walter, she also brought a bag of herbs and two limes, and a stick of butter. After hugging Walter everyone took a chair and watched Elzie.

It took me a few minutes to realize that this was "the show", and certainly not the first time it had been seen. Like with the bream, the snapper had already been cut along the belly to under the mouth. The gills had been removed but the gill plates were still in place. The scales were still on the fish. Elzie had me help him by holding the snapper with its back against the table, belly up. Elzie cut several slits along the backbone, into the meat. He told me to note that he didn't cut all the way to the skin, never break the skin, and then he pushed pieces of the butter into the slits and squeezed lime juice over the meat. The herbs Cloud had brought covered the inside, and slices of un-squeezed lime were included with the herbs. Elzie then tied the snapper with the butcher's twine the same way he had with the bream. The fish then went back into Mark's cooler.

"We'll put this bad boy on the last hour the meat cooks." Elzie was satisfied.
We all gathered in the big screened-in room, under the fans, away from the heat. Stories began, as well as laughter. I felt like one of the men. They treated me like one of the men. Around 2:30 Tess came looking for me.

"I see you've fit right in!"

"Yes ma'am, but I don't tell lies that these guys do!" That got them to laughing and they started making fun of me. Tess dragged me away and said she needed some help. Back at her house, on the back porch, I asked what I was to do.

"Kiss me! Kiss me Now!" That was a job I could do. We sat on the back porch and held hands; she told me all that she and her Mom had prepared for the meal. It sounded like a lot of food and I asked why so much? "Because there will be lots of people here! And most all the women will be bringing just as much."

"Wow, how many people will it be?"

"Between 40 and 50."

"Are they all family?"

"Yes, some closer than other, but all related."

"Are they all Taylors? Is this a pow-wow?" I couldn't hold back my smile on that one.

"No crazy! They're not all Taylors, and this is not a pow-wow, but it has become a family tradition. I think you'll have fun."

"As long as I'm with you, I'll have fun!" That one came from the heart.

We stayed on the back porch for over an hour until Alida gave us instructions to start taking things to the big room. Other family members started arriving, unloading items for the meal. The counters were covered with all sorts of vegetables, salads, breads, and several things to drink. Laughter was everywhere. I was introduced to everyone, I'd never remember their names. The women set the tables, the men told big tales, the children screamed and played. It was a festive event. I wasn't there when Elzie put the snapper on to cook, but at 4:30 he removed the metal lid, and with hot gloves, he and Mark placed the pig on the table, along with the red snapper. Platters were immediately brought for the meat and Elzie cut and sliced until several large platters were stacked with pork. The snapper was placed on its on platter, twine was cut, and the skin and scales pulled back to present the beautiful fillet.

Everyone started serving their own plates and taking a place at the tables. Elzie, Cloud, Tess and I sat at a table that could seat six. Mama Sol joined us at one end of the table. There was no beginning prayer like before, just lots of laughter and happy sounds. Tess and I had our backs to the houses and shortly after everyone started eating Elzie and Cloud started smiling, staring at something toward the houses. At first we didn't turn to look, but when Elzie and Cloud and Walter, who was at another table, stood up, we turned to look. Dad was coming through one of the doors into the screened room. He was wearing jeans, he hardly ever wore jeans, and a khaki short sleeve shirt. He was carrying a wrapped package, a present. I didn't know what to do. I stood fixed, just staring at him. Finally I raised my hand as if to say "I'm over here." He smiled at me, but he didn't come directly to us. He went directly to Mama Sol, she remained seated. He bent down, took one of her hands in his and said how wonderful it was to see her again. He presented the present to her. A big smile came over her face, she leaned back as if to focus on his face, and then gestured for him to lean down closer. She reached up, patted his face and said,

"You're a good boy!" He kissed her on her forehead and then turned to us. He walked directly over to Tess and me, directed his attention to Tess and said,

"Hi Tess, I'm James Drugar. I'm Matthew's dad."

"How do you know my name?"

"I know a lot about you. First, I know that you're Alida's oldest daughter. I know you're a cheerleader; I've watched you over the last few years. I know that you are going to be the Junior Class President this next year, and I hear that you like my son."

"No sir, I love your son!" My heart stopped. My mouth got dry. I didn't know if I was about to cry or scream. My beautiful girl, who lives on Owl Creek, who just met my Dad, said, in front of her entire family, that she LOVES ME!

The room went completely quiet. The silence held there as if we were watching a glass fall from the ceiling, waiting for the expected crash. Finally, Dad cleared his throat, as if trying to find his voice and said, "Well, I hope you'll allow him to come visit his mom and me often!"

The room cheered! Really, they cheered! Most didn't even know me, but they cheered. And then there was laughter. Tess went to fix my Dad a plate while he shook Elzie's hand, gave Cloud a hug, and then went to Walter and shook his hand. He then joined us at the head of the table. The room noise returned. Tess reached over and put her hand on my leg; I took her hand and squeezed it, then leaning over to her I whispered, "That was the most beautiful thing I've ever heard. I love you." Sitting there, looking around at these people, watching the kids and hearing their laughter, I felt like I belonged. It felt like family.

Conversations continued at our table, Dad asked about the Bristol game but before I could answer Tess told him I was the hero. Dad just smiled and said it wasn't the first time. My hat size just grew. A few minutes later I noticed that there was a vacant seat next to Walter, so I excused myself and went over and sat by him. He sure looked happy. "Boy, you've fallen right in it haven't you?"

"Sure feels like it!" We both laughed. But I had a plan, "Walter, you said that we needed to put in the dove field first part of August. Can I come and help?"

"Why certainly!"

"Also, there's a full moon the first week of August, and you said that the baby turtles should be hatching. Would you mind if Elzie, Cloud, and Tess joined us?" He leaned back in his chair, a smile crept across his face. I could see the wheels turning!

"Why don't you let me work on that a bit, and I'll get back to you."

"Thanks Walter. I really appreciate it." And I went back to join Tess and the others. It was well past dark when the party broke up. Piles of food were divided up and wrapped to be taken home. Tess fixed Dad a couple of plates and told him to be sure to share with Mom.

Dad thanked her and actually gave her a hug. I walked him to the door and as we walked out he stopped and looked at me, "Son, I'm very proud of you. And, I hope you'll bring Tess to visit with us soon. I know your Mom wants to meet her."

"Mom knows about Tess?" How could all these adults seem to know so much?

"Certainly she knows about Tess!"

"I think Elzie will be taking me home either Sunday evening or Monday morning. I'll see if she can join us."

"That would be fine. Now, help out up here and have fun." And he walked away. Everyone had turned in by ten o'clock, Tess and I were on Cloud's screen porch, her leaning back against me in the chaise lounge. We kissed often but mostly just sat there holding each other. We didn't even talk much. The evening had cooled, the cicadas were sounding off so loud we could hardly hear each other whispering. We were both tired, it had been a long and busy day. She was about to fall asleep when I told her to wake up, I'll walk you home.

At her back door she kissed me again. She held my face between both of her hands and whispered, "This is just the beginning!" I think I floated back to Cloud's and to my bedroom.

Saturday and Sunday flew by like lightning strikes. Elzie and I fly fished Saturday morning for about an hour; Tess and I canoed again that afternoon. Saturday night Tess and I got to be alone for a few hours. Our intimacy was so strong, it was extremely hard to control our passion. We touched, we played, we held each other. We both fell asleep on the back porch. I woke around 2 AM, walked her back home, and made my way to my bedroom. Sunday was mostly a blur, but I told her about my conversation with Walter. She immediately said we had to talk with Cloud. Cloud was in the kitchen when we found her, we said we needed to talk to her. Her faced looked like we may have just thrown water on her. "What have y'all done?" a stern look toward each of us.

"Nothing!" Tess laughed. I was afraid to talk. I wondered what Cloud might have thought we had done. Tess continued,

"Matt has a plan. Tell her Matt." All eyes turned to me. I'd better make this good. Those stern looks from Cloud had power.

"While I was staying with Walter on Little St. George I got to see a turtle crawl and lay her eggs. Walter said that the baby turtles should be hatching around 60 days. The first week of August will be 60 days. Also, Walter said we need to put in a dove field the first of August. I asked Walter if I could come back to help with the field and to possible see the baby turtles hatch. I also asked Walter if you and Elzie and Tess could join us."

"Well, aren't you the master manipulator?" and a smile spread across her face. Cloud's smiles always made me feel like I should smile. I tried! Cloud, like Walter, said that she would work on it and get back to us. She did add that she hadn't been on Little St. George in several years. Tess later told me that the twinkle in Cloud's eyes was a real good sign. The decision was made that I would stay over Sunday night and Elzie, Cloud, and Tess could take me home on Monday morning. I called my folks and told them I should be home Monday morning around ten o'clock. Sunday evening was a blur, I didn't want to go home, but I knew I had to. I was sad until Tess told me I had to grow up, we couldn't be together all the time. It didn't stop me from being sad, but it did make me act like I was better. We did have a couple of hours together on the back porch.

When we got to my home in Apalachicola, I now felt I had two homes, both of my parents were there. Dad had come home from work just to be there when we all arrived. I did not know that Mom had met Elzie and Cloud until she and Dad met us at the back door. Mom opened the door and immediately said, "Hi Cloud, it's been a very long time since I've seen you. You look wonderful as always."

"You're the one who looks wonderful!" Cloud replied. "I love what you've done with your hair." Mom reached up as if to adjust something with her hair and said she was trying a new hair style. Cloud told her it certainly suited her. All this before we even got inside the house.

Inside, Mom said hello to Elzie and then Dad took over and said he was honored to introduce Tess to Mom. Mom smiled, Tess smiled. Elzie and I acted like we had ants in our pants. In the short time I had been with Walter and Elzie I had learned to be uncomfortable with manners. I think it showed. We all sat around the living room mostly listening to the women. Tess was remarkably comfortable. Cloud and Dad talked school stuff, Mom asked Tess about school, cheerleading, and if she wants to go to college. Tess assured Mom that she definitely was going to college. All in all, no one got offended, no one said a curse word, and Elzie, Cloud, and Tess left me alone at my Apalachicola Home. Later that evening when Dad got home from work I asked if we could talk a little.

"Dad, I didn't know that you knew Mama Sol, how long have you known her?"

"Son, when I was young, maybe ten or eleven, I started having a hard time. Walter and Elzie were doing the best they could to give me a stable home, but without a mother there, it got hard. I had been having some terrible dreams, I was misbehaving at school, until finally Elzie took me to Owl Creek to meet Mama Sol. Over the next few years Mama Sol treated me like I was her kid. She taught me many things, but most of all she taught me to respect other people, and to take pride and responsibility for my actions. She was the mother I didn't have and she guided me through lots of tough times growing up. I only spent weekends there, and not every weekend, but she got to me and helped me see a future." I didn't know what to say, but I told him I understood. I'm not sure that I did.

I called Tess each day, I practiced baseball and played two games, and by Friday I was really ready to escape. The weekend was upon us and I had no way to get to Owl Creek. The phone rang about five o'clock, it was Tess. "Hi? What are you doing?"

"I'm doing nothing but missing you. I hate staying here all weekend without seeing you."

"Well, why don't you come have dinner with us?"

"Because I don't have a car and I don't have anyone to drive me up there."

"Well, put on some clean clothes, we'll be by to pick you us in five minutes."

"What? How? Where are you?"

"We're at the Gibson, and Elzie's buying!"

"I promise, it won't take me five minutes." I hollered for Mom, told her I was meeting Tess at the Gibson for dinner, changed my clothes, and was standing out by the street when they drove up. I hope Mom heard me! "What did I do to deserve this?" I asked as I got into the car.

"Nothing! It wasn't you that made the decision." said Elzie. That sure provoked a laugh from me and Tess. Cloud gave Elzie that woman look! Elzie smiled and told me he was glad I could join them. The Gibson's a really cool old hotel and restaurant. It sits at the foot of the bridge, has three stories, a large porch, and balconies on the second floor.

There were a couple dozen visitors having drinks on the porch but only two couples eating in the dining room. We were shown to our table and as we sat down the waitress asked if anyone wanted a drink. Cloud said water was fine, Tess and I said the same; Elzie had a beer. There was small talk, I couldn't keep my eyes off Tess, so Elzie told me that my eyes were going to freeze that way if I didn't occasionally look around the room. Tess laughed, Cloud punched Elzie on the arm, I think, I wasn't sure because I was still starring at Tess. I was so happy; this sure beat staying home and watching Gun Smoke. Our meals were great, I had grilled shrimp and Tess had broiled grouper. I don't even know if Elzie and Cloud ate. Remember, my eyes were fixed on Tess. But as we finished our meal, deserts were ordered. Cloud suggested that Tess and I try the chocolate bourbon pecan pie. That sounded dangerous so we decided to split one. My god, it was just about the best thing I've ever eaten. I fear I was making a hog of myself because at some point Tess stabbed my hand with her fork. "Remember, we are supposed to share this!" Remember what I said about manners? I even embarrassed myself. Everyone got a good laugh at my expense, but as we finished Cloud said that Elzie had some news for me. We all turned out attention toward Elzie.

"No I don't!" Cloud punched him.

"Oh yea, that dove field project, and turtle babies hatching sounds like fun. I think we've got it figured out. And Walter will call your Dad." Tess grabbed my hand and said she was so excited. I couldn't stop grinning. We finished up inside and as we were leaving Elzie said it was still early so we found chairs on the porch and Elzie ordered another beer. Cloud said she would do the driving going home. A cool breeze was blowing from the bay, locals and visitors were visiting on the porch, and Tess and I held hands. This sure felt right. We talked about Apalach, its history, the seafood, and the Seafood Festival.

We all thought that we should plan something for the festival, but that would wait for another time. It was pushing nine o'clock when they dropped me off at home. I gave Tess a kiss and thanked Elzie and Cloud so much I think it embarrassed them. They headed back to Owl Creek, land of enchantment, land of love. I went in to reruns of Gun Smoke.

It was the third week of July, we had baseball practice on Monday and Wednesday, games on Tuesday and Thursday. I had talked to Tess every day, we were trying to figure out how I could get up there for the weekend. When I called her late Thursday night I was hoping that she and Cloud might come pick me up on Friday. She informed me that I couldn't come up there this weekend. I felt crushed, "Why not?" I know I sounded pitiful.

"Because you have a surprise coming."

"What? What kind of a surprise?"

"You'll see tomorrow morning."

"Are you involved with the surprise?"

"Nope! It's a guy thing."

"Will I be seeing you this weekend?

"Nope! Like I said, it's a guy thing."

"But I want to see you."

"You will, just not this weekend." It just amazed me how I could be a leader on a baseball team, a football team, even in my class at school, and yet a beautiful girl who lives at Owl Creek knew more about my life than I did. At some point you feel that you just exist, being swept along by the currents of life, not in control of anything. But some cute little girl, well, a beautiful girl who lives at an enchanting place, knows more about what I'm going to do than I do. I told her that I would call her if I lived through it. Just before falling asleep I decided that one day I would surprise her!

Dad stuck his head into my bedroom as he was headed for work, "I'll be home around one, be ready to go. And, you might need a light jacket, and some rubber boots.

"Where are we going?"

"Tess didn't tell you?"

"No, just that it was a surprise. What's up?"

"We are going shrimping, we will be out all night." And he went out the door. Walter had done it, he put the whole thing together. No one had even mentioned it to me. I'm telling you, everyone was running my life except me. But, I sure was having some fun.

We got to the fish house at 1:30; Walter and Elzie were at the table with Mr. Siglio having coffee. "Paisan", you finally made it. My Dad couldn't help himself,

"Well, some of us have to work for a living!" Mr. Siglio was quick,

"Well, some of us are more successful than others!"

Walter and Elzie had to laugh. Dad did take himself way too seriously. Dad took a chair, I dropped to the floor. They talked for just a few minutes until Mr. Alonzo Salvatore walked in. He looked to be about 5 feet 6 inches tall, shoulders wider than mine, dark, dark hair, dark eyes, and a three or four day old dark beard. He wore a T-shirt tight enough to see every muscle in his chest, and there were plenty. His arms looked like weight-lifter's. His smile was a big as his muscles. "Paisan! You gonna stay here all day or go to work with me?" Immediately Mr. Siglio jumped up, gave him a hug, turned to us and said, "I teach him all he know!" And we went shrimping!

His boat's name was Sweet Maria, she was fifty-eight feet long, and sixteen feet wide. The wheel house covered the first third of the boat, with walk-ways around both sides and room at the bow. Twin structural steel outriggers were attached to each side of the wheel house, they stood almost thirty feet tall and Mr. Siglio explained to me that when fishing they would stretch at least twenty-five feet out to the sides of the boat. From each outrigger a forty foot wide net would be pulled along the bottom. Cables and winches controlled the nets. The size of the net is measured across the mouth of the net, and doors, the name given to the metal and wood devices used to spread the net, are attached to each side of the net opening. These doors are designed to pull downward and outward.

A chain was attached from the inside bottom of a door to the other door. Its purpose is to kick up shrimp from the ocean floor so the nets can work best. The chain is called a tickler chain. The back two thirds of the boat is all deck, work space. When the nets are brought in, the catch is dumped on the deck and then the crew separates the shrimp from the trash fish. The trash fish, often called bycatch, are shoveled back overboard through openings along the sides of the deck called cull holes. Once the shrimp are collected they are placed below deck in the large ice compartment. The bottoms of the ice boxes are solid, usually 6 inches thick. After the shrimp are placed in the ice compartments more shaved ice is spread over the shrimp to preserve them. A large boat like the Sweet Maria can stay at sea usually five to seven days without risking spoiling the shrimp.

As we eased away from the docks and headed toward the gulf I went in to talk with Mr. Salvatore, "Mr. Salvatore, I..." He stopped me.

"You call me Sal. No Mr. Salvatore."

"Yes sir, Sal. How fast does this boat run?"

"Lots of power, but not fast. We run about eight to ten knots while heading out or coming in, but when we pull the nets, maybe three or four knots."

"How far out will we be going? Are we shrimping at night?"

"Oh, maybe twelve to fifteen miles from the Islands. Yes, we shrimp at night. We'll catch some brown shrimp, and if we're lucky, we'll catch lots of hoppers."

"What are hoppers?"

"A hopper looks a lot like a brown shrimp, except they actually lighten up to blend more with the bottom. They are firmer, easy to peel and really taste good. Brown shrimp don't change colors, but they taste good too. They tend to be a little softer."

We followed the Intracoastal Waterway until it turned east but we headed due south to Bob Sikes Cut. There was no one fishing in the cut, but I told Dad about the turtle crawl Elzie and I staked, within a couple hundred yards of the jetties. Elzie, Walter and Mr. Siglio were leaning against the railing along the back deck so Dad and I joined them. By the time we entered the gulf I had moved to the bow. Sal had turned our heading south by southwest. There wasn't much wave action and within the first mile from shore, dolphins joined us. They were riding the bow wave from the shrimp boat. I called Dad to come and watch. As he reached the bow a couple of the dolphins broke from the wave riding and jumped alongside the boat. They were in and out of the bow wake for a couple of miles. Sal said we should be in the grounds before dark. I asked him how deep we would be shrimping. "Maybe fifty or sixty feet."

It became very obvious why the big shrimpers stay out for several days, running fifteen to twenty miles one way wasn't a hike around the block, it took hours. As the sun set the gulf got very calm, the evening light lasted it seemed like a long time. We first dropped the nets just as the sun dropped below the horizon. Sal said we needed to settle in because it would be an hour before we pulled the first net. We sat on the back deck, just talking and watching the sky. Stars were everywhere, from one horizon to the next. Mr. Siglio had brought sandwiches for everyone, so we sat on deck looking at the sky and eating some kind of Italian sausage sandwiches and drinking cokes. It was so beautiful. I was thinking that someday I might like being a shrimper, and then Sal turned on the lights.

The sky disappeared. There was nothing outside the deck of the boat. It even took a while before we could focus our eyes on the water behind the boat. After a while it got better. We started seeing fish, at least their shining eyes, darting around the back of the boat, and out by the cables leading to the nets. Dolphins, as well as sharks, appeared alongside the boat. The gulf was alive. Close to the hour mark Sal said to get ready; Mr. Siglio took over net duties. The winches started turning, cables pulling the first net to the surface and into the boat. We only pulled one net, the catch was dumped on the deck, and then the net was returned to the bottom.

Mr. Siglio showed us how to separate the bycatch from the shrimp. He looked at me and pointing his finger he said, "Matthew, put on a pair of heavy gloves. Watch how I separate the fish and trash from the shrimp, using this paddle," a board about a foot long with a handle on it, " you push it to the side walls and then shove it out the cull holes. Now watch how we handle the shrimp." He had another piece of wood that was narrow, with a handle, and he slid it under piles of shrimp and lifted up about a foot. Long stringy tentacles that attached to the shrimp head were wrapped around the stick. With his other hand he grabbed the tentacles and lifted up; a bunch of shrimp hung there like you were holding a bunch of grapes. He slid them into one of the baskets he had nearby and turned to me again. "Matthew, if you get stuck by the shrimp," and he showed me the pointed spine at the head of the shrimp, "or you get stuck by some of the fins on these trash fish, you won't be playing baseball anytime soon. Your hands will swell and hurt like boiling water had been poured over you."

I reached for the gloves, a paddle, and one of the narrow sticks. I thought that maybe I didn't want to be a shrimper after all. It took the five of us working steadily for close to 30 minutes before we culled the trash and the trash fish and had the shrimp on ice. Then we pulled the other net and did it again. We made four double pulls over the next 5 hours. We were all whipped. Mr. Siglio had a talk with Sal, and shortly after that our heading changed to north by northeast. We washed the decks with a hose used for such, brushed down the deck to get rid of any jelly or trash left on deck, and went into the cabin.

There were two bunk beds, one on each side of the wheel house when you entered. Another bed was past the helm. Mr. Siglio took the bed past the helm and told Sal that he would relieve him in a couple of hours. The rest of us crashed. It was just getting daylight when I woke. I could smell coffee. The adults already had a cup, and I accepted one when someone asked if I wanted some. They had no cream, but a little sugar hit the spot. Sal stirred and took over the helm. We were back at the dock before nine o'clock. We all thanked Sal and started to the fish house, but I turned and went back to see him, "Sal, a few weeks ago I was standing on a big sand dune on Little St. George Island and saw three shrimp boats anchored a few miles off shore to the southeast. I thought it looked like a fun thing to do. Working on a shrimp boat, seeing all the sea life, being on and a part of the sea, I just thought that I would love it. Tonight taught me that I'd better get a good education. I think I'm more sore now than after the first day of football practice."

Sal got a kick out of that. He said that you get used to it. And he asked that I drop by and see him sometime. He also said he would see me after some football games this fall, and that I had better throw some touchdowns. When Dad and I got home, I went to bed, even before calling Tess. It was after four o'clock before I woke up. I had a shower, which helped some, but I was still tired. The salt air actually dried my skin, and even with the shower I still felt sticky. Dad was in the living room so I joined him. "That was a lot of fun, wasn't it?" Dad offered.

"It sure was but I'm glad I don't have to do it again tonight!" Dad got a kick out of that. I continued, "I don't know what people pay for shrimp, but I'm sure it's not enough."

"It does make you appreciate how these people live, and work." Dad even looked tired. We both just sat there not saying much until Mom called us for supper. It was fried shrimp. I don't know if Sal or Mr. Siglio gave some to Dad, but where ever they came from, they were outstanding. I still didn't know if they were brown shrimp or hoppers.

After supper I called Tess. She sounded happy; I think she always sounds happy. "Did you catch any shrimp?"

"We caught a few hundred pounds!"

"Did you bring any home?"

"That I don't know but we did have shrimp for supper, and they were great."

"Well, you'll have to bring us some one day soon. Was it fun?"

"It really was, but it sure was hard work. You have to squat on the deck to separate the shrimp from the bycatch, that's the other fish that get caught as well, and after a few hours of that I could hardly stand up. We got home just before ten this morning. I passed out and didn't get up until 4 this afternoon."

"Well, I'm glad you had fun. And, I can't wait to see you."

"I miss you like crazy! Maybe I can get up there next weekend. And, this next week will be our last baseball games for the summer."

I hope you can come up, and you know what? It's less than two weeks until first of August." Wow! I hadn't even given it any thought, only two weeks. I hope Elzie has called my Dad.

"Do you know if Elzie called my Dad?"

"I don't but I'll ask Cloud tomorrow. We have got to make this trip happen. I can't wait to see the Island, and where you worked, and the rock pile, and the tire swing, and hopefully we'll see some baby sea turtles." Just listening to her got me excited. I really hope we get to go, and I really hope we see those baby turtles. We talked on for a few minutes and then said our goodbyes. Before ten o'clock I was already asleep.

Chapter 6: The Invisible Sands

The next week plodded by, we had a light practice on Monday, a game on Tuesday, another light practice on Wednesday and our final game on Thursday. We played St. Joe again for our final game. They beat us six to two, but it was our only loss for the summer. I ended up hitting just over 400 for the summer, with three home runs. With August approaching talk turned to school and football. Practice was to start on the fifteenth. We wanted to start earlier, but Coach said it was some school rule. But he did say that he would make some equipment available if we wanted to go throw the ball around a little before actual practices started. The fifteenth was on a Friday so a few of us decided we needed to start working on some pass plays; we would start on Monday the eleventh.

Our last baseball game was on the twenty-fourth, Thursday. I hadn't seen Tess in almost two weeks. I felt like Owl Creek was calling me. After a few phone calls, a small amount of pleading with my parents, and Tess begging Cloud, they came and picked me up in Apalach on Friday morning. I could stay until Monday morning. Elzie wasn't with Tess and Cloud, but Mom and Cloud talked for a bit while Tess and I walked around our neighborhood. It was less than thirty minutes before we were headed home. Elzie did show up late that afternoon and he brought a nice mess of freshwater catfish. Cloud fried them for supper and Alida and Sage joined us for supper. The next morning Elzie and I went fly fishing for a few hours. It was a hot morning but we did catch a dozen nice big bream. We cleaned them on the bank and headed to the house. As we were starting onto the back porch Elzie grabbed me by my shoulder and said wait! Cloud and Tess were sitting on the floor, cross-legged, facing each other, their arms stretched over their knees, their hands opened and facing upward. It looked as if their fingers may be touching each other's hands. I could not tell if their eyes were open.

Elzie guided me around to the front of the house, he told me to wash up and he would put the fish in the refrigerator. I washed my hands, changed my T-shirt and met him in the front room. He motioned for me to follow him; we went to the big screened room, and settled under a fan. "What were they doing?" I asked.

"It's a type of meditation. Cloud says it helps her with her visions."

"Visions? What visions?" This was strange and new to me. Elzie seemed a little cautious, as if he was hesitant to tell me something. I could see the wheels turning in his head; after a little thought he began,

"Matt, Cloud has had visions since she was a small girl. Sometimes she sees things that have happened in the past; other times she has visions of what may happen in the future. It's not voodoo stuff. It's not bad. It doesn't make her do strange things. But it does help her make decisions about things. It also helps her help other people." Okay, that was new. She certainly seemed normal to me! Well, maybe I should think about that some. She did paddle by herself from Owl Creek to Elzie's house boat. But she is respected; everyone around here considers her the tribal leader. My thoughts were running wild, I didn't know what to say but,

"What does she see? I mean, does she see people, events, signs? What?"

"She's told me about seeing her ancestors, how they lived, how they hunted, fished, even how they cooked. Other times, she has premonition about events that are about to take place. She knew you and Tess would fall for each other." Okay, now that's a little weird!

"How would she know that?"

"She just gets feelings. That's about all I can tell you. But I've grown to respect her gift. You might want to respect it to."

"Should I talk to her about it?"

"I think you should wait until she approaches you about it."

"Why was Tess with her?"

"Well, you might want to talk to Tess about that. You see, she has visions too." What? What am I hearing? Is this some kind of joke? Maybe this is too weird. Am I just blind?

"Elzie, does she see weird stuff? Is this some kind of joke?"

"No, it's no joke, but it's not something to freak out about. Listen, I've been on the river most of my life. I've seen some strange things. I've felt some strange things. Not once in my life have I had thoughts, feelings, even visions that hurt me. And it won't hurt you. And they, Cloud and Tess won't hurt you. If anything their love is the strongest thing you'll ever feel. Now put on your big boy pants and let's go have some lunch."

When we walked back into the front room we could hear them talking in the kitchen. Elzie hollered something about starving to death. I trailed along, trying to get my mind around what just happened. They were laughing when we walked into the kitchen. Tess came to me and gave me a quick kiss, and asked what I wanted for lunch. I suggested a hamburger, French fries, and a large chocolate milk shake. She thought that sounded good! But probably not going to happen. We had soup and cheese sandwiches, and ice tea. After lunch Elzie and Cloud retired to the bedroom for a nap. Tess and I went to the back porch, but before we could even sit down she suggested we go for a walk. I say that tongue in cheek, I think she just said "come on." We headed back to the hill overlooking the creek. At the bench between the two trees we sat down. We held hands, and after several minutes she turned to me and said, "Yes?" I said yes what? And she said, "What do you want to ask me?" Damn! How does she know!

"Did you hear me and Elzie this morning when you and Cloud were on the back porch?"

"Yes."

"What were you doing?"

"Meditating."

"You never told me you meditated."

"Well, for the most part, when we're together we talk a lot, and we don't seem to be able to keep our hands off each other, and we have lots of fun, and meditation requires quiet." I didn't have any reply to that. I sat there not really knowing what I should say next. Thanks goodness she knew, "People all over the world meditate. Cloud has been teaching me to meditate for years."

"Why do you do it?"

She thought for a moment, then said, "In a baseball game, when you are on deck, or even standing back by the dugout, I've notice that you hold the bat a certain way and close your eyes. What are you doing?"

"I'm visualizing a pitch."

"Bingo! That's what meditation is. It's mind visualization. It makes you better at what you're trying to do." I just couldn't help myself,

"Elzie said you and Cloud have visions!"

"So do you! You just told me you visualize pitches."

"That's not the same."

"Sure it is. It's just that it's expanded, enlarged, broader than looking at a single pitch, it's seeing the whole game." OK, I'm way over my head. This girl who's only a few months older than I am, says that she can see the whole game when I can only see a single pitch. I wish it didn't hurt so much to think.

"What do you see?"

"When?"

"Now."

"I see you kissing me." How does she know these things?

74

We sat there for a long time, we didn't say much, but finally the mud in my brain softened a little and I began to talk, "I don't understand, but I want to know, learn. You've got to teach me. Can it make two people closer?"

"Certainly!"

"Can you teach me?"

"What I can teach you is nothing to what Cloud can teach you. Cloud loves you; all you have to do is ask her."

"Elzie said he thought I should let Cloud approach me."

"Why don't you let me and Cloud visit a bit this evening, maybe I can help." We held hands and talked. A nice evening breeze picked up, the big oaks and hickory trees swayed with the breeze, singing songs of the swamps. We strolled along the trail, not in a hurry to get back to the house, but when we entered the back porch Elzie and Cloud were there. They acted happy. Elzie pretended to beg for fried catfish for supper; Cloud pretended not to listen. Tess and I just sat there and laughed at them.

Soon, Elzie and I were on the porch and the girls were frying catfish. "Elzie, I talked to Tess this afternoon regarding our talk earlier. She's going to talk to Cloud and see if Cloud will with talk with me. Maybe teach me."

"Boy, you sure do amaze me. You go from thinking they're witches to thinking you want to be one." He smiled, looked real satisfied, then said, "You'll be happier."

The next morning after breakfast Cloud asked me to join her on the back porch. As we settled into chairs she asked about my conversation with Tess. I told her what Tess and I had talked about and that maybe Cloud could teach me how to meditate. She smiled and said she would be happy to share what she's learned over the years. I was beginning to think that this couldn't be much, after-all, I do play sports. Cloud began,

"Before we start sitting on floors and crossing our knees, let's just talk a bit about the process, and what you might learn or at least experience. It's not like learning English, or math, or even athletic plays. It has a lot to do about who's inside you."

"What do you mean, who's inside me? I'm me! I'm inside me."

"Do you dream?"

"Sure I dream. Don't most people?"

"Most do. Some don't. But what do you dream about?"

"Lots of things. Sports, school, even sometimes about things or people I don't even know."

"Why do you think you dream about people you don't know?"

"I don't know. It just happens sometimes."

"If you were awake and saw someone you didn't know, but then you looked away or blinked and then they weren't there, what would you think?"

"I guess I'd think that they weren't there to begin with."

"But if they had been there, then what?"

"Then I'd probably get spooked."

"What happens if you get spooked?"

"Nothing. I'd probably just forget about it."

"Well, let's talk about if the people had been there, but when they were where you saw them, it had been another time for them. Are you understanding what I'm saying?"

"I'm not sure, but go ahead."

"If you were walking on a beach and found footprints, what would you think?"

"I'd think that someone had been on the beach and they had walked where the footprints were."

"So, it's easy to understand footprints?"

"Sure."

"What if I told you that there are different type of prints, not just footprints. People prints, event prints, life prints. Try for now to imagine that if you are on a beach and if you left the beach you would not just leave footprints, but also your prints. Not on the sand, but also in the air, the scene. Can you imagine that?"

"I think I understand what you're saying, I just don't understand how you would see the human prints. What would the prints be on?"

"You know how jets leave a stream of smoke across the sky?"

"Sure, but isn't that the exhaust?"

"Yes, but what is it on?"

"Just the air."

"If it didn't leave the smoke trail, it still would have been there? Right?"

"Sure."

"So, we see footprints, trails, lots of things if they are left on something. Now, I want you to imagine that there is an invisible force that exists all over the world. Think of the force as invisible sand. Where someone or something was, there are prints left behind. That's what we want to explore. When you meditate, or visualize, you can see the prints left behind. I know that sounds far-fetched, but sometimes it's easier for some more-so than others to see these things. Just as you practice sports to become better, meditation and/or visualizing takes the same discipline. The more you connect to the un-seen world, the more you will see."

My head started to hurt. That sounds way too deep for me. It's hard enough to keep up with things that I can see, how would I handle things I can't see. I'm sure that dumb look on my face gave me away. Cloud smiled, then said I should sit on the floor next to the wall and lean back and relax. As I took my position on the floor she pulled her chair over next to me, and began, "Now let's practice a little. Cross your legs to where you are comfortable, lean back and get relaxed. Close your eyes and think about your breathing; just breathe slowly and steady." This was making me feel silly; I started to laugh, but thought better of it. Ok, I can do this.

Cloud began speaking in a soft voice, slowly, giving me time to try to picture her descriptions, "Now, I want you to think about a beautiful creek, the color of the water, the tree's branches hanging down and over the creek. See the small bream swimming close to the bank. It's a hot day, but the breeze cools you. Look up at the sky, it is so blue that it reminds you of a deep, deep, ocean. Now look up the creek, as far as you can see, until the creek turns and disappears behind the bank and trees. Keep staring. Breathe slowly, keep staring. Now picture a canoe appearing way up the creek, slowly coming into view as it comes around the bend. Slowly, slowly, it keeps coming into view. Soon, the entire canoe is visible. Its dark green, it blends into the tree-lined bank and its color almost disappears into the water and foliage." By now my breathing had slowed, I felt really relaxed, and I was actually beginning to imagine the scene. "The canoe keeps coming toward you. Slowly it emerges from the shade into the sunlit glitter of the creek. There is a girl paddling the canoe. She's very beautiful, with dark hair, and a light blue handkerchief tied around her head. She raises her hand and waves to you. Then she disappears."

"What?" My pulse was faster, my mouth went dry. My eyes were wide opened, "Why did you stop?"

Cloud smiled at me, "Could you see Tess?"

"Yes, why would you stop?"

"Was she there when you opened your eyes?"

"You know she wasn't!"

"But you could see her?"

"Yes, I told you I could."

"Now, do you believe in visions?" What do you say? Nothing! It sure felt real, I didn't want it to stop. She played a joke on me! Maybe I should listen more, talk less. Finally, I asked her how I could do what she just did without her help. She smiled at me again, and said "Practice!"

After lunch Tess and I went canoeing. The creek had a lot more influence on me since my morning session with Cloud. I became very aware of the water color, even the sky, and how the banks and trees blended in colors, shapes, and sizes. I started telling Tess about my training session with Cloud and when I got to the part about the creek she started giggling. "Why are you giggling?" I felt a bit hurt, after-all it was her idea that I meet with Cloud.

"Because she used the same scenario on me; the same creek, the canoe, and you appearing in the canoe."

"Did you ask her why she stopped?"

"I did!" and then we laughed together. We decided that we needed to play a trick or two on Cloud. That would require some thinking and planning. The afternoon and evening passed way too fast for me. I was feeling low late in the evening when Tess reminded me that Friday we would be going to Little St. George. "My Dad hasn't said anything about me being able to go." Now I was getting depressed.

"You're going." Tess said matter of fact.

"How do you know? Did Elzie talk with my Dad?"

"Nope, Cloud did. How could your Dad say no to Cloud?" That made sense. As I laid in bed that evening I tried to visualize Tess and me on Little St. George. I don't think it worked, but I sure did sleep well.

Cloud and Tess took me home the next morning. Dad was actually there when we arrived. After brief hellos and courtesies Cloud asked Dad point blank, I think for my benefit, if it was okay for me to join them on Little St. George the next weekend. Mom and Dad both agreed. Happy birds flew around inside my head. They left shortly thereafter; I started packing that afternoon. In four days we would be back on Little St. George. I sure hope Walter is prepared.

I was to meet Elzie, Cloud, and Tess at the fish house Friday morning at ten o'clock. Dad said I was to have an ice chest with me. I had my bag packed with extra shorts, T-shirts, a bathing suit, two pair of tennis shoes, in case we did any wading, a light jacket, and I also brought an extra baseball cap in case Tess needed one. Dad went inside the fish house with me to wait on the others, they were already there.

"Paisan!" welcomed us as we entered. Without any questions Mr. Siglio took the ice chest and went into the freeze room. He returned a few minutes later and gave the ice chest to Elzie. "You tell Walter that I hope he enjoys!" We visited for a little and then as Dad got ready to leave us he turned to me and said, "You help out a lot, OK?" I nodded that I would and he was gone.

We loaded the ice chest and my bag into Elzie's boat, I untied the bow and stern lines, and we were off on another adventure. Tess and Cloud both had on shorts, light blouses, and tennis shoes. Neither had on caps. I took my two caps out of my bag and gave one to each of them. They acted impressed with my manners. After passing under the bridge, Elzie accelerated the boat to plane. I started telling Tess about the bay, pointing out the buoys, and how you navigate between them. The bay was calm, skies were clear, and it was a hot August day. I was so excited I could hardly contain my emotions. I had spent a couple of months running back and forth to Owl Creek, not giving Little St. George much thought, until now I realized that I had missed it. In June it felt like a prison; today it felt like a luxury vacation. I hadn't seen Walter since the Fourth of July. Maybe I could get him to grill us some more oysters.

At the turn of the Intracoastal Waterway we turned west; I told Tess about the Intracoastal, and about Bob Sikes Cut, and about the turtle nest just a couple hundred yards from the cut. We passed Pilot's Cove, the Government dock, and then Elzie idled us in toward Walter's covered boat house. We unloaded our gear onto the dock inside the boat house, and then I helped Elzie turn the boat around and anchor the boat outside the boat house. There wasn't enough room for both Walter's and Elzie's boats in the boat house. Elzie used double anchors attached to the bow, and he had me tie double stern lines to the docks under the boat house. He educated me to the perils of wind and tides when anchoring around structures. I knew I'd better pay attention.

Walter came out to help us with our gear, and shortly we were unloaded. Entering the house Walter instructed Elzie and Cloud to take his room, Tess was to have the second bedroom, and Walter and I had the front porch. Back on the porch again! I noticed that Walter had another cot on the porch; I sure hope he doesn't snore. I dropped my gear and then helped Tess with hers. While the adults visited a bit I took Tess out the back. Walter had finished the concrete under the pole barn. It looked really good. And sitting on the concrete was a tractor with a disk attached to the back. Next to it was the jeep. And, the generator had been placed under the barn, and Walter had run the lines to the house underground. Seeing it all again filled me with pride. It had been hard work, but wow, look at it now. The tire still hung from the pine tree, and as soon as Tess spotted it, we had to go have a look. She pushed the tire into motion, then turned and asked, "Do you really throw a football through the opening while it's swinging?"

"And also while running," I offered.

"Maybe you can show me while we're here?"

"If you're standing there watching me, I doubt I could even come close."

"Sounds like an excuse to me. Where's the rock pile?" So, we walked back around the house to the rock pile. It wasn't near as many rocks as when I started the batting practice. I gave Tess the approximate size and height of the rock pile before I started the hitting rocks into the bay. She found it hard to believe, but she said I could show her how it was done while we are here. I suggested that I could also give her some lessons. "Maybe so," was her reply.

Back in the house Walter was spreading some sandwich makings on the table; Cloud called for us to join them, and shortly we were back on the front porch having lunch. A nice west wind had the porch cool. As Walter settled in a chair he turned his attention to me, "Well, how does it look?" I knew he was talking about the barn, so I bragged on it, and then asked,

"Where did you get the tractor?"

"I found a guy who wasn't using it right then."

"How did you get it over here?

"I found a guy who wasn't using his barge right then." You'd think I'd learn. Elzie thought it all made sense. Cloud and Tess just laughed at us.

After lunch Walter said we had a lot of work to do and that we should get after it. We all headed out the back to the pole barn, Walter took charge, "It's going to take me a while to drive this tractor to the dove field; Matt, why don't you take the others to see the light house and then come on down the beach to the dove field. I'll take the tractor through the timber." Elzie and I grabbed a few snacks and a couple of gallons of water, then we all piled into the jeep. I took the driver's seat, Tess took the other front seat. Elzie and Cloud just stood there like they expected to be up front. Tess and I didn't budge, just motioned for them to get in the back. The seconds seemed like minutes. They stared at us, we stared at them. Finally, they consented. They piled into the back seat and we headed off to the light house. I felt like a tour guide.

At the light house I pulled the jeep around to the shady side and we unloaded. As we opened the door to the stairway, Cloud said we should go on up. She had been up in the light house before. Elzie said that he had had to haul batteries up that damn thing a few times and swore that he'd never climb up there again. Tess and I headed up. At the top Tess gasped, "Wow, this is beautiful."

The breeze had the surf up, the waves were crashing along the shore, and looking to the east, the white foam from the waves looked like white ribbons floating on a green sea. It was the same to the west except the sun's reflection made it harder to watch. We stood there for several minutes, she was leaning against me, and I held her close. The sand dunes stretched on for miles, sea gulls were working the shore line, and the sea oats were beginning to turn golden on the sand dunes. I whispered "Amber waves of grain" and then told her how the sea oats would be in full development and color by October. It really does make you think of amber waves of grain.

She turned around to me and gave me a kiss, then said "I am so excited to be here. I'm glad it worked out."

I thought about something she had said to me once, "And this is just the beginning!" I whispered. We talked a few minutes about how the light actually works, about the Coast Guard and the batteries, then headed down. Elzie and Cloud were in the light house keeper's old house, so we joined them. Elzie explained how the fireplaces worked, how each hearth was vented into a central chimney, and then he talked about the timbers the house was made from. Cypress lumber, from Cypress trees out of the river swamps, cut at a local mill in Apalachicola. He told us how he and Walter had timbered the swamps, how they had floated rafts of logs down the river and to the mill. Until right then he had never told me how he and Walter had worked the swamps. I got a cold chill listening to him, realizing for the first time that he really was a river rat. Walter did it because it was what they had to do to make a living; Elzie did it because he loved it. He was part of it, the swamp, the cypress, the frogs, and even the gators. Dad had said that I had a lot to learn, I realized I had some good teachers.

Back in the jeep, we headed toward the west end. We hadn't gone far when I noticed the nest where Walter and I watched the sea turtle dig her nest and lay her eggs. I drove over to it and we all got out. I explained the wire mesh and the stakes, and gave them detail by detail of the mamma turtle crawling to her nest, the digging, and then the laying. I told them about the tears she shed, and the slow crawl back to the sea, and how I waded out with her until the waves covered her and she was gone. They all listened, never saying a word, and as soon as I finished both Tess and Cloud made wishes that we would see the babies hatch while we were on the Island. Back in the jeep we drove on to the dove field, along the way I kept pointing to nests we had staked. At the end of the big timber and just past the big sand dune we turned in toward the dove field. Walter had already gotten there and was wrestling with what looked to be a drag. Elzie and I jumped right in to help. The drag actually turned out to be a drag, just heavier than the ones we used when dragging the infield for baseball. Walter was trying to attach the drag behind the disk, thinking, according to him, that he could disk and drag at the same time.

Elzie suggested that we take turns disking the field and once disked, we'd drag it. He thought the dragging would be much faster after the field had been disked. Once agreed, Walter started the process. Cloud suggested that she and Tess would just be in our way so they decided to go for a walk on the beach. While Walter started the disking Elzie and I walked over the field looking for logs, stumps, anything that we thought should be moved before the disk arrived. Walter's first run was a perimeter disk. Outlining the field made our trash removal easier. The field ended up being approximately 100 yards wide by 300 yards long. Walter had finished about a third of the field when he stopped. Elzie took over while Walter and I had some water and discussed the field. "Matt," Walter began, "if we finish the disking this afternoon why don't we come back tomorrow and spread the seed?" It wasn't a question, he was just letting me know that there would be more work to do.

"Why don't we spread the seeds today after we finish with the disking and the dragging?"

"Because I need y'all to be awake when we go turtle hunting this evening." I'd forgotten about the turtles. Walter continued, "And we have a full moon tonight. I have a good feeling about this."

The girls showed up just a little later, the field hadn't completely been disked yet, so Cloud said they were enjoying the beach walk, they had walked to the end at west pass, and decided that they would walk back toward the light house. She said that we could pick them up on our way home. Elzie finished the disking and then we disconnected the disk, and rigged up the drag for the finish work. They showed me how to drive the tractor, not to make sharp turns with the drag, and turned me loose. I had pulled drags for a few years at the ball park, just not with a tractor. It took a little getting used to, but I adjusted quickly; pulling the drag was a lot faster than disking. It took just over half an hour to finish. We hooked the disk back to the tractor, wrapped up the drag and tied it to the top of the disk, and Walter headed back home through the timber.

Elzie and I went to pick up the girls. They were well over a mile down the beach when we caught up to them; both had shells in their hands. They loaded quickly and we headed back to Walter's. Elzie and the girls had gone inside. I rinsed off the jeep and had put it under the pole barn by the time Walter arrived. He acted pleased. So, of course, I rinsed off the tractor and the disk. We rolled the drag off the disk and put it under the barn as well.

By the time I got inside I could smell the shrimp frying. Elzie and Cloud had taken over the kitchen. Walter went to lie down for a few minutes on the porch, so Tess and I walked to the boat house and sat on the inside dock in the shade. The west wind was cool, small minnows could be seen swimming under the dock and around the stern of the Walter's boat. Gulls were working the shoreline, calling and chasing whichever bird had a minnow. Tess held my hand, leaned against me, and whispered that this was wonderful. "I'm so glad we got to come here," she said. "Today was beautiful. Cloud and I really had a good time during our walk. She's very happy for us." She leaned up and kissed me. I held her close. It did seem perfect. Sitting there together was perfect.

Then I said something I probably should have thought about before opening my mouth, looking into her eyes, I said, "Tess, I don't think I ever want to grow up!" She started laughing, tried to stop, then started laughing again.

Finally, she said, "I know, I think growing up will mess everything up." We were both laughing when Elzie called us for supper.

Fried shrimp, hushpuppies, cheese grits, and green salad. You know, growing up on the coast sure has its advantages. We were all stuffed. The grown-ups got to go to the porch, Tess and I washed and dried the dishes. The sun was setting by the time Tess and I joined the others on the porch. Before we could even sit down Walter turned to me and asked if I remembered where he kept the waxed paper. I told him I did, so he sent me to get it and also asked that I look in the drawer next to the knife, fork, and spoon drawer, and also bring a small bag that had rubber bands in it. He shuffled inside, returning in a couple of minutes with 4 flashlights. "We'll need these tonight if we find the turtles," he began. He explained that baby turtles when emerging from the nest are drawn to light which is supposed to be the moon shining on the gulf. Sometimes some of them get confused and go the wrong way, never getting to the gulf. He said our intention is to help the little buggers along to the gulf. He also explained that the flash lights were too bright to be shinning on them especially if we were close to them. So, to diffuse the light we would wrap the plastic paper over the head of the light secured by a rubber band. He said that if we did get to find a nest as the turtles are hatching then we could shine our lights and back away from them guiding them to the gulf.

The sun was gone for the day, but the evening light still held when we climbed into the jeep. Walter drove, Elzie joined him up front, Cloud, Tess, and I sat in the back seat. At the light house Walter turned east and headed toward the cut. We didn't even check any of the nests going in that direction. Just about the time we reached the jetties at the cut, the full moon crested the eastern sky. Walter turned off the jeep and we all just sat there and stared at the moon. I heard that in Africa the monkeys do the same thing! No one said anything. Tess held my hand, squeezing it often. I was beginning to wonder if squeezing my hand somehow was helping the moon climb up out of the gulf.

It's times like this that you need Elzie to guide the conversation, "Well, that's nice, let's go!" So, we headed back toward the west. This time Walter didn't drive down by the water, he stayed well up on the sand so we could see each nest site. We stopped at each one, got out of the jeep and inspected the nest site. Walter explained that sometimes a few of the babies will appear before the whole batch comes bursting out of the sand. Also, we were to look for tracks.

"They're small, so look very carefully." We took our time on the first nest, Walter showing us or pointing out something we need to be aware of. At the second nest it went a little faster. There was only one more nest before the light house. Nothing so far. The nest where Walter and I saw the turtle lay her eggs was the first one past the light house. It was well down the beach, but it was the first past the light house. The moon was getting higher in the sky by the time we reached that nest. The sky was so light, and the moon shine off the white sand so bright, we didn't even need the jeep lights on to drive. But, Walter kept them on anyway. As we had done with the other nest, we parked the jeep a little ways away from the nest, and higher toward the dune line. As we approached the nest on foot Walter said to stop, turn on your lights and look very closely.

The sand under the mesh was bubbled up in spots, kind of like popcorn just before it pops. Walter took control, "Matt, help me with the mesh. Let's get it up and move it back behind the nest to the dune." We snatched the stakes up, picked up the mesh and moved it to the dune. We then gathered in front of the nest, facing the nest, our backs to the gulf. Within just a few minutes the sand began to move, slowly at first, then the first few babies broke the surface. Tess and Cloud both squealed, then giggled. Walter said for us to be careful because as the rest of the babies burst out of the sand, it's hard to see them and we don't want to step on any. The few babies were moving slowly at first, but within seconds after they emerged from the sand, the rest of the nest came to the surface. Literally more than a hundred baby turtles burst out of the sand, all headed toward the gulf, their little flippers pulling them along.

Walter reminded us, "Shine your lights toward them and keep backing up toward the gulf. As the babies get closer to the gulf they will spread out, we have to do the same, leading them into the water."

I would not have believed that little baby sea turtles could move very fast. The mother had moved very slowly, dragging her weight, but these rascals had one thing to do, and they were doing it in a hurry. We were having to keep moving, backing up, then spreading out the closer to the water we got. The girls were squealing the whole time. We were all laughing, so excited to watch the marvel of the hatching, the running to the sea. Within a few minutes they were all gone, running directly into the waves washing the shore. Walter went back to the nest site to check than none got caught in anything, making sure there were no tracks leading off in the wrong direction. As we gathered back at the jeep Walter claimed, "They all made it! That's rare. Good job." We celebrated, we laughed, Tess and Cloud cried tears of happiness. Then we regrouped and started again. We found no other nest hatching but we sang, and laughed, and rode the beach with the full moon lighting our way. It was magic!

Back at the house we all gathered on the porch and talked until very late. Walter suggested that Tess and I make a turtle run the next morning, just to check for tracks around all the nests. Tess and I thought that would be fun. The others decided they'd rather sleep in.

It was just getting light when I woke. I laid there for just a few minutes just remembering the night. The morning was cool, the sky clear, and I felt excited. I slipped on my bathing suit and a T-shirt, when and brushed my teeth, then got some cereal and milk ready, then went to wake Tess. She was already awake and said she'd join me shortly. We sat at the table having cereal, whispering softly, until Walter arrived. He put on coffee and was about to go back to the porch when I said that Tess and I were going for the turtle run. He reminded me not to drive fast in the soft sand, and have fun.

Tess grabbed her beach bag and we were gone before Elzie and Cloud got up. Tess had on her bathing suit as well, but a large T-shirt over it. We turned at the light house toward the cut, I drove closer to the water because the sand was packed and we could make time. At the cut we turned around and started checking nests, headed back to the west. Stopping at each nest, we checked for tracks just like Walter had instructed. At the nest from last night we stopped and checked it again. We just stood there staring at the site, remembering every second of it, wondering what happened to the babies after they got into the gulf. Walter had told us that the babies swim straight out into the gulf and keep swimming until they find floating sea grass beds. They live there until they get much bigger. Tess turned to me and said, "I am so thankful for last night, for getting to come here, for you. I love you!"

"And I love you!" We headed west again, checking each nest, looking for tracks. We found no other activity. At west pass we turned around and headed back, but when we got close to the big sand dune I knew she had to see it. I put the jeep in four wheel drive and we creeped up to the top. We got out and I was showing her where I had seen the shrimp boats, telling her how it felt that day, up here looking out over so much beauty, so remote. She turned to me and kissed me. I didn't want to turn her loose. We stood there for several minutes, holding each other, not saying anything. I didn't want to leave this spot, she said the same. She reached into the jeep and brought out her beach bag. From it she produced a large beach towel. We spread it over the sand and sat down. We kissed again. She knew, I knew, and she said it's time. And there, on that high sand dune, with the beautiful world of sand and sea, and swaying palms, and gulls calling, and with a west wind blowing, we made love. I held her beautiful body against mine, we stared into each other's eyes, we whispered I love you. Neither of us wanted to leave, but we left, and on the way back to the house we stopped on the beach and went for a swim. We were still wet when we got back to the house. We both knew that the others would know what we did, that by our smiles, our looks at each other, they would know. And, they didn't pay us one bit of attention.

After a light lunch Walter said we had to catch supper, so he told me to get the castnet and a sack and work the government dock, and he and Elzie would go pick up some oysters. Tess and Cloud decided to join me, and shortly we were on the dock. Walter and Elzie took the jeep and headed to Pilot's Cove. I had to instruct the girls not to walk ahead of me because they would scare the mullet. They laughed and made fun of me, but thankfully they held back while I eased along the dock looking for mullet. The tide was low so I had to get well out on the dock before I started seeing small schools of mullet working around the dock.

Remembering what Walter had taught me, I waited until I had a small school headed away from me then cast the net. I made a decent cast covering most of the school. As I brought in the net the girls saw the mullet start kicking against the net, they laughed a bit, but gladly helped as I retrieved the net and removed the mullet individually and put them into the sack that Tess was carrying. I had six that first throw. We kept working our way out on the dock, stopping and throwing, and within several minutes we had ten mullet in the sack. I knew that was plenty so we headed back to the house.

The girls headed to the porch, I took the mullet to the boat house and found a suitable place to clean the fish. The heads, backbones, and guts left for the crabs, I took the filets back into the house, then went to wash out the net. By the time I cleaned up and changed into some clean clothes and joined the girls on the porch I heard the jeep returning to the house.

Walter and Elzie had a nice tub of oysters. It looked to be another night of good seafood. We gathered on the porch, listen to Walter and Elzie tell some stories of their youth, appreciated the cooling west wind, and watched as the sun began to set. Walter said it was time to roast some oysters, Cloud said she would take over the kitchen and fry the mullet. Tess joined Cloud and within minutes we could hear them laughing in the kitchen. Elzie was in and out preparing sauces for the oysters, and I was directed to provide them with beers as reward for their skilled harvest. Island living! Just a couple of months ago all I wanted to do was be home; now, it felt like home.

The meal was wonderful, the stories and laughter comforting, and the prospects for another happy time certain. We sat on the porch until late, enjoying the cool breeze and the full moon. Tess and I were to make the turtle run the next morning, and as I drifted off to sleep dreams of baby turtles crawled across my brain.

The next morning, Sunday, was just like the day before, I was awake by daylight, Tess and I had a bowl of cereal, and were headed out the door when Walter got up headed to the kitchen to put on coffee. Again we started at the cut and checked each nest all the way to the west end. No sign of tracks. Without discussion we drove back to the top of the big sand dune, the towel retrieved from Tess's bag, and again, with the sun shining bright, a west wind blowing, and gulls crying along the shore, we made love. It was even more passionate and intimate than the day before. Afterwards we lay there looking up at the sky, holding each other, both smiling uncontrollably, when Tess turned to me and said, "You're right, we don't need to grow up!" We laughed and held each other for several minutes, then headed back to the beach. We didn't swim, but waded in the gulf, washing the passion from our skin, but smiling. Love is a beautiful thing.

Back at the house, Walter was inside when we arrived. Elzie and Cloud were out on the Government dock. Walter asked about the nest, we told him no tracks, he said that the other nests should hatch over the next week to two weeks. I asked if he would try to see anymore when we're gone, he said no, but he would check each nest for the next couple of weeks and as they hatched, he would check for stragglers each day, and remove the mesh and stakes from the beach. Tess and I agreed we wanted to stay and turtle watch. Walter thought that would be a good idea, but didn't think our parents would approve of us leaving home just to take care of turtles and an old man. Elzie and Cloud returned, we had a nice lunch, then returned to the porch.

By four o'clock the tide was low so Cloud suggested we take a walk along the bay. Walter and Elzie declined, but Tess and I joined her. Along the bay from in front of the house to the Government dock we found lots of pottery, made by Indians who lived here several hundred years ago. Most were small pieces, but we did find some pieces that were larger, with markings. Cloud explained how the pottery was made, what some markings meant, and how the Indians used the pottery bowls and plates, even cups. Holding history in your hand gives one a whole different impression of what once was. Cloud also explained how the clay and different soils were brought down the river for the pottery making, often traded for fish and shell fish, and how the Indians traded food, furs, tools, even techniques on how to create utensils. The different tribes along the Apalachicola, Flint, and the Chattahoochee rivers were all considered Creek Indians, but the different locations dictated different sub-tribes. Of course those Indians who lived in the lower Apalachicola River basin and on the islands that creates our bay are the Apalachicola Tribe. Cloud's knowledge impressed me and intrigued me. "How do you know so much about the Indians that lived in our area?" I asked.

"Still live in our area!" She smiled. I felt so....embarrassed, stupid, dumb! But she consoled me,

"I study history! I am a history teacher. But, you should know that there are others just like me throughout the river basin. I have friends who live along the Flint River and the Chattahoochee River. Their families are like our families. They suffered. Many were killed. They assimilated to survive, just as we did."

"Do you stay in touch?"

"Yes, but we don't visit often. When there are problems or individuals have needs we always try to help.

"Do they use different names as you do?" As soon as I asked the question I knew that I was stupid. Cloud looked at me as if looking at a child, she smiled, then turned and stared back looking along the shore for pottery. We moved together, looking at the shells, hoping for pottery, me biting my lip. Tess, squeezing my hand. I bet she really wanted to laugh out loud at me. Finally, Cloud spoke.

"Matthew, it's hard to hold on to traditions, to embrace the past, to honor the customs. Life is moving so quickly now, new inventions, new communications, different people from many different places are now living around here. When you don't know where you came from it's much harder to know where you're going. Our people were here a thousand years before the white man arrived. They brought new customs, new religions, new methods of killing, and diseases. So many of my people were killed either by the white man's guns or from their diseases. They wanted our land, and in the beginning, our labor. Once they became established they wanted us gone. We weren't allowed to stay in our home areas, own our land. It became white man's law. Our tribe are spiritual people, we honor the land, our rivers, the animals and the fish. We taught the white man how to grow our vegetables, how to harvest fruits, nuts, even honey from our swamps. And still, in order for us to survive, we had to act like white men. They did not honor us, respect us, or respect our women. It was die or adapt. What I know about the past is not limited to books, it's been taught to me from many generations, from others and their knowledge of how their tribes survived. There are many women, Indian women, like me, who have become the spiritual leaders of our communities. We have taken it upon ourselves to preserve the past, to hold our customs sacred. It has been easier for the women to do so than the men, because when an Indian man is known as a leader, the white man feels threatened and often, the men are killed. Even today."

I have felt small and stupid a few times in my life, but not like I was feeling at that moment. Tess held my hand tightly. Our walk slowed along the beach, Cloud seemed distant, not looking for more pottery or shells. We turned back toward the house, the west wind meeting our faces. Finally, Cloud spoke to me again, "Matthew, what I can teach you, what I am teaching Tess, are connections to life, to feelings not generally felt by modern folks, visions of the past, visions of the future. Having a connection to the unseen elements of life, that touch your soul, that allows you to know the presence of people, animals, events, sadness, even joy, will guide you through your life's journey. You'll be able to see the invisible sand."

There was no more talk until we returned to the house. The sun was dropping fast, evening colors were washing over the bay, and I realized that my life had changed, I was now on a journey. A journey to the past. By the time we got back to the house Walter had a fire going in the fire pit, building a bed of coals for roasting oysters. Cloud went directly to the kitchen to begin supper. Tess joined her. I sat on the porch with Elzie while he had a beer. After a bit Elzie said, "Find some pottery?"

"We did, and Cloud explained how it was made and what some of the markings meant."

"Yep, she's tried to educate me to those things. But, you can't eat pottery!" And that about summed it up. At some level, I knew that I was right there with Elzie.

The setting sun cooled the evening, Walter's oysters smelled of briny wonders, and when we gathered at the table for fried mullet, smoked oysters, more cheese grits, and hushpuppies, I had to give thanks for life, for love, and good food. Tess and I cleaned the kitchen, then joined the others on the porch.

Walter said that we had to get the seeds on the dove field the next morning before we head to town. Head to town! I'm not ready to head to town. There's baby turtles to watch, fish to catch, rides on the beach, and Tess. My heart sunk. It's passed so fast, there's so much more to do, Tess hasn't even seen me hit the rocks, throw the football. The evening past quietly, I think I wasn't the only one not wanting to go back to civilization.

The next morning just before sunup Walter stirred, headed to the kitchen to put on coffee. I stayed in bed. It was a lot easier to get up when I knew that Tess and I were on turtle patrol! By sunup we were all up and preparing for the end? The beginning? The ride back to responsibility? What should I do about the tire swing? The rock pile? Cloud prepared some pancakes while Walter and I went out and loaded 200 pounds of millet seeds on the jeep. At breakfast Walter said that if Tess and I would help him it wouldn't take any time to spread the seeds. Shortly thereafter, we were piled into the jeep, Walter driving, Tess in the front seat, me in the back seat. We rode through the timber because it was faster than going all the way to the beach before heading west. At the field Walter had Tess and me sit on the back of the jeep, the sacks of seed between us, and as Walter drove slowly up and down the plowed and dragged field, Tess and I threw handfuls of seed behind and on each side of the jeep. We spread them as evenly as we could while bumping along on the back of a world war two jeep, always staring at a beautiful big sand dune where memories were made, dreams fulfilled. Walter was right, it didn't take long to spread the seeds and head back to the house.

When we returned, Elzie and Cloud were finishing loading their stuff into Elzie's boat. Cloud said for us to hurry and get our stuff ready and loaded. As we loaded our bags and prepared to leave Walter came out and said he would follow us back to Apalachicola, he had provisions to buy and needed more gas for the jeep, as he had turtles to tend to. The ride home seemed twice as fast as the ride over to the island. We went directly to the fish house, tied up and as we got out of the boat to go inside, Dad and Mr. Siglio came walking out to the docks. "Paisan, I thought you would have been here sooner?"

From Elzie, "Walter made the kids spread seeds on the dove field this morning. He has no respect for people's vacations." That brought some laughter. Elzie went to help Walter dock, tied his bow and stern lines, and then we all entered the shade of the fish house. Elzie took my ice chest to the cooler and without the help of Mr. Siglio he loaded several pounds of shrimp, iced them properly and then had me help him load them in his boat.

"I promised Cloud's family I'd catch them some shrimp."

Mr. Siglio replied, "Looks like you made a good haul." More laughter. I never saw any money change hands. We all visited for a little while, Cloud and Tess told Dad and Mr. Siglio about the turtle hatching, all the good food we had to eat, and how much they enjoyed the shrimp he sent with us. It felt like the last scene of a really good movie. And then they were gone. Dad and I went home. I think I collapsed on my bed when I took my bag to my room.

At supper Mom grilled me on all that we did. I told her about the turtles, the dove field, the fishing, the food, but I didn't tell her everything. Dad asked about football practice. That made me think about what day it was, it was Monday, August 4th, one week before we start the unofficial football practice. I knew that from here on all times would relate to football practice and games. School would start after Labor Day, Tuesday, September 2nd, and our first game would be on Friday, September 5th. My junior year, I always expected it would be great. I never could have imagined what a year it would be!

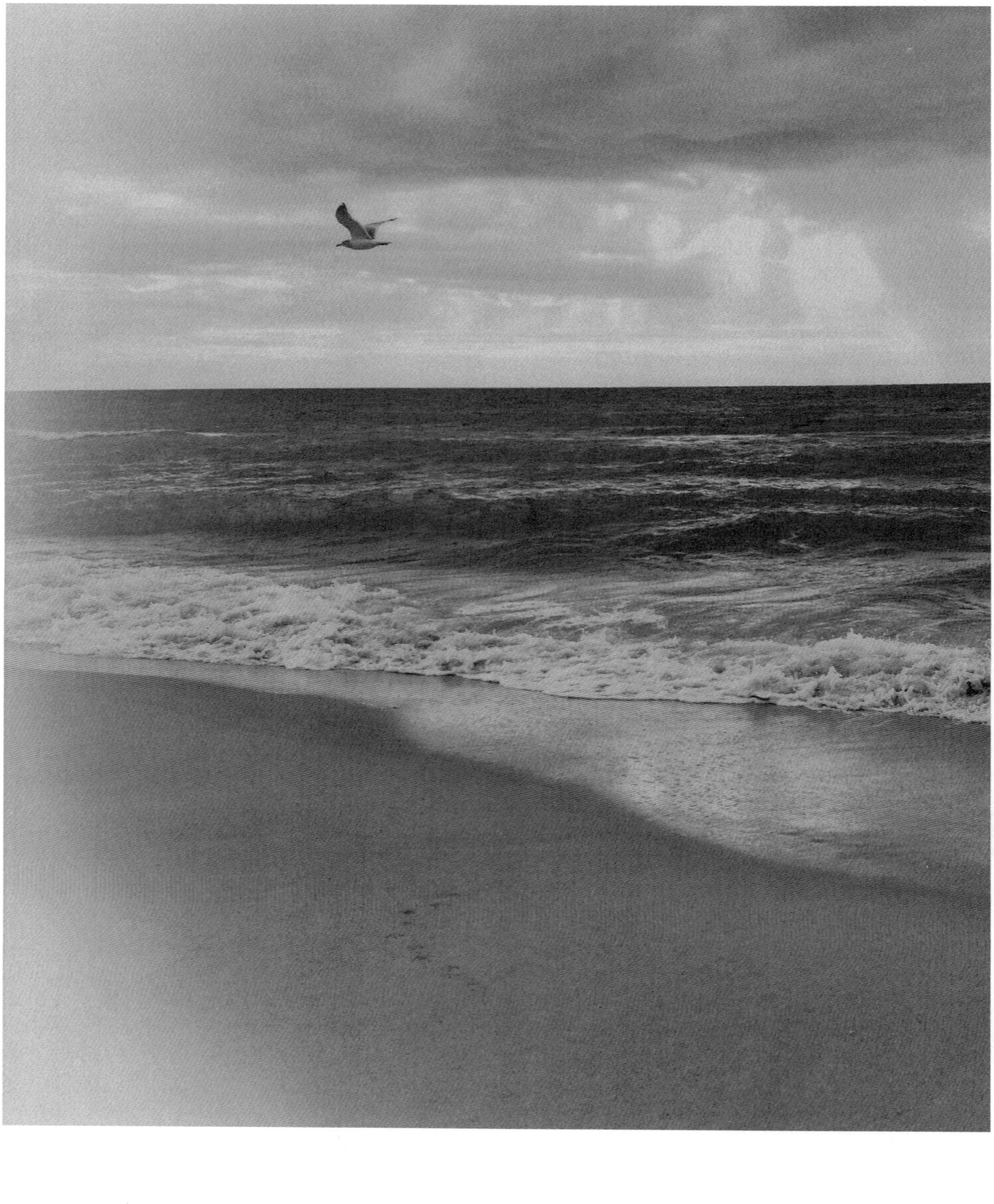

Chapter 7: It's an Inside Game

I called Tess each day, we asked Cloud to intervene, and as she explained to Dad, it would be our last long weekend for some time. So, Friday morning she and Tess came to pick me up. I promised my folks I'd be home Monday morning. There were no big plans for the weekend, but Cloud said that if we, Tess and me, wanted we could do a little visualizing, maybe talk about ways to focus our attention to help us in school, even sports. Tess was further along than me at the visualizing, but I said I was ready, as long as we didn't have to make Tess disappear from the canoe again. I think Cloud may have said I was hopeless.

Elzie showed up around 5 that afternoon, he was soaking wet, I thought he may have fallen over board when getting out of this boat. We all asked what had happened. He said, "Nothing!" and looked at us as if we were the ones all wet.

"Then why are you so wet?"

"Well, some of us have to work!"

"Doing what?"

"Driving pilings."

"Where?"

"On East River."

"Why?"

It was always like that, Elzie took great pride in making people work for answers. Finally Cloud had enough and told him to quit playing games and tell us what he had been doing.

"I just did!"

"OK, let's try this again, why were you driving pilings on East River?"

"To tie the barge up to!"

"Are you moving the barge?" I couldn't help myself. I think he's rubbed off on me.

"Just like every year, end of the summer, we move the barge to East River for the fall and winter hunting. And by the way, Matt, I'll need your help over Labor Day weekend to help me move the barge."

"That's great by me. You might have to talk to my folks. They already think I've left home." Cloud suggested some ice tea, so we all moved to the porch. Minutes later Alida arrived home, Sage was with her. Cloud suggested we have supper together, everyone agreed, then Elzie asked what we were having?

"Whatever you're cooking!" from Cloud. We all laughed at that, but Elzie said he was all wet and would think about it while he showered. After his shower he told us we were not allowed in the kitchen, even suggested we go for a walk, or go play with the kids. It was almost eight o'clock when he called us to come serve our plates. He had made a shrimp and sausage gumbo from a roux, lots of onions and peppers, and finished with gumbo file` seasoning. Rice in the bowls, plenty of gumbo on top. It was really good.

Saturday morning, after breakfast, Cloud asked if I wanted to talk a little; of course I said yes, and as we moved to the porch Tess came in the back door. Cloud said she could join us. We sat in chairs, not on the floor, and I didn't have to cross my legs. I figured we must be just going to talk. The first thing Cloud said to each of us, "What do you see in your future?" We each had to answer, I said,

"Ladies first," so, after sticking her tongue out at me, Tess began.

"I see a fun year of cheerleading, with happy holidays including Matt, a really wonderful Christmas, and a Spring Prom with Matt." Boy, I thought, ole Matt's gonna be a busy boy.

"How about you Matthew?" Cloud turned to me.

"I see a winning football season, I see making some passes to win ball games, I see a fall and winter where I learn more about hunting and fishing, and I also see holidays filled with happiness and Tess. Spring baseball is going to be special."

Cloud sat back, a thoughtful look on her face, and focused on both of us,

"Each of you see happy times, things that will make you happy. Things you want. Now, I'd like you to tell me what you are going to do to make those things happen." Tess said I had to answer first this time.

"I'm going to practice hard, learn my plays really well, ask Elzie to teach me about hunting in the river swamps, and I'm going to hit a lot of rocks before baseball practice begins." Tess' face had changed, she looked almost puzzled, thinking hard as to what she wanted to say.

"I am going to encourage the other cheerleaders to work hard together, I'm going to do my best to lead. I'm going to help others prepare and enjoy the holidays, and I'm going to focus on making others happy, believing that happiness begets happiness." Cloud looked at both of us, smiled, and said that we should think about what we just said we wanted and what we were going to do to make it happen.

Then she started talking as much to herself as to us, "Being happy starts inside, it's an inside game. Some people live very poor lives, but are still happy. Becoming aware, and living it, that happiness is not about having things, doing things, going places, or being with someone. Happiness is a state of mind, a state of being. When thankfulness of being, whether it be in life or even in death, permeates all that you are, then happiness will be one of the by-products. Happiness is not the end result, nor should it be." Cloud's focus changed, she looked at each of us, her smile warmed the room, "Being in love certainly makes people happy, but if a loss occurs, it should not prevent you from being happy. Your connection to that person lives on. It can center you, help you focus on the being, even if there can be no sharing. Love is also a by-product of being. The process, the art, the learning that Mother Earth connects us to all things, living and not living, present and not present, should be your quest. Your life, your love, your happiness will merge, all as one being."

I sat there listening to Cloud, reaching and touching Tess, not knowing what I should do, or not do, but I was sure of one thing, my journey was afoot. There would be no turning back. Early afternoon Tess and I went for a walk, back to the trail that had the seat between two large trees, overlooking the creek, we didn't stop there, but continued on following the trail overlooking the creek. It was a bright day, hardly any clouds in the sky, but the tall trees on the ridge cast such long and full shadows that gave the feeling of evening. A few hundred yards further up the trail from the bench we stopped. There were two very tall white acorn trees on the creek side of the trail; they were fairly close together and in looking up into their branches it appeared that they grew together. Branches intermingled with other branches creating a canopy of large leafs with very little sunlight showing through.

Tess suggested we stop there. We both sat down next to each other but leaning back against the same tree trunk. We said nothing. After several minutes Tess turned to me and said, "Let's try meditating together." I agreed, so she repositioned herself in front of me, allowing me to continue to lean back against the tree. We crossed our legs, arms across our knees, palms up, but touching each other. There was silence; only the breeze through the trees could be heard. After a few minutes I asked Tess how we should proceed, I didn't have a clue. She smiled at me and said that we should first try to visualize our time together on the big sand dune overlooking the gulf and west pass. We closed our eyes, but within seconds I suggested we needed to visualize something else. I was beginning to get excited. She giggled, reached out and touched my face, but agreed we needed to focus on something else. Moments later she suggested we visualize standing on a high hill, looking out over the Apalachicola Bay, the sun just beginning to set. She said that as the sun dropped below the horizon there would be a moment where green light would flash just as the sun disappeared. We should both try to catch that moment, and then tell each other about it.

We both closed our eyes, I continued to lean back against the tree trunk, my mind actually slowing down, my breathing softened, I became very relaxed. And then I fell asleep. Something splashed across my forehead, wet and warm. It startled me, I jumped; it scared Tess, she leaned back away from me and then started laughing almost uncontrollably. "What is it?" I almost yelled.

"It looks like a squirrel just pooped on you!" More laughter. After a bit and some wiping of my face, I even laughed as well.

"So much for visualization," I said. "Maybe we should head back."

Tess was still giggling, "Wait until I tell Cloud about this one!"

"Please don't do that," I begged. "She already thinks I'm a lost soul, or maybe just stupid." The first thing Tess did when we got back to the house is run tell Cloud. They both started laughing at me, I felt stupid all over again, but I couldn't just stand there and take it, so I said, "I was getting in touch with nature! I just didn't know nature smelled so bad." They both really laughed at me that time, but Cloud said that was good. I past my first test! "Test? Why didn't you tell me this was a test?" Of course they laughed at me again. I decided I should go find Elzie.

Elzie was over in the big screened in room talking with Mark about some kind of timber contract when I walked in; they didn't stop talking but after waving me over to join them they changed the subject. Elzie turned to me and said something along the lines of, well, did you get enough of those women's education? He couldn't help but smile, Mark joined him. I wish someone around here had a dog I could be friends with. I settled in one of the bigger chairs and decided I should listen more, maybe talk less.

The sun was setting when Cloud called us for supper. Tess, Alida and Sage joined us. We all ate on the back porch; I tried not to talk too much. At some point Elzie had me over next to him and he started telling me about how he always moves the house boat to east river each fall because he likes hunting over there and it's just a short run down to the marsh at the bay where he duck hunts. Moving the houseboat is not hard he offered, except when going through east river cut-off, where the currents are stronger, and it takes more than one boat for guiding the houseboat. Three boats are usually better. "So, who helps you?" I finally couldn't keep my mouth shut.

"You, for starters! But Walter comes to help, and if Mr. Siglio is available, it really helps if he brings one of his smaller shrimp boats. We'll see. I should know the plan within a couple of weeks." It just all sounded so exciting to me, I wanted to be part of everything. Especially the hunting.

"Elzie, will you teach me to duck hunt and deer hunt this fall and winter?"

Elzie looked at me surprised, "Did you think I wasn't going to?"

"We've never talked about it." Now I felt stupid all over again.

"Damn, boy, do we have to talk about everything? I swear, sometimes you're as bad as those girls." Maybe I should have stayed home this weekend. I could have mowed the yard, maybe hit some rocks, maybe hit the rocks in my head.

"When do we start?"

Another one of those almost smiles from Elzie, "Why don't we worry about that after we get the house boat moved to east river?"

By ten o'clock everyone was off to bed except Tess and me, we stayed on the back porch, held hands, and I tried not to talk too much. She finally got me to stop acting like I had gotten my feelings hurt and we settled on a chaise lounge and snuggled close. She kissed me, I held her close, but we didn't take things very far. We had become closer than I ever imagined, and her family treated me as if I was one of them, I didn't want to mess that up. We talked about that, but we also whispered about our future times together, and the love we have for each other.

By eleven-fifteen I walked her next door to her home, and I went back to my bedroom.

Sunday mornings, at least the ones that I had experienced this summer at Owl Creek, were generally calm, and quiet. No one, that I saw, dressed up and went to church. Usually there was some of the group that either ate lunch or supper together, but that was about it. I realized that Cloud was a spiritual person and served as the spiritual leader of the community, but there was no church, no preaching, no organ or piano playing, and no spiritual hymns. So, I was surprised when around 10 O'clcok the women started bringing their children to the screened in room. A couple of family members who did not live here in the community also showed up. They were all women and their children, at least the children under the age of 13. The children were both boys and girls. The mothers, women, stayed with them in the screened in room. Tess came over to see me about the time the women and children gathered in the room.

Cloud had gone to the meeting room about 30 minutes earlier and stayed to wait for the others. Tess explained to me, as I stared out the front door, that usually once a month the women and the children gathered together here and Cloud spoke to them about the Indian ways. Tess was very adamant that Cloud was NOT preaching. It was an education process, a learning of the past, their heritage, their tribe's beliefs. It also was to educate the kids on how to act and avoid confrontation and conflict with other people, white, black, or other nationalities, and their religions. It is a long, educational process to prepare the tribe so as not to attract attention or conflict, and to be able to function in our society. Assimilate Cloud had told me. Adapt or die!

Tess and I went to the back porch so we could talk. Elzie had left early in the morning, so we had the house and the porch to ourselves. I realized there was so much that I didn't understand, I had lots of questions, but Tess was patient with me, and more importantly, honest. We pulled a couple of chairs close together and as we sat down I started with my questions, "Did you go through the training while growing up here?"

"Yes, but it isn't training! It's educating. I'm not trying to be callous here, but please try to understand, many people think that if you don't believe what they believe then you are crazy, stupid, even dangerous. So many people are just afraid; they're afraid of mean people, black people, different nationalities. Think how they would react if they found out that you were of Indian ancestry and that you had a different understanding about religion, or Christianity. Some people that you consider friends would turn on you, not even associate with you."

My mind was racing again, but I had to ask, "Are you not a Christian?"

"Probably not in the same way you are a Christian, but what our nation, our tribe, believes is not anti-Christian. It's probably closer to what Christ preached than what the different Christian religions preach today."

"So what does Cloud teach them?"

"The same thing that she's teaching you and me. Love. Appreciation of life. A connection to our world, our universe. The totality of being! It's what Christianity is supposed to be, but without the salesmanship and the judgment." I was trying to take it all in, understand, not be judgmental, but I had so many questions.

"How did you deal with your friends when they asked about this community?"

"I just told them that our family had gone together and purchased the land a long time ago, and it's always been home."

"Did your friends ask about you going to church?"

"Sure they did. I told them we went to church in Eastpoint, or Apalach, or even in Hosford. Sometimes I told them I didn't like going to church. Many of them understood that."

"Do your friends know of your Indian heritage?"

"Some do, but everyone has a heritage. Me having an Indian heritage doesn't mean that I wear feathers in my hair, at least not in town," I had to smile at that one. "Or that we beat drums and dance around fires, we don't do that in town either, or shoot white folks with our arrows."

I was beginning to see her point, even if I couldn't get my head around having to deal with classmates who might be so judgmental. "And anyway," she continued, "I make really good grades, I'm the head cheerleader, and going to be class president next year. Do you think somebody in Bristol wants to try to beat me up over that?"

"OK, I'm sold, where do I sign up?" She did smile at that. "But, how long does it take to educate those children, to protect themselves, to fit in?"

"Not long, though most attend these classes with Cloud from about age 3 until 13. Some often come back for more counseling, like you and me!" My mind went into overdrive again, I kept thinking about all of the people everywhere that had to deal with others not like themselves. We were quiet for a bit, while I sat there plowing through thoughts, trying to be non-judgmental, trying to be mature. I had never spent much time thinking about people who were not like me. Thinking about people of other races and cultures having to adjust their lives just to survive in a world that I was able to walk through without much care was a new, and troubling concept. I knew this was something that I would need to ponder for a while.

The meeting broke up just before lunch. Tess and I decided to prepare some sandwiches for Cloud and Tess's family. We all gathered on the back porch, there was an atmosphere of celebration. Certainly not the same feelings I experienced coming from a Baptist Church sermon.
After lunch Tess and I went for another canoe outing, we paddled further up Owl Creek than I had been on the water. Soon I recognized the stand of large white oak trees we had sat under the day before, pointing them out to Tess, my hand automatically rising to wipe off my face. Tess took that as a joke, I laughed with her, but down inside I was still embarrassed. We took our time, listening to the wind, the birds, the river sounds, and watching the small bream work along the bank, underneath the overhanging branches.

I got to thinking it's Sunday afternoon, I have to go home tomorrow. Unofficial football practice starts tomorrow afternoon. Regular practice starts Friday afternoon. Our time together will be much shorter. Tess sensed my mood change and asked what was wrong? "I've got to go home tomorrow, football practice starts tomorrow, we won't get to see each other as much."
That realization hit me harder than I had expected it would.

Tess turned around in the canoe and said, "I know we won't see each other as much as we have this summer, but I assure you, we will see each other weekly. I can drive, you will be driving in just a few weeks. This isn't going to stop. It's just going to get stronger, even better! And, I've been thinking, maybe I can come stay with you and your folks some?" Wow, that hadn't even crossed my mind.

"I'll start working on Mom and Dad tomorrow night!" Already I felt better. The rest of the afternoon flew by, our evening with family was great, and the next morning Tess drove me to Apalachicola. Cloud had other things to do. When we arrived at my Apalachicola house Tess came inside with me. Mom was there, Dad was at work. Mom seemed surprised that it was just Tess and me, but I explained that Cloud had something she had to do. Mom seemed satisfied. There was small talk, Mom, always the worrier, seemed comfortable around Tess, and we even discussed holidays, especially Christmas, and how we could all be together. By the time Tess left to head back to Owl Creek I was feeling really good, especially about my Mom's attitude. Four o'clock arrived in a dash.

Coach met us at the field with some equipment, said he couldn't stay, but he gave me a short list of exercises to warm up, and three sheets of paper with pass plays illustrated. He said he couldn't turn on the lights until at least Friday, and then he took off. We huddled around in a semicircle to review the plays. Rob Gant, our catcher on the baseball team, is also our center.
Left end is Gillis (Lefty) Brown; he's a tall kid, only lived here for the past two years, but he's tough and he's smart. He has good hands, but he's not fast. His nick name, Lefty, is because he's the only

left handed player on the team. Right end is Bud Carlson, also our first baseman on the baseball team. Our backfield consisted of Bob Riley, Left halfback, and also the shortstop on the baseball team; Billy Smith, right halfback, and also the third baseman on the baseball team, John "Bull" Read, fullback, and of course me, quarterback. Our fullback, Bull, got his name because he's about 5 feet 11 inches, 225 pounds, not an ounce of fat; his legs look like tree stumps and his hands look like lighter knots. He doesn't run the ball much because he's such an excellent blocker. He's not real fast, but runs especially strong; when needed, he most always can pick up a few yards. He can catch too. We've all been playing ball together since we were in junior high, some of us since elementary school.

We all had our cleats, and were dressed in shorts and T-shirts; we ditched the exercise list and I called out a few warm ups and then we ran 40 yard wind sprints for several minutes. We gathered around and reviewed the pass plays, most were the same as the previous year, and ran them for about 40 minutes. They were all pretty basic routines. At that point we took a break, got some water, and then discussed our upcoming season. I really wanted to get these guys turned into more of a passing game than what we normally run. We always passed some, but I felt that we could step up our play with some good pass plays. I was hesitant as to how to approach the guys with my ideas, but came up with a plan. I started, "I know some of you weren't involved with the shit-stomping judge back at the end of school this past spring, but some of us had to pay penance for our wrongs." That got a laugh from everyone, even those not guilty. "My Dad thought it best that I spend some time with a coach that he knew. I was required to work on my hitting for baseball as well as my passing for football."

I doubt that any of them knew Walter, but if they did, I doubt they would consider him a coach; probably best I not give any names. "Anyway, I didn't have the luxury of receivers so coach rigged up a tire swing, and I had to run roll-out passes through the tire for a few hours a day. Standing still throwing through a tire isn't very hard, and roll out passes through the tire wasn't that hard either, but after I got my confidence up, coach had me running roll out passes but I had to throw through the tire when it was swinging back against the grain. It got me thinking, we could do that with our pass plays. Something most guys in our conference have never seen."

That did it! Billy and Bob both started with ideas of plays, with Bud being the primary receiver but they would cut back inside of his route, running in the opposite direction. It ought to work. Agreed. We ran several varieties of the plays for the next couple of hours. Lefty was looking good, and Bull showed us he wanted in on the show too. There was a lot of enthusiasm, and for the next three days we practiced more of our own plays than the ones Coach provided. When Friday's practice arrived, we were pumped!

The beginning of official football practice is always exciting, there's friends you haven't seen all summer, and there's always a few new people, some just moving to town, and others, like Gooch, who are just becoming part of the varsity squad. We don't practice in pads until four or five days of conditioning. We all start by doing stretching exercises, plenty of jumping jacks, push-ups, sit-ups, and always some strange exercise that Coach has read about, saw at a conference, or dreamed up during a fitful night of sleep.

After half an hour of that we break up into squads, or special teams and work on certain drills. I took over punting duties last year, so Coach sent me and Rob, and a couple of receivers to one end of the field to work on my kicking, with the receivers, usually Bob and Billy, catching the punts. The linemen always work with our assistant coach, Paul Blackmon, who believes that any lineman worth having on your team needs to be pushed to the point of exhaustion to prove they deserve to wear a uniform. The rest of the team work with Coach on special exercises, special past defenses, special running defenses, and special anything he dreams up in those fitful sleepless nights, as long as they are special.

After about 45 minutes Coach blows his whistle, we all gather around him and he then directs us to run different special dreamed up exercises that he forgot to order last time. Usually, about that time, he sends Rob and me, with the ends and backs, to the other end of the field to work on pass plays. Normally, Coach goes with us, leaving the rest of the team under the direction of Coach Blackmon to exercise and run drills designed specifically to test the limits of the human body. Under Coach's directions we ran the same old pass plays as last year, but as soon as he left to dream up more special plays, we went back to our pass plays we'd been running for the previous four days.

After another 45 minutes of these exercises Coach and Mr. Blackmon gather us around them for a pep-talk. Coach gives us an overview of the rumors about our competition for the season, of course, this is designed to make us want to work even harder to be prepared, to be willing to sacrifice, to earn the right to wear the uniform. Then, Mr. Blackmon takes over and lectures us about the sin of drinking carbonated drinks, the need to be in the best shape of our lives, and the reason behind pushing us to the limits of the human body. After that, we get to run 50 yard wind sprints until no one on the team can catch their breath. At that time they call it a day, but as we crawl off the field, Coach says we should run on our own this weekend and be back at the field at 3:30 Monday afternoon. Practice has begun!

The sun was down before I got home, but the evening light was still good. Lights were on in the house, and as soon as I got inside Mom told me to hurry with a shower, that supper would be ready soon. Body cleaned, breathing restored, I came into the kitchen to the smell of hamburgers and French fries; order and tradition had been restored. Dad seemed to be in a good mood, he asked about practice, about any new players, what I thought the team's prospects were, and was I going to Owl Creek this weekend? I had talked to Tess most nights of the week, but we hadn't discussed it because of football practice. I told Dad I didn't know but I was to talk to Tess in a little while, I'd find out what was happening.

I thought about this while eating, and even before calling Tess, I kept feeling that my parents sure are understanding about my desire to be with Tess and her family. I didn't know any of my friends whose parents would agree to allowing them to spend so much time with a girl friend's family. I felt happy, almost honored, that my folks would give me such freedom. I didn't want to screw that up. I called Tess a little later, she answered on the second ring, "I've been waiting on your call."

"Mom had supper just about ready when I got home, I took a quick shower, and just finished supper. Guess what we had?"

"Hamburgers and fries?"

"Yes, routine is back on the menu." We both laughed at that. Tess then changed the subject, "Will you be able to come up here this weekend?"

"Will you be able to come get me?"

"I'll be there before breakfast!"

"Better let me make sure. Can I call you right back?"

"I'll be right here waiting."

I went into the living room to talk with Dad, "Dad, I just talked to Tess, she wants me to come up there for the weekend. Is that alright?"

"How will you get there and when will you be back? And, is Cloud there?"

"Yes sir, Cloud will be there, and Tess will pick me up tomorrow morning. I'll be back on Monday morning. We have practice at 3:30 Monday afternoon."

"OK, but I need to know that I can reach you if I need to."

"Just call Cloud's house or Alida's. I'll call Tess back and let her know. And Dad, thanks."

Tess got there at 9 AM; she and Mom visited a little and then we took off for Owl Creek. I kept telling her about my conversation with Dad, how I was so impressed that they trusted me enough to allow me to spend so much time with her and her family. "Why wouldn't they trust you?"

"Well, I guess they should. But, they did have to come get me out of jail the end of May." I thought I was making sense, but Tess got to laughing so hard she almost had to stop the car.

"I never considered that I was dating a jail bird!"

"Then maybe we need to question your judgement!" That did it, silliness took over, and we laughed almost all the way home. Elzie and Cloud were on the back porch when we arrived, so of course we dropped into chairs like we belonged there. Elzie had to say something,

"Boy, you sure do need to get a driver's license. Seems this whole family has to change their schedule just to haul you around."

Tess came to my rescue, "But he's worth it!"

Cloud to Elzie, "You're one to talk about having people change their schedules!" Tess and I weren't too sure what Cloud was referring to, but we laughed anyway. Home again. It sure felt right. We sat around for a while, then Cloud suggested we go ask Alida to join us for lunch. Minutes later, Alida and Sage joined us on the porch. When you're an only child, having more than immediate family around felt like a party. That's the feeling I got sitting there, listening to Elzie tell some stories, watching Cloud and Alida laughing and talking, and Tess teasing Sage. After lunch Alida and Sage went home, leaving me and Tess on the porch with Cloud and Elzie. It was a hot day, the fans on the porch sure felt good. There wasn't much conversation, but at some point Cloud turned to Elzie and asked, "Why don't we go for a boat ride tomorrow?"

"Where you wanna go?" Elzie acted like it might take some efforts.

"How about you show us where you're going to move the house boat to?"

"I can do that, if you promise to make some lunch to take with us."

"Don't I always?"

"Sure, but just checking. I hate to run off entertaining and such and starve to death."

"There's not much chance of that happening, and losing a few pounds wouldn't hurt you!" Tess and I sat there just laughing at Elzie. I think he liked the attention. Not long after that Elzie went to take a nap. Cloud stayed on the porch with Tess and me. "So, wouldn't you two like to take a boat ride tomorrow?" Certainly, we both said yes. "Good, I think you'll like East River. It's one of my favorite places to stay. And, it's got magic." That got my attention,

"What kind of magic?"

"History type magic."

"Please explain."

"Well, the site is on the east side of the river, which is part of the mainland. The west side of the river there is all islands, long ones, but still islands. But most importantly, within a couple hundred yards of where Elzie ties up the house boat, there are old Indian mounds."

That got me excited, "Real Indian mounds?"

"Yes, real Indian mounds. And there's a beautiful creek just north of where the house boat will be called Thank You Ma'am Creek."

"Why is it called Thank You Ma'am Creek?" You'd think I'd learn.

"Your guess is as good as mine!" Tess got to asking Cloud some questions about something, my mind was in high gear. Thank You Ma'am Creek, Indian Mounds, what magic must be there? I was ready to go. When Elzie joined us after his nap I asked him about the mounds. He told me not to get too worked up, the majority of the mounds had been dug up and haul to the fills on both sides of the long bridge from Eastpoint to Apalachicola back in 1935 when the bridge was built. He said the mounds were used to establish the base for the roads that were built leading to the bridge. He also said that for years people would hunt around on the fills to find pottery and arrow heads.

He used to have a box full. Of course I asked if he still had them, but he said he thinks an old Indian came and stole them from him. A little later in the afternoon I told Tess that I thought we were going on a fishing expedition. She said maybe so, but sure sounds like fun.

The next morning after breakfast we loaded the lunch that Cloud had made and some ice and cold drinks into Elzie's boat and headed out. After idling out of Owl Creek to the big river Elzie brought the boat to plane, headed south. Cloud sat next to Elzie, Tess and I sat together in the stern of the boat. The river was calm, glass like, the sky was clear, and the swamp's tall trees cast long shadows along each bank. River lilies could be seen in the shadows, and the passing vegetation blended such colors that it appeared like a painted canvas, a moving painted canvas.

As we passed Fort Gadsden and Bloody Bluff, Cloud pointing each out and calling their names. Later she would tell us about their histories, but said that legends didn't always agree with the history books. We continued pass the mouth of the Brothers River, on toward Mark's Point. As we approached Marks Point, I pointed out to Tess that the big river continue to the right and we would be taking the left fork, Big St. Marks, and the house boat would be less than half a mile on the left. I also showed her Humphrey Slough, and told her that's where I gigged the gator. She just patted my arm and smiled. At the house boat Elzie stopped, we tied up and got out. Elzie went inside for a few minutes and came back with some bug repellent and a pistol. "What's the pistol for?" I asked.

"In case I have to shoot something!" I knew not to continue with this conversation, we'd had it before. We loaded back in the boat and headed toward East River Cut-off. Elzie backed off the speed as we entered the Cut-off and told me to look for logs under the water's surface. "We'll be bringing the house boat through here in a few weeks, so look for snags, any logs or stumps. We don't want the house boat hung up in here. We'd lose it for sure." That sure got me to thinking; how would you save the house boat if it got hung up in this swift water. Elzie took each curve very slowly, telling me that most snags and logs typically would be found on the curves. "Watch the water, look for whirling water, signs of different currents, that's signs that there are logs or snags there."

East River Cut-off isn't very long, maybe a quarter of a mile, but the current is swift, and there are some sharp curves. Elzie knew these waters, but I noticed that he was making mental notes at each curve, each snag, any logs that were lying against a bank. As the Cut-off opened into East River, the river was much wider, the current slower. Elzie told us that the river right there was over 60 feet deep. "When the winters are really cold, and the water temperature drops way down, you can catch some nice catfish right here in this deep water." I needed to remember that.

Elzie took us back to plane and within a few hundred yards we passed under the rail road trestle, the same track that we passed on the big river. We continued south for maybe a mile, around a few bends, and then Elzie backed us off plane, and then to idle. Up ahead we could see the wooden pilings that had been driven on the eastern bank. We were maybe a couple of hundred yards from them when Elzie took the motor out of gear, "Look to your left, that's Thank You Ma'am Creek." The entrance to the creek was very narrow, and had some willow bushes growing along the bank. A tupelo tree had a branch that hung low over the water.

"Can we get in that creek?" I had to ask. It looked like it would be hard to navigate through there.

"Yep, it's a little shallow in the mouth, but the creek opens up once you're inside. Before hunting season we'll cut that limb. I have to cut it almost every year." We eased on down to the pilings, like the ones on St, Marks they were about 10 feet apart and maybe 3 or 4 feet off the shoreline. Elzie pulled the bow of the boat between two pilings and had me jump out onto the bank and tie the bow line to a tree. He tied off both sides to the pilings so the boat would not drift into either piling. The girls and Elzie joined me on the bank. Immediately Elzie showed me what brush he wanted cut, where the fire pit would be, and told me to remind him that we needed to bring the walkway with us from St. Marks. I was needed! Manual labor! But I was happy to be a part of it.

It was August and the bugs were out. Cloud and Tess had worn shorts on the trip down, but before we got out of the boat they each pulled a pair of jeans on over their shorts. Elsie and I were wearing jeans. We all sprayed down, Cloud had brought some large kerchiefs for us to tie around our necks and used to cover our mouth and face if need be. I brought baseball caps for me and the girls. Elzie wore an old hunting cap, dark brown, with pull down flaps to cover his ears if needed. His pistol had a holster so he strapped it to his belt and tied it off around his leg to keep it tight against him. He told us to watch our steps, to please follow along behind him, and in single file, with Cloud behind Elzie and me behind Tess we eased off from the bank, headed into the woods but angled off slightly to the north.

There was a fairly wide ridge that ran along the river's edge. Oaks, hickory, pines and cypress trees covered the ridge, a fairly thick underbrush filled in under the trees. From our start the ridge also ran east, headed into the woods. We followed Elzie along that ridge for a little over 100 yards, finally stopping in an area for no obvious reason. Elzie called me to him, and in a low voice said, "Matt: now take a look around you, notice the trees, not just at eye level, but also notice the tree tops. On this ridge there are lots of pines and live oak trees. They don't lose their leaves in the winter. Remember that when it's winter. The cypress trees will be bare, most all the gum trees will be bare, even the white oak will be bare of leaves. It's important to get familiar with the tree tops, because at night you can't see much on the ground, but if you know your tree tops you can find your way out. But look around and tell me what you see."

We were all gathered around Elzie, I noticed that when each of us spoke, we whispered. The swamp sounds were like most woods sounds, the breeze through the trees, the birds singing, crickets, cicadas. It's as if we were afraid to interfere, disturb the natural state. I kept looking around, trying to see something out of the ordinary, trying to figure out what he wanted me to see. He didn't say anything, just waited on me. After a bit I think the girls were getting bored, but I just stood there, looking at the trees, the brush, the ground. I looked at up the sky, the tree tops, near and far, and then I saw it. The tree tops were opened in a line if you looked south, but only the tall trees. There was brush and smaller trees under the opened areas. I turned to Elzie, "We're standing on an old road." His smile startled me. He reached over, grabbed my shoulder and squeezed. The girls immediately asked where? Elzie showed them, explained how the road had been here to haul the mounds back to the bay for fill for the bridge, but time had grown the underbrush and disappeared the road. I will say, that felt good. It was the beginning of my training, with the exception of outlawing catfish and gigging gators.

We turned back toward the north, toward Thank You Ma'am Creek, and Elzie lead us down the unseen road to the mounds. I don't know what I was expecting, but some disappointment ran through my mind as we neared the remaining mound. It wasn't much more than a raised ridge, it ran from east to west, I assumed parallel to the creek, probably 40 to 50 yards long. As we approached the mound I could see that it was covered with brush, vines, thorns, a few small cedar trees, and a couple of taller trees with vines hanging to the ground. There were a few animal trails leading from our side to the other side. Elzie lead us along one of the trails to the top of the mound. From that I figured the height of the mound above the normal ground level was maybe 4 to 5 feet high. The ground was covered in growth, most of it looked like a type of moss. As we topped the mound and moved toward the other side, the elevation dropped at an angle, not steep, but dropped more than 6 or 7 feet not back onto a ridge, but into bottom land, real river bottom swamp.

There was not much brush, but some short cabbage palm, and green grasses covered a large expanse. Cypress trees sprinkled the entire site. We stood there in silence, listening, watching, waiting, for what I don't know, but I felt that I should not move, nor speak. Just listen. Tess moved closer to me, reached for my hand and squeezed it, I think she felt it too. After several minutes, Elzie came over to me and whispered, "I've sat here on several cold mornings and had a flock of turkeys feed right by me. Get you some warm camo before hunting season."

At that moment Cloud came over to me and whispered, "Invisible sand." I felt it, I knew it, this was where I was supposed to be. I was the student, Elzie and Cloud were the teachers. All I had to do now was wait until hunting season arrived. But hunting season was a long way off, I had much to do until then. I remembered what Tess had said to me, it's just the beginning. I was ready.

Chapter 8: Little Pearls of Desire

The ride back to Owl Creek was serene, the river was calm, the colors beautiful, Tess sitting next to me. I felt like I belonged here, this day, this time, with these people. I had learned so much this summer, mostly about growing up, accepting responsibility, and knowing the meaning of love. I now felt that I had two families, two homes, both guiding me along a path to some ordained meaning. I had always heard that growing up was hard, tough, many times painful. Maybe so, but this part of my growing up sure is fun.

Back at Owl Creek I helped Elzie clean up the boat while we discussed moving the house boat around to East River. He said he had spent probably 15 or 16 of the past falls and winters at that site. It was an easy run to his duck hunting blinds, provided good squirrel and deer hunting, and the creek held some good fish. He said Thanksgiving would be fun. I hadn't thought about Thanksgiving, it was still a long way off, and he hadn't said anything about me being invited. I really didn't want to be assuming, at least not let him think that I was assuming, but I had to ask, "Will I be able to join you at Thanksgiving?" He gave another one of those almost smiles and said

"Well, I guess that will depend on your folks." Ah, reality, it always boils down to that. I'm still not grown up. But, it sounds as if Elzie wants me there. Maybe we should get through the Labor Day house boat move first, and maybe through football season. Then ask. Maybe have Elzie ask as well. We'll see.

Cloud fried catfish for supper, as always I ate too much, but Tess and her family joined us on the back porch. It was a great evening with lots of laughter. Cloud brought up school, our junior year, I hadn't even thought about the dates. Two weeks from this Tuesday, school starts. By ten o'clock everyone had gone to bed leaving me and Tess on the back porch together. It seemed we both had a lot on our minds. There was no passionate kissing or even holding each other, just sitting next to each other and talking.

Football season controlled Friday nights, so we made the assumption that we would be together on Saturdays and Sundays. We again talked about her coming to stay with me in Apalachicola on some weekends; I still needed to talk to my folks about that. My birthday was on the twenty-eighth, I could take my driver's test the next day, so I, hopefully with Dad's permission, could drive up here instead of someone coming to get me. We talked about the holidays and hunting season; I told her I really wanted to hunt a lot with Elzie, but that would take time away from us being together. At that point she looked straight into my eyes and said, "Hunting and fishing has been a part of our family traditions all of my life. It's been a part of our tribe's traditions for generations, even longer. I expect you to go. It needs to be a part of your tradition. There will be times I might even join you, but you need to go, and to learn. I will always support that."

Well, that did it, I now knew that I was in love with not only the most beautiful girl in the world, but the most supporting one as well. She seemed to never put herself first, like every other girl I had known. And, she loves me! We stayed up until eleven-thirty, then I walked her home next door, and I went to my bedroom. As I lay in my bed, before dropping off to sleep, I gave a prayer of thanks. Happiness filled me like fried catfish! The next morning, Monday, August eighteenth, Tess took me home. Three more days of practice before we put on the pads.

Monday, Tuesday, and Wednesday were repeats of last Friday. There was one constant: sweat. Coach Blackmon called the beads of sweat little pearls of desire. I felt way down inside he must have had a tough upbringing. And then came Thursday, first day with pads. One would think that once you put on the pads we'd start running offensive plays, working on defense, punting and passing, getting ready for the first game. But no, each year just before we put on pads, Coach has another really bad night of fitful sleeping, and during those nights he dreams up exercises to test the strength of the equipment, and the metal of our souls. His favorite? Figure eights. This is where three guys lay on the ground, side by side, about 3 feet apart, and when Coach blows his whistle the first guy on the right side has to jump up, make a dive over the middle guy, while the middle guy rolls in the direction the first guy just jumped from, and the other outside guy has to roll away from the middle guy, and when the first guy hits the ground he has to roll in the direction of the third guy, who has to dive over him and then roll, while the original middle guy has to jump up, dive over the rolling guy coming in his direction, all with the intent of making a far-fetched figure eight. Sounds like fun, doesn't it?

Well, we get to have all this fun until Coach blows his whistle again, which usually is about let's say 10 hours, at least that's what it feel like. And when you think you can't get up off the ground because you hurt all over, and you're soaked with sweat, Coach Blackmon starts screaming "Little pearls of desire! Little pearls of desire!"

After at least one thousand hours of that Bud Carlson whispered loud enough for a few of us to hear, "I wish he'd stick that whistle up his ass!" And, because some of us laughed, Coach thought we were having fun, so we had to continue for another 1000 hours! And then, after many thousands of hours of figure eights, Coach breaks us up into pairs. We have to lay on the ground, on our backs, head to head. Except he puts a football between our heads. Coach designates one of us to be a ball carrier, the other a defensive tackler.

When he blows the whistle, we have to roll over, one grabs the football, the other tries to separate him from the football and his helmet, and his breath, all while Coach Blackmon screams "Little pearls of desire!" God, I just love football practice! And then, with 15 or 20 minutes left of sunlight, we run some actual scrimmage plays. And as dark closes in on us, we ran 40 yard wind sprints until no one is left standing. Then coach blows his whistle and tells us it was a good practice. Friday was a repeat of Thursday. At the end of practice someone reminded Coach that our first ballgame would be in two weeks, on September 5th, which prompted Coach to remember and tell us that Monday, September 1st, Labor Day, we would have practice, to be at the field ready for practice at 3:30.

After I got home and showered I called Tess. I told her I could not come up there the next day, Mom said I had to go to Tallahassee with her to buy school clothes. Tess thought I was just kidding when I told her I told Mom that I had plenty of jeans and T-shirts, and even after I swore I was not kidding, she still laughed at me. I'm sure there is a female conspiracy when it comes to clothes. But Tess, being Tess, said she understood and that we would see each other soon. I said I'd call her tomorrow night after collecting my vast and exciting wardrobe. She didn't even giggle.

Now shopping with Mom is a lot of fun, if you like splinters under your nails, or snake bites. Mom is a great Mom, she's almost always supportive of me, she's a good cook, and she's a great person. But she thinks I need to dress nice to go to school. She believes that guys wearing jeans, T-shirts, and tennis shoes degrades the education process. She believes that JC Penny was the founder of the High School Dress Code. So, first thing on Saturday morning Dad sees us off; he was smiling, I think because he knew he didn't have to shop with Mom. I had my restricted driver's license, so I drove. With Mom driving it normally takes right at two hours to get to Tallahassee. I got us there in an hour and a half, driving the speed limit. We only had to make one stop, Mom's one stop shopping, JC Penny.

After trying on ten thousand pairs of pants and at least three hundred pairs of shoes Mom agreed to two pair of khaki pants, two new pair of blue jeans, three button up shirts, and a pair of shoes that had non-slip soles, I think they called them deck shoes.

There was a cute girl, I think probably a college girl, that waited on us. She seemed to know the score and every time I stretched the truth a little about the clothes, she smiled and agreed. She must have said "that's what all the guys are wearing now" at least twelve times.

I think Mom said something along the lines of "degenerates" but in keeping with her firmly held belief in JC Penney as the sartorial sage of boys school attire, she opened her wallet and paid the bill. Back in the car, ready to head home, Mom said, "WAIT! You have to buy a new belt."

"Mom, my belts are fine. If they break I can just tie some cord around my waist."

"Degenerates!" she said in a whisper.

I called Tess when we got home and told her the whole story, at first she laughed, but by the time I finished she said she agreed with Mom, "degenerate!" I'm telling you, there is a conspiracy among women about clothes.

Saturday night dragged by, I think I called Tess ten times. On the last one she said she had to go to bed. We could start again tomorrow. Sunday mornings we normally go to church. I hadn't been to church all summer, didn't want to go to church. Mom wasn't pleased. Dad hid in the living room, reading the paper, not helping me one bit. After a heated exchange I promised Mom that I would not grow up to be a degenerate, that I would get a good education, a good job, and never cuss or tell a lie. After a while she gave up, and she and Dad went to church. After listening to Cloud and Tess, I just didn't think I could handle another Baptist Church sermon.

Until this summer I had always hated Sunday afternoons. I don't really know why, but it just always felt depressing, probably because I had listened to a Baptist Church sermon that morning. Most families stayed around home, most guys weren't available to throw a baseball or football around, and I was never really good at entertaining myself. This summer had been different, really different. Tess was in my life, their family was a happy family, their happiness was contagious. But this Sunday I was back home, and the depression crept back in.

I wanted to be on Owl Creek. Or even Little St. George Island. It got me to thinking, Walter and Elzie spend a lot of their time alone. It doesn't seem to bother them, matter of fact, I think they prefer it most times. How could these two old guys, brothers, be so content, even happy, living alone? What had Cloud told me, meditation, visualization would help me connect, be more complete. Happiness is a state of mind, a state of being. I went to my room with the intent of meditating but I lay on my bed, got relaxed, and fell asleep. An hour later I awoke and went looking for Dad. He was in the living room. "Dad, can we talk a little?"

"Sure, what's on your mind?" He put the paper down and turned his complete attention to me, which was a bit surprising.

"Dad, Cloud has been teaching Tess and me about their tribe. I know it sounds strange talking about a tribe in today's world, but she holds on to beliefs, traditions, customs that, well, that you don't hear in a Baptist Church. She doesn't force anything on me, but she shares information, suggest we consider other aspects to our lives that you just don't hear anywhere else. Have you spent much time around her?"

"Matt, as I told you before, I met Cloud because of Elzie. Walter and Elzie raised me after my folks were killed, Cloud came on the scene several years after that. She's probably three or four years older than me, but she's got great insights, strong beliefs, and I'm not talking about religious beliefs, but living beliefs. She and I have had many conversations over the years. She has confided in me regarding her family, her beliefs, goals, well, maybe life goals, and she has become a leader in her community. She's also very well respected in the school system."

"I know some of that, but Cloud has an understanding about life, death, living, loving, guiding others that I certainly don't find in church. But there is a happiness about her, a sharing of her living experience, that makes me want to know more, maybe live differently."

"Live differently how?"

"I don't know yet, Dad, but I'm gonna find out. When I'm around Cloud I feel different. I feel happier, more confident, but always wanting to know more. She's allowed me to make her home my home. She never said anything along those lines, but I've always felt welcome, and I know that she always looks out after me."

"Son, that's what families do. We do the same for you. The difference, I think, is that our attention is directed solely on you, where Cloud's is spread throughout her entire family, her tribe. And, I would suggest that when you speak of her to others, don't use the term tribe. That is their vision. It's not the vision others may have. And, when speaking of her around others who don't know her, don't refer to her as Cloud. She's Anne Taylor."

"I know and understand that Dad. I didn't know that Mom knew Cloud until she came here to pick me up one time. When did Mom meet her?"

"Probably right after you were born. She and Elzie came to visit us, to see you. We see her every so often. As I told you before, we see her at educational seminars. Remember, your Mom was a teacher until you were almost 10. We decided that she probably shouldn't teach at the same school where I was the principal, so she stayed home."

"Dad, y'all have given me a lot of freedom this summer. I'm glad I got to spend time with Walter and Elzie, to get to know them. I hope they will allow me to continue the relationship."

"They will son, we just had to wait until the right time to get y'all together. We just didn't know the circumstances were going to be what they were." We both had to laugh at that.

"The point, Dad, is that I really do appreciate what you've done for me. I won't let you down."

"I know you won't son."

"Dad, a couple other things, Elzie has asked me to help him move the house boat to East River next Saturday. Can I go and help?"

"Certainly you can. I didn't tell you but Elzie called me last week to discuss it. It's all set up."

"I don't know how I'm going to get up there, probably with Walter, but I think it's really going to be fun."

"Well, I'm sure you'll find a way to get up there."

"One other thing, Dad, I've been going up to Owl Creek all summer to see Tess. Do you think she could come stay with us some this fall? We have the extra bedroom. And, she and Mom seem to get along well."

"That is something that your Mother and I have already been talking about. We think it would be a good idea for her to come visit as often as y'all can work it out."

There are times that parents just impress the stuffings out of their children. Mine just did that to me. I told Dad how much that meant to me and was about to leave but thought of something I had wanted to ask,

"Dad, how do you know Alida?"

"Before I met your Mom, on one of my trips home from college, she was with Elzie and Cloud in Apalach. I thought she was the most beautiful girl I'd ever seen. I was in hopes of dating her, but she informed me that she was already dating another person, and those girls don't change directions. She was married to him before I got out of college."

"Did you know her husband?"

"I did not, but Elzie told me he was a fine fellow. The logging accident was really sad." I don't really know what happened the rest of the day or evening, except I did call Tess and tell her about mine and Dad's conversation and how Mom and Dad thought it would be really nice for her to come stay with us this fall. There wasn't any more depression around our house for some time to come.

The next day, Monday, August 25th, football practice changed. We had solid warmups but the entire practice centered on offensive plays, and defenses against what we knew about Port St. Joe, our first game to be Friday, September 5th, at home, under the lights. I was throwing well, the receivers were catching well, our running game was shaping up, and our attitudes improved. It was Wednesday before we showed Coach some of our new pass plays. At first he acted like we were rebellious, but after we ran a couple with our defensive backs trying to cover the receivers, we got his attention. And he didn't even have to draw them up for us.

The practice sessions drew out, we started at 3:30 and most nights we didn't finish until 7PM. We were all getting in good shape, I guess from all those pearls of desire, and more importantly, we were becoming the team we should be. Many of us have played together for years, we should be ready.

On Thursday, August 28th, it was my birthday, and finally 16, I could get my driver's license. As I headed out the door about 2:45 to go to the gym to get dressed for practice Mom said she was making me a cake, it should be ready to have after supper. I told her thanks and headed out. Practice was intense, our defense was working really hard, and Coach Blackmon was tasking each defensive lineman and the linebackers to look for certain formations St. Joe would run generally on certain downs. Coach was allowing me to run any pass plays I wanted to test our defensive backs. Even when they knew what we were going to run I was still completing passes. Our receivers were hot, they all had good hands, and most could run well. Those that couldn't we'd hit them with short button-hook passes for short yardage.

Practice ended just before seven, by the time I dropped my pads at the lockers in the gym and caught a ride with Bud, it was still just after 7 when I arrived home. Bud asked who all the vehicles belonged to, but I said I didn't know and headed in. Just outside the garage was a new boat on a trailer. It was a Roy Smith boat, one of the local boat builders, the best; it was 14 feet long, 56 inches wide, had a model bow, steering at mid center, and a 35 horse powered Mercury. It was painted duck boat brown. I checked it out and was thinking that I hoped I could get a boat like that one day while I walked in the back door. There was Mom and Dad, Walter, Elzie, Cloud and Tess, and they all sang Happy Birthday to me as I came in the door. Now that will knock your socks off! I couldn't believe it. I was actually having a birthday party. Elzie spoke first, "Well, what do you think of her?"

"I love her, you know that!"

"Not Tess, dummy, the boat!"

"It's beautiful. Whose is it?" Tess broke in,

"It's yours silly."

"Mine?" I couldn't believe it, my eyes began to water, a knot formed in my throat and I couldn't speak. I thought I was going to cry. Now that would look pretty bad for a 16 year old quarterback. I finally got my composure and said that I want to turn the lights on it, but I'd first like to take a shower. They all laughed at me, but I headed to the bathroom. Fifteen minutes later I was back, not stinking, feeling like someone had just given me a million dollars. We all had to go outside, turn on all the outside lights, and talk about every inch of her. I climbed in the boat, sat at the wheel, rubbing my hands up and down the railings. I was proud I didn't wet my pants. After several minutes gawking, rubbing, and bragging about every inch of her, we finally went back inside. Mom had supper ready, hamburgers and fries, and it wasn't even Friday. Afterwards we had chocolate cake and ice cream.

After so much laughing and talking, Walter spoke up,
"I'll be by to pick you and the boat up around 10 0'clock in the morning. You have to have lessons before we turn you loose to terrorize the river and bay."

"I've got to get my driver's license in the morning, but I should be back by then. The motor vehicle office opens at nine, I'll be there 15 minutes early so I'll be first in line." More laughter, the excitement was in the air. Elzie spoke up and said that I now had a way to get to the house boat to work on Saturday morning. Plans made. Tess and I went back outside to look at the boat some more, I was so excited I grabbed her and hugged her so hard until she begged me to stop. She got up in the boat, sat behind the wheel, even asked if she would be allowed to run the boat. I said of course she could as soon as I checked her out. She smiled and asked what I meant by that. I told her she would have to wait and see.

It was the best birthday ever. I explained that I had to help move the house boat on Saturday and wouldn't be going up to Owl Creek. She said she understood and that I shouldn't worry about it. And then she smiled. I took that as an invitation and kissed her. It was past ten o'clock when the party broke up, I told Tess I'd call her tomorrow, and Walter that I would meet him at the house at ten. I was still thanking everyone as they drove away. Once back in the house I asked Dad if he bought me the boat. I didn't know who it was from. He told me it was a joint effort, from all parties, and that I had better take good care of it. Everyone there was expecting a ride. As I lay in bed that night, just before dozing off, I sat up, crossed my legs, arms across my knees, palms facing upward, and I visualized Tess and me running the river in my new boat. And then I gave thanks for family, friends, loved ones, and the promise of being.

Friday morning I was up by seven, had finished a bowl of cereal by seven-thirty, and read over the driving test questions until Mom said she was ready to go. We arrived at the Court House at 8:40. The motor vehicle office is located in the basement of the Court House. Mom said she would be at Austin's Store and for me to pick her up when I was finished. I paced the floor until 8:56 when the director arrived. He smiled and said something along the lines that I must be anxious. Forty questions took me eighteen minutes, then the Director had me drive him around to the Post Office where I had to park between two other cars. From there back behind the Court House where he had cones placed for the parallel parking test. I'd been practicing the parallel parking in our drive way for a few weeks when I had time. No sweat! The Director filled out my license, told me the State would send me a hard copy for my wallet, but my paper copy made me legal.

At Austin's Store I found Mom in the women's department, she was visiting with one of the ladies that worked there, but I interrupted their conversation and told her we had to go. I had another appointment. As we headed out of the store Mom told me I shouldn't be so rude. We drove into our drive way at 9:55, Walter was already there and had the boat hooked to a dark blue ford truck he was driving. Mom invited him in while I ran to change clothes, but he said he'd wait in the truck, which took about two and a half minutes. I was so pumped I'm surprised I didn't run alongside of the truck on the way to the boat basin. At the boat basin Walter got out and told me to back the boat into the water. He disconnected the boat from the winch cable, then instructed me to launch the boat next to the launching pier. I had never launched a boat before, but I had backed up a vehicle with a boat attached. It looked a lot easier than it was. After three or four minor adjustments I got the boat in the water, Walter slid the boat off the trailer and tied it to cleats on the pier. I parked the truck across the street and joined Walter at the boat. "Whose truck?" I asked Walter.

"Elzie and I bought it, but we've turned it over to Mr. Siglio, since he needs it more than we do, but it's there when we need it." That made sense. They aren't there much and anytime they came to town they docked at Mr. Siglio's. Walter gave me some instructions about the boat, how the motor would respond, how I should idle out to the channels, and how to maneuver around other boats and channels. Then he turned directly toward me, gave a sincere look directly into my eyes and said, "If I ever see or hear that you ran this boat without a life preserver, I will make sure it is taken away from you. Do you understand?"

"Yes sir." And I did.

"This life preserver may not save your life, but it will make it a lot easier for us to find you." And that was a lesson I would never forget.

The motor came to life at the touch of the switch. I idled out of the basin, into the mouth of the river, Walter signaled for me to head up the river. As I gave it some gas he motioned for me to move over to the far right hand side of the channel. Under the bridge he had me take it back to idle so he could instruct, "Matt, from outside of the basin to up about where that buoy is," as he pointed to a red buoy about 400 yards up the river on the right hand side, "is considered a no-wake zone. Now you will see lots of guys running pretty fast along here, even the marine patrol, but note that they always run way over on this side of the channel so as to not cause much wake along the docks. You don't ever want to create wakes along the docks."

Got it, and I eased back to plane. Walter would stop me every so often to point out different channel markers, where flats were, and how to look for logs and other debris. He had me speed up, then slow down, then make different turns, and then he directed me into a marsh area. I stopped well before reaching the marsh line, but he told me to ease into the marsh. I again stopped right at the marsh. He turned to me again, "Did you not hear me? Into the marsh." I eased into the marsh as far as we could go, the boat stopped its forward motion. At that point Walter turned to me again, "Good, now back out." I put the motor in reverse and gave it some gas. The foot of the motor reared up and propeller actually came out of the water. I backed down in a hurry. Again Walter, "See what happens when you use too much power in reverse? It will happen every time. Always ease back in reverse."

Following instructions I brought the boat out of the marsh. Got it! And then Walter said, "Ok, now do it again." Back into the marsh, back out again, just like an old pro. From there he guided me through Crooked Channel which opens into East Bay. East Bay is open water, where all of the finger rivers empty into the bay. The right hand side, south side, is the bridge between Apalachicola and Eastpoint, including the fill areas. The north side is the mouth of Little St. Marks, Big St. Marks, East River, and also Sam's Cutoff. Between each river channel there are flats, lots of flats, which I ran up on as soon as we entered East Bay. Next lesson, Walter had me turn off the motor, tilt up the motor and lock it in place, then he handed me an oar and said "Pole us back to deeper water." He continue, "Matt, I can't teach you the bay in a few hours, you've got to come over here on some low tides and run aground a bunch, pole around enough until you learn where the channel are and which flats are the hardest to work around."

After we got back into deeper water Walter said we should make a long run before heading home. We started out again, with Walter sitting beside me showing me where to turn and pointing out the flats and the channel, we ran into the mouth of Big Bay. The channel hugs the left, west bank, and before you enter the actual Big Bay there is a channel which runs northeast, which we took, which empties into Big St. Marks. Once on Big St. Marks we ran north until Big St. Marks joined Little St. Marks. Walter backed me down and cautioned that in the bend where the two rivers meet there is a log jam, always be careful, slower speeds needed and generally hold closer to the east bank. After the rivers joined we ran up to the house boat. Elzie wasn't there so we turned around and headed south.

Walter said he would show me a quicker way to get home instead of running the big river. Headed south we passed under the rail road trestle and continue south until the tree line began turning to marsh. Walter backed me down and started pointing out trees and marsh lines that I should remember. Within a few hundred yards Walter had me make a wide turn from the middle of the river toward the western bank. As we were well into the turn I saw a creek. Walter had me stop for explanation. "Matt, this is Four Tree Cutoff, it connects Little St. Marks to the big river. It's narrow and has some sharp curves, slow down on the curves. If another boat is coming from the opposite direction you can't see it until you are right on each other." And it was, narrow, and hard to see, but it only took a few minutes to reach the big river. Where we entered the big river was almost directly across from the creek that leads to Bay City Lodge. Just a few minutes run and we were back in the boat basin. Walter gave me the truck keys and said to back her in and we'll load her up. Again, it took a couple of tries but I was getting better. Once we got home and unloaded Walter said he would see me Saturday morning at the house boat, and then he drove away.

Mom wasn't home, so I had a light lunch and was getting my practice clothes together when she returned. We talked briefly and then I headed to practice. Friday's practice was a duplicate of Thursday's practice, the same offensive plays, the same defensive plays, but it was Friday and everybody's attitude was great. At the end of practice Coach called us all together for a pep talk, at least that's what he called it. He started, "Guys, you've really been working hard, it will pay off. One more week and we test our mettle. Next week we'll practice under the lights on Wednesday and Thursday nights. Thursday will be without pads. Monday and Tuesday will be totally game related. Now I don't want you going out this weekend and getting into any trouble. We can't afford to lose anyone on this team. Don't go nuts, not drink a bunch of carbonated drinks, you've worked too hard at getting in shape to do stupid stuff. If you happen to run across anyone from St. Joe, don't start any fights. I'll telling you, they'll send guys over here just to get some of you in trouble. We can beat these guys, but you all have to be ready. So think, think, think about winning. We'll see you Monday at 3:30."

As we walked off the field Rob said he was going to think about growing wings so he could fly the hell out of here. Bob and Billy said that we needed to all get together with a couple of pickups and drive over to St. Joe and ride around and paper the St. Joe player's yards with toilet paper. Somebody else said something about getting a judge to stomp on a bag of shit, and then, after a lot of laughter, everybody shut up!

At home Dad and I were talking about me helping move the house boat the next day when I realized that we didn't have any way to put the boat overboard, it startled me so much I almost yell, "Dad, how can we put the boat over board, we don't have a trailer hitch?"

"Well, son, shouldn't you have thought about that?"

"Dad, until seven o'clock last night I didn't know we had a boat. What are we going to do?"

"I had a trailer hitch put on my car this morning. I think it will do for now." It's wonderful to have a great Dad! I told him again, "Thanks!" I went to call Tess.

Tess answered on the second ring, "How was practice?"

"Wonderful, if you like suffering!"

"Yes, I know you're suffering," You could hear the sarcasm. "Like most ball players, you'd pay to suffer like that." Well, I guess she did have a point.

"I think we're shaping up. We'll be ready for St. Joe next week. So, what do you have planned for tomorrow?"

"I don't know. Why don't you get your folks to let you come up here tomorrow after you help with the house boat?"

"I'll ask. Heck, I can even run my boat up there now. I'll call you back in a little while."

"Ok, but I sure miss you. I hope it works. Call soon."

I went to talk to Dad, "Dad, I just talked to Tess and she asked if I could come up there after helping with the house boat. If Elzie is going I could go with him, or I could run my boat up there."

"If it's not too late when y'all finish, it's ok. But if it's late, then either stay with Elzie or come home. Either way, I want you home by early afternoon Monday. It maybe Labor Day but you still have practice at 3:30."

"Thanks Dad, I'll let Tess know."

I called Tess, she said she would see me tomorrow. I told her I hoped so. Dad agreed to put me overboard the next morning. I told him I wanted to be on the water early. He nodded; I don't know if it was a yes nod, or a maybe nod, but the next morning I was already packed to stay a couple of days, had cereal for breakfast, had the boat attached to the trailer and was waiting for Dad to get up at 7:30. I was at the breakfast table when he came to the kitchen for coffee. I told him I was ready to go, all packed, boat attached to car, can we leave now? "My lord, son, can't I at least have some coffee first?"

"Dad, you can drink your coffee in the car. I need to get on up there. You know how Walter and Elzie are, they'll be half way to East River before the sun gets up."

"I doubt that son. Mr. Siglio will be helping and he doesn't get up before the sun." I started to asked how he knew that, but surprisingly, I already knew the answer. But Dad understood, and within a few minutes he got in the car, the passenger's side, and I drove us to the boat basin, backed the boat into the water, got out, disconnected the boat from the trailer winch, and slid the boat off the trailer and tied it to a cleat. I think I even impressed Dad.

He told me to be careful. As I put on my life preserver, I told him I would. As I idled out of the boat basin I was so excited I could hardly keep from yelling at the world, "Look at me!" I ran up to Four Tree Cutoff and cut over to Little St. Marks, I took my time through the cutoff just as Walter had instructed. As I entered Little St. Marks the sun was well up, the sun's reflection on the river looked like a gold mirror. I headed upriver, the sun at my back, running into a glow of inspiration. I slowed through the curve at Big St. Marks, then accelerated toward the house boat. Just as I was approaching the house boat I noticed a small shrimp boat headed down from Mark's Point; it must be Mr. Siglio.

Walter was standing on the back porch as I eased up to the house boat, he reached for the bow line I tossed him, tied me off, and then said come on aboard. I asked where Elzie was and he said they are on the front porch. I climbed aboard and was about to ask who they were, when Tess stuck her head out of the screened front porch and said, "What took you so long?"

"How did you get here? When did you get here? Why didn't you tell me?"

"I wanted to surprise you!"

"Well, you did!" And about that time Walter hollers,

"OK, it's time to get to work. Mr. Siglio doesn't like socializing until the work it done."

Mr. Siglio was idling just off the bow of the house boat. Elzie told me to run my boat around to the front porch and he would tie me off there. Walter went to the back porch and waved Mr. Siglio to him. Mr. Siglio threw a heavy rope to Walter which Walter tied to the middle cleat on the stern. Mr. Siglio had a cross beam installed behind the wheel house used to pull shrimp nets, which he used to tie the rope to the house boat. I ran my boat around to the stern and Elzie tied me off to the middle cleat. Walter and Elzie's boats were on the river side of the houseboat; Walter tied a line from the stern of his boat to a cleat near the stern of the house boat, and Elzie did the same from his boat but tied his line toward the bow of the house boat. I climbed aboard the house boat while Walter got in his boat. Elzie had me help him quickly untie the ropes that ran from the house boat to the pilings along the shore. Then Elzie jumped in his boat, and signaled for the motion to begin.

Walter and Elzie pulled the house boat very slowly out toward the middle of the river, while at even a slower pace, Mr. Siglio pulled the house boat toward East River Cutoff. Once the house boat was well away from the pilings and the shore Elzie had me untie his line to the house boat and he ran around to the other side of the house boat and had me tie his line back to the house boat about center of the boat length. I asked Elzie if we were going to turn the house boat around so the front porch would be leading, but he said that it didn't matter with the barge design and when we got to the pilings on East River, we wanted the front porch to be facing upriver.

I was really impressed, it was obvious they had done this before. Mr. Siglio was towing the house boat from the stern, while Elzie and Walter were on both sides of the house boat. Then both Walter and Elzie eased their boats up against both sides of the house boat and while Mr. Siglio pulled the barge, they push and pulled, which ever was needed to keep the barge in a straight direction. Just as we entered East River Cutoff Mr. Siglio shorten up his tow line to where he was only about 10 to 15 feet from the barge. Walter and Elzie were tight against the sides. Slowly we eased along, making the curves slowly, but steady under power. At one point on a curve the house boat looked as if it would drift onto the bank but Elzie loosened his line and pushed the bow of his boat into the stern area on his side of the house boat and with a little extra power maneuvered the house boat back into the middle of the cutoff. It didn't take much longer than 30 minutes to make it through the cutoff into East River. Once in East River Mr. Siglio lengthen his tow line and Walter and Elzie returned to the sides of the barge and we moved along down the river, under the trestle and on toward Thank You Ma'am Creek. Cloud, Tess, and I moved to the back porch which was facing Mr. Siglio and the direction we were going.

It was impressive, watching these watermen maneuver the barge so smoothly gave me a whole new sense of what I needed to learn, what I wanted to be a part of. At one point Elzie called me over to his side of the house boat and gave me instructions, "Matt, as we approach the pilings we are going to have to stop the barge, and Walter and I are going to push it into the pilings just like we pulled it away from the other pilings. There is a line already attached near the stern, and another near the bow, you will need to tie each of those to a piling and pull it pretty tight. We'll make the adjustments after we are stationary."

And that's exactly how it was done. As we approached the pilings Mr. Siglio slowed to a crawl, taking his boat out of gear to move the house boat so very slowly. I untied Elzie on his side and he ran around to the other side of the barge and then Walter and Elzie both eased their bows up to the barge. They directed me and Cloud to wrap their lines around a cleat but not tie, so they could push slowly. Then, with Cloud and Tess tending the lines on the river side, I ran around to the bank side, and as we slowly eased up against the pilings I wrapped a couple of loops around each piling and tied the lines off. Home at last. Once I signaled we were secured everyone gave a yell and moved all the boats to the river side and tied up against the house boat. Cloud immediately went to the kitchen and put on a pot of coffee; she knew Mr. Siglio would want that as a prize.

Elzie had some unique methods of tying the boat to the pilings where the boat would rise and fall with the tides without disturbing the ropes. It confused me a bit, but he said he would show me later. Once completely secured we all gathered in the living area of the house boat and had a cup of coffee. Even Tess and I had coffee, with tupelo honey in it. Mr. Siglio really acted happy. We listened to the old guys tell stories about other house boats they had owned, how they moved them from site to site depending on the time of year, or when moving from one job site to another. Timbering the swamps always made it into the conversation or story telling, but I had never heard Walter talk much about the old river boats they used when he was young.

He had worked with my grandfather almost three years before Elzie was old enough, or at least big enough to work in the swamps. They mostly worked off barges which had very large winches attached to the barge decks that were powered by steam engines. Having the huge power winches allowed the timber guys to work further back in the swamps; they cut and trimmed the trees, mostly cypress, and then long cables were drawn to the trees and strapped in line so they could winch several logs at a time to the river's edge. Generally the logs were floated down the river. Logs that were too green to float remained on the banks until they dried enough to float. The logs were floated down to mills in Apalachicola, cut into lumber and then shipped all over the world from Apalachicola. Elzie described an old, fairly large barge that was built to house and feed the workers, and he said that he once worked on one of the river boats, called a pusher, I imagined like a tugboat, that pushed the large barge from one site to another. Some of it was hard to imagine, but Walter and Elzie had enough stories to keep anybody's attention, and enough stories that made you laugh so hard it didn't matter how perfect the descriptions were.

For almost two hours we sat there listening to the men's stories, but Mr. Siglio said he had to get back to town, and then Walter said he needed to get back to Little St. George, and before I could even start to ask the thousand questions I had running around inside my brain, they were up and loaded into their boats and headed back toward town. As we settled back in the living area Cloud said, "Well, that was certainly entertaining!"

Elzie replied, "Yes, and some of it was even true." A pause, then, "Well, maybe not a lot of it." Tess giggled and then said it just sounded like hard times to her. Elzie agreed to that. Elzie suggest lunch, but Cloud said there wasn't much to work with. We had Elzie's standby favorite, Sardines and crackers. After lunch Elzie required my help. I hadn't even noticed that he had strapped the walk-way, which connected the house boat to the bank, to the counter on the back porch. We carefully carried it around to the front porch.

The long support timbers were strapped above the front screened wall to the support post attached to the roof trusses. On one end of each support timber Elzie had installed a U-shaped connector which he attached to a welded base on the edge of the barge by running a large bolt through the pre-drilled holes. Once the timbers were attached to stakes driven into the ground on the bank, the timbers and the walkway on top of them would raise and lower as the tides affected the house boat. Of course I had to get into my boat to get to the bank. Elzie stood on the front deck, threw stakes and an axe to me, told me where each stake had to be driven. Once driven he slid the support timber to me, connected them to the boat, and then with Cloud's help, slid the walkway on the support timbers to me. He carefully eased over to the bank, nailed the timbers to the stakes I'd driven, and then attached the walkway to the timbers with screws. Then he suggested Cloud and Tess try it out, just in case he missed something. Cloud had heard that song before, so after Elzie walked back and forth a couple of times, Cloud and Tess joined us on the bank.

Minutes later Elzie had me cutting brush, trimming trees, and clearing the area for the fire pit. He had not brought the stones for the pit. By middle afternoon I thought we should be headed up to Owl Creek, so I asked when we were going. Elzie said he was ready when everyone else was. But Cloud suggested, "Why don't we stay here tonight?" Tess jumped in saying she thought that was a good idea, she had never spent a night on a house boat.

"But we don't have much in the way of supplies." Elzie offered. He was always thinking about eating. Cloud wasn't having it,

"You seem to have plenty of flour and meal. Can't a river rat like you catch us some fish?"

"Sure, but what are we going to eat besides fish?"

"How about cabbage? The swamp is full of it." I could see Cloud's eyes sparkling.

"Yea, we can do that. Matt, we need to make a run back to East River Cutoff." I promise, I could not help myself,

"Are we going to outlaw some catfish?" Even Tess howled at that one.

We were back in less than 30 minutes, six nice fresh water catfish, retrieved from a wire mesh trap. Elzie did have a responsibility to feed us! After cleaning the fish, Elzie grabbed his axe and a machete, told me to bring the five gallon bucket, and as we headed into the swamp Cloud and Tess came out with a basket and a long knife. "Where are y'all going?" I asked.

"To pick some flavors to go with the cabbage." Cloud replied.

"Flavors?" I asked. But Tess told me to tend to our business and they would tend to theirs. Elzie and I walked along looking at cabbage palms, the swamps are full of them, but Elzie couldn't just pick one and start cutting, he had to pursue perfection. He finally found some the right height, the right width, the right smile for all I know, they all look alike! From the ground to the top of their palm fronds was only about six feet. He cut four of them off just at ground level, then took the machete, whacked off the fronds where they grew out of the trunk, then split the trunk opened, peeled away layers of bark, then pulled the tougher inside layers away from the center. At that point he cut everything away from the center until he had a nice, white elongated core. He did the same with the other three, putting all four into the five gallon bucket.

Back at the house boat Elzie washed the palm cores really well, sliced them into bite size pieces, put a little bacon fat into a pot, added salt and pepper, then enough water to cover the cabbage and started cooking. Minutes later Cloud and Tess arrived, their basket full of something. As they took their findings out of the basket to wash Cloud explained what each plant was. First there was purslane, and then bitter cress, both grow best in the swamps along the edges of the ridges. Both will be used in a salad and can be eaten raw. To the salad makings they had picked some small muscadine grapes, the vines which grew draped through the oak trees throughout the swamps. The last item Cloud called betony, which meant nothing to me. They were white grub-like tubers, she then clarified for me as wild radishes. I was really getting into this. Eating off the land! Can't be a true river rat unless you can do that. Cloud suggested that Elzie and me go to the front porch and let the women folk tend to the cooking. Elzie jumped at that and almost knocked me down getting through the front door.

Soon the smell of fried fish drifted out to the screen porch, my mouth started watering, Elzie began pacing the floor. After much torture and fading patience Tess came and asked if we would like to join them for dinner. This time I beat Elzie through the door. A dinner for kings! We had fried catfish, hushpuppies, swamp cabbage, and a salad made from vegetables grown in the river swamps. Cloud had washed the purslane and bitter cress, dried it, then chopped it. To that she added the muscadine grapes, and last she sliced the wild radishes thin and spread over the salad. To that she sprinkled salt, pepper and a dressing she had made. It really was a dinner for kings!

After dinner Tess and I cleaned up the dishes and the kitchen; Cloud and Elzie went to the front porch. We joined them as soon as we finished cleaning up. The last light of the day was fading fast. River sounds began, the occasional strike of a bass, the cicadas continuing buzz, and of course, the owls. There must have been a convention of them. They hollered, hooted, and carried on like they had just eaten some fried catfish, hushpuppies, and magic vegetables from the swamp. The evening sky was a mass of tiny pearls. Darkness settled in like a fog; the filling moon not yet above the horizon. Tess sat next to me on my daybed. Elzie and Cloud were in chairs but pulled close together. No one talked. The silence was peaceful. By 9:30 Elzie and Cloud went to bed. Before 10 Tess went in to the couch in the living room. I made my daybed ready to sleep. I lay there awake, taking in the sounds, feeling the night. About 10:45 Tess came out onto the porch and got in bed with me. She whispered, "They're making love."

"What? How do you know?"

"Because I could hear them."

"Damn!"

"Well if they can, we can too." And we did, but we were much quieter, and we didn't rock the boat. The next morning when Elzie got up to put on coffee, Tess was on the couch in the living room, I was on the porch, on my daybed with a smile on my face.

We all drank a little coffee, some of us had tupelo honey in ours; Cloud made some pancakes. Tess and I cleaned up, packed our clothes, Elzie secured the house boat, and we all headed to Owl Creek, Tess with me in my boat, Cloud with Elzie in his boat. I felt like a big shot. The ride was beautiful. Sunday afternoon and Sunday evening were slow and easy. We were with family. Children were playing in the field in front of the houses, parents visiting with other parents, even Mama Sol came out and sat with us some. Her hair was pulled back like Cloud and Tess wear theirs often, the wrinkles in her face seemed deeper, but there was a glow about her that always seemed to amaze me. She had a peace about her; I felt that she epitomized everything that Cloud was trying to teach us, me and Tess. The evening came on quickly, Tess and her family joined us at Cloud's. We all sat on the back porch, had dinner together, and everyone had left Tess and me on the porch by ten o'clock. We snuggled on the chaise lounge for a while, just listening to the night sounds.

By eleven I had walked her home and gone to bed. I was up by daylight, it was Labor Day, and I had to go home. Football practice starts at three-thirty. Tess came over and had breakfast with me, she knew I had to leave. I called my Dad at nine o'clock and told him to meet me at the boat basin at ten o'clock. Tess walked me to my boat, I kissed her goodbye and headed home. The ride was beautiful, but a bit sad; it always felt a bit sad when I had to leave Tess, Owl Creek.

There were folks on the river, some just riding and sightseeing, others were skiing, some folks fishing. I waved, they waved. People do that when they're on the river. Dad was at the boat basin when I idled in. We loaded the boat and headed home. When Coach blew the whistle to start practice, I had to stop punting and join the others.

Chapter 9: Chapman High

Tuesday September 2nd, first day of school for my Junior year was a lot like the last day of my Sophomore year which ended in May, for me, for the rest of my class, with the exception of Bud Carlson, Bob Riley and Billy Fields, it ended June 4th. We all stood around the school yard of Chapman High School waiting for the bell to ring, telling summer time stories, talking about this year's football team, and wondering who was dating whom. It was small talk and it didn't take long before the bell rang. Our class of 30 had been together for the past four years, with the exception of a couple of people leaving or new people joining us.

Our homeroom teacher was Richard Blaylock who also was our math teacher. He was an old retired military guy who thought numbers were much more important than people, especially if the people were high school students. He often would assign us numbers instead of calling us by our names. For instance, Billy Fields he often called 6, as in deep six, because he thought Billy certainly needed to die by drowning when he went into one of his laughing fits. Bud Carlson was number 7, as in lucky seven, because he should have dropped out of math long ago, but somehow pulled off miracles on the last test of the semester. Of course, he called me one, as in number one on the football team or the baseball team, but mainly because my Dad was principal who was number one. I often thought he didn't think that through because by using reason I'd be number two. I didn't mention that to Mr. Blaylock because I didn't particularly want to be number two.

Mr. Blaylock had short grayish hair, cut in the traditional flat-top style, broad shoulders, but was developing a pot belly which didn't become him. He was military through and through. He gave instructions like he was calling commands, and when he addressed you he expected you to stand and answer him by first saying SIR! I think I could have gotten all A's in math if I had saluted him. After a few minutes of calling roll and quieting us down he brought us to attention, "Ok, class, let's get this year off to a good start. First days of school are for organization. Nothing, nor no one, functions well without organization. Our goal this morning will be to elect class officers, develop a class motto, for every junior year needs a motto. A good motto guides you into your senior year. And, we will need to determine a fund raising project for the first semester. Fund raising will be foremost this year in all that we do, because you have the full responsibility to raise enough money to put on the very best, by anyone's standards, the senior prom next May."

Billy Fields immediately stood up and said, "SIR! I suggest our first project should be a dunking contest where teachers sit up on a platform and students throw baseballs at a target and if they hit the target the teachers get dunked!"

"Sit down six! Let's don't start this year, like last year, with your suggestions."
The first day was much different than most days, we would spend the first three hours completing the items Mr. Blaylock outlined, then we would move to our regular classes except they didn't last an hour, just long enough to pick up our books for the class and the outline of work required broken down by week, or in some cases, by six weeks when report cards came out. It took just over an hour to elect officers, it always took just over an hour to elect officers, because every year we elected the same people, just not for the same position as the year before, with the exception of Bud Carlson who was always elected treasurer for the sole reason his Dad was the local bank president. And I've seen Bud not be able to make change.

After the officers were elected, Cynthia Chriswell, newly president elect, took charge and said the floor was open for suggestions for motto. Six jumped up and suggested, "If you think you can, you might; if you believe you can, you will!"

Actually I thought that was pretty good, but of course all the girls laughed at Billy, and Mr. Blaylock told Billy to see him after class, I assume he wanted to sign Billy up for the Army. We hemmed and hawed for more than half an hour, but finally one of the girls got up, went to the blackboard and wrote, "From a single seed, the mighty oak!" I really don't know what that had to do with our Junior Class but it passed the vote. After class Billy asked if we were the seed or the oak? Money earning projects were the same as every other class that has ever passed through the halls of Chapman High, car washes, cake bakes, hot dog sales at the Seafood Festival, raffles, and of course, more car washes.

I was ready to get on with it long before the bell rang for our next class, History. History I liked, especially since I had met Cloud. Our history teacher was an institution in her own right at Chapman High. She had taught my Dad, and everyone else's parents in our class. She didn't just teach history, she was history. Emily MacFadden, everyone called her Miss Mac! She had a birth defect which prevented normal growth, she was only 4 feet 8 inches tall, but she commanded her class and her teachings in such fashion that even Mr. Blaylock was jealous. When she began classes and told us to turn to a certain page, then proceeded to march around the room quoting history from memory, it would be word for word by the book. She must have written the book, especially on the Civil War.

After we settled in she handed out books and a course outline broken down in six week sections, but she then told us that 50 per cent of our grade would be determined from an essay we would be required to write. She said it was strictly up to us as to what the subject would be, as in a person, a battle, a political position, an event, as long as it had to do with the Civil War. And, if it included Apalachicola we could get extra credit. It had to be typed, double spaced, and be at least five pages long. It would be due at the end of the semester before Christmas. It sounded pretty easy. After Miss Mac's class we headed to Government. Edward Lawson was the teacher. I didn't know much about Mr. Lawson, but in his introductions he said we would learn about City governments, County governments, State government and the U.S. government. He handed out our books, our work outline, and said he's see us tomorrow. And we were excused for lunch.

The lunch room at Chapman High sounded much like a machine shop, there was a constant buzz of talk, laughter, and the occasional plate dropped to the floor like a hammer landing in a bucket. The food wasn't much, but the yeast rolls were outstanding, and if you smiled just right, and your Dad was the principal, many times you could get extras. After lunch, and before the bell rang again for classes, we all gathered again out in front of the school to visit. It was the first day when Jill walked up to me and said, "Where have you been all summer? I thought I'd at least see you at the canteen." She was looking really good, but that flame was out. I asked if she heard about the fire stomping incident, and when she laughed and said that she did, I told her that Dad had put me on restrictions for the summer, and put me to work. Before the conversation went any further the bell rang. I was actually glad it did.

After lunch we had English and Chemistry. English was taught by Barbara Morningstar. She stood close to six feet tall, slender, dark, dark red hair, always in a bun, and burning green eyes. I didn't know if I should think that she could be beautiful or if I should fear her for my life. When she stared at you those eyes would pierce the toughest armor. She graded like it was a death sentence. You could have the best story, the best characters, the best scene, but miss a few commas, quotation marks, and god forbid a period or a capital, and you had a C at best. She handed out a couple of books, one on basic English, the other, plays by Shakespeare. Oh boy, won't Billy have fun here?

After English, Chemistry. The teacher, right out of college, was Dale Chu. He was American born from Chinese parents. His English was better than anyone in our class. He didn't even have a southern accent. I bet Billy a dollar that Mr. Chu couldn't even say ain't! My chemistry background was fair at best. The book Mr. Chu handed out might as well have been in Chinese, I didn't recognize anything from the pages I flipped through. Junior year was shaping up to be hard, and we hadn't even begun classes. Thank goodness the bell rang about that time and I could go do something that I liked, throw the football.

Tuesday's football practice was solid. We worked on offensive plays, including at least seven different pass plays, punt returns, kick-off returns, and then defense. Coach Blackmon drilled the linemen and the linebackers on what to look for when St. Joe lined up certain ways. I also played some as a defensive back so I took part in the defensive drills. St. Joe was known to throw some too, so I ran their pass plays against our defense. By the end of practice we were feeling pretty good about our play. Of course we then had to run 40 yard wind sprints for at least a thousand hours or until no one was standing. Little pearls of desire were sprinkled all over the field.

Wednesday classes started the regular schedule. Football practice was exactly like the day before. Wednesday night I called Tess. She had been going through the same thing I had, she said her cheerleaders were ready for ball games, and we talked about me going up to see her on Saturday or her coming to see me. I told her that would depend on whether we won on Friday night or not. She asked why, and I told her that if we didn't win I didn't want her to be around me when I cried all day Saturday. She laughed a lot at that one. I didn't tell her I was serious, but I was.

Thursday's classes were uneventful, and Thursday's football practice was without pads. We ran every play we had in the playbook at least twice. I threw at least 50 passes, and we reviewed kickoff returns and punt returns. We finished with wind sprints, but Coach was easy on us, and told us to get to bed early, we would need to be at our best tomorrow night. I really don't remember classes on Friday, my mind was running in overdrive, but I do remember that for the last period of the day we had a pep-rally. The cheerleaders ran up and down the aisles in the auditorium, cheering for the players, often by name, and we all had to sing the school's song. Some of the teachers spoke, promoting us to victory. Finally, Coach got up on the stage and told the whole school that we were the finest team he's ever coached. That sounds like a great compliment until you realize that he's said that about every team he's ever coached. He gave the same speech last year; he'll probably give the same speech next year. Maybe it's the only speech he can remember.

After school I walked home and tried to take a nap, but my mind couldn't slow down. I visualized every play of our play book, I visualized every pass play we had including the ones Bud, Bob, Billy and I dreamed up. We had to be at the gym by six to get ready, I was there at 5:45, and I was one of the last to show up. Everybody was pumped. Both coaches taped ankles like it was the salvation for our team, everyone got their ankles taped. If the cheerleaders had been there they would have taped their ankles as well.

By 6:45 we headed to the field. The field is three blocks north of the gym on 14th street, we walked it just like we do every day. Some of the crowd was already there and they started cheering us as we entered. We took the eastern goal, closest to the street; our team and fans gather on the southern side. We lined up five across, four deep, with me and Rob Gant out front leading exercises. Fifteen minutes of exercises and then we broke up in teams, ran a few plays, I passed some, punted a few times, all while watching the St. Joe school bus enter the football field grounds and unload. They unloaded and took the western end of the field. They had at least 10 to 15 more players than we had. Coach Blackmon kept walking around telling us that they can only play 11 at a time.

At 7:45 we jog to our sidelines and Rob and I walk to the middle of the field for the coin toss. The referees gave us their names, which I've never remembered, showed us the coin and flipped it into the air. St. Joe wins the toss and the refs tell us to shake hands and play a good game. St Joe defers to the second half, so we will get the ball first. As we shake hands it's Joe Shuler standing there smiling at me. "Drugar, it's pay back time." He never stopped smiling. Billy Smith and Bob Riley are back for the return. Billy takes the kick and returns it to the 35 yard line. I jog onto the field and the first play I call is Banana Right, it's a pass play where the right end, Bud Carlson, goes down and angles deep right. The left back, Bob Riley, is in the slot right which is behind the right end, but just outside and in the back field. His job is to take out the defensive end. We roll right and Bull rounds the end and angles to the right flats. The intent is for Bud to draw the defensive back into following him leaving the flats open for Bull. The play works like a charm, I hit Bull and then instead of running for lots of yardage he turns and looks for someone to run over. The safety is the man, so they butt heads and Bull picks up 12 yards instead of maybe 20 or 25.

I was watching Bull ramble downfield when someone hit me from the back, it felt like a truck. I was flat on my face, helmet pushed into the dirt, when I heard someone say, "Pay back, Drugar! Every play, your ass is mine!" Shuler was laughing as he trotted back to his team. I had to take my helmet off to shake the dirt out of it. The next play we ran a cross-buck play where I fake to Bull, then hand off to the running back which runs off tackle. I had just handed the ball to the running back when Shuler hit me from the back again. "I told you Drugar, your ass is mine! See you next play." Again I had to take my helmet off the shake the dirt out of it.

The third play was a rollout left where the left back ran the same banana route that Bull had run to the right. I had stopped after the throw watching Bob dance through the defensive backs for about 10 yards. Bam, I was face down again and Shuler was laughing at me, singing his same old song. Back in the huddle I said someone's got to get to Shuler, he's killing me. "Give me a shot at him," Bull said. His voice wasn't panicked, wasn't loud, just matter of fact. I gave him the nod, then called the play.

"Bud, I want you to make a button hook about 8 or 10 yards downfield directly behind where Shuler lines up. He's middle linebacker and he's coming right up the middle. Bull, I want you to line up directly behind the left end, slightly inside, I'm going to drop straight back to throw to Bud. Rob, slow Shuler up just half a step, we want him to think he's got me dead to rights. Bull, at the snap you break back toward the middle, Shuler should be coming through the line intent on killing me, you take your shot. Lefty, run a deep pattern toward their safety. If Bud gets the ball, then take out the safety. If the safety comes for Bud you should be opened deep. Ready, on two."

We lined up, Shuler was directly over the center, I could almost smell his breath. He had a smile big enough to stuff a watermelon in. Rob snapped the ball on the second count, I dropped straight back, planted my foot, and before I could throw the ball, Shuler was stretched out, full bore, coming at me. He had just cleared our line when Bull hit him, helmet first, right on Shuler's right knee. I heard the knee pop before I heard his scream. I hit Bud over the middle, we picked up 15 yards. I went over to Shuler, the referee wasn't even there yet, and I leaned over and looked him in the eyes, they were mostly closed, pain burning across his face, he could hardly breathe, and I said, "Shuler, I really hope you have a great Senior year!" and then we huddled up for another play. They carried Shuler off the field, two of their linemen holding him up, his leg bent outward, the knee's cartilage definitely torn. Two plays later we were in the end zone. Without Shuler slamming me every play we picked St. Joe apart. We were up two touch downs by half time, and we finished the game 26 to 6. I threw three touch downs, and ran the fourth. By the time I called Tess late that night I was still pumped.

She laughed at my enthusiasm, "So I guess I don't get to see you cry!"

"Not tonight! I hope not all season. I will see you tomorrow."

Dad let me borrow his car so I could go to Owl Creek. I got there around eleven o'clock, Tess had run an errand for her mother. I put my bag in my bedroom, Cloud was not there but her car was so I walked out front; she was in the big screened in room talking with Mama Sol. As I headed over to see them it was obvious that Mama Sol was saying something important, Cloud was sitting there like a student listening to a teacher. Cloud's face was intent, Mama Sol's had the glow I'd become used to seeing. Her right hand was holding Cloud's left hand, their voices were low, neither even acknowledged my presence when I entered the building. I knew not to interrupt so I sat at the first chair I got to, and waited. I could not understand what they were saying, but their expressions were intense, their eyes soft, occasionally Cloud would nod. Fifteen minutes later they both turned to me and smiled and said I should join them. I went over and as I sat down beside them Mama Sol reached over and padded my hand, "You're a fine young man, young Drugar."

"Thank you, Ma'am!" Cloud took over the conversation and asked about the football game, she had already heard, but she wanted me to brag about it. I tried to act nonchalant, but my excitement gave me away. "We got the job done!" They both smiled at that, then Cloud asked about school. Immediately I thought about the history project and began, "Ms. Mac, our history teacher has given us an essay assignment that's going to be 50% of our grade for the semester; it can be about most anything as long as it involves the Civil War, and we can get extra credit if it involves Apalachicola. I wanted to get some ideas from you." Cloud said she appreciated that I would ask her, which surprised me, I thought she would expect me to ask her. But she then asked what interested me the most. "I don't really know, we've read a lot about General Lee, the Confederacy, a few battles, but mostly it's about Abraham Lincoln."

"I don't think you would get much of a grade from Miss Mac if it's about Abraham Lincoln." That made me laugh, Miss Mac certainly didn't want the Northern aggression to override good southern story telling. We discussed several ideas including Fort Gadsden and the role it played during the Civil War, Apalachicola and its role during the war, and even some of the people who lived in Apalachicola during the Civil War period. Nothing really appealed to me. Maybe history wasn't as appealing as Cloud made it sound. I thought we were about finished with the ideas until Cloud said, "Well, you could write about the lost gold that probably cost the South the war."

"What gold? I never heard anything about gold."

"There's a lot about the war, the south, that didn't make it into the history books; and there's a lot of stuff in the history books that isn't accurate. I'll tell you what I'll do for you, I'll get some notes and some references to get you started. The rest will be up to you on how you proceed. Sound fair?"

"You bet it does, I'm like an old hound dog, once I get a scent, I can track'em down!" That made Mama Sol and Cloud smile.

As we were leaving the screened room Mama Sol turned to Cloud and said, "Send him to see Yellow Bird." I had not heard of Yellow Bird, and I felt that I should wait and let Cloud tell me who or what Yellow Bird was. One thing I had learned this summer, Cloud worked on her own time frame. Me pestering her wasn't going to speed up anything. As we were about to go into Cloud's house Tess drove up and parked at her house next door. I went to greet her. She gave me a big hug and said how happy she was that we won. As we went into her house her Mom came out onto the back porch and the two of them made me tell all about the game. I tried not to brag, at least I tried a little not to brag, but I think I told them every play including when Bull took out Joe Shuler. I don't think they were too impressed with our meanness, but I explained it was self-defense! I don't think they bought that either.

Later in the afternoon Tess and I went for another walk along the ridge overlooking the creek, we talked about school, different classes, even the teachers. I told her about Mr. Blaylock and the numbers he assigned students; when I got to Billy Fields she almost cried she laughed so hard. She told me about her classes, a few of the teachers, and she told me about Bristol's game against Carrabelle. Bristol won 32 to 12. She said that Carrabelle didn't have much of a team this year. She wouldn't tell me if Bristol did. I told her I would find out in two weeks, that's when we played Bristol, in Bristol. She immediately said that she wanted me to stay over after the game, I said I'd run it past Dad. The afternoon passed so quickly, it seemed my whole life was passing by so quickly, I wish I could figure out how to press on the breaks when we were together.

After supper we sat on the back porch at Cloud's until late in the evening. Elzie wasn't there that day or evening, I asked Cloud where he was, she said he was doing something with Walter. Cloud turned in by ten o'clock, we held each other until a little past eleven, not wanting the time to run out on us. It always does. Sunday morning the mothers and the kids showed up again at the screened room. Tess and I went to Cloud's back porch. We had just settled in when I thought of Yellow Bird, "Tess, who or what is Yellow Bird?"

"She is a who! She's an old friend of Mama Sol's, they were raised together in or around Columbus, Georgia. She serves her tribe in a similar way that Cloud serves ours. Why do you ask?" I told her about my conversation with Cloud yesterday, about the history assignment I had, and the recommendation Cloud had given me. She said she had never heard of the lost gold either. Then she offered to help with the research. I told her I'd pay in kisses. And then I gave her a down payment. She said that if we found the gold it would take more than kisses for her share! One of the things I like most about Tess is how much we laugh together. I can start a conversation or a funny story and she picks up on it, adds to it, embellishes it, and we both laugh at the outcome.

The morning flew by, we had lunch, and by two o'clock I was headed home, it takes just over half an hour for the trip. As I came across the Apalachicola Bridge and the fill ways I thought about the Indian artifacts, all of the pottery, arrow heads, and history buried there. And I thought about how the white man, my ancestors, desecrated Tess's family's burial grounds, their artifacts, their history. I found that I could not come to terms with that knowledge, there was no explanation that made sense, no excuse good enough to excuse the sacrilege. I felt shame, and it wasn't from anything that I had done. That night as I lay in bed I prayed to be made stronger, to make a difference.

The first complete week of school was boring, five classes a day with the sixth class a study hall. The one course that was the exception was Government with Mr. Lawson, we started right off with government operations for cities, specifically Apalachicola. Our real first assignment was to know who the mayor was and each City Commissioner. Our goal, to be discussed in class, was to know who was elected, when and for how long. Were political party affiliations needed to be commissioners? We needed to know who ran City Hall and what departments made up the city operations. And, how did the City make and manage the money needed to run the City. By Wednesday we needed to know those things, to be able to discuss in class, and by Thursday there would be a test.

Monday evening I asked Dad for some assistance. He knew all the politicians and the personnel at City Hall. Tuesday's class was fun. Billy Fields, right out of the blocks, made it be known that he would be Mayor of Apalachicola one day. Someone in the back of the room suggested that it would be when hell froze over. Mr. Lawson agreed. By Wednesday we were discussing City finances, how each property owner was assessed based on property value, and how the Tax Collector collected the taxes at the end of each year and passed those assessments on to the City. Another source of income came from water, sewer, and garbage collections. There was some discussion about those on city sewer and those who had septic tanks. I had never even thought about people within the City not having central sewage collection. Mr. Lawson explained how anyone could go to the County Property Appraiser's office, look up an individual property, and find out what the value was for tax purposes. He also explained that the City and County gave certain exceptions to lower the valuations, such as age and homestead exemptions. He informed us that after we get into County government we would have an assignment to go to the Court House, to the Property Appraiser's Office, to pull a property card which would be submitted to him, and to go to the Tax Collector's office and get a breakdown as to what taxes would be due, or has been paid in the past.

I talked to Dad about that and said that I didn't have afternoons off because of football practice and I needed to know what to do. There were several other players in the same boat. Dad said he would make it possible for us to go during sixth period, study hall. Now that sounded like the kind of educations I was after.

The next week we got into County government, and three afternoon study halls were skipped to go to the Court House. The first day, Monday, none of my teammates went with me to the Court House. I asked Dad if I could borrow his car, he agreed and by 2:15 I arrived at the Property Appraiser's office in the Court House. Entering from the back of the Court House, the Property Appraiser's office was the first room on the right, first floor. The office entrance was a large room, a couple of desk, but lots of filing cabinets covered two walls. There was a room to the left, a sign over the door read "Map Room". At one of the desk in the main room a woman sat, talking on the phone, the name tag on the desk read, "Hilda". She appeared to be a fairly large woman, her pale blonde hair was somehow spun to the top of her head like a cone of cotton candy. She wore the brightest red lipstick I had ever seen, and she was loudly talking to someone about something in County politics. She looked at me, but made no effort to address me. I stood there for just a little bit, then took a seat in a chair located just inside the door. She kept talking, but about every minute she would look over at me, not smiling or even appearing to be helpful. I got the feeling that she was sizing me up for something, I hesitated to think for what. After several glances toward me, while still talking on the phone, her face lit up, a big smiled expanded those bright red lips, she told the other person on the phone that she had to go, hung up, then directed her attention to me. "Honey, what's your name?"

"Matthew Drugar."

"I thought I recognized you. Aren't you one of the boys that pulled that shit stomping joke on Stinky? I mean the Judge."

"Yes Ma'am, I'm afraid so."

"Honey, that's the best damn thing that's happened around here in ages. Marsha, Marsh, come in here."

A woman appeared from the adjoining room, she appeared to be in her late 20's or early 30's, she was cute, with dark hair, a big smile, and neatly dressed with skirt and blouse. She came toward me as Hilda rose and came around the desk toward me. When Hilda rose from behind her desk, I thought the sun may be blocked. She must have been at least six feet tall, very large frame, but the hair surely gave her a few extra inches. She had on spiked high heel shoes, a skirt that must have taken help to put on, it was straight and tight, and her blouse looked like shoulder pads had been inserted. Together they stood over me like giants. I didn't know what to do, should I stand, sit, or high tail out of there. As my thoughts were racing for an escape plan, Hilda continued, "Honey, I just want to shake your hand. That judge needed a comeuppance. Why he treats us like hired help, and we don't even work for him. He's always running over here and yelling at us to do something for him. You'd think that being County Judge made him King! Well, from now on he's Stinky! That's all everyone in the Court House calls him anymore."

About that time the thought occurred to me that we might have opened a can of worms that would follow us around for years. The thought was not appealing. But Hilda continued, "Honey, what can we do for you?"

"I have a class assignment to get copies of our family property records. Can you teach me how to look up the information?"

"Hell yes we can! Marsha, show Mr. Drugar our map room and property cards and give him a full explanation. And Honey," directing her attention back to me, "if you need anything from this office you just give me a call." I thanked her, then followed Marsha into the map room. She explained how all the properties in the County could be found on plats, and all properties had file numbers. From there we went to the property card files, and based on the file numbers, we could pull the property cards to find the legal descriptions, the last deeds to the property listed in Official Records Books in the Clerk's Office, the property description, the improvements, the assessed value and the tax value. She explained to me that often the tax value was less than the assessed value because of credits given to property owners, like homestead exemptions. Marsha made me a copy of the property card, I thanked them both, then headed home to get ready for football practice.

We were to play Carrabelle Friday night in Carrabelle. Scouting reports said that Carrabelle was weak this year, so Coach said we wouldn't be running anything but basic plays just in case another team had scouts there. Friday night finally arrived, we beat Carrabelle 36 to nothing; I only threw two passes the entire game, both were for touchdowns. Saturday morning Tess came to see me, and stay the night at our house. Mom and Dad actually acted happy that Tess was coming to Apalachicola instead of me going to Owl Creek. After visiting with Mom and Dad for a little while we walked to town, to Buzzett's Drug Store, for a chocolate shake. Several of the team members were there.

As we entered the building I told Tess that I'd forgotten my pocket knife, she asked why I needed a pocket knife, and then I explained how I needed it to fight off the guys from stealing her away from me. She thought that was funny until Bud, Rob, and Billy Smith surrounded us. They immediately started asking her questions, wanted to know why she was wasting her time with me, and suggested that any of them would be a step up from me. She politely told them that she wasn't interested, that she was planning to become a nun as soon as she graduated from Catholic Bishop High. They left us alone after that. We laughed about it all the way back to my house. Mom and Dad got a laugh over it too, but I think it elevated Tess's status with them after that story.

And then, after supper, we went to the Canteen. The place was packed, from 14 year olds, to 18 year olds, from sophomores to seniors. The music was loud and the buzz of talk and laughter drowned out the music. As we walked into the main room a silence dropped over the crowd like Jesus himself had walked into the room. Everyone turned to look at us. Tess whispered, "Jeez!" I had not been to the canteen all summer. The music "All I Have To Do Is Dream" was playing, so without giving any acknowledgement to anyone, I swung Tess around in front of me, took her right hand, wrapped my right arm around her waist and started dancing.

The noise returned, and while we were dancing Tess asked me why everyone was staring at us. "Because they've never seen anyone as beautiful as you." She told me I was really full of it. After the dance Bud and Rob came over with their dates and introduced them to Tess. Both the girls with Bud and Rob were cheerleaders, and within a few minutes they had connected with Tess, remembered her from Bristol games, and like every other time in mixed company, Bud, Rob, and I went to talking football.

We were all having a good time, dancing some, having a coca cola, and then Jill walked in, with none other than Joe Shuler. I almost broke out laughing. Shuler was on crutches, Jill was holding on to him. I told the others to come on, we have to show our manners, and with Tess holding my hand, the others in tow, we marched right over to Shuler and Jill and I said, "Shuler, it's good to see you. How's the leg?" He was actually nice, and even Jill smiled. I introduced Shuler to everyone, Tess to Shuler and Jill, and then, right on cue, the song "Magic Moments" came on, I took Tess to the dance floor and told her, "This is perfect!"

We stayed at the canteen for a couple of hours and then rode around a little while I pointed out the Judge's house where the shit stomping took place, where the jail was, where I went to school, and our own Dixie Theater. Mom and Dad were still up when we returned home, we told them about the evening and even Mom was smiling at our rehash of the evening. Mom asked us to join them for church the next morning, but Tess said she had to get back home, so I stayed to see her off.

The next week we were to play Bristol, at Bristol, so we made plans for me to stay there after the ball game. She told me she would be cheering for Bristol, but pulling for me. She left about 10 minutes to noon, before Mom and Dad got home. We typically have a nice dinner on Sundays, and we did today. Mom and Dad both kept telling me how much they liked Tess. I told them that I agreed. That night before I went to bed I called Tess just to check on her, she said everything was great, that she and her Mom had been talking about her trip to Apalachicola. I told her about my conversations with my folks. We both agreed we had the best parents ever! Before we hung up I asked her to do something for me, I asked her to talk to Cloud and see if I could visit with her next weekend, maybe even talk about the gold report I had to write. She said she would, we would talk again within the next couple of days.

The week moved along like waiting for water to boil, each day seemed to get longer and longer. Billy Fields reverted to his pre-junior year antics, always doing something in class to get attention, which always got him in trouble, which lead to him being sent to the principal's office, my Dad. Dad had often said that Billy needed structure, that he seemed to be a bright guy, but he just couldn't keep it between the railings. It, I suppose, was acting like he had some sense. He mouthed off in English class about something which triggered Miss Morningstar to remove her glasses, shoot body piercing rays of green molten contempt straight through his heart, then sent him to the principal, who told him he had to keep it between the railings.

Football practice became intense, Bristol always played well against us; they were usually a good team, decent size players, and always tough. We had scouting reports showing their defense to be especially strong with their linebackers, a little weak at defensive backs and safety, but mean through the middle. They had one running back that could scoot. They liked to run sweeps to either side, and usually the fast running back switched sides in the backfield to run the ball for the sweeps. Coach Blackmon drilled the line and linebackers to watch for the sweeps; the fast guy was the key. By Friday we were ready to play. The week had crawled along to the point that everyone was on edge, with pent up excitement, anticipation was boiling over, our focus getting blurred. It was moments like these that I learned to appreciate the jobs coaches do.

Thursday afternoon, after running a thousand plays, being drilled on what we had to expect out of Bristol, focusing on our offensive game plan, and running the mandatory wind sprints, the coaches had us sit down while they gave us advice and inspiration. Coach began, "Guys, we drill you like we do for one reason, to prepare you for what you'll see from the other team. It's always the same process, not the same game plan, but the same process. You know your plays, you know you're in shape, you know we're tough, and you know how to control yourself. Tonight, eat well, and get a good night's rest. You don't have to worry about anything, Coach Blackmon and I will do that for you. Tomorrow we will leave the gym at four o'clock. Get here a little early, bring a bag for your clothes so we can change before coming home. We'll win this one, just like we're going to win all of them. We're a team."

That night before going to sleep I sat up in bed, crossed my legs, arms across the knees, hands up, and visualized every play that we run. I saw the roll out passes, the drop back passes, and especially the pass plays where the receivers run against the grain. Friday night was going to be eventful. Mom and Dad were going to the game so I had them bring my bag of clothes for the weekend. Tess would take me home Sunday afternoon. As we headed to Bristol we were full of all the grit, determination and high spirits of a busload of teenage boys heading into gridiron battle on a southern Friday night.

Bristol is a little over an hour's bus ride, we pass through Sumatra on the way, the turn-off to Owl Creek just before that, nothing but woods to see. We arrived at Bristol's gym between 5 and five-thirty, of course the coaches had to tape ankles for thirty to forty minutes and then we went through warm-ups, passing some, kicking some, and finally gathered on our side of the field. Most all of our fans were there and cheering for us. Bristol's team had the same number of players as us, 22, it's a curse of small schools. Rob and I met the Bristol captains and the referees at mid-field for the coin toss. We won and deferred the ball until the second half.

We were lining up for the kick-off before I saw Tess on the other side of the field. Just seeing her made me feel happy and excited. I was ready to play. Bristol tried to run sweeps the first three plays, one picked up five yards, the other two lost yards, and we received their punt on our 35 yard line. Our first play I had Lefty split wide left, his job was to see what their right defensive back would do if he started across the middle. We ran our Banana Right play, throwing to Bull. Bristol had scouted us and knew the play, but it's not easy to stop Bull. He picked up 12 yards. Back in the huddle Lefty said that the defensive back didn't rush him or even give him much attention, so we sent Billy Smith in motion toward the left side of the field. At the snap I took one step back and fired a shot to Lefty who was angled slightly in toward the middle of the field. Their defensive back was worried about Billy, Lefty took the ball down to Bristol's 20 yard line before the safety ran him down. The next play we put Rob in motion to the right side, I rolled out behind Bull and Billy, Bud ran a down and out deep, Rob cut back across the grain behind Bud, I hit him around the 10 yard line and he took it in for the score.

We had scored in less than one minute since we got the ball. The Apalach fans stood and clapped as we jogged off the field. Bristol was tough and they fought hard, and even scored on us in the second quarter. We scored in every quarter and twice in the third quarter. After the game, as we were all leaving the field, Tess came over and walked off the field with me. I don't think the Bristol players thought much of that, but that's life, to the victor belongs the spoils! Except I couldn't tell that to Tess, if she even thought that I referred to her as spoils, I might not be able to play next week. Mom and Dad, and Alida, with Sage, were waiting for us as we exited the field. I changed in the locker room quickly, left my uniform and pads with Coach, and met the family outside. By then Elzie and Cloud had joined the family. Sage told me again I was the best player ever. I felt like it! It's hard to describe that feeling of winning, of knowing you've done a good job, that all your hard work has paid off. I felt happy and content on the ride to Owl Creek.

It was already late when we got to Owl Creek, I showered quickly and joined Elzie, Cloud, and Tess on the back porch. Everyone seemed happy about our win and my passing. Cloud fixed me a sandwich and some ice tea, and while I ate they talked about the game, some of the plays, and especially about the pass play where I roll out and throw back against the grain. With a mouth full of sandwich I gave all the credit to Walter. At that Elzie said I had to be lying, Walter had never thrown a football in his life, matter of fact the only thing he's ever thrown is a castnet, and only then when he gets hungry. That got everybody laughing, I promised to tell Walter what Elzie had said. It was a great night, the win, the ride back to Owl Creek, and family.

Just before Elzie and Cloud headed off to bed Cloud asked about talking in the morning, I told her I appreciated it, and whenever it was convenient for her. Finally, left alone on the porch, Tess sat next to me, kissed me long and slow, and then told me how proud she was of me and the game I played tonight. She said some of the Bristol cheerleaders were jealous of her because she had the cutest quarterback of all. Boy, that's a name a tough quarterback wants hung around his neck, cutest! We weren't there long before Tess said she was going home, I think I must have dozed off. I walked her home and returned to my bedroom. I think I was asleep before my head hit the pillow.

The next morning Cloud fixed me some breakfast and juice, and I had a cup of coffee with tupelo honey in it. Coffee drinking was becoming a habit, but only when I was here or with Elzie or Walter. By the time I had finished and cleaned up my dishes Cloud asked if I was ready to talk a while. I said I was ready. We took our seats on the porch, a small table and lamp between us. The first thing she did was hand me a sheet of paper with a few notes written on it. The first item was a reference to a newspaper article written several years before out of Columbus, Georgia. It didn't give a name of the article but it did give the name of the newspaper, The Columbus Enquirer.

The next was a book about the Civil War, and the South's relationship with Spain and France. There were some references to the State of Florida Division of Historical Resources, and lastly a name, a family name in Apalachicola, McKenzie. I glanced over the names and references, none of which meant anything to me, and waited on her to begin. "Matthew, to make any story interesting one of the first things you should try to do is bring in characters, people of interest, so your readers can identify with them. It aids the story, and once people are involved, the tactics and turns of the story are easier to follow. I read an article many years ago about the Civil War as it related to Columbus. Columbus became a manufacturing center during the Civil War, it also had a foundry. The foundry melted iron to be cast into weapons. It also melted and cast gold into coins and blocks to exchange for goods, ammunition and all types of things. But before you can get to the gold you have to understand the need for the gold, the despair of the Confederacy, and where they were seeking help. You are going to have to read a lot, research a lot, and if you do those things then the story will develop in your mind, and from there to paper. I have one other name I want you to write down, we are not going to talk about this person until you are well along in your research. The name is Alice Robertson."

I wrote down the name, then sat there waiting for Cloud to continue, she didn't. "Is that it?" I questioned.

"It is for now, until you read enough till you have more questions than answers. Then, and only then, will we talk about the gold." I sat back, trying to get my head around this, trying to decide if this one paper, 50 % of my grade, was worth all this reading, this research. Why wouldn't Cloud just tell me about the gold? Why all this mystery? I'd been around Cloud all summer, talked to her endlessly, asked for her help, her guidance. Why does a stupid story about gold have to be so mysterious? I knew I might as well shut up and do the work. Then she would talk to me. I was about to get up and go find Tess when Cloud said, "I thought there was something else you wanted to talk to me about?" It caught me off guard, I had to think for a minute what I wanted. It finally dawned on me what I was going to ask, but after the mystery of the gold, maybe I'd be better off not jumping in to something else. Cloud, being Cloud, sensed my hesitation. "Maybe you should share your thoughts before making up your mind if you want to drop it or not."

I started to just say, "drop it", but I'd been having these strange feelings, knots in my stomach, about how I was feeling. Those Indian artifacts buried in the bridge fills, those feelings I had about the people, white people, that had destroyed the Indian Mounds. I was feeling guilty about not going to church with my folks. I didn't even know how to get started. I think Cloud felt my discomfort, she said, "How would you feel about Tess joining us when we have this talk?" I didn't have any problem with that, I could talk to Tess about anything.

"Sure!" I replied.

"Then go get her. I'll be here when you're ready." Tess came out as I knocked on her back door, said good morning, then asked if I wanted breakfast; I told her Cloud had already fed me. As we sat down on the porch Tess asked me if I had had my talk with Cloud. I paused, then decided to tell her what had happened.

"Cloud just gave me a list of references, not one thing about the gold. I thought maybe she would share the story and then I could write about it. I don't know what to think."

"Well, you need to know something about Cloud, she believes people should research things, not just take someone else's story. Remember, she's a teacher." That made sense, maybe I was just expecting things to be easier. But there was more,

"Tess, I also want to talk to her about several other things, things that have been bothering me. She asked if I was ready to discuss anything but I just couldn't get started. She asked if I would mind if you joined us. Of course, I told her not at all. So, will you join us?"

Tess sat back, looked at me a little strangely, then asked, "What other things?"

"I'm sorry I haven't talked to you about it, but I'm having a hard time getting my head around this Indian religion. I don't know what to think. And, last weekend when I went home, as I crossed the fill ways of the bridge, thinking about the devastation that white folks did to the Indian mounds, I got sick at my stomach. I felt so ashamed."

"Whoa, you need to slow down a little. First, no one has said anything to you about an Indian Religion. I don't know where that's coming from, and next, what took place more than 20 some odd years ago hasn't got anything to do with you. You sit right here, I've got to finish something for Mama and I'll be right with you. We do need to talk." And she left me on the porch, feeling stupid as usual, me thinking I should just run and hide. Maybe Elzie will come fetch me up. Within a few minutes we were on Cloud's back porch, waiting for her to finish something, me thinking that I was stirring up discomfort. I probably was, but the discomfort was mine.

"OK, I'm back!" Cloud entered the room and took a seat directly in front of us. "So, what's on your mind?" Before I could say anything Tess spoke up,

"Matt seems to think that our discussions are about an Indian religion, and what white men did when they built the bridge to Apalachicola was wrong and it was his fault." Well, that made me feel even more stupid. Where is Elzie when you need him? Cloud turned to me, a strange look on her face, and said,

"Matthew?"

"Where's Elzie?" I blabbered.

"He can't help you here." Cloud replied. We sat there in silence for a couple of minutes, me trying to figure out how to start the conversation without sounding like a complete idiot. Cloud sat there quietly, waiting on me to process whatever nuts were running around in my head, but luckily she spoke first, "Matthew, I may have an idea as to what's gnawing on you. Let's start by me asking you some questions." I nodded approval. "Matthew, do you believe in God?" I said I certainly did. "And what do you believe God's plan is for you?"

"I have no idea."

"Do you think of God as a person? As in a physical being?"

"I guess so. Jesus was a physical being, and the bible says that we are made in God's own image."

"Do you know of any other time God has revealed himself/herself to humans?"

"I guess Mosses on the mountain, the ten commandments."

"I don't think a burning bush qualifies as a revealed human. But, let's talk about Jesus for a few minutes. Jesus was the son of God, but the Bible says that there is a trilogy, Father, Son, and Holy Ghost. Many scholars believe that Jesus was God's human form. Do you agree with that?"

"I guess so." I was feeling way over my head here.

"In thinking of Jesus, how do you think of him?"

"As the savior of the world."

"Certainly that could be his mission, but what did he do while on earth?"

"Well, he healed the sick, forgave sins, taught his disciples Christian principles."

"Good, so you agree that Jesus was a teacher?"

"Yes."

"Did Jesus teach to be religious? Or did he teach to love one another?"

"To love one another."

"OK, now tell me what religion is."

"I guess it's the belief and worship of God."

"That's very good. But throughout the world people get confused about God. Matter of fact God's known by many names, Yahweh, Allah, Jehovah, Adonai, Brahma, and many more. So when people worship God, by whatever name they have for him, it's called religion, and because there are so many names for God, we end up with many different religions. The problem most people have is they suffer over not having a personal relationship with him. They can't see him or touch him. And when bad things happen, we never understand how God could allow those things to happen. You would think that a loving God would not allow bad things to happen to those who love and worship him. One of the problems we have as humans is it's hard to totally believe, have total faith in something that we can't feel or touch. We have to have faith. Faith is something everyone has to face by themselves, remember happiness is an inside game? Well, faith is too."

I didn't know how to respond, I kept thinking what does this have to do with Indian religion? How is the Indian religion different from Catholics or Protestants? After a couple of minutes of silence, Cloud continued, "Matthew, in your life, what you ultimately end up believing will be totally and directly tied to your faith. No matter what religion you choose or religious beliefs you may have, that journey can only be traveled by you. Our ancestors did not have a name for God, they did not see Jesus, nor any other physical being, known as God. We have always referred to God as the Great Spirit, for spirit is the only thing we could associate with a non-physical being. To this spirit we give thanks for all that is given to us. And that is what I want to educate you to. Before I begin, do you have any questions?"

I was afraid to open my mouth for fear that I'd blabber some foolishness, or beg for Elzie again, so I nodded no. So Cloud continued, "Matthew, what we have been given is the gift of sight and feel, not only the physical sight and feel, but the metaphysical reality as well. It's what visions are, it's that state where you feel the presences of something or someone, but you cannot physically see or feel that someone or something. There will be times that you know something is about to happen, or that something has already happened. It is a knowing. It is not a religion or a religious belief. It's a gift that not all people possess. But I believe that you do possess that gift. I just want to help you discover it. Remember, invisible sand."

I sat there not saying anything, I had no idea what I should say, if anything, but I knew, I felt it, it's part of my journey. Tess reached over and squeezed my hand, Cloud smiled at me. Moments later I said, "I'm ready!" We sat there for several minutes not saying anything, just me holding Tess's hand, Cloud smiling that smile that says everything is right. She broke the silence first.

"We can't do everything at once, and where we're going is a long journey, so why don't the two of you go out and have some fun. Elzie is supposed to be here for supper, what would you like?"

I started to say "humble sandwich" but decided I'd made a big enough idiot of myself already. Tess said she would love some smoked ribs. I agreed with that. Cloud said she would work on it, and shoved us out the back door.

Tess asked her Mom to borrow the car, that we wanted to ride around to Wright Lake, and off we went to the lake. Wright Lake is less than a mile away, all on dirt roads, and we didn't even have to go back to the paved road. Leaving the Owl Creek road we turned left instead of right to go back to the pave road, Highway 65, and within a couple of hundred yards we took a right that leads to the lake. It's not a big lake, but it's popular in the summer time. Today no one was there. "We use to come up here and camp when I was in the Boy Scouts," I began as we parked by the lake. "We, scouts, use to swim across the lake when we camped here. There used to be a big rope swing off that cypress tree," I pointed. "I once tried a back flip off the swing, landed directly on my back, had the breath knocked out of me, and one of my buddies had to retrieve me."

Tess was patient with my stories, she's grown up around here, swam there hundreds of times, but today, we had it to ourselves. We walked around some of the trails, even waded in the shallow areas, but ended up back in the car. It was like pent up hunger for each other, never having enough time together, just getting glimpses of what could be, and today we had each other.

The sun was still up, but not for long, by the time we returned home. Elzie was there and had a fire going in the fire pit, putting seasonings on racks of ribs, sipping a beer, and waving for me to come help. Before I could even get over to him some of the women were bringing plates and silverware to the screened room. By the time the ribs were ready platters of vegetables, jars of sauces, pitchers of ice tea, and lots of laughter was waiting on us. It seemed that almost every meal eaten in this community was like a party; I sure liked being a part of it.

Sunday morning was quiet, the women and children were not meeting in the screened room, Elzie had gotten up very early to go somewhere to meet somebody about some timber, so by the time I walked to the back porch, Cloud was sitting there having coffee. She offered breakfast, but I told her I'd rather have some coffee first. She nodded and I went to get some with tupelo honey in it. We sat there not saying anything, just sipping our coffee, listening to the birds, my mind completely focused on Tess and our afternoon together yesterday. After a little while Cloud said she would fix me some breakfast, and disappeared into the kitchen. I kept thinking that I should go see Tess, but it was still early, and I figured I should at least act like I wasn't impatient. As I finished breakfast Tess walked in, hair pulled back to a pony tail, wearing shorts, a light green blouse, and barefooted. Just seeing her got my pulse up, she smiled, and then poured herself a cup of coffee, with honey.

We sat on the porch for a while, not saying much, until Cloud addressed me, "Matthew, I don't want to get into a lot of discussion this morning, but I want to get you to start doing something. It's not a chore, it's not a test, and it's not me teaching you, it's something you can do to help yourself, to center your thoughts, help to make things clearer with your thinking. There's always confusion, with everyone, at all levels, but when you have those moments, times, I want you to feel that you can always come a talk to me. I may not have the answers you're seeking, but I can probably offer suggestions that might help you balance the scale. I want you to start finding 20 to 30 minutes a day, or at night, to be completely alone, in your room, outside, it doesn't matter, but you need to be somewhere that you will not be disturbed. You don't have to cross your legs, go into some yoga position, or anything like that, but I want you to be in a place where you can be completely silent and still. Then I want you to relax and visualize a peaceful place. Try not to think, don't try controlling your thoughts, or solving anything. Just be quiet, visualize that peaceful place, and listen. Usually when we listen it's for outside things, by that I mean outside of our bodies, but I want you to listen for inside things. Just listen, nothing else. Don't expect to hear a lot, but listen. We'll talk more about this over the next few weeks." I sat there thinking I was in the land of cuckoo! Tess saw the look on my face and came and rescued me.

"Come on, let's go for a walk." It wasn't a question, not even a command, it was what we were going to do together. We started toward the river, the high ridge, and the big oak trees, she held my hand. I was ok as long as she was holding my hand, that was one thing I was sure of. At the bench between the two big oak trees we sat down. We had not said a single word to each other since we left the house. At the bench I asked her what was Cloud even talking about. She just kept smiling at me, like an adult might look at a kid.

Finally she said, "After Dad died Cloud spent a lot of time with me, I was really having a hard time dealing with his death, him being gone forever. Mom cried a lot, I cried a lot. One day Cloud sat me and my Mom down together, gave us the talks she has given you, talked to us about the happiness, the knowing, the being, and then she told us to do the same things she just asked you to do. I'll admit, about the only thing I heard was me crying for the first week or so, but after a while, when I felt I couldn't cry any longer I started to hear things. Not really 'hear things' like sounds, but knowing things in my mind, like I knew I heard something, but really just knew it instead. I know that doesn't make any sense, but try it, at least for a while. If it doesn't work, you haven't lost anything. If it makes you think clearer, then it will certainly be worth it. And you can tell me about it."

"Tess, I don't know what I would do without you. You make things that don't make sense, make sense. It's a good thing they threw me in jail!" At that she laughed so hard that I couldn't help but laugh too. The walk back to the house was much louder than the walk away from the house. After lunch Tess took me home. She stayed for a while and visited with my folks, but by 4:30 she was gone. I went to my room, pulled out the notes Cloud had given me to start my research which is supposed to lead to the gold. Gold in them there swamps!

Monday, it was already the fourth week of September, cool weather would be here soon. For the sixth period study hall I asked to go to the library to do some research, I was given permission to go there each study hall for the week. At the library I found several books about the Civil War, but none addressed the relationship the confederacy had with Spain or France or any other foreign country. I would have to keep looking, but I did look up the family named McKenzie. There was only one listing in the phone directory, Patricia McKenzie, who lived in Apalachicola, on Ave E, just past 16th street. I needed to talk to Dad about her.

Football practice was getting more and more focused, we had to exercise, run a lot, but a couple of the guys had some injuries, not real serious, but it was enough for us to stop scrimmaging. We couldn't afford to lose anyone, but we ran our plays, I passed a lot, and Coach Blackmon worked the defense really hard. We were to play Crawfordville at home this coming Friday night. We got a good scouting report on them, they were strong, fast, and had a couple of running backs that were a threat. Each practice we would be looking at the formations Crawfordville ran, how they lined up, what their strong plays were, and how we thought they would respond based on our defense. We would need to show them something they had not seen before based on the scouting they had. It would be a good game.

At supper that night I asked Dad about Patricia McKenzie. First thing Dad said was she's very old, from a very old family, been around Apalachicola for at least four generations. He wanted to know why I was asking, when I told him it was for a history paper I had to write, he just said, "Well, talk to Miss Mac, she's knows more history about this area and the people than anyone alive." I guess when the time came I'd have to ask Miss Mac about her. But, I'd better have some idea what I was asking for or about. I called Tess around 9:30, told her about my day, told her I loved her, and then told her I'd gotten started on my research for "that gold in them there swamps!" She got a kick out of that. We didn't talk long, but it felt good. I went to bed a little early with the intent that I would clear my mind and listen. As I lay back on my bed I tried to clear my mind, tried not to think even of Tess. I was immediately aware that I sure move a lot when going to bed, my foot would itch, my neck would hurt, my nose needed blowing, there was everything wrong with me that stopped me from relaxing. What seemed like hours lasted maybe 10 minutes, but finally I got relaxed, cleared my mind, and woke up the next morning not having any idea what, if anything, I might have heard. Well, at least I'd gotten relaxed. I'll try it again tonight.

For the rest of the week, except Friday, I went to the library for sixth period, I needed to research, but not sure where to even look. We had a new librarian, right out of college. She was from Tallahassee and had graduated from FSU. She was also really pretty and helpful. Her name was Joyce Whithers. I explained to her that I had to write a paper about a Civil War person or event, and if it included Apalachicola I could earn extra credit. I gave her an overview of what I was thinking about:
1. I wanted to include some Indian history as it related to the Apalachicola Indians.

2. I wanted some information about the South's relationships with foreign nations who might have helped the South in the Civil War.
3. I wanted information about some battles that affected our area, and I expanded our area to include the river system of the Apalachicola, Chattahoochee, and Flint Rivers.
4. And I wanted to know about gold and other currencies that the South used in the Civil War.

Miss Whithers acted like she was impressed with my thought processes, but she quickly said that I wasn't going to find that information in our Library. She suggested we contact the State Division of Historical Resources. She told me to write out my search requirements and she would send the request for me. She also said that one of her relatives could pick it up for us when it was ready. That night I made an outline of information I was seeking; Miss Whithers send out the request the next day. I still went to the library each day for the rest of the week except Friday. Football practice continued to be intense, Thursday's practice, as always, was without pads. Coach added an extra running play to our play list, it was an unbalanced line, either right or left, and Bull would run the ball off tackle. I was feeling good about our prospects. Friday, the last class of the day was another pep-rally. The only thing I remember about the pep-rally is that Jill would not even look at me. It surprised me, but it didn't matter.

The work up to the ballgame, the increasing tensions, excitement, bragging, and of course, praying for help, continued to heighten. The evening was cool, the fans arrived early, and at the gym Coach actually taped Bull's ankles twice. As we entered the gates onto the football field area our band was in mid-field playing the school song. We went through our normal warm-ups, then gathered on our side of the field. Crawfordville had 26 players, and their fans were there in numbers. Rob and I went to the middle of the field for the coin toss, we won and deferred the ball until the second half. On the kick-off one of their scat-backs took the ball to our 45 yard line. Six plays later they scored. It was a bit of a shock to not only our team but to our fans as well. The intensity of the fan's cheering increased, both coaches looked panicked.

Billy took the kick off back to mid-field. Our first play from scrimmage I rolled left, then threw back to Bud who was cutting across the middle. Bud took it down to Crawfordville's 25 yard line. The second play we ran our banana right pass play, Crawfordville had scouted us well and every receiver was covered leaving me room to run. I took it in from the 25 yard line. The clock showed it took us 45 seconds to score. That got everyone's nerves settled and our defense picked up the pace. We held them to less than 6 yards and they had to punt. Coach called for a return left, which means our blockers set up an alley on the left hand side of the field. Billy received the punt and took it to the end zone. At half we were up 20 to 7. The second half was a head knocker, both teams rushed up and down the field, but no score in the third quarter.

By the fourth quarter little pearls of desire were scattered all over the field. There wasn't a dry jersey on either team. We had the ball on our own 40 yard line when I called an unbalanced line left, Bull picked up 15 yard, so I called for an unbalanced line right. Crawfordville adjusted to the unbalanced line, but instead of giving Bull the ball, I told Bull I would belly the ball to him but pull it out as he hit the line and I would follow him through. Crawfordville doubled up on their linebackers to the unbalanced side and jammed the hole Bull tried to get through, leaving me room to run. I took it to the end zone. We walked away from that game 27-7. After the ball game Coach asked where I got that play. Of course I told him from him. Mom and Dad took me home from the game, Mom fixed our favorite meal, Hamburgers and fries. September was coming to a close. The next morning Dad let me take his car to Owl Creek.

On the way to Owl Creek I got to thinking about all that had happened to me over the last four months, it seemed like a life time. Last May all I could think about was that by the time school started I'd be able to drive and maybe start dating. Now four months later I had a whole other family, a beautiful girl friend, adult friends that treated me like family, and a focus I'd never even considered. Who was I, what was I, where am I going, were thoughts I'd never gotten friendly with, now they were everyday challenges, everyday insights. And in front of me, opportunities I'd never heard of or considered.

Tess was on her back porch when I drove into their yard. Her mother and Sage came out to visit with us for a while, we talked about the ball game, how Bristol played, and what plans we had for the weekend. I told Alida my plan was to be right here! She loved that. Tess walked with me to Cloud's to say hello, and for me to drop off my clothes bag. Home again, Home again! Elzie was on the back porch, reading about our ball game, drinking coffee. "Come on in here, Champ! I see that you had another good night?"

"Yes sir, we all did."

"Well, I think play like that deserves a reward! Why don't you take me fly fishing in the morning?"

"That's a deal." And about that time Cloud appeared, all smiles, and told me she was proud of my victory. I responded that it wasn't just my victory. She said that when I was here, it was. Okay, I can live with that. As we settled in I told Cloud about my research and the request we had made to the Division of Historical Resources, she was pleased and said she looked forward to reading my report. I did not tell her about falling asleep during my listening session. I would imagine she already knew.

Elzie reminded me that Dove season was to start next Saturday, October 4th, but unless a good cold front came through we would wait until it cooled off. He said he would keep me posted and for me to tell my Dad what we had planned. Also, he said I should discuss with my Dad about bringing another father-son team. Wow, the millet should be up by now, hopefully with seeds. Tess said that she thought she and Cloud should be allowed to go, and she said she wanted to learn how to shoot a shotgun. Elzie smiled at her, that smile that looks like he's about to laugh, though I knew that he knew better. Cloud did not respond. I felt that she and Elzie had had that discussion before. I told Tess that I could teach her to shoot a shotgun, that I have a single shot 20 gage. "That sounds like a big gun, a 20 gauge?" I explained that it wasn't a big gun, that the larger the number usually meant the smaller the gun.

Elzie broke in, "A single shot 20 gauge? Is that what you use to shoot doves?"

"Yes sir, that's what my Dad bought me a few years back when he started taking me squirrel and dove hunting."

"Well, we'll have to see what we can do about that." About that time I think Tess had enough of hunting, guns, and whatever men talk about, and said she was going home, that her Mom was going to town and she had to take care of Sage. I took the hint and said I should help. Cloud smiled and went back into the main part of the house, Elzie gave me another one of his smiles, but didn't say anything.

Alida did have to go to town to do some shopping leaving Sage with Tess and me. Tess fixed us some lunch, Sage told me about school, and I relaxed on her back porch until Tess woke me to eat lunch. I must be a ball of fun, or much more tired than I thought I was. After lunch Tess suggested we take Sage for a canoe ride, which Sage got really excited about, and shortly we were paddling up Owl Creek. Tess turned our outing into class, pointing out and naming flowers, different plants, and showing Sage the tupelo trees where the bees get the nectar for their honey. I pointed out small bream, places where they hang out to ambush bugs, and the different trees and which ones make the best lumber for different things. All in all, it was a perfect grown up afternoon. As we returned to the landing, I kept asking myself, what is happening to me? Later in the day I told Tess about my thoughts, she really laughed at me and said that maybe, just maybe, I might be salvageable.

The next morning Elzie and I left women folk behind and returned to the emancipated state of male freedom, we went fly fishing. We didn't talk much, just enjoyed the coolness of the morning, the glass like conditions of the creek, the changing colors of the leaves, and the intensity of the strikes from such small fish, the bream. We kept 18 nice large ones, I took five home with me when I left. I stayed until after lunch, Tess was a bit out of sorts, and when I asked her if something was wrong, she explained that it was just the time of month. I understood, but I could not comprehend. Mom and Dad acted really pleased when I brought in the bream, Mom fried them for supper, and Dad and I talked about the dove hunt coming up. Fall and the first cool snap would soon be here. I could hardly wait.

Wednesday was the first of October, it was hot and wet. It rained all day, football practice was held in the gym. Mostly it was strength training, some warm ups, and then walking through plays, different blocking arrangements for some of the same plays, and of course, offensive plays that Sopchoppy ran. We were to play them Friday night in Sopchoppy. Scouting reports said they were weak this year, but they had one running back that if he breaks free he would be hard to catch. Thursday's practice was normal, no pads, but we were able to get back on the field. Again we went through Sopchoppy's plays, their defense, and what we should look for, then our plays, and I threw quite a bit.

Friday's classes were entertaining, Billy Fields got sent to the principal's office three different times, one from history class, the second from English class, and the last one from chemistry. The one from English class wasn't even his fault. Wayne Barker, our left tackle, and Billy are pretty good friends, though Wayne hardly ever gets caught doing things that require a trip to the principal's office, but today Wayne was in rare form. He sits behind Billy in English class, and he and Billy usually have something going most every day. They thump spit balls at each other, they pass notes about everything, they make fun of everybody, but today Wayne decided to pull a good one on Billy, well, sort of.

Our school is old, no air conditioning, but the two story building has very large windows that slide up and down to help with a breeze. So, Wayne, being bored, makes an airplane out of a sheet of paper, and, while Miss Morningstar had her back to the class, writing something on the black board, Wayne shoots the airplane out the second story window. A few of the class saw it and giggled a little, but it was not big deal, until Miss Hicks, the Home-Ec teacher, storms into our English class and tells Billy to come on, he's going to the principal's office. We found out a little later that the paper plane that Wayne threw out the window, made a U-turn on it's descent, and flew into Miss Hicks' class directly below ours, and flew all the way to where she was standing at a black board and flew into her. Her class broke out laughing and they told her the plane came from upstairs. Of course, she knew who it had to be to be disrupting her class like that. Billy took the blame like a trooper, never ratted out Wayne, and became a legend for class pranks, even those he didn't commit. Wayne had to tell the story to the entire football team at least four times on the bus while traveling to Sopchoppy for the game. When a football team gets off a bus laughing and carrying on, it's a sure sign they're relaxed and ready to play. We won that one 28 to nothing. The fast back Sopchoppy had almost broke free three times, almost!

Saturday morning Dad let me use his car again to go to Owl Creek, this time I took my 20 gauge single shot and a box of number eights bird shot. Hopefully I could give Tess a lesson on shooting a shot gun. Tess was waiting on me when I drove into her yard, she came out smiling and gave me a hug as soon as I got out of the car. "That's for my bad attitude from last week."

"I didn't know you had bad attitudes?" I offered, smiling of course.

"Well, you keep on believing that," she replied. I thought that I surely must be learning something here, it just escaped me as to what it was. I told her about the 20 gauge, she acted happy, but said we'd see what we could do after lunch. Alida was home, Sage was playing in the big field with some of the other kids, but I didn't see any activity over at Cloud's. Tess went with me to drop off my clothes bag.

Cloud, according to Tess, had gone to Bristol for something. Elzie was not there. When we got to the bedroom Tess said she wished we could stay there for a while, but I said I didn't want her mother to use my 20 gauge on me. We laughed about it headed back to her house, but she did say her Mom knew how to shoot a shotgun. I kept telling myself, calmer heads prevail. We joined her mother on the back porch, we talked about the football games, who we played next, and even about the Seafood Festival. The festival is always the first Saturday of November, and this year Alida wanted to get a few of the family together and be a part of the activities. Tess told her Mom that she would be staying at my house. I'd forgotten about how we discussed it with my folks when she was there before, but the idea of her and family members there got me excited. I'd got so use to being a part of everything that took place at Owl Creek, its party atmosphere, so right then I decided that my folks and I needed to do something special for them. I'd talk about it with Dad and Mom when I got home.

After lunch Tess and I drove over to an open area close to the road that leads to Wright Lake. I got the shot gun out, showed her how to hold it, where the safety was and how to aim to shoot. I loaded the gun, told her to watch how it kicks, and how to hold it tight to prevent it from kicking too hard. I took off the safety, aimed at a pine cone in a tree and fired. I then showed her that the first thing you do is put the safety back on. I handed her the gun and a shell, she loaded it, raised the butt to her shoulder, pushed the safety off and fired at another pine cone. Her pine cone exploded, mine just hung there shot up a little. "That's perfect. You sure you haven't fired a shot gun before?"

"I'm sure, but I have a good teacher. Let me shoot again." And for the next half hour we shot pine cones, plus I threw some where she had to shoot them on the fly. I was impressed, she hit more than half of the ones I threw. She then said that one day she wanted to go dove hunting with me. I said it was a deal. I knew then I needed to talk with Elzie about getting us a place to dove hunt up here. That would be worth borrowing someone's tractor who wasn't using it on a particular day. After shooting we drove down to Wright Lake, but someone was camping there. I think I heard Tess say, damn!

The evening was delightful, Cloud came home with a box of peaches and ice cream makings. Someone brought out an old ice cream churn, and Tess and I started peeling peaches. Just at dark Elzie arrived. He had four or five real nice fillets of grouper, so Cloud mixed up a marinade, let the fillets rest in it while in the refrigerator. Alida brought over a Greek salad and a loaf of homemade bread. The fillets were broiled in the oven, Cloud made a dipping sauce for the bread, and after the wonderful meal Tess dished up homemade peach ice cream for dessert. I kept thinking that I should be putting on weight, but those little pearls of desire must be keeping it off. Sage said that Tess made the best ice cream ever! Tess and I cleaned up the dishes while the others stayed on the porch.

By ten o'clock Tess and I had the porch to ourselves. We snuggled on one of the chaise lounges, trying not to make too much noise, but that started becoming a problem, so we decided to slow things down. I whispered in her ear, "I told you I don't ever want to grow up, but damn, I think everyone is forcing us in that direction!" She giggled at that, then said that maybe growing up was going to give us more freedom. "Freedom! How will we ever have that if we have to be responsible too?" She really laughed at that. I walked her home a little after eleven. As I lay in bed that evening I tried to picture us as grownups, with our own home, but try as I might, I couldn't see that far into the future, nor picture us as adults. Being non-adults was much more fun, that made me smile as I dropped off to sleep.

I had coffee with Elzie the next morning. He said that he had not heard of anyone seeing any doves so far. I told him about Tess shooting my twenty gauge, and that we wanted to go hunting together one day, and asked if he knew anyone around Bristol area that might have a dove field. He said he knew a couple of farmers and would check with them to see if anyone had planted peanuts, he said if they had then we might get in a shoot the second half of the season. We talked some about the upcoming hunt on Little St. George, he said it would all depend on a cold front, and that as soon as he knew he'd call dad and me. I asked if he was coming to next week's game, we're playing Blountstown in Apalachicola, he said he was planning on it. Cloud joined us and said she wanted to see the game. I took that to mean that if she wanted to see the game, then Elzie was planning on it. Tess joined us shortly and after hearing us discussing the game said that Bristol had an off week and she wanted to go as well. I'd better let my folks know that Tess would be staying with us. Just having that conversation picked my spirits up, having more family at the game would be great. And then Tess suggested peach ice cream for breakfast. Could it get any better?

The morning flew by, and by two o'clock I was headed home. I told myself as I got closer to the bay that I was not going to think about the Indian mounds and the bridge fill. There were more things to get excited about. At home I told Mom and Dad about Tess shooting my twenty gauge, and I told them that Cloud, Elzie, and Tess would be at the game, and that I wanted Tess to stay over at our house. They were in agreement with that.

I was about to head to my room to put my clothes away when I thought of the Seafood Festival. "Mom and Dad, we were talking about the Seafood Festival on Saturday morning and Alida said she wanted to get some of the family members and come for the Festival. Dad, you know how they all gather for just about anything, they eat together, play together, it's almost like a party all the time. And, I've gotten to enjoy so much of it. I was thinking, could we do something special for them when they come to the festival?"

Dad looked at Mom, Mom gave a nod, and Dad asked what I had in mind. I told him I didn't know but just a fun gathering would be great. He said he and Mom would work on it, but to plan that it's on. I called Tess before dark and told her the plan, and that I was excited that she would be staying at our house the next weekend. Before hanging up I told her that I was committed, for the time being, to enjoying non-adult status for as long as we could. She laughed, told me she loved me, and hung up. My next big challenge lay ahead, beating Blountstown.

Monday morning home room, Mr. Blaylock handed me a note from Miss Whithers, it read, Matt: your information from State of Florida Historical Resources will be at the library for your sixth period. As I tucked the note into my shirt Billy Fields asked what's up. I explained that I had ordered, or at least Miss Whithers had ordered for me, information from the State of Florida Division of Historical Resources which I hoped would help with my history report. Billy wasn't the least bit interested in that but just hearing Miss Whithers name got his mouth to running. "Miss Whithers? Wow, she is beautiful. You know she graduated from FSU? I need to spend more time in the library. You know she even has a degree in encyclopedia?"

"What? Encyclopedia? Do you mean Library Science?"

"Yea, that's what I meant!" And another day at good ole Chapman High! It would be so boring without Billy.

Sixth period finally arrived, I met Miss Whithers in the library, and unloaded the box of information the State had sent me. She explained that most of it was books and documents that needed to be returned to the State and that it would have to remain in the library, but I could come over every day, sixth period, to review. She offered to help me. I told her that would be great, and then I got to work. My plan was to read everything I could, within a reasonable time period, and then make an outline of what I wanted to write about. I still didn't have a plan but I decided to make notes as I read, then come up with an outline, then put the specifics together in an interesting report. My goal was to get people's attention, and be entertaining. I had reviewed my notes from talking with Cloud, she had not mentioned Indians in relationship to the Civil War, but I felt that I should research Indian history at least to see if they were involved in the Civil War. That's where I started first, then I would get to the war itself, look at battles, find out which foreign countries were friendly with the South, and why gold was a key item, according to Cloud's taunting challenge.

Today's sixth period was the fastest of all. I had barely gotten started when the bell rang. Miss Whithers worked from behind a tall desk, where she checked books in and out for students, and she designated a shelf for me and my materials. She promised not to let anyone else bother the materials. At the bell I headed to the gym.

Blountstown was bigger than Apalachicola, had more students, more players, and they always seemed to be tough. Scouting reports said they were balanced, big and fast. They had a quarterback that was a good runner, and could also pass well. Practice was focused. It was obvious the coaches were worried about Blountstown. Coach Blackmon separated the defense from the start of practice, they moved to one end of the field, and he had them line up in game positions and started walking through plays that Blountstown would run. From our end of the field, the offense, you could see Coach Blackmon, pointing, shoving the linemen into blocking positions, directing the linebackers on where and when to rush or drop back for pass plays. On our end of the field Coach started describing Blountstown defense and where their weaknesses were, which running plays would work, and which pass plays we could use in certain circumstances. He told us to look at what their linebackers would do when running certain plays, and if we could pick up a pattern he thought that our cross-buck play would be a key play for the game. He gave my receivers and me full authority to mix it up as weaknesses showed on Blountstown's defense.

From Monday's practice until the game, there was no joking, laughing, or horse play, this was serious, and we had our work cut out for us. When the team rejoined, Coach Blackmon told us all about a play that Blountstown ran for extra points. He had our defensive line and line backers line up in playing position, he had our offense line up in Blountstown's offensive positions and then he walked us through their big play. Blountstown's quarterback was a good athlete, and the play called for them to unbalance a line to one side or the other, and then the quarterback would take a running leap over the line into the end zone. We practiced defense for that play every day until the game. Each day was more intense than the day before. I kept my appointment in the library every day, including Friday, which was the time scheduled for a pep-rally.

I was at the gym by six o'clock. Most of the team was already there. Ankles were taped, our all blue uniforms were ready, there was no laughing and horse play. A sense of determination filled the gym. This would be our biggest challenge so far. At the field the stands were packed on both sides, Blountstown dressed out twenty-eight players. Both teams had their bands there, Blountstown's sounded much better and louder than ours. Blountstown won the toss, deferred to the second half, and then the head knocking began.

Both teams moved the ball up and down the field, I made some good passes, but at the end of the first half, neither team had scored. At the half-time break Coach gathered us past our end zone and away from the crowd. Coach Blackmon circled up the defense, Coach circled up the offense. We went over plays, talked about different formations, and ideas for different pass plays. When it was time we return to our sideline there was no hooting and hollering like in some games, no pumping of fist, no waving at family or friends, we just walked in single file back to our benches and sat down until the referees signaled it was time to play ball.

We kicked off to them, they returned it to their thirty-five yard line, and the head knocking resumed. After the game my Dad said you could hear the pads slapping during the blocks and tackles. No score in the third quarter. They punted to us to begin the fourth quarter, Billy took it to our forty-five yard line. We ran an unbalanced line left, and I bellied the ball to Bull, then took it out when he hit the line and took it to Blountstown's thirty-five. We had run Bull often during the first half, either off guard, or off tackle. Their linebackers were keying off Bull. From the 35 we ran two plays, a cross-buck where I fake to Bull then hand off to the half backs cutting behind Bull and to the other side of the line. Blountstown had not seen these plays, and they worked like a charm. We scored, and then Bob Riley kicked the extra point. The stands came alive, the band struck up a fight song, and the attitudes returned to the players.

    We kicked off to them, and seven plays later they took it to the end zone. Damn! They lined up, unbalanced line to the left, their quarterback back in a shotgun position, our line and linebackers adjusted to the play. At the snap every player on our defense dived into the unbalanced pile, a wall of pads and helmets, met their quarterback. He literally could have walked around the other side of the formation for the extra point, but he ran their play, and it failed. I was standing on the sidelines next to Coach Blackmon for the play, when Blountstown failed at the extra point, Coach Blackmon grabbed me by my arm, got his face right in front of mine and said, "Drugar, we've got them. All we have to do is make first downs. Keep running that cross-buck, keep making yards. We've got them!"

    They kicked off to us, Billy ran it out to our 30 yard line, and then we began pounding out yardage, three and four yards at a time. We ran Bull left, then cross-buck right, Bull right, cross-buck left. We slowed our pace, using every second we could between plays, got up slow after the play, and when time ran out we were on Blountstown's 20 yard line. I was so thankful that game was over. None of us on our team were celebrating like after other games, we knew we were well matched. I walked over and shook the quarterback's hand from Blountstown. I didn't know it then but later in life he would become one of my best friends.

    Tess met me on the field and walked off the field holding my hand. My parents, Elzie and Cloud, and Alida and Sage met us off the field. Tess and I rode with Mom and Dad to the gym, I changed quickly, gave my uniform to Coach, and then we met the rest of the family at our house. Mom even cooked late night hamburgers and fries.

    After everyone had gone I had Tess rub some BENGAY on my right shoulder and back before I went to bed. I knew it was going to take a few days to get over that game. When I woke Saturday morning I was as stiff as a board, my back hurt, my shoulder hurt, even my right hand hurt. I struggled out of bed, went to the bathroom and stood under a very hot shower until we ran out of hot water. Boy this football sure is fun!

    After breakfast Tess and I walked down town to Buzzett's drug store, I knew many of the players would be there. As we approached the building several players were standing outside including Coach Blackmon, when he saw me he said there he is, and all the players turned to say hello. The attitudes were back. I introduced Tess to everyone, and soon the conversation was all about football. Everyone agreed we were lucky to beat Blountstown. Tess and I went to get a shake and to our surprise Mr. Buzzett said they were on the house because of our good play. I love small towns! We stayed downtown for a while then walked back home.

    Mom and Dad were relaxing in the living room, we sat around visiting with them most of the day, but Saturday evening we went to the Canteen again, this time no one stopped talking to look at us as we entered the room. Rob, Billy and Bud were there and as we entered the room it began, "Droo! Gar! Droo! Gar!". Then all laughter. Tess laughed too. About 9:30 Tess and I left, we drove across the bridge to Eastpoint, turned on South Bayshore and drove to the ferry landing. No one was there. We stayed there, looking out over the bay, holding each other, until almost eleven when we went back home. I kissed her good night before we went inside, Mom and Dad were already in bed. Tess went to her room, I sat in the living room for a little while just appreciating where we were, not just at home, but where we were in our lives. The football, the cheerleading, the weekends together with family, for the first time in my life I think I finally realized how good we had it. And as Tess always said, it's just beginning. The next morning I needed BENGAY again.

We had a late breakfast and right after Mom and Dad headed to church I drove Tess home. We went directly to Wright Lake, no one was there, so we stayed for a little while. As we were getting ready to head to her house she leaned over to me and said, "Thank goodness we had this time. I might not get to see you next week, and that's hard to handle."

"Why won't you see me next weekend?"

"Because you are going dove hunting."

"How do you know that?"

"Because I heard Elzie talking about in Friday on the way to Apalachicola."

"I sure hope a cold front comes through."

"Boys!"

Chapter 10: Harvest Time

Time was flying by; we had already won six ball games, only four more and the season would be over. Dove season was opened, only five more weeks and hunting season would be opened. I looked over at Tess and said, "We need to slow this train down! It's happening too fast." She agreed.

Back at Owl Creek I told Cloud about my bounty from the State, and that the only problem I had was that the report was due in two months and I didn't think I could read all that info in two months. She looked at Tess, and together they said, "Boys!"

I went to talk with Elzie. He said he thought the game was one of the best he'd ever seen. I switched the conversation to dove hunting, but all he would say was it depends on a cold front. Not long after lunch I headed home. At home Dad reminded me that our six weeks report cards should be out by Friday. All I could think of was I hope we don't lose any players because of grades. Classes had been going well, I was really enjoying Government, suffering with Chemistry, but maintaining decent grades. I had been thinking of asking Miss Morningstar if she would review my history report when I finished it, but decided I'd better wait until I was close to finishing it first. I didn't want her hounding me for the report along with Miss Mac reminding us every day. How does anyone get behind when the teachers hound you daily? And on top of it, Mom and Dad were both teachers.

By sixth period the next day I was running to the library; I was ready to start my outline for the Indian part of my report, but I just couldn't get my mind around how to handle it. The more I read about the Indians on the Apalachicola River, the more confused I became. They were part of the Creek Indian Nation, but along the Apalachicola, Chattahoochee, and Flint Rivers there were more Indians from other nations. Through the 1700s they all traded, fought, and even married explorers from Spain, France, and England. As the country moved into the 1800s the Indians continued to trade, and often fight with the Spanish, French, and English. They also were run out of their homeland by the new settlers moving in to the south. By 1830 reports said that they had been completely run out of the south, moved to the western side of the Mississippi River, but some had their own reservation in middle Alabama. I hadn't gotten to the Civil War yet, but at the way the reports were reading I was beginning to think the Indians were right in the middle of the war. I wondered which side they would have taken. I sure hope it starts making sense.

Football practice had a feeling of relief, we were all pleased we beat Blountstown, but none of us wanted to play them twice a year like we do Port St. Joe. Friday's game would be against Greenville, at home. Scouting reports were not kind to Greenville, maybe it would be a fun game; it's always fun when you score touchdowns. Coaches put us through the routines, Greenville's defensives, their offensive plays, and what threats they might have. A few of our boys were beat up pretty good, but all should be ready by Friday night. Also, homecoming was Friday night. Jill was selected as the senior home coming queen, right tackle George Walker, a senior, was the home coming king. I wondered if Joe Shuler would be there?

Each day was a repeat of the last, but late Wednesday afternoon a nor'wester blew through, we had a little rain, but lots of wind. The temperature Thursday morning was 56 degrees. Thursday's afternoon practice was without pads, but we needed long sleeve jerseys. When I got home that afternoon late there was a 12 gauge Browning automatic laying across my bed. I asked "Dad, whose is this?"

"Yours!"

"Mine? Really? Where did it come from?"

"From Browning Arms I would guess."

"No, really Dad?"

"I'm not sure, but I think it's a gift from Walter and Elzie."

"Wow! I wish we had a short wave radio. But I can call Elzie and thank him." And I did, he was at Cloud's, and he said I'd better take care of it. And he would pick me up Saturday morning at Mr. Siglio's. At supper Dad and I talked about the hunt for Saturday, he said that Bud and his Dad would be joining us, we would be leaving the docks around ten o'clock. He also said that he bought us a case of number eight bird shot. It's great to have a good Dad. And good friends.

After supper I called Tess, she already knew. Those women know everything. But she felt my excitement, and that made her excited. She said that we had better win the game Friday night or the dove hunt might not be so much fun. I told her no sweat!

After last week's game, none of us were particularly boasting about how great we were, but there was an air of excitement and relief at the gym. We certainly weren't taking Greenville for granted, but we figured we could run a more open game, more passes, maybe a trick play or two. A few of the guys were joking around, teasing Walker about being the king, some getting some grief over their grades, we didn't lose anyone but a couple had some problems. The tape brigade taped everyone's ankles, and the walk to the field was cool, really cool, and it felt great. Our band was playing in the middle of the field when we got there, the stands were happy, the girls in the home coming parade were all decked out, just another big time event in small town America.

We lost the coin toss, Greenville deferred, and after Billy took the kick-off to our forty-five yard line, I started with roll out pass to the right; Bud was down and angled deep, Billy was out of the backfield and sharp right, Lefty was angled deep over center. Greenville's safety followed Bud leaving Lefty open and I hit him on a dead run. Their safety wasn't any faster than Lefty, so it was a race of the turtles down to their twenty-five yard line.

The next play we ran a cross-buck with Rob getting the ball over right center, that picked up another eight yards, and we followed that with Billy in motion left, Lefty breaking deep over the center, with Billy breaking back toward center shallow. I hit Billy just inside the ten yard line and he scored. The extra point was good, and the team strutted off the field with the swank of an NFL franchise. At half time we were up twenty-one to nothing.

Big George Walker sashayed to the middle of the field to crown Jill Miss Homecoming Queen, we all cheered from our designated retreat behind the end zone, and in unison chanted hoot, hoot, hoot, hoot, as George made his way back to us when the crowning was complete.

The second half we worked on our button hook passes some, we ran our banana patterns a few times, and Billy and Bob showed their stuff on some sweep plays. We finished homecoming thirty-nine to nothing. I figured it was time to go hunting.

The next morning Dad had me up by seven-thirty, I ate a bowl of cereal, put on my hunting clothes and boots, cased up my new twelve gauge Browning automatic, and Dad and I met Bud and his Dad at Mr. Siglio's at quarter to ten. Of course Elzie was already there, drinking coffee with Mr. Siglio, "Paisan!" was the first words we heard as we entered the fish house. Mr. Siglio started bragging on me as soon as we walked in, he had gone to the game the night before, and his happiness showed. "Hey, you shoot doves like you throw those passes you do pretty good today! Eh?

"Yes sir, I will. Do you want me to bring you some doves?"

"Yes, you bring me four." And he held up four fingers just so I'd know.

"I'll do it." I turned toward Elzie, he was all smiles. I figured he'd slipped back into Mr. Siglio's cold storage room for some shrimp, but he gave me a slap on the back and said he read all about it.

Minutes later we were in Elzie's boat headed to Little St. George Island. It was a little choppy, but not bad. There were still some clouds left from the front, but the wind was directly out of the northwest, nice and cool, my excitement was rising. Returning to Little St. George Island was like another homecoming, I felt welcomed and a part of it. I was proud of the work I had done for Walter, and now Walter treated me like family. We unloaded under the boat house, then I helped Elzie with the anchoring. Walter came out to meet us, and shortly we were on his porch making plans for the afternoon shoot.

Walter began, "I drove to the field yesterday, plenty of doves. As long as this wind doesn't pick up too much you should have a good day. Even saw a couple dozen teal pitch into Sand Island pond."

"Is it alright if we jump shoot those?" I asked.

"I doubt your Dad would want you going to jail again!" And that got the day started. After a little socializing Walter said for us to come out back. He had a fire going, the oyster rack already set up. He had a table set up close to the fire, napkins, paper plates, forks and spoons, all lined up, two boxes of saltine crackers, and in three bowls he had sauces for the oysters. On one end of the table he had smoked mullet laid out on trays, and on the ground next to the table he had a large ice chest full of beer and cokes. Off to the side he had an ice chest full of beautiful oysters, extra oyster knives, and gloves. He and Elzie jumped in and within a few minutes they had two trays covered with oysters on the half shell. I asked to eat a few raw so Elzie shucked me several, I ate them straight from the shell, just added a little hot sauce and lemon, they were great.

On the fourth oyster I ate, at least tried to eat, I bit into something hard. I spit it into my hand and there was an off-white large oyster pearl. I'd seen lots of small pearls in oysters before, but they were always brittle, this one was large and hard. I put it in my shirt pocket.

Walter put the two trays of oysters on the fire, gave them a minute or two to warm, then started basting them with the sauce, and as they began to curl, he sprinkled parmesan cheese over them. A minute later they were ready. Bud asked his Dad if he could have a beer, his Dad said yes if he was going to swim home. We ate like it was our last meal. The salty brine taste of the oysters went perfectly with the hint of horse radish and hot sauce. After the first couple, my Dad told me to wipe the drool from the corners of my mouth. Bud and I jumped in to help with the clean-up. When we finished, the big guys were on the porch so Bud and I walked around a bit. I showed him the swinging tire target, and I also showed him my rock pile and explained what I did at each. "You mean that coach that helped you last summer was Walter?" I admitted that it was, but I made Bud promise he wouldn't tell anyone. I explained how we poured the concrete floor, how Walter taught me to throw a castnet, and how I ran the turtle patrol every morning.

We were about ready to pull out the fungo bat when Walter said that he needed to take the first of us to the field, we all couldn't fit in the jeep. Bud and I got our guns and shells, piled into the jeep and Walter hauled us to the field. When we got there Walter said it was about shooting time, but the birds might not fly for a while. He suggested we walk through the field and jump shoot some. He told us to be careful, reminded us that those guns have safeties, and we had better use them. When I pulled my new 12 gage Browning from the case Bud whistled, "When did you get that?"

"Yesterday," I replied.

"Did your Dad buy it for you?"

"No, actually Walter and Elzie did."

"Why?"

"I don't know. I told them I had a single shot 20 gage, but they said I probably could do better."

"Tell them I want to do better too."

As Walter drove away Bud and I loaded our guns, spread out across the field and started walking toward the Sand Island trees at West Pass. We had gone a little more than a hundred yards when seven doves flushed. I killed one on the right side of the bunch, Bud killed one on the left side of the bunch. We were off to a good start. We went to the end of the field but jumped no more birds, so we returned to where Walter dropped us off and waited until the rest joined us. We talked about football mostly, but also things that had happened in school. I told him about Billy Fields thinking that Miss Whithers had a degree from FSU in encyclopedia. At that Bud howled, he couldn't stop laughing. He was still laughing when our dads arrived.

We gathered at the jeep, Walter had brought the ice chest with the drinks, and there was plenty of water. Walter explained that there was a flight on and that more doves should be showing up this afternoon. He said to look for bunches flying fairly low and often they would be flying along the dune line. They're traveling South, the cold front is pushing them. He directed his attention to Bud and me. "If you start seeing bunches flying over those dunes," and he pointed to the low dune line just past the edge of the field, "run over there and squat down behind the dune, get where you can just see over it and where you can see the bunches flying. As they get in range one of you take one side of the bunch, the other take the other side and start pounding away. There are doves here that have already found the feed, they'll start feeding around three to four this afternoon. He turned his attention to me and Bud, "Boys, Elzie and I are going to move the jeep back over next to the timber, I'm going to try to catch some mullet, Elzie will be at the jeep if you need him. Since we aren't going shoot, why don't the two of you shoot our limits for us?" Of course that sounded just great for Bud and me.

Elzie cut in, "After you get several birds give me a wave and I'll run over here with the jeep and pick up the birds. I doubt we'll see any game wardens, but let's not take any chances." We all agreed that was just what we wanted to do, so Elzie and Walter drove off, My Dad and Bud's Dad walked down the field and spread out. Bud and I dropped down next to the ice chest and had a coke. Just before three o'clock the doves started to move. Bud and I spread out and started taking any shot we could. Our Dads started shooting as well.

We'd been at it for 45 minutes or so when Bud hollered at me, "Look, bunches along the dune line." So I ran over to him and we jumped behind one of the dunes and squatted down. Within minutes the first flight came toward us. We raised up and both of us dropped a couple. We picked them up quickly and got back in position. It wasn't long between flights for the first hour, but after that it slowed down. While waiting Bud asked me,

"How do Walter and Elzie have so much?"

"What do you mean?

"Well, they have really nice boats, new motors, good guns, how do they make their money?"

"I don't know. I think Walter gets paid for being the light house keeper, he owns the cabin he lives in, and he told me that he bought that when they sold a house my grandfather use to have, and it was extra money left over after they paid for my Dad's schooling. And Elzie lives on a house boat, and he sells catfish to the fish camps."

"You still have to buy fuel, groceries, and they have a lot of equipment."

"Yea, but that equipment is older than you and me. It's all government surplus, World War 2 stuff. I guess if you aren't buying an expensive house, and you don't have a family to raise, then it doesn't take much to live. I lived with them most of the summer and I'll promise you, we lived off the land a bunch."

Another flight came by, we downed a few more and when we returned behind the sand dune Bud said we should count our birds. He had 14 and I had 13. We walked back to the field and gave a wave to Elzie and he came and picked them up and said for us to keep it up, there's hungry people out there. The birds worked all afternoon, and they were still flying when we limited out and had to call it a day. We had six limits, 72 birds. It was a beautiful day and the best dove hunt I'd ever had, and my new 12 gauge Browning was the ticket. Elzie ran Bud and me back to the cabin first and then went to pick up our dads and Walter.

When they returned, Walter unloaded a sack full of mullet, I think we counted 38, but it seemed like more. While Walter and Elzie cleaned the mullet, we cleaned all the birds, Walter making us put all the feathers, guts, and bird parts not kept in a cardboard box. As we washed up the birds and divided them into batches Walter burned the box of bird remains, saying that burning would keep the coons and maybe even a boar hog away. The dads and Walter had a beer, Elzie had a coke with Bud and me. Everyone agreed it was a perfect afternoon and hunt.

Walter kept a dozen birds, and told us to come back soon for another hunt. The sun had just begun to set when we headed back home. Mr. Siglio was still at the fish house when we got to his dock, we unloaded, then Elzie took a dozen birds and headed up the river. He told me he was headed to Owl Creek, I made him promise to share the birds with Tess and her family. I gave my dozen birds to Mr. Siglio who seemed mighty proud to have them, Dad's dozen we took home. Bud and his Dad said it was a great afternoon and took off. Dad and I stayed with Mr. Siglio for a bit before heading home, Mr. Siglio was in good humor, and he and Dad talked about football, how well I was doing, and some about the shrimp season. I remember Mr. Siglio saying there was so many shrimp in the bay this fall that the price of shrimp was down to 12 cents a pound. Years later I told that to folks but they wouldn't believe me, shrimp were $2.50 a pound then. When Dad and I got home I offered to clean Dad's gun as well as mine. I think he really appreciated it.

After supper Dad and I were sitting in the living room and I asked him how Walter and Elzie made their money. "Well, son, Walter gets paid something for tending to the Light House, it's a government job so I guess he gets paid fairly and probably has some retirement benefits. Elzie runs catfish traps, and I think he still works some timber leases occasionally. Why do you ask?"

"Bud had asked me that today and I told him about the same thing except about the timber, but Bud didn't know how they could afford good boats, new motors, and whatever else they may want. I just didn't know what to say."

"I guess if you don't have a normal house, or raising a family, it shouldn't take much to live." That's what I figured, but it bothered me that Bud would think they had a lot, but mainly why he would care. I guess being a son of a bank president makes you wonder about that kind of stuff. I called Tess a little later to tell her about the shoot, but Elzie was already there and had told them about it. She seemed happy for us, but said next weekend I needed to be with her. I agreed! When I got undressed for bed I remembered the oyster pearl, retrieved it from my shirt pocket and placed it in box where I kept cuff links and stuff, it sure seemed out of place.

As I lay in bed that night I kept thinking about Bud's questions, how do Walter and Elzie afford such nice boats, motors, guns, and what about the things they helped supply me with? They chipped in for the boat I was given, I don't know how much it cost, but it wasn't cheap, and Dad wouldn't say how much he put in, and the shot gun was not a cheap model, and every time Elzie showed up at Cloud's he always brought something. It was something I wanted to find out, maybe Tess can help. Hopefully next week we could talk about it.

Sunday was one of the slowest days ever, I wanted to get back to my research paper, but all of the study materials were locked up in the library. I thought about going to the city library but it was closed on Sundays as well. Mom insisted on me going to church with them, which I did, but half way through the preacher's sermon he lost my attention, so I decided to focus on pleasant things in hopes of not going home depressed. I just couldn't go home, like I had so many other times before, thinking that I was a sinner and going to hell. I'd much rather be up the river, meditating on a beautiful girl in a canoe paddling toward me.

After lunch Bud called and said someone had seen a bunch of doves out at the airport, so we took his truck and our guns out there to check in out. We saw way more hunters than we saw birds.

A few of the other players were out there so we ended up over on one of the runways throwing bottles , cans and whatever we could find to shoot at. We ran out of shells after a little bit and headed home. After I cleaned my gun again I called Tess just to complain about Sunday afternoons. She said she felt the same way but at least we could be miserable together. I did have my English book at home so, out of boredom, I began reading A Midsummer Night's Dream. Within fifteen or twenty minutes of reading I realized that the setting was a woodland and in the realm of Fairyland, under the light of the moon. Well, that didn't take me long to compare it to Owl Creek, and once I started thinking about Owl Creek, Shakespeare wasn't very important. I put the book down and went to watch TV.

I was actually glad to get back to school the next day, classes were uneventful, but by sixth period I ran to the library. I realized I was confused about the Indians and if or when they actually participated in the Civil War, but there was lots of ground to cover, so I started reading about the battles, the timing of the war, which conflicts helped the South, which ones hurt the South, and since I needed Apalachicola to be in the middle of it, I started researching cotton being shipped out of Apalachicola before, during, and after the war. I found cotton shipping receipts from 1840 to 1860, nothing during the Civil War. Looking back at war encounters, military strategy, I found that the Union army tried to blockade the passes between the Gulf and Apalachicola Bay. I say tried because I also found information leading to the assumption that the South ran the blockades often using lighter, faster, schooners. Of course no one was documenting helping the Confederacy by sneaking cotton past the Union soldiers. Now I had to find out who the Confederacy was shipping cotton to, and if they were supporting the war. That would have to wait because the bell rang.

Football practice was more routine than focused, we reviewed the scouting reports on Wewahitchka, they were not strong, but we still needed to know what to look for. Coach Blackmon took us through the defensive positions they would run, and Coach took us through the offensive plays we would see. We went through our defensive strategy, then our offensive plays, we ran some, we passed some, ran some sprints, then called it a day. Some of the guys were still beat up a bit so we didn't scrimmage at all. Sprits were high, attitudes good, all we had to do was not get hurt, run our plays, and win. But, we had to play in Wewa, and sometimes that wasn't good for morale. I think I heard one of our players say that they cheat, at least the referees do. But we couldn't control that, we could only control our play.
For the rest of the week I spent more time researching Civil War stuff than anything else.

We gathered at the gym at five o'clock, ankles taped, lots of laughing and teasing and team spirit. The bus trip took almost an hour, we took the field to warm up at 6:15. There weren't many fans there, theirs or ours, and our band had stayed home. We warmed up, ran some plays, I passed a bunch, and kicked a bunch, and by 7:15 we were ready. It was a very cool evening, and as we sat and waited, we all got cold. By 7:45 Coach had us warm up again. I was beginning to think no one was going to show, but by 7:45 folks started flooding the field and stands. Their band came marching onto the field as they entered the park, playing, I guess, their school song. Both teams were ready for the coin toss but the referees hadn't shown up yet, so we waited on the sidelines. And waited. And waited. Finally at 8:15 our time the referees made their appearance. Rob and I went out for the coin toss, the referees informed us that Wewa was an hour behind us, I knew that, but the game was scheduled for 7:30 Wewa time. OK, maybe our Coaches didn't bother to check. We won the toss and deferred to the second half.

We kicked off and one of their backs darn near broke it all the way, I say darn near because Bud Carlson barely got a hand on him and it was the face mask he got, so Wewa, after the penalty, started on our 40 yard line. Six plays later they were in the end zone. They ran for the extra point but our line shut them down. Coach called us together on the side line and told us to settle down, don't start thinking, just play ball.

Billy took the kickoff back to mid-field, three plays later I hit Lefty in the end zone, Bob kicked the extra point, and we got our spunk back. We were up 21 to 6 at the half, and we finished that one 41 to 6. The ride back home was cold, the bus had no heat and being all sweaty, it had gotten really cold. We didn't get to change after the game, just a cold ride home. It was almost midnight when I got home. Dad had stayed up waiting on me just to make sure everything was okay, I said I was fine but I needed a hot shower. Dad went on to bed, I finished my shower and went to the kitchen looking for something to eat. Cold roast beef was perfect; I ate a sandwich and some chips, drank lots of water and was sound asleep by the time my head hit the pillow.

Mom and Dad let me sleep the next morning, it was almost ten o'clock when I got up. I had promised Tess I'd call her when I got home from the game, so I called her even before eating breakfast, she understood but wanted to know if I was still coming up to see her. I told her to hold on and I'd find out, I checked with Dad, he said I could, so back on the phone with Tess she sounded happy. I told her I would see her after lunch and hung up.

Mom and Dad joined me at the breakfast room table, we talked about the game, the cold ride home, but soon they changed the subject to the next weekend. Seafood festival time! We would be playing Chattahoochee next Friday in Apalachicola, Seafood Festival was the next day, Mom and Dad had a plan and wanted to go over the details with me. They started with a list of who would be there, together we started naming our guests: of course Tess, her Mom and sister, Elzie and Cloud, Mama Sol, and Dad suggested we invite Walter to join us. I thought that sounded just fine, but I also suggested we invite Mr. Siglio. Dad liked that idea as well. "What are we going to do for entertainment?" I asked. Dad took over,

"Well, most of the outings at Owl Creek revolved around food, so we were thinking of putting on a seafood feed. We can set up tables outside in the back yard, have oysters on the half shell, as well as grill some too; your Mom wants to make a seafood gumbo, and I was in hopes of getting Walter to smoke some mullet for us. We can eat on the back porch, and in the house if some want to, but our plan is to make it simple and comfortable, no fancy sit down dinner where most people are uncomfortable."

"That sounds great to me, just remember that Tess will be staying with us." They said they knew, and I took off to go pack my bag.

It was just after one when I left home headed to Owl Creek, the weather was cool, the bay was slick, not a cloud in the sky, St. George Island looked like a dark gray line between the bay and sky, the marsh was turning brown quickly, the tree line up the river taking on a gray hue. Fall was here. That thought alone excited me, I love the cold weather, migratory birds arriving, hunting season coming in, holidays to follow, harvest time! That's it, harvest time! Time to collect all that you planted. The concept stuck in my brain, I thought that I am collecting all that I planted, friendship, family, love. It's a satisfying thought. Maybe I'll run that idea past Tess, who knows, she might even think I'm progressing.

She was waiting on me outside when I drove into Cloud's yard. She gave me a hug and we went into Cloud's back porch, taking my bag to my room, Cloud and Elzie were there, and the first thing I heard was Elzie, "Well, our hero returns! Heard you won another one?" Of course I dropped the bag and Tess and I took a seat.

I had to tell my story, "The winning wasn't the hard part, trying to keep from freezing after it was over was." I told them about the time scheduling mix-up, the ride home in the bus with no heat, and getting home in the middle of the night. They thought it was funny, and of course Cloud said it sounded like all the other coaches she's seen come and go from Bristol. And then I set the hook, I started telling them about what was in store for next Saturday's Seafood Festival and the plan Mom and Dad have for festivities at our house.

Elzie got excited, told me to tell Dad to get some blocks and grates for grilling and he would help while the rest of us went to the festival. Then he said that he froze the doves from last week's hunt and that he would thaw them out and prepare the best grilled doves anyone has ever tasted. Of course I had to ask how he was going to prepare them, and of course, he said they would be dove poppers, and that if I wanted to know how to prepare them then I'd have to work for it. I told him that Dad was going to invite Mr. Siglio which really got Elzie excited, he automatically decided that Mr. Siglio would bring shrimp, and that he, Elzie, knew the best method for grilling shrimp that had ever been invented. Elzie was so excited it got me excited, and it was all about food, which made me hungry. Cloud and Tess just sat there watching the whole thing, and by the time Elzie got to talking about shrimp, my mouth got to watering, so Cloud and Tess went to the kitchen to start fixing something to eat before we even had a chance to ask.

We had lunch on the porch, and after lunch Tess wanted to go for a walk, so we took off. I never even took my bag to my bedroom. We headed toward the creek, the high ridge, and we stopped at the bench. The big white oak trees were beginning to lose their leaves, some of the leaves were as big as a pie plate. There was no agenda, we just sat and talked and held hands. We had been there maybe 30 minutes when my brain kicked into gear, "Tess, do you know how Walter and Elzie make their money?" Tess gave me a strange look, said that was a strange question, then asked why I asked. "Well, last week when we were dove hunting Bud asked me the same question. I told him I didn't know but I didn't think that it took much money based on how they live. He kind of agreed, but he point out that they both had good boats, new motors, and lots of equipment. I said that if you don't have a regular home and a family to raise it shouldn't take a lot to live and you could afford special things."

Tess agreed with me, but said that she would ask her Mom or Cloud if I needed the information. I told her not to, it wasn't important, I was just thinking about what Bud had said. We changed subjects, but back in my brain, the question still stuck. There seemed to be conflict as to how things appear and how things usually develop. But, it wasn't important.

Back at the house Alida was busy sewing so Tess and I took Sage out to the swings and stayed out of everyone's way for a couple of hours. Later in the afternoon, as the temperature started to drop some, Cloud suggested we grill some hamburgers so Elzie and I went to the fire pit and got things started. By the time the coals were getting right Tess, Cloud, Alida, Sage, and Mama Sol came to join us. Each had a dish to carry and I was sent to bring the ice tea. We gathered in the screened room and discussed the next weekend as we had supper.

The excitement was growing; Mama Sol said she had not been to Apalachicola in over 20 years. I told her I doubted it had changed any. After supper we took chairs outside and sat around the fire, Elzie told us stories about logging the river swamps, shrimping with Mr. Siglio, and he and Walter's one trip to New Orleans. He didn't get very far with the New Orleans story until he realized he shouldn't be talking about it with mixed company; Cloud suggested he get it out of his head, even recommended shock therapy if necessary. All the while Elzie had that little grin on his face as if he was about to laugh, maybe even pull a joke. I noticed the grin disappeared after Cloud suggested shock therapy. We all laughed a lot, the evening ended well, and after everyone had turned in Tess and I were left on Cloud's back porch.

Sitting there together on a chaise lounge I told her about my thoughts when coming up here today, about fall, the change of colors, and harvest, and that harvest was collecting all that one had planted. I told her I didn't know just exactly what I planted but that I was harvesting family, friendships, and love. She put her arms around me, kissed me, and said, "I think you have the makings of a farmer! And that's a good thing. Maybe we're both harvesting the love." Look at that! The thoughts ran through my head, fear flashed in front of me, I said to Tess,

"Damn, this is getting way to close to growing up! We need to run away or something." Tess laughed and said,

"Ok, if you don't mind being hungry!" I told her,

"Come on, I've got to walk you home."

Sunday morning the Mothers and children gathered at the screened room to meet with Cloud, Elzie had gone back to East River, so Tess and I drove over to Wright Lake. We had it to ourselves. It was a great morning, and as I headed home after lunch, I thought about the harvest of love, and how much fun it was going to be next weekend when all of my family was there in Apalachicola.

The last week of October is a lot like the week prior to Thanksgiving or Christmas. Folks get into a festival state of mind. Halloween was Friday, the night we played Chattahoochee in Apalachicola, and the next day is the Seafood Festival. The students not playing ball worked on floats in the afternoons after school, the band marched up and down streets practicing for Saturday's parade, and our football practices were light. Chattahoochee was actually the Chattahoochee School for Boys, a reform school, the one me and my cohorts almost got a scholarship to last June. They were not expected to be challenging, the scouting report said they had good size, but no discipline, and poor coaching. The report didn't show any particular plays that stood out, so we ran our usual defensive plays and offensive plays for practice. Coach said that I should throw a lot during the game.

Sixth period every day, even Friday during the pep-rally, I was at the library. I was struggling with my report, I had some information about the native Indians, the military battles, the cotton trade through Apalachicola, and was researching money used during the war, but I couldn't find a foreign nation that was aligned with the Confederacy. I still had a month and a half before the report was due, but I wanted to have time for the typing, for having it reviewed by more than just me, and hopefully let Cloud review it as well and make suggestions if I needed to make changes. Not being able to take the State information home with me surely restricted my time for research, and I was needing to start bring this thing together soon.

After school I went home, Mom had made a sandwich for me, so after eating a little, I laid down to rest. I dropped off between four and five o'clock, mom woke me at 5 and said I'd better get my gear together. I walked into the gym at six o'clock, the coaches were already taping ankles, there was a lot of laughter and camaraderie. Bud walked over to me, "Dru, I have a suggestion."

I looked at him, he looked serious, so I replied, "What?"

And Bud, with a straight face, said, "I think we should take it easy on these guys tonight, we don't want to piss any of them off, you know we almost could have been playing on their side tonight, and if we happen to end up there someday, I don't want anybody holding grudges." I couldn't help myself, I started laughing, and laughing so hard I almost cried. About that time Bob walked over to us and asked what we were laughing about, I gave him a quick take, and he started laughing as well.

At some point Bob turns to Bud and says, "Bud, do you think I should run the wrong way every so often tonight so maybe they can score too?" and the laughter started again.

We must not have seemed serious enough for the coaches because Coach Blackmon walked over to us and said, "Y'all think this is just some sort of joke? It's still a game and we have to be mentally prepared! You need to cut out that joking and carrying on, get with the plan, after we win tonight you can laugh all you want." And he went back to taping somebody's ankles.

As he left, I turned to Bud and said, "Bud, if I call a pass play for you and I say down and back, you'll know that I want you to run 3 steps forward, then turn and run hard back toward our goal, I'll hit you when you break free of our backfield."
We laughed about that one all the way to the football field.

As usual, our fans were out in numbers, the band was playing on the field, Chattahoochee hadn't even shown up yet. We warmed up, went through our drills, and were about to go to our sideline when Chattahoochee drove into the field behind their stands. They unloaded, warmed up for about 10 minutes and then the referees called for the coin toss.

We kicked off to them, held them to very little yards, and they punted on the fourth down. The ball rolled out of bounds on the fifty yard line. Our first play was a rollout pass to the right, Bud was down and out to the flats. Lefty was deep over the middle, their safety nowhere to be seen, so I hit Lefty around the thirty yard line and he took it in for the score. The extra point was good. The second set of downs was a repeat of the first; we scored with another pass on the first play. Chattahoochee, unable to get organized, ran three plays and out.

By the time we took possession of the ball the third time I began noticing the Chattahoochee players. There was no fight in them. One of their defensive linemen ran off the field to be replaced by another player. When they met at the sideline he took off his helmet and gave it to the incoming lineman. They didn't even have enough equipment to suit up the entire team. In the huddle a couple of our linemen were bragging about dominating their competition, almost yelling that we could score sixty or eighty points. I thought about who these guys were, from Chattahoochee, thinking that it could have been me and my buddies in crime, without influential parents to intervene for us. And I thought about what it means to compete in sports, that pride plays an important role in competition, and without pride, competition is meaningless. These guys didn't have family there to support them, to go home with, to celebrate or commiserate after a game. They didn't deserve our abuse. Our huddle was uncontrolled and loud. I stepped into the middle and hollered, "Shut up!" They hushed. I looked each one of them square in the eyes and said, "Hell no! That's not who we are. And I'll be damned if I'll throw dirt in their face." I stepped away from the huddle, motioned to a referee for time out and jogged off the field. At the sideline Coach asked what the matter was. "Coach, we can score anytime we want. This isn't competition. Send in the second team."

A smile came across Coach's face, he reached up and patted my helmet and told me to take a seat on the bench. He immediately called the second team to take the field. Chattahoochee had no stands, no band, and, of course, no cheerleaders. By the second quarter some of our fans went over to sit on the Chattahoochee side just so it didn't look so bad for them. After the game we shook hands with almost all of the Chattahoochee players. I think their coach appreciated it. Back at the gym Bud came over to me and said he made a couple of new friends from the Chattahoochee team just in case. I told him that if he really wanted a scholarship there I could ask my Dad to help. He didn't even think that was funny.

Dad had been at the game and was waiting on me when I left the gym. On the way home he said he was proud of us for not running completely away with the score. I told him about Bud, he didn't seem too impressed. I think as a Dad and Principal it must be hard to laugh at stupid stuff your kid does, especially when the law gets involved. At home, I called Tess, she said they would be at our house by 9:30 tomorrow morning.

Chapter 11: Festival

The Seafood Festival started as a Harbor Day in the late 1940s to early 1950s. Visitors from up river would come down the first Saturday of November each year and the men's and women's clubs would put on a fish fry and oyster eating event. A few hundred people from all the way to South Georgia would make a boat trip to Apalachicola. It became an annual event, later being called the Apalachicola Seafood Festival, and in 1965 it was incorporated as the Florida Seafood Festival. But even in 1958 the festival parade had bands from around NW Florida, politicians from local, state, and even national representatives , and many of the local organizations and churches would set up food booths. Watching women shucking oysters and the men frying mullet, all wearing white oyster boots was a sight to see. Watching South Georgia residents stuffing their faces with seafood was better than watching children eating cotton candy at a fair.

By 7:30 I was awake and getting ready for the day. I had a quick bowl of cereal, then went out back to help Dad set up the tables and fire pit. He had lots of concrete block, and oven racks used for cooking, and a stack of oak wood Elzie would be proud of, plus plenty of fold-out chairs. Mom provided some table cloths, and said she was setting up a serving table on the big dining room table, more chairs and small tables would be on the porch. By the time Tess and family showed up Walter and Mr. Siglio were already in the back yard with Dad. Dad had a large ice chest with oysters packed in ice, Walter had brought two dozen smoked mullet, Mr. Siglio brought 10 pounds of shrimp. Elzie unloaded another ice chest which contained the marinated doves, and other food stuff. It was beginning to look like a party.

After several minutes of visiting I took Tess, Cloud, Alida, Sage, and Mama Sol with me to go watch the parade. Walter, Elzie, and Mr. Siglio stayed with Mom and Dad. Our plan was to be back sometime the middle of the afternoon. We all packed into Dad's car and drove to Main Street a couple of blocks away. The parade always started at 14th Street and Main Street next to the high school; from there it went all the way to the middle of town and turned toward the bridge but disbanded just before the bridge at the park where the festival is held. I took three folding chairs for Mama Sol, Cloud, and Alida, I figured Tess, Sage and I could sit on the ground if necessary. The parade began just after ten o'clock, there were four bands, a couple of the homecoming floats with the homecoming queen, a festival queen, and several young girls all dolled up, waving at everyone. Jill was on the Homecoming float, waving to everyone, when she saw Tess and me she turned toward the other side of the road and kept pumping her hand. It was funny and sad all at the same time. Politicians walked between the bands and the floats waving at locals and shaking hands with those they recognized.

The parade lasted just over an hour, from there we loaded back up in the car and drove to the park. Booths were set up to serve food, fried fish, oysters, and all sorts of hot dogs, hamburgers, cold drinks, and some folks had displays of art, and crafts. The park filled with folks, children running wild, lots of laughter, and of course, politicians were speaking from a podium, making promises they surely couldn't keep. The boat basin was filled with all sorts of boats from small river boats to larger cabin cruisers. It was a grand event. By three o'clock we were all ready to get home. Back at the house the women gathered inside, I joined the men folk out in the back yard. Dad and Elzie had erected a fire pit, stacked blocks, with several racks for meats, and the fire was building a great bed of hot coals. Dad had brought home at least three folding tables, one to work off of while cooking, the second for serving oysters on the half shell as well as grilled oysters, and the other for the additional items to be cooked on the grill.

Elzie was working on the third table, taking dove breasts out of the marinade, laying the split breasts on sheets of waxed paper, putting slices of jalapeno peppers and goat cheese on the breasts and rolling them in bacon then skewered with a tooth pick. All total he had 24 poppers, that's what he called them. Next to Elzie, Mr. Siglio had peeled the shrimp, and was skewering them on long skewers, and basting them with a combination of lime juice, honey, a little olive oil, and seasonings. There were probably 5 or 6 shrimp per skewer, and lots of skewers. Knowing that Mom had made a seafood chowder, and with all the food I could see, I went and asked Dad if I should call up some more people to get them to come eat with us. He just laughed and said no, but we would send lots of left overs home with everybody. While Dad and Elzie put the oysters, shrimp, and dove on the grill, I took almost 5 pounds of shrimp inside and told Mom that Dad said to boil them.

Tess had taken her bag to her room and was returning to the kitchen when I gave Mom the shrimp, she offered to help, but Mom said she had it covered in the kitchen. Mom's seafood chowder was something she was really good at, and it was one of my favorite dishes, it just might get lost in all this food. Mom's chowder was made from a redfish, with a great broth, but she also included potatoes, cut into small cubes, along with the onions, peppers, garlic, and other seasonings. This one, however, she also added shrimp, oysters, and some mild sausage; I think the only thing that made it a chowder instead of a gumbo was the potatoes, and it didn't have roux in it. Mom also made a huge salad, we both liked salads, Dad not so much.
Around five o'clock we started preparing our plates, as we found a seat, and after everyone oohed and aahhed, Mom asked Cloud if she would give a blessing. To me that was natural as I know Cloud, but I never would have guessed Mom would have asked Cloud to give a blessing. Cloud looked surprised, but acted quickly. She looked around at everyone and without standing, she lifted her arms out in front of her, palms upward, looked upward, and prayed, "Great Spirit, we give you thanks for all that you provide us, look down upon this family, and bless it; raise us up to do your will, and keep us strong. Amen!" Everyone said Amen, and as I watched each one there, I felt that we were a family. Tess was sitting next to me, she reached over and squeezed my leg, she felt it too.

I think we all ate until our bellies were about to burst, and then we waited a few minutes and tried to eat some more. There was laughter, smiles, and it felt good. I was so proud of my parents. At Owl Creek the family gathered regularly, but this was the first at our house that we had shared so much with so many. It felt right. Around nine o'clock everyone headed home, Walter went with Mr. Siglio, I think he was staying at his house for the night. Elzie drove the rest home to Owl Creek. Tess stayed with us. Tess and I jumped in to help with the clean up, Dad went out and doused the fire, and sprayed off the tables with the water hose, Mom put the left-overs in the refrigerator. She had packed boxes of food to take to Owl Creek, and at least two large bags of food each for Walter and Mr. Siglio. I think everyone was glad to take some home. Before everyone left, my folks suggested we plan something around Christmas; everyone agreed.

After my folks went to bed Tess and I stayed up. We sat in the living room for more than an hour, just sitting there, holding hands, not saying much of anything. The only thing I remember saying was how great it was, I probably repeated that one sentence at least a dozen times. Before we went to bed Tess said that we should go back to Owl Creek a little earlier tomorrow, we might need to check out Wright Lake before going home. I told her I thought that was a great idea. As I lay in bed before going to sleep, I prayed, "Great Spirit, please give me sight, and lead the way."

We left for Owl Creek by ten o'clock, no one was at Wright Lake so we stayed there until almost one o'clock. I just knew that everyone would know when we drove into the yard at Tess's house, certainly they could see it in our eyes, the way we looked at each other, but entering Tess's back porch Alida looked up from the paper and said that we sure looked happy. We both said that it had been a great weekend. We visited with Alida a short while, then went to see Cloud and Elzie, but Elzie was gone, Cloud said they had a wonderful day yesterday and Elzie was still bragging about the food.

I left for home about three o'clock, called Tess from home about four O 'clock to let her know I was home safely. She said she was already lonely and missing me, I told her I felt the same. Mom and Dad had been somewhere but came in about the time I hung up the phone from Tess. They were in a good mood, and I told them how much everyone enjoyed the gathering, and that Cloud said Elzie was still bragging about the food. I think that made their day. We had left overs for supper that night, it was still really good.

Monday morning, November third, last week of football season for us, school was humming, there was a chill in the air, everyone was still excited about the festival, Dad even went on the loud speaker reminding everyone that our football team remained undefeated, and Port St. Joe wanted to end that run. The rivalry was fueled at St. Joe Paper Company, where approximately forty-five percent of the employees were from Apalachicola and Franklin County, the rest from Port St. Joe and Gulf County. Every day, seven days a week, the men ragged each other, made bets about the games, and generally nagged each other from one sport to the next. This being the last football game of the year was big! We beat them twice last year, and they just couldn't stomach the possibility of losing to us twice again this year. Bets were getting bigger. Classes were just normal, Billy Fields didn't get in trouble one time during the week, but football practice was intense.

We had updated scouting reports, we went over every new play they had, and we worked really hard on our offense to keep their defense off balance. I expected to be throwing a lot during the game, so Coach had us run every pass play we had at least a thousand times. We had to play in Port St. Joe, and their crowds were just as loud and rambunctious as ours, it was going to be eventful. Monday through Friday sixth period was spent at the library, my report was still struggling; maybe after this week I could get more focused on it. God I hoped so. I tried talking to Tess every evening, she kept telling me I would do great, but I kept feeling like I was forgetting something important to the game. It wasn't Joe Shuler, he was still limping around and dating Jill, but I just needed to connect the dots, if I could find the dots.

By Thursday night I was nervous, I tried watching some TV with Dad, but I just couldn't sit still, by 9:30 I told Mom and Dad I was going to bed. In my room I lay on my bed, then sat up, crossed my legs, arms across my knees, palms up, I took long slow breaths, focused my mind on the game, and started running plays. I ran cross-bucks, sweeps, then sweeps and passing, I visualized the unbalanced plays where I handed off to Bull, then again bellying in with Bull, then taking the ball and finding my hole. I saw drop back passes, roll out passes, and then I visualized running a roll out past to the right, but first putting Bob in motion to the right taking him several yards past Bud at right end, then have Bud go down about 10 yards and button hook, I would hit him there, but Bob would break down field at the count but angle to Bud. I expected the safety to come up and hit Bud at the button hook, so Bud would lateral the ball to Bob, the ole hook and ladder pass play. We had never run it, I knew St. Joe had never seen it, and when I got to school the next morning I grabbed both of them and walked them through the play.

At sixth period I didn't go to the library, I got Rob to join Bud, Bob and me outside the gym, and we ran the play 20 times. We worked out the kinks, but I told them not to tell Coach, he would flip out if he thought we were making up plays.

We gathered at the gym at six o'clock, got our ankles taped, put on our uniforms and we were on our way to St. Joe at 6:30. We were off the bus and on the field to warm up at 7:10. Our fans started showing up by 7:30, and our band came marching through the field entrance by 7:45. The emotions were boiling, we were ready to play.

Referees called for the coin toss at eight. St. Joe won the toss but decided to take the ball first, I'm sure they had a trick play to start the game. We kicked off deep to their best receiver, he started up middle field but then quickly broke to the left side of the field where their team was setting up an alley to run, except a couple of our defensive players got to their receiver before he could get to the sideline. Their first play from scrimmage started on their 25 yard line. They gained 15 yards before we held them, forcing a punt.

We started our offense on our 40 yard line. The first play we ran was unbalanced line left, Bull took it to mid-field. The next play I faked an off tackle right play again to Bull, but pulled the ball and hit Bud in the flats for another 10 yards. We kept knocking out yards with cross-buck plays, short button hook passes, and sweeps. Eight plays later we were in the end zone, the extra point was good, and we gathered around Coach on the sidelines. He gave instructions to watch for the sideline return, and we went back to head knocking. There was no other score in the first quarter.

In the second quarter I hit Lefty in the end zone and we took the score to 14 to nothing to finish the first half. Halftime entertainment lasted longer than usual, their band put on a show and then our band put on a show, we were getting cold by the time the second half had begun. They kicked off to us and Bob Riley took it back to just inside their territory, three plays later we ran a unbalanced line left again but I bellied in with Bull and as their defense piled up the left side I took the ball out, took a couple more strides, found my hole and shot through, immediately reversed my field back to the right, their linebackers were on the ground, and it was open field for me to the end zone. After we kicked off to them they made a really good drive down field and scored on us with a reverse we hadn't seen before. At the end of the third quarter we were up 20 to 7.

The fourth quarter started slow for us, they made some good drives but we held them without scoring until midway through the fourth quarter when they threw a long pass to their right end, our defensive back fell down, and they scored. There were less than 5 minutes to go, the score was 20 to 14, and we were on their 45 yard line. In the huddle I had to explain the play to the rest of the team, first telling the line that it was a pass play, they couldn't leave the line of scrimmage, telling the backs what to do for blocking, but then calling Bud to button hook, Bob to go into motion and the hook and ladder play. When Bob went into motion to the right, their whole defensive backfield moved in that direction. At the count Bob broke down field, Bud went 10 yards, button hooked, I hit him as soon as he turned toward me, their safety came up quickly to tackle Bud, Bob crossed right in front of Bud facing me, Bud made an easy toss to Bob and all the stands on both sides went to their feet.

Our side went to hollering and yelling and cheering as Bob took it to the end zone. St. Joe's side got real quiet, real fast. The extra point was good, and we walked away from that one 27 to 14. As we walked off the field and headed to our bus Joe Shuler was waiting on me in the end zone. Jill had already joined him, he held out his hand and I shook it, he said good game, I said thanks, and then he said he'd see me in the spring. I told him "Yes, you will."

The St. Joe Paper Company employees from Franklin County got to collect their bets the next week. Coach didn't even mention the play until the next week; I gave him all the credit. Mom and Dad were at the game but I rode home on the bus with the players, and they picked me up at the gym. They both complemented me, said how much they enjoyed the game, then asked when Coach came up with that last pass play. I told them he didn't, but I would show it to him again next week for next year's plays. They got a kick out of that. At home I called Tess, she had already heard that we won. I told her I'd see her in the morning. I was ready for a good night's sleep.

It was just past ten o'clock when I drove into Tess's yard. I didn't see anybody at her house so I took my bag over to Cloud's, no one was on the back porch, but as I entered the kitchen on my way to my room, everyone hollered "surprise" and started singing "our hero's come a courtin'," whatever that means. But it was fun and it took me a few minutes to figure out that they were giving me a party for going undefeated. Cloud had baked a cake, and even Mama Sol had come to enjoy the celebration. What a way to end the season. I think Tess was more proud than me.

After everything settled down Elzie called me to the porch and said that squirrel season comes in next Saturday, and we need to put up some duck blinds. If things work right we could kill a mess of squirrels in the morning, then put up a couple of blinds during middle of the day, and could be back here by late afternoon, maybe cook up a squirrel stew. I told him it sounded like a plan and that I'd be there unless Dad had me arrested. He got a kick out of that.

Later in the day when Tess and I had a chance to be alone I told her about my visualization for the game, how I went through all of our plays, and then about the pass play I came up with, the hook and ladder play to Bud and Bob, and how it scored the last touchdown. I think she was impressed. Then she said, "Maybe you can visualize all that gold in them there swamps!" which really killed a perfect morning because it made me realize I was way behind on my research. She said I'd get over it, especially if we drove over to Wright Lake! I told her just thinking about that made me get over research. We didn't get to Wright Lake that weekend but it was a wonderful time, and I was already looking forward to the holidays.

Monday's classes were upbeat, the teachers all seemed to be in a good mood, all the students were happy about the football season, but the underlying atmosphere was that the holidays were fast approaching. Hunting season is a big deal in our county, and when you combine hunting season with holidays it just spells fun. Every day for sixth period I went to the library, I knew I needed to get my report finished by Thanksgiving or I'd be slammed trying to get it typed and reviewed at least twice. By the end of the week I stayed after school in the library until Miss Whithers locked up. My research, I felt, was coming together, I had a pretty good idea what I wanted to say about the Apalachicola Indians, I had an outline regarding the battles in the Civil War, I had plenty of material regarding the cotton trade and Apalachicola's importance to that industry, but I still needed information regarding a foreign nation that supported the Confederacy. And somewhere in there I needed to find out information about gold!

Friday came way too fast, but I was still excited. Thursday night I packed my hunting clothes, prepped my boat, and as soon as school was out on Friday I took Dad's car and put my boat overboard. Dad said he would get his car later in the day. My run to the houseboat was exhilarating! I decided to run across the bay to the mouth of East River and then up to the houseboat. The bay was calm, a light north wind blowing, and the sky was as blue as the gulf. I counted the power poles that paralleled the bridge until I got to number eight, then turned due north which took me to East River channel. As I entered the mouth of East River a dozen green-wing teal flew directly over me, then pitched into East River pocket. I promised I'd see them on Thanksgiving morning.

Elzie was sitting on the front porch when I arrived at the house boat, he didn't even come out to help me. I tied up to a cleat, unpacked my clothes, shotgun and shells, and of course my boots. I dropped them on the couch inside then joined Elzie on the porch. He had that almost smile spread all over his face, "Well boy, did you remember to bring some shot gun shells?" I told him I did, then he said, "Did you bring enough for me?" I told him I'd share, but I wanted to do most of the shooting any way. He got a kick out of that, then said we needed to gather up some fire wood. By the time dark rolled around I could hardly sit still, so I got the fire started, while he started on supper. Supper was baked beans out of a can, and sausages, and a loaf of white bread. That's it! But there was plenty of it, I got my belly full. I think Elzie drank more beer than he ate. I decided it was best I not be too close to him during the night, beans and beer didn't have a good effect on Elzie. I decided to sleep on the front porch. It was still dark when I woke the next morning, and I could smell the coffee. Elzie was already dressed and having coffee when I entered the living area. "You sleep alright?" Elzie asked me.

"Yes sir, except when the owls started hollering at one another."

"They do get loud; I wonder what owls talk about? Must be a lot cause they sure make a lot of racket."

"Are you going to hunt this morning?" I asked.

"If you'll loan me seven or eight shells, I'll help fill up the pot."

"That's all the shells you want?"

"That's all I plan on killing. I figured you'd kill your limit, so that'll be plenty for our stew."

Just when it got light enough we could begin to see into the swamps we left the fire burning and slipped into the woods. Elzie said he would work out to the old road bed and I should work along the river. He told me to move slowly and listen a lot. Over the next two hours I shot my limit of 12 squirrels, Elzie shot eight. We were back at the houseboat by nine o'clock. We worked together on the back of the houseboat cleaning the squirrels, then iced them down.

Elzie then pulled out a couple of machetes and said we needed thirty palm fronds, and to keep the limbs pretty long. The swamps are full of palm trees so that didn't take long. We piled the palm fronds close to the bank back at the house boat. While Elzie moved his boat around to the bank side of the houseboat he had me shaving the sawtooth edges of the palm fronds so they wouldn't cut our hands when we stuck them into the muddy bottom to build our duck blinds. As I finished trimming each palm frond Elzie stacked them into his big boat.

Less than an hour later we were back at the mouth of East River, he was in his big boat, I was in mine. We transferred 15 palm fronds into my boat, then he joined me and we idled into East River pocket. East River pocket is an open but shallow area surrounded by marsh just off the channel, it's easy to get to if the tide is up, but it takes an oar to pry your way into or out of the pocket when the tide is down. Lucky for us today the tide was up. Elzie directed me to a point jutting out from the marsh, there we pushed my boat into the marsh using an oar, then stuck the palm fronds completely around my boat, blending them with the marsh grasses and reeds. We left the stern of my boat clear of the palm fronds but stuck a couple on both sides of the boat so we could close in the stern when we stooled out to hunt.

After finishing that blind we retrieved the rest of the palm fronds and repeated the process over in the next bight, Sam's Bight. We flushed at least a couple of dozen teal when going into Sam's Bight. Just building the blinds was exciting, knowing that within a week and a half we'd be stooled out waiting on the ducks. I had never done any duck hunting, but Elzie was teaching me, and giving me advice about blinds, tides, and how to place the decoys when hunting. The whole process didn't take us long and shortly I dropped off Elzie back at his boat and then we headed back to the house boat. I grabbed my clothes and gun, Elzie put the ice chest and squirrels in his boat, secured the house boat and we headed to Owl Creek.

Tess and Cloud met us at the landing site, helped with my bags and shotgun, and Elzie and I carried the ice chest and squirrels to Cloud's; it was still early afternoon. We settled on the back porch for a little while, Cloud fixed us a light lunch, and Alida and Sage joined us. I just kept thinking that it felt like a holiday, everyone was happy, the breeze was cool, and the fall colors washed all the trees. You could hear the kids playing out at the swings.

Eventually Cloud got around to asking about my report. I gave her the overview, where I was, and how I was having problems with the foreign nation or nations that supported the Confederacy, and where gold fit into the picture. She gave me a couple of references which I wrote down, then said that the next weekend she would have a contact which should help me clarify my story. I told her I appreciated it, and I sure hope it helped because right now it was still a blur. She just laughed at me. Tess reached over, squeezed my hand, and said I shouldn't let Cloud get to me, she does it to her all the time.

Around four o'clock Elzie directed me to come on, we have supper to prepare, and the two of us left the women folk on the porch and we took possession of the kitchen. He put me at a counter, pulled up a stool, and had me start slicing and dicing onions, peppers, and mushrooms. He pulled out a large pot and a frying pan, then started working on the squirrels. He first cut them into quarters, spread them out on the counter, then covered each quarter with salt, pepper, garlic and paprika. In the large pot he poured enough olive oil to cover the bottom, then placed my cut vegetables in the oil and took the heat to high; after a few minutes he turned the heat to medium, then turned his attention to the squirrels. He put oil in the frying pan, turned the heat to high, then shook each quarter of squirrels in a bag of flour, then laid them out on the counter again. As the oil in the frying pan got hot he started browning each quarter until they were brown all over but not completely cooked, then returned each to the counter and added more quarters to the oil. By the time he finished with browning the quarters, the vegetables in the big pot were wilted, so he added some flour to the pot, stirred in the onions, peppers, and mushrooms, and continued stirring until the flour turned a golden brown color. He then added some water and continued stirring until all of the water and vegetables combined into a gravy, then he added the squirrel quarters, turned the heat to low and covered the pot with a lid.

At that point he turned to me and said, "I think I'll have a beer!" I was thinking that I sure would be glad when I got old enough to join him with a beer. We rejoined the girls on the porch, Elzie exclaimed that his work was finished and should be ready to eat within a couple of hours, and that the rest, which included rice, and another vegetable and some bread, was the girl's responsibility. Standing there, listening to Elzie, thinking about the squirrels, realizing that I'd never really seen him cook vegetables, brought me to the conclusion that Elzie figured his responsibility was to meat, that's all, just meat! Maybe that would be a good plan for me to adopt. I will say, the meal was outstanding, the squirrels as tender as any meat I've ever eaten. I bet it's even better with beer!

Tess and I cleaned up after the feast, Alida and Sage went home early, Elzie and Cloud disappeared by 9:30 leaving me and Tess on the back porch. We settled on a chaise lounge, snuggled, and talked until almost 11:30. As I lay on my bed that night, before dropping off to sleep, I thought about the duck hunting, the marsh, and when the big migration would happen. We had seen a few ducks, but nothing compared to what Elzie said would show up when the big cold fronts pushed them down to us. I pictured big flocks of ducks pitching into our decoys, cold north winds bending the marsh reeds, me making excellent shots with my new 12 gauge Browning.

I think I was still shooting ducks when I heard Elzie in the kitchen. I made my bed, packed my gear, and joined Elzie and Cloud on the back porch. I thanked him for everything, it had been a great opening day. Tess joined me on the porch for a while, but by 10:30 she helped me take my gear to my boat, I kissed her good-by, and I headed home. Dad met me at the boat basin, and I talked his ear off all the way home. I don't remembering him saying anything, I don't think I gave him a chance. At home I repeated everything all over again to Mom. After lunch I laid down on my bed to relax, it was almost five o'clock when I woke up. The owls hadn't kept me awake. At supper I told Mom and Dad all about squirrel stew. Dad seemed interested, Mom, not so much.

Sixth period on Monday I reviewed the references Cloud had given me with Miss Whithers, and she said she would do her best to get me the information from the State as soon as possible. I decided I should start putting what I did have from my notes into report form; I started with my outline, but started expanding it with sub-sections under each section of the report. I figured that if I had enough sub-sections under each heading the actual written report should fill in pretty easily! My first section was about the Indians that inhabited the land along the Apalachicola, Chattahoochee, and Flint Rivers, with subsections about their tribe names, where they were located, and how Apalachicola relates to a certain tribe. The next sub-section would outline the Indian's introduction to the white man, the relationship with the Spanish, the French, and eventually the English. The relationship with the white man began as trade, but the Indians were drawn into battle and conflict from each foreign nation. Next, I noted the introduction of white settlers and the pressure to move the Indians out of their land. Lastly, I wanted to address the Indian Removal Act of 1830 and discuss how written history didn't always reflect the actual outcome of that act.

The next section of the report was to be about the Civil War with a condensed version of the battles and time lines as it related to areas along the tri-rivers. As a subsection I hoped to bring out the significance of Apalachicola as a shipping port, the importance of the river system, and the close relationship between Columbus, Georgia, and Apalachicola. I didn't know why at this time, but I felt I needed to emphasize time lines as it related to the end of the war and hopefully a foreign influence that could change the outcome of the war. I just needed to find the information that Cloud alluded to.

And lastly, I needed to tie gold to the war and the foreign nation. I now had some semblance of an outline, but lacked some needed information. I hoped the information Miss Whithers would give me would solve some of these questions.

The rest of the week crawled along, nothing really exciting happened, and every sixth period I was at the library working on my report. Thursday afternoon's sixth period I received the material ordered from the State. Payday! I found a report that answered my questions about what foreign nation was amenable to helping the Confederacy: Spain! I went back to my outline, and added a section to address foreign influence that could have changed the outcome of the war. How did it come about, and what happened? Now all I needed was information about the gold. That information would come after Thanksgiving, I just never imagined how I would get it.

Friday after school I had my boat ready, my bags packed, gun and shells, and Dad let me use his car again. By four o'clock I was at the house boat, Elzie was again sitting on the porch. "Did you bring me some more shells?" he began.

"Of course I did. Did you bring something besides beans and sausages for supper?" He laughed at that and said he brought leftover squirrels and gravy. I told him that would do. At five o'clock, with just over an hour of daylight left, we eased into the swamps to shoot a few squirrels. Again I headed up down river along the bank, moving slowly, listening for any sounds. About 150 yards from the house boat there is an oak grove that begins at the river's edge and extends several hundred yards back into the woods. It's where I killed the squirrels last Saturday, and it's where I stopped when I heard the first squirrels barking at something. I picked my way along the ridge, killing one every now and then, and minutes before it became too dark to see, I headed back to the house boat, my game pouch feeling mighty full. Elzie and I gathered on the back porch to clean the squirrels, he had ten and I had twelve. While cleaning the squirrels he suggested we do a little fishing the next morning instead of killing more squirrels. I agreed that it was a good idea.

That night as I snuggled down in my sleeping bag on the front porch, I listened to the owls holler, the occasional strike from a fish, the gurgling of the running river, and I felt that I was at home. It's where I belonged. And that night, the owls didn't keep me awake.

The next morning Elzie and I sat on the front porch drinking our coffee, the sun not yet above the horizon, the river looked like a sheet of glass, not a leaf moving on any trees; it was so calm neither of us even said anything, we just sat there drinking our coffee, enjoying the silence, in no hurry to go fishing. When the sun finally got above the horizon, lighting up the river, a mist rose above the river and was thick enough you couldn't even see the bank across the river, only the trees well above the water line. Elzie finally spoke up and said we didn't need to get in any hurry and went to start some breakfast. It was almost 8:30 when we loaded up in his boat and started down river. The mist was mostly gone, but the chill stuck to you like a wet cloth as we ran down river into the rising sun.

At the point where the tree line stopped and marsh began Elzie slowed the boat, then idled to the west side of the river and had me tie the bowline to a tree limb hanging out over the river. As he cut the motor he said, "The river along here drops off to around 16 feet right off the bank, the reds love feeding along here." Within a few minutes we had our lines overboard, weights taking shrimp to the bottom, and in no time we were catching nice size redfish, most of them running 15 to 20 inches long. We sat there in the sun, fishing for just over an hour, until Elzie said we had enough and he wanted to clean them before heading to Owl Creek.

Back at the house boat I started scaling the fish as Elzie filleted them, we had 10 beautiful redfish, 20 slabs. We packed the fish in ice along with the squirrel from the evening before, I cleaned up the kitchen, and we were headed to Owl Creek even before lunch. I followed Elzie in my boat, it was my transportation home for tomorrow. And like the week before, Cloud and Tess were waiting on us at the landing site.

This time Elzie had Tess and I take squirrels and fish to everyone in the community. For supper with Alida and Sage, Elzie grilled some redfish and Cloud fixed grits and hushpuppies. As we gathered on Cloud's back porch for supper, Elzie looked over at me and said, "And duck season hasn't even begun yet!" I could hardly wait. I started talking about meeting Elzie at the house boat on Wednesday afternoon, he said that the season began at noon on Wednesday and we could hunt that afternoon, and we would spend most all of Thursday, Thanksgiving Day, in the blind. My mouth must have been running a mile a minute talking about duck hunting, but at some point Cloud interrupted me and said not to get too excited because I couldn't hunt all weekend. I asked why, and she said that Tess and I were going to Columbus, Georgia on Saturday. "Columbus? Why Columbus?" I asked.

"Because that's where your answers are for your report."

Chapter 12: Columbus

I looked at Tess, she looked at me, then Tess asked if Cloud was going to give us instructions on where we were going and who would we be seeing? Cloud said of course, she would give us that information next Friday. I can't tell you what happened after that, I can't recall, except I thought that I'd be duck hunting all of the next weekend, but now I was going to Columbus and it all seemed like a mystery, an exciting mystery.

The next morning when I was preparing to head home Elzie came over to me and said he had a bag of redfish fillets for me to take to my parents. I told him thanks, that I was sure my folks would enjoy them. I didn't leave until just after lunch, I told Elzie I'd see him early afternoon on Wednesday, and I told Tess I'd see her next Friday. She said she would get us a map for our trip. The boat ride home was nippy, but I was loving it. On my way home I decided I really wanted to run by East River Pocket, just to check it out, kind of put in my mind how everything laid out so when I was running to my blind in the dark I'd have a better idea as to where I was. At Mark's Point I took Big St. Marks down to East River Cutoff, then headed south on East River, I passed the house boat and continued toward the mouth of the river. As I got to the juncture where the river splits, I took the east channel, which is also the way to the pocket, then cut my motor at the pocket cutoff.

I decided I would just sit for a few minutes to see if any birds were flying. I had been there less than half an hour when a bunch of teal, maybe 30 birds, flew right over me. I had anchored where I could see not only the pocket area, but Sam's Bight as well. A few birds were coming and going out of Sam's Bight, circling out over the pocket, and on toward the bay. As I continued to look I noticed more birds circling over the bay, it seemed more birds were showing up. I happened to look up at the sky and way up, at cirrus cloud level, I could see small v-shaped waves of ducks beginning to descend from the sky toward the bay. It took me a minute for the sight to register in my mind as to what I was seeing. It was the migration, thousands of birds, hundreds of V's coming from the northwest, headed to our waters. It was the most impressive thing I'd ever seen.

I decided I wanted to get out into the bay so I could see where all the birds were going. I pulled my anchor, cranked up and ran around to the mouth of East River. I moved out further away from the marsh but still in East River channel. I anchored again. The tide was falling fast and a light northwest wind had sprung up. Once the anchor caught my boat swung around, the bow facing the marsh. I could see from Little Bay in the west to the mouth of Blount's Bay to the east. The V's of birds continued to descend to our bay. They came in bunches, flight after flight, forming big tornado waves as they descended to calm water. I watched in awe as wave after wave, circling our marsh, filled it with activity. Flight after flight, bunch after bunch, birds flew over me, all looking for a place to light, a place to feed. The majesty of the moment moved me. I got so excited I started yelling. I stood up, outstretched arms, and yelled "Yeah, Yeah, Yeah. Come on! Come on home. To my bay! Yeah, come on home."

The wind in my face, the puffy clouds at high altitude, the fall migration, I didn't want to go home. I stayed there until almost four o'clock, then finally I cranked up and headed home. The northwest wind had picked up, the temperature was beginning to drop. At home I grabbed my gear and gun and went inside. Mom was at the stove preparing supper, "Mom, you should have seen it! The fall migration is on. I saw thousands of ducks coming to our bay this afternoon. It was beautiful!"

"Well that's nice Matt. I'm sure you'll enjoy your hunts." Dad was in the living room reading the paper.

"Dad, they're here! The ducks, this afternoon, I saw them. The fall migration. Thousands of birds!"

"That's good son. It should be a good Thanksgiving." I went to call Tess, she responded to my excitement with the same enthusiasm,

"Wow, I want to see it. How long will it last? You've got to show me."

"I don't know how long it lasts, but I promise you, one day you'll see it." That night as I lay on my bed before going to sleep I realized that my folks didn't share my passion, my excitement, my desire to be part of the calling. I prayed "Great Spirit, help me to honor these traditions, these sacred gifts."

I could hardly contain my excitement. A hard nor'wester blew through the next morning. Monday and Tuesday were like my first days on Little St. George, time moved so slowly I could hardly stand it. Some of the guys at school would also be hunting ducks over the break, so we talked about where our blinds were, and who would be where. The anticipation was worse than waiting on Christmas, but finally Wednesday came. I had been packed since Monday night, my gun was cleaned at least three times, I had five boxes of number sixes, and Dad had bought me a pair of waders. When the bell rang at noon the hunters burst out the doors like we were running from a fire! We said our good-byes, would see you in the marsh, and good luck. I launched my boat at one o'clock and headed to East River. The weather had turned cold, but my excitement was boiling hot, I was ready to get to the marsh.

Elzie was waiting on me at the house boat, I say that with a bit of sarcasm because I had to wake him up when I got there. He said he had been working hard and was really tired. I asked where he had been working, but he said he didn't remember. After I unloaded my gear Elzie had me transfer some duck decoys from his small boat to my boat, said he was going to hunt with me this afternoon to get me started, he'd hunt in his boat tomorrow.

I put a dozen decoys in my boat, then showed Elzie my waders, he said they sure were nice, but I'd better not wear them in East River Pocket. I asked why not, and he said that if I didn't have them on I would remember to never get overboard in East River Pocket. He cautioned that the bottom may feel solid, but it was not. If you start down you might not ever come back up.
It was almost three o'clock when we headed to the marsh. The tide was medium, rising, with high tide around eight o'clock tonight. We ran straight to East River Pocket and were able to idle into the blind. I cut the motor, kicked it up and Elzie put out the decoys as I poled us around. He gave me some tips, talked about wind direction, and said I should always leave a space opened in front of the blind for birds to land. We only had 12 decoys so his statement didn't make much sense to me, but by the next afternoon I'd understand.

After the decoys were out I poled into the blind. I adjusted the extra palm fronds behind the motor, and settled in. As we loaded our guns Elzie began instructing me. He made me pay attention to the wind direction and told me that ducks like pitching into the wind to land. He then said he would call the shots, because sometimes the ducks will pitch in low over the decoys just to check them out, especially going downwind, and then circle back into the wind to land. Shooting at them going down wind is nothing but wasting shots.

He had a couple of duck calls hanging around his neck and suggested I listen to him when calling. He gave me a sample of what to expect, he started with what he called a high ball call, then a feeding call, and explained what a simple quack sounds like and had me try it on his other call.
I was really getting excited about this when two pair of teal shot over our head from behind us, flying down wind, Elzie gave a quick high ball call then told me to get down.

We hunkered down behind the palm fronds, the teal seem to accelerate in speed, increased altitude, then circled back and pitched into our decoys. Elzie said for me to take the ones on the left, he'd take the right. He kept whispering to wait, wait, wait, then NOW. We both stood up, picked out our first bird and pulled the trigger. My first bird folded so I switched to the other who was by now headed straight up and climbing. My second shot missed, but my last shot connected, he folded and splashed down in the middle of our decoys. I looked over at Elzie, he was already reloading his shotgun, I looked toward the decoys, his two teal were belly up in the decoys. I tried to give him a high five, but he just looked at me like I was waving or something. He told me to back the boat out of the blind and let's pick up the birds before the wind blows them into the marsh.

I moved the palm fronds, backed out of the blind, we picked up the four teal, and had just gotten back into the blind when Elzie said, "Get down! Keep your head down. There's a nice bunch of mallards circling us." I squatted in the boat, pressed my face against the palms and looked for the birds. They were out front and to our left, still pretty high, but looking for a place to land. They made a couple of passes over the pocket, kept their altitude, then dropped down fairly low over the creek out front, and pitched toward our spread. They had their feet down for landing when Elzie said, "take'em!" There must have been ten or twelve of them, we left four belly up in the decoys. I backed out of the blind again, we picked up the four mallards, and returned to the blind. I was beginning to think this was pretty easy, and exciting. Elzie spoke up about then and said that these birds had just come in on the cold front. Then he said, "Give'em a few days and they get real picky about pitching in to decoys."

I checked the time, we had been in the blind less than 30 minutes, it was just getting to four o'clock, and we already had eight ducks in the boat. Elzie told me not to get to cocky, opening days tend to be like this, but later in the season you really have to work to get your shots. I decided this was my kind of work.

Over the next hour and a half we picked up six more birds, one was a male pintail, a beautiful bird. It was still not dark when I asked Elzie what the limit was for ducks, he said that depended on where the game warden was. So, I asked what the limit was if the game warden was right here with us, he said we were two over. I suggested we head to the house boat. He said he was ready for a beer.

At the house boat Elzie said we wouldn't completely clean them this evening, but we gutted them, washed them real good, then put them on ice. We would pick them after our hunt, and he would show me how to use hot water to help with the picking. After supper we sat around the fire, Elzie told me lots of duck hunting stories, and said that tomorrow I would be on my own. He thought I should hunt in the Sam's Bight blind, and he would give me 12 decoys, he'd take six. Our plan was to hunt in the morning until about 10:30 to 11, then head back to the house boat. We would hunt again in the afternoon.

Elzie woke me at five o'clock, he was already drinking coffee, I had a cup with him. After a quick breakfast, I put on my insulated underwear, grabbed my wool scarf to wrap around my neck, pulled on my heavy hunting pants and coat, and we started getting our boats ready. I was already in my boat when Elzie pulled his small boat from behind the house boat. As I warmed up my motor, Elzie checked his gear, started his motor and while he let it warm up, he came over to me and gave me some directions, "You follow me down to the pocket, don't get too close in case I have to stop or avoid a log or something. At the pocket I'll give you more instructions." And we were off, the night was dark, no moon, but the sky light was enough to see the outline of the tree tops, and some reflection in the river.

I stayed at least 100 yards behind Elzie. We actually ran faster than I had anticipated. At the pocket Elzie cut his motor and motioned for me to come closer. As I eased up to him, he grabbed my boat railing, I cut the motor and listened to him. "As you head out the east channel you'll notice some thin marsh on your left, go about forty or fifty yards past where it ends, then cut across the flat right there, there should be enough water so you can jump the flat. If it's not, then cut your motor, kick it up, and pole across. If you can't do that then put on your waders and pull the boat across the flat. It's not wide there, and as soon as you get back in deep enough water to run it's clear all the way to your blind. Good luck. I'll see you around ten o'clock."

When it's your first time of running in the dark, and jumping flats, it makes you pay attention. I followed Elzie's instructions and when I passed the marsh I took a guess at forty to fifty yards and made a sharp cut across the flats. The motor kicked up some mud, shook a little, but I made it into deeper water. The run to the back of the Bight was easy. The back end of Sam's Bight has a few reed islands out from the bank, we built my blind on one of those.

As I got close, I cut the motor, then poled around while placing the decoys; I remembered to leave an open area directly in front of my blind. The decoys in place, I poled my boat into the blind, adjusted the palm fronds, loaded my shotgun, then settled in to wait on daylight. The first bunch of birds flew into my decoys before daylight, I could hear them, heard them splash down, but could only see outlines of them from my blind. I had to wait, but daylight was coming on fast. Long before the sun hit the horizon it got light enough to see and shoot; the birds that had flown in earlier had moved over closer to the bank, they were in range but I didn't want to shoot them on the water. About that time a couple of mallards pitched into my decoys, I hadn't even seen them until they were right on top of me. I picked out the green head and dropped him with my first shot; at my shot the birds on the water flushed and a couple flared right over my decoys, I took another green head. I reloaded, looked around a bit, then moved my palm fronds at the back of the boat, then poled out and picked up the birds, two beautiful green head mallards. A fine start.

I was just getting back into my blind when a bunch of teal strafed my blind, circled out over the large part of the bight and then pitched back into my decoys. My first shot dropped two, my next two shots must have been salutes because I didn't cut a feather. I picked up the two teal, got back in my blind, and went to scouting the horizon. I could hear Elzie shooting some over in the pocket, it was a great beginning for the day, and the sun wasn't even above the horizon yet.

Elzie had given me one of his calls to use, it was hanging from a lariat around my neck, I had not even thought of it. Birds started working out toward the mouth of the bight, so I decided to see if I could attract their attention. I began with the high ball call just like Elzie had shown me and low and behold, it worked! As they came closer I went to a feeding call. It looked like they were committed to my decoys so I shut up. They pitched in over the decoys down low, I picked out the first bird and dropped him the first shot, the others headed skyward, I pulled on the closest bird, fired and he turned loose. As I poled out to retrieve the birds I saw that both were male pintails. I returned to my blind, spread out the six birds on my floor board, and realized I had my limit. I sure wanted to keep shooting, but I unloaded my gun, cased it, then sat there for the next hour and a half watching birds come and go out of the bight.

The sun's reflection on the water turned the bight into a scenic movie. Birds were continually circling over the brown and green reeds, mullet jumping occasionally, and the sun's heat created a mist along the marsh edge. It was one of the most beautiful mornings in my life. I practiced with the call some, but mostly just watched the birds, where they were coming from and which direction they were headed. In one of our discussions Elzie had told me that if I would spend time in the marsh just watching the birds, watching their flight patterns, and find out where they were feeding, I'd kill a lot more birds than just always sitting in a blind. Today it all made sense. It was almost 9:30 when I picked up the decoys and headed back toward the pocket.

Elzie was already anchored in the channel, he had his limit too. We headed back to the house boat, as we unloaded our birds and gear, placing the birds on the back porch table, Elzie looked over at me and said "Happy Thanksgiving!" It was the best ever. We gutted the birds, washed them really good, and iced them down. While doing that Elzie made a suggestion about the afternoon hunt, "I saw a lot of birds flying over the marsh island out in front of the pocket this morning, I don't think they were feeding out there, but it sure looks like a flight pattern. Why don't we try a shoot out there this afternoon?" I told him it sounded good to me, and he continued, "It's a big flat out there, and the tide will be down this afternoon, so let's take a couple of crates with us to sit on and we'll just sit in the marsh, and maybe get some pass shooting. Let's use all 18 decoys."

Around 3:00 we headed back to the bay, we passed the pocket cutoff and ran just another couple hundred yards to the edge of the marsh island that lies between the main channel of East River and the eastern channel, both of which empty into the bay. The marsh island is about 4 acres in size. We pulled my boat into the marsh at the edge of the channel, anchored it well, broke some marsh reeds over it for camouflage, then hauled the two crates, a bag of decoys, and our shot guns and shells around to the bayside of the island. We spread the decoys fairly wide, but laid them out in a half circle, leaving a landing site for the ducks right in front of our blind site. We hunkered down and started waiting, the tide was dropping, exposing some flats, but we still had some water in front of us, the wind was picking up out of the northwest. No birds were moving so I started a conversation with Elzie, "Have you ever used a retriever for duck hunting?"

That almost smile crept over his face, "Oh yeah, Walter presented me with a gift one year just before duck season started, probably 20 or more years ago. I was working on my duck boat, getting it ready for the season, and he walks up and hands me a rope. On the other end of the rope was the damnedest looking Chesapeake Bay Retriever you've ever seen. He must have weighed 100 pounds. So, the dog walks up to me and bites me."

"What?"

"And Walter said, look he likes you."

"That son-of-a-bitch drew blood. Walter thought it was funny. But that dog sure could retrieve. Blind retrieves were a snap, you could wave him in any direction. But he had a bad disposition. One day we were headed over to the marsh, the bay was choppy, and some of my decoys were bouncing around in the boat. I reached to move a couple and the dog turns around and bites me again." By this time I was already laughing at Elzie,

"So what did you do?' I asked.

"I threw the son-of-a-bitch out of the boat, and went on to my blind."

"You left him?"

"Well, I tried to, but he swam along behind me and by the time I got my decoys out and started into the blind, the dog swims up and climbs in the boat. I was afraid to try to throw him out again, I figured he'd bite me again."

The first bunch of birds to check us out were about a dozen teal, flying down wind, cruising along just a little faster than the speed of shot gun pellets; I say that because Elzie told me to take a shot, then laughed at me when I didn't cut a feather with three shots. "I just wanted to see how you would do!" and he laughed some more. I reloaded, checked for more birds in the air. Seeing none I asked again about the dog,

"So the dog worked out okay?"

"No, he made it a habit of biting me. But I figured I'd pay him back one day. We were sitting in the blind over by Long Point Bight, the tide was way out, the decoys laying over on their sides, and the dog goes to whining. I looked out on the flats and there's a big boar coon. I mean a really big coon. So, I decided that it was about time for that dog to get his ass whopped. I smiled at the dog and said fetch. Out he goes and the closer he gets to the coon the faster he gets. The coon started to run but the dog had him cut off from the marsh, and in just a few steps the coon realizes he didn't have anywhere to run to, so he bows up for a fight. About that time the dog hit him, he hadn't slowed up yet. They rolled I bet you 25 yards. When they stopped the coon was dead. So, the son-of-a-bitch picks up the coon and brings him back to me and drops him at my feet and goes and sits back down on the bow of the boat. Acted real satisfied about the whole thing."

The next bunch of birds came along about then, made the same rocket diving pitch over our decoys, headed down wind, we let them pass; they sailed out over the bay, turned around and sailed back into our decoys bucking the wind, we dropped four. I made the retrieve, reloaded my gun, then asked again about the dog, "So everything did work out?"

"Not exactly, Walter called me one day, he was already staying a lot on Little St. George, and said that some geese were watering in Sand Island Pond, and that I should come harvest a few. The dog and I met him that afternoon at his house on Little St. George. The next morning well before daylight I took the jeep to the end of the timber, then the dog and I walked the rest of the way to the pond. It was still dark when we got there, so we found a dry spot with cover and settled in to wait on the geese.

The wind had picked up quite a bit out of the south, the surf sounded like thunder. The sun was well up when geese arrived, there were at least a dozen birds. They didn't even circle the pond, just set their wings and sailed in directly over me. My first two shots dropped birds, but my third shot was off a bit and, though I hit the bird, he locked up and sailed toward the gulf. The dog immediately broke for the bird headed toward the gulf. I screamed at him to stop. He never even slowed. I reloaded, picked up the two geese closest to me and headed toward the gulf to get the dog. The sea was pounding the beach. I followed the dog's tracks to the gulf, to where he went into the gulf. I stood there for what seemed like a long time, I yelled for him several times, but couldn't see him anywhere. A deep sadness came over me as I realized he was gone. I decided I should go, hell that dog had caused me enough trouble anyway."

"You left him? He died?" I couldn't believe that Elzie would leave the dog, how could he? That almost smile returned to Elzie's face, he turned toward me and continued,

"Well, I thought he had. I was about half way back to the jeep when I heard the damndest commotion coming up behind me. I turned around and here comes that big son-of-a-bitch carrying that goose. The goose was still alive and his one good wing was flapping and beating the hell out of that dog, and the goose started honking and yelling with every bound the dog made. Right then I would not have taken $10,000 for that dog." Elzie directed his attention back toward the bay, reflective thoughts tightened his eyes.

"What happened?" I needed to know.

"Well, I reached down and took the bird, and that son-of-a-bitch bit me again." I started laughing, trying to picture Elzie and that dog. It seemed they would have made a perfect pair.

Over the next couple of hours we had several bunches of ducks check us out, some decoyed, most did not, but before sunset we picked up six more birds, mostly teal, and called it a day. Back at the house boat Elzie said he would gut the birds if I would gather some firewood and get us a fire started. I was just starting the fire when he said he'd fix supper.

I sat by the fire until I couldn't stand smelling the food cooking any longer, I went in to see what he was fixing. He was about ready to serve when I walked in, he had brought some left over greens from Owl Creek, but he had taken two teal, cut the breast and legs off of each, sautéed them in butter and soy sauce, then made a brown gravy from the remaining sauce, then simmered the breast and legs in the gravy. For the greens he had a pepper sauce, and the teal were placed over toast, and covered with gravy.

The first bite sat on my tongue for as long as I could hold it, the flavors melting in my mouth, the pepper sauce from the greens blending with the soy gravy. The freshness of the duck breast was unlike any meat I had ever eaten. Only hours before those birds had come in from the north, an annual pilgrimage followed for thousands of years. It was the best Thanksgiving meal ever.

Later that evening, while sitting around the fire, I asked Elzie what ever happened to the dog. He told me that Walter knew a guy that owned a farm just north of Marianna, and he wanted a dog. So, Elzie gave the dog to the farmer. According to the farmer the dog turned out to be the best dog ever. He seemed to like having a job looking out for the cows and sheep the farmer raised. Elzie said the farmer told him that the dog would often stay out in the field at night just protecting the sheep. He never bit the farmer.

Friday morning Elzie and I traded blinds, he went to Sam's Bight, I went to East River Pocket, he took the 12 decoys, I took six. Just at daylight I had five wood ducks land in my decoys, where they came from I have no idea, they were on the water before I even saw them. I downed two as they exploded off the water as I stood up to shoot. Both were males, their colors were awesome. Just before the sun hit the horizon six mallards circled the pocket at least twice, then pitched into my decoys. They were feet down when I made my first shot, two were close together and I killed both on my first shot, then got a third as the rest headed toward the bay. After that the activity came to a halt, according to Elzie that's normal, the birds start shying away from the marsh after the first couple of days of shooting, but I had five and I was pleased with my first opening of duck season. I was anchored in the channel when Elzie came from Sam's Bight, I followed him back to the house boat. We gutted the ducks, packed our gear, secured the house boat, then headed to Owl Creek. I followed Elzie in my boat.

Cloud and Tess were not at the landing when we got there, so we made a few trips back and forth from the landing to the house, but we were still completely unpacked, and ready to pick the ducks before lunch. Cloud and Tess had gone somewhere so Elzie and I took the ducks to Cloud's small barn behind her house. Elzie had a butane gas burner there and a large pot, he filled the pot with water and put it on the burner to heat. He pulled out a folding table, covered it with some waxed paper, and placed the ice chest next to the table. As the water got hot Elzie put a small amount of liquid detergent in the water and turned the temperature down so the water wouldn't boil. He retrieved two stakes about 18 inches long and gave me one, then told me to pay attention. We both had crates to sit on, and Elzie placed a large wash tub between the grates.

Elzie took one of the ducks, held it by its head and using the stake he submerged the duck's body and held it completely under water for about a minute. He then held the duck over the wash tub for another minute to drain and then began picking the feathers from the duck's breast first, then the back and legs. He explained, "The detergent helps cut the oil in the duck fat making the feathers easier to pluck, but never use too much detergent, you don't want ducks tasting like soap. Also, don't submerge the ducks in the hot water very long or they'll begin to cook. Don't worry about the wings, not enough meat there, we'll cut them off." He gave me a duck and said get started. After picking each duck, we cut the wings off, trimmed the legs at the knuckle above the feet, and severed the head at the neck. We then stacked them on the wax paper to drain and cool. I think we had 28 ducks, it took us just over an hour, but wow, they looked great. We took them to the kitchen to wash and clean really well, then put them in the refrigerator to get cold, some would be frozen later.

About the time we finished Cloud and Tess drove into the yard. Tess was all smiles, waved a map in front of me, and said we had a plan. I agreed but she first must come see our ducks. After lunch Tess let me rest for a little while, but by four o'clock we were on the back porch, Cloud was with us. She first started by telling us that we would be meeting with Alice Robertson. I recognized the name, she was the person Cloud mentioned when we were discussing my report. Cloud gave us directions, signs to look for as we got close to Columbus, then more directions to Mrs. Robertson's house, and particularly what to look for regarding the subdivision she lived in. We got her address and her phone number in case we got lost. Cloud said Mrs. Robertson would expect us between ten and eleven Saturday morning. It should take us around four hours to get there. After Cloud finished with all the directions she asked if we had any questions, I said I had one. She gave me a questionable look, raised her eye brows. I asked, "What am I supposed to ask her? How is she connected to the gold or the war?"

Cloud sat back, looked at me and said, "Well, I guess I never did tell you about her did I?" I shook my head no, so she continued, "Remember me telling you about Columbus during the Civil War? Remember it had a foundry, and Columbus was an industrial center in the South before and during the Civil War. Lots of material, guns, ships, merchandise was shipped to Apalachicola from Columbus during the Civil War. The bulk of the cotton shipped to foreign nations during the Civil War came from Columbus and through Apalachicola. The Union Army tried to blockade the Apalachicola Bay and River, but there were a few sailors, with fast ships that could outrun the Union Navy, that worked out of Apalachicola. The relationships with foreign nations centered around those sailors and the cargo they delivered. Toward the end of the Civil War, when it appeared that the Union could out-man the Confederacy, Jefferson Davis sought help from a foreign nation."

At that point I spoke up, "Wasn't it Spain?" Cloud smiled and said she was proud that I had done my research, then she continued with her explanation.

"That effort to enlist foreign help centered around Columbus and Apalachicola. Mrs. Robertson's grandmother worked at the foundry, and she has information that I believe will help with your report." I couldn't put it together in my head, but I trusted Cloud, matter of fact, I figured Cloud had all the answers but just wouldn't give them to me, she expected me to work for it. I figured I'd get through with this report work and then start working on something that's really important, like decoying ducks in late season. The evening went quickly, Tess and I made plans, and by 10:30 everyone was down for the night.

Elzie woke me at 5:00 the next morning. Our plan was to be on the road by 6:00 AM. I got dressed, had a bowl of cereal, and was ready well before 6:00 when Tess showed up. While waiting for Tess, Elzie called me to the back porch. I sat down next to him, he reached into his pants pocket and handed me $50. I said, "Wow, that's a lot, we're not going for the weekend, just up there and back." He smiled at me and said it's always smart to have a back-up plan. Tess arrived within a few minutes, she had a note pad with her, all the instructions and telephone number. Elzie, Cloud, and Alida all gathered at the car to send us off. As we got into the car Tess turned to her Mom and Cloud and said, "We're not leaving for college, we're just going for the day; we should be home before 5 this afternoon." They smiled, but the look on their faces showed the concern. We waved good bye as we drove out of the yard in Cloud's car.

As soon as we were out of sight Tess slid over and kissed me on the cheek and said, "This is fun!" The car was full of gas, Tess said she and Cloud had filled it up yesterday when they went to Bristol for the map, so we headed north on Highway 65. We took 65 to Quincy and on to Bainbridge; at Bainbridge we took Highway 27 North to Blakely and continued to Columbus. We were still a ways away from Columbus but Tess pulled out her notes and started reading, "We're supposed to look for the first sign for the National Civil War Navel Museum, from there it's approximately two miles to Morgan Road, on the left, we're to take Morgan Road to the first left, approximately one half mile, then turn left on River Road. A few hundred yards down the road there is a small subdivision on the left, across the street from the river, we're to turn in there and go to number 224. That's Mrs. Robertson's home."

We followed the instructions without any problems and when we knocked on Mrs. Robertson's door it was 10:15. The door opened within a minute and there stood a small, elderly woman, almost the exact image of Mama Sol. Their faces weren't just alike, but their build, the way they wore their hair, the way they carried their bodies, they could have been sisters. Mrs. Robertson's hair was gray, very long, and pulled behind her head and tied, not a pony tail, just pulled together and hanging down her back. She wore a simple day dress, and sandals. She smiled at us, and I started, "Mrs. Robertson?" She nodded, "My name is Matthew Drugar, Cloud sent us to see you. This it Tess Crawford, she's Cloud's niece." She smiled again and said for us to come in.

The first thing I noticed when we drove into her yard was that the house looked exactly like Mama Sol's. It wasn't the same color, but the construction was the same, the same house plan. Inside it was the same floor plan as Mama Sol's. Mrs. Robertson directed us through her house to the back porch, it also was just like Mama Sol's. We took seats on the porch, she asked if we wanted tea or anything, we said no, so she sat down and asked what she could do for us. I felt that I should explain everything, but before I started Tess took over, "Mrs. Robertson, my mother is Cloud's sister, her name is Alida, she's a Taylor." At that, Mrs. Robertson smiled and nodded like it had special meaning. Tess continued, "Sol is my grandmother, my mother's and Cloud's mother, they all send their best wishes to you." I felt that I should say something as an opening, a special appreciation, but I didn't have a clue.

I started to speak, stopped, then started again, but before I could Mrs. Robertson turned her attention to me and said, "Young Drugar, you look very much like your Papa and Grandpapa!" Okay, I sure didn't see that one coming, but it was very obvious she knew a lot more about my family than I did hers.
I finally got my mouth to work and asked, "How do you know my father and grandfather?"

She smiled at me, then at Tess, then continued, "I knew your grandfather when he was a powerful timber man here in Columbus; I saw your father when he was just a boy."

"Are you and Mama Sol related?" I asked. Mrs. Robertson's expressions never seemed to change, she never quite gave a big smile, though she did smile some; there was a calmness about her, a tranquility. She directed her attention toward me again.

"No, we are not blood relatives, but we are from the same tribe. We were raised around here. Sol went to Florida around 1926." I kept trying to think of something to talk about without jumping right into why we were there.

I wanted to be polite, but my mind was focused on only one thing. I finally just jumped in, "Mrs. Robertson, the reason I needed to talk to you is because of something Cloud told me. You see, I'm working on a report for my history class, it's about the Civil War, and Cloud suggested that I write my report about something you don't find in the history books, it's about gold and a foreign nation that might have changed the outcome of the Civil War." She nodded as if she understood, so I continued, "I've read a lot lately, and just recently found out that Spain was sympathetic to the Confederacy. I believe they may have desired to intervene in the war." She smiled again, somewhat, so I continued again, "What I don't know, what I can't find is why they didn't, or what even stopped them from intervening. I've never seen anything written giving a time line when Spain may have attempted to intervene, or where they would intervene, or who they may have worked with in the Confederacy." Mrs. Robertson sat there listening to me, nodding occasionally, almost smiling, being very polite, but not talking. So I decided to shut up and wait for her to talk. She didn't, she just sat there, I assume, thinking, but she didn't say anything for what seemed like a long time. I looked at Tess, she smiled at me, but no one talked.

After a few minutes that seemed like hours Mrs. Robertson got up and walked out of the room. She didn't tell us to wait, or go, or anything. I gave Tess my "what now look", she shrugged her shoulders in "I don't know" fashion, and we just sat there. After a bit Mrs. Robertson returned carrying what looked like a ledger book. Before sitting down she suggested we all have some tea, Tess said that would be lovely, I just nodded. Mrs. Robertson put the ledger book down then turned and went into the kitchen, she returned shortly with a pitcher of ice tea and three glasses. She poured each of us a glass then sat down. I sipped on my tea, trying to think, but I realized that much of my life I always found myself in situations that I just didn't know what to say or how to keep a conversation going. It puzzled me, it always puzzled me. Tess complimented Mrs. Robertson on the tea, I nodded and smiled, I said nothing. Finally Mrs. Robertson began, "Matthew, my grandmother worked at the Columbus foundry during the Civil War, she was young, beautiful, and she had learned English very well, she spoke without an accent. She and her family had assimilated very well in the white world, it's how they survived. She had other family members that worked at the foundry. Some of them worked in the metal division, they made weapons, tools, ship parts; others helped with melting and minting of bullion and coins.

Columbus was a major center for industry and shipping before the war and during the war. In late 1862 the Bank of Louisiana sent a few million dollars' worth of gold to the Iron Bank of Columbus because they expected the Union forces to overtake New Orleans. For the next two plus years that gold helped fund the war for the Confederacy.

My grandmother worked for a woman who oversaw and managed some of the melting and minting, but directed most of the shipping. My grandmother was smart, but she always knew she had to be careful exposing what she knew, how she knew it, and what information was most important. The people at the foundry did not know she was of Indian ancestry. Every night when she returned home from work she would write down the information she thought was important, and she wrote it here." And she patted the ledger book. By then my mind was running a thousand miles an hour, I wanted to see everything, know all about everything, I had so many questions I didn't even know where to start. Thank goodness I didn't open my mouth, I'm sure I would have sounded like a babbling baby or a sick dog.

After another long silence Mrs. Robertson continued, "When shipping anything, my grandmother's boss would have her send letters to the intended receiver days before the shipment to confirm the shipment date. Many times my grandmother would also send letters after the shipment to make sure the shipment was received. She knew most all of the merchants and sailors that she corresponded with regarding shipments. As for shipments to Apalachicola she also had a sister there and she corresponded with her often; her sister was very involved with the war efforts on the part of the Confederacy.

By the time 1865 arrived the war was not going well for the Confederacy, the Union forces had seized most of the South's shipping ports, arrested and jailed many of the Confederate soldiers, and were moving lots of troops into Alabama, Georgia, and Florida. The Confederacy realized it needed foreign help. Jefferson Davis requested help from leaders in Columbus to explore avenues to reach possible foreign leaders who would intervene on the Confederacy's side. My grandmother's boss knew who to contact. The best sailor in Apalachicola, who was most efficient at blockade running, also delivered most of the cotton shipped to Apalachicola to the Spanish authorities in Cuba. His name was Frederick Buck.

Mr. Buck did make contact with the Spanish soldiers and evidently an agreement was made; funds to support the war were to be delivered to them in Cuba. The shipment was scheduled, the correspondence sent, and the shipment was sent to Mr. Buck on or about the 5th of March, 1865." And then she opened the ledger, spread the pages and turned them around to where Tess and I could see the notations. It read $364,000 in gold sent to Frederick Buck, March 5, 1865. Confirmation letter sent to S. McKenzie, February 15, 1865. Follow-up sent March 7, 1865. $300,000 in bullion, $40,000 in American gold coins, $24,000 in Spanish gold coins.

McKENZIE ! That's the name of the lady in Apalachicola. I almost yelled with excitement. Cloud had given me that name, never told me anything about her, and now I find out that the family in Columbus was connected to the family in Apalachicola. I had to see Miss Mac first thing on Monday, I needed an introduction to Mrs. McKenzie in Apalachicola.

Thank goodness Tess was there, my mind was running a mile a minute, I had more questions than I could ask, but Tess had her pad in hand and writing everything she could as fast as she could. My first response, after reading the amount of gold sent, was what happened to the gold? Mrs. Robertson flipped a few more pages of the ledger and read aloud to us, "Shipment interrupted by Union forces near Fort Gadsden, ship severely damaged, twelve of the fifteen man crew found dead, ship ran aground down river. Union forces thought to be a patrol, including free black men, sixteen men found dead. No one remained. Gold missing from ship."

I sat back in my chair, trying to visualize the scene, wondering who and how someone reported the event. I finally had to ask, "How did the information get back to Columbus?" Mrs. Robertson smiled at me, kind of like Cloud smiled at me when I asked if Spain was the foreign country, then explained that letters and different communications were sent separate from the shipments. If shipments went by water, down river, then communications went by rail, if available, if not, then by horse, the old pony express. And in some parts of the South there was the telegraph. There were communities between Columbus and Apalachicola, communications were relayed through them. I sat there listening, trying to take it all in, trying not to ask stupid questions, but of course, I had to ask, "Did anybody ever find out what happened to the gold?"

Again, Mrs. Robertson smiled at me, then shook her head no, but then added, "Many people have speculated about the gold, some say the Confederate troops that didn't get killed on that trip took the gold; others say the Union troops took the gold, though they would have had to have a boat to get across the river where the Confederate ship ran aground. Some say the gold is at the bottom of the river just waiting on someone to find it." I tried to imagine each scenario as she described it, considering the weight of the gold the only one that made any sense to me was that it was on the river bottom somewhere.

After a bit, I asked, "What do you think happened to the gold?" She just kept smiling at me, it made me feel stupid again. She reached over and had a sip of tea, asked if we needed more tea, we both nodded no, so she turned her attention to me again.

"Matthew, Indian legend says that the Apalachicola Indians, those that remained behind and lived in the swamps, found the ship that had run aground, and they found the gold and hid it in the swamps. No one has seen or heard of the gold since." I didn't have anything else to say or ask. Cloud's approach to me was a mystery, now I understood why. It was a mystery, an unsolved mystery. Somehow I had to put it in writing, build my story, entertain my audience, and earn an A in history. We sat there a bit longer, my mind was deep in thought, I was already enlarging my outline. Finally Tess reached over and touched my shoulder, it brought me back to the present, so I turned to Mrs. Robertson and thanked her so much for sharing her knowledge with us. I asked if there was anything we could do for her, but again she just smiled and said she was glad that she could help.

Tess and I were getting up to leave when the lights kicked on again in my brain, I turned to Mrs. Robertson and asked, "Mrs. Robertson, I'm not trying to be nosy or disrespectful, but can I ask you a question?" She looked at me without smiling and said certainly. I wasn't sure that I should even ask, but I did, "Mrs. Robertson, are you Yellow Bird?"

It was the first big smile I had seen out of her, she reached and took my hand and said, "Yes, that is my given name. And you can call me Yellow Bird anytime you speak to me. Thank you for asking, and thank you for coming to see me. I trust we will meet again." Finally I felt I had done something right. She walked Tess and me to the door, and as we started out, Yellow Bird took my hand again and said, "Ashwanna!" We smiled at her, then left.

As we drove away from her house she was on the front stoop, waving good-bye. Tess turned to me, "How did you know she was Yellow Bird?" I reminded her that Mama Sol had told Cloud to send me to see Yellow Bird. It all made sense, they were all from the same tribe. We were south of Columbus when Tess asked me a question, "Matt, what was the difference in American gold coins and Spanish gold coins? I thought gold was gold, that it didn't matter who minted it."

"From what I've read Spanish gold coins were the preferred currency from the 1700s to until the middle 1850s. The United States demonetized foreign currencies in 1857, but gold coins from other nations remained in use up to the late 1800s or even the early 1900s. The original Spanish gold coins were not minted like the circular coins we recognize, they were stamped into different shapes, but the controlling factor was weight. The US gold coins had face values, as in a $5 gold piece, or a $20 gold piece. The Spanish coins were based on weight. They were called escudo denominations, or pieces of eight. They were minted in one, two, four, and eight escudos. If it was an eight escudos, they were called doubloons. From what I can determine that's about an ounce of gold."

"Well, if I had my choice it would be a gold necklace."

Chapter 13: The Report

It was 4:30 when we drove into Cloud's yard. She and Elzie, Alida and Sage were on the back porch, everyone seemed really pleased to see us; maybe it was just relief that we weren't broken down somewhere in South Georgia. We gathered on the back porch and were asked a thousand questions, we kept saying it was just a long drive, but they wanted to know everything. Before we even got to the part about Yellow Bird, Mama Sol came over to hear our story.

Tess pulled out her notes and everyone got gold fever. It was lots of fun, I got the feeling it wasn't the first time the discussion had happened on this porch. Elzie didn't have much to say, he just sat back and grinned a lot. I told Cloud and Mama Sol about asking Mrs. Robertson if she was Yellow Bird, and her reaction; they were tickled with the story and glad I did what I did. I turned to Cloud and asked, "Cloud, what does Ashwanna mean?" That got Mama Sol's and her attention, she asked where I heard the word, I told her it's the last thing Yellow Bird said to me as we left. Cloud went into teacher mode, Tess and I tuned in.

"Ashwanna is an old term, it means different things in different societies. Some people believe it means 'God's gift,' our tribe always used it to say 'may the great spirit lead you' as if on a journey, or through an ordeal. It's considered a holy word, it transcends different people and places." That got me thinking, a journey? I hadn't thought of this report as a journey, just a project. Maybe an ordeal? That it had been. But I still had lots to do, and I needed to get it finished by the end of next week. Tess said she would type it for me, but I had to get it written.

The evening passed quickly, and by ten o'clock the next morning I was loaded in my boat and headed home, I had Tess's notes with me. Dad picked me up at the boat basin and hauled my boat home. I unpacked quickly, put my shot gun away and started working on my report. I reviewed the outline, wrote more notes on it, then got started. I needed to talk to Miss Mac the next morning to get an introduction to Mrs. McKenzie, hopefully she could help me with any missing details, or at least substantiate the correspondence and maybe the shipment. I still wasn't sure how, or even why, I wanted to introduce the Indians into the report, but I felt I needed it, especially now that no one ever found the gold. Cloud had said there was a lot that didn't end up in the history books!

After reading my notes for the fourteenth time I decided that I should begin my report with a preface. I began by stating that Indians lived along the Apalachicola, Chattahoochee, and Flint rivers for more than a thousand years before the white man ever set foot on our shores. The first documented contact with the Florida Indians was from Hernando de Soto's expedition of Florida in 1539, but no colonization took place until the mid-1600s, and those were primarily Spanish missions.

By the 1700s France was sending expeditions to Florida as well. Most of the 1700s the Indians traded with Spanish and French explorers, often drawn into battles on both sides, but by the late 1700s to early 1800s English explorers appeared on the scene. In 1819 Spain ceded Florida to the United States, but the transfer did not occur until 1821. By then European settlers were coming in droves to the rich farm land of the South. Their economic futures depended on a new trade, cotton. But before a cotton culture could develop along the interior valley, the Indians had to be removed from their land.

At first the Indians sold large parcels of land to the United States. Soon after the United States suggested the Indians be moved to reservations in the South. But in 1830 the United States created the Indian Removal Act of 1830. Most Indians did not want to leave their land and by 1836 the Creek War broke out, and by 1843 Niles' Register proclaimed that all of the Indians had been removed from the South. However, a small group of Creek Indian descendants remained in their tribal land and currently live on a reservation which is 57 miles from Mobile, Alabama. What the history books don't tell you is that many of the larger tribes broke into small family size groups and never left their homeland, they moved into the swamps, off the fertile farm land. History proves that they assimilated into the white man's world.

For my report introduction to the Civil War I wanted to first give an overview to the reason for secession, the wealth that was created from cotton, and the reaction to the abolitionists. By 1828 the first bales of cotton appeared on shipping receipts in Apalachicola, by 1830 2400 bales were shipped, and by 1836 51,673 bales were shipped to Europe, and in 1845 153,392 bales were shipped out of Apalachicola. Cotton was king! Wealth was being created all over the South. Brokers and cotton merchants traded on existing cotton shipments and also future cotton production. From farms connected to the Apalachicola, Chattahoochee, and Flint Rivers to the Banks that financed the cotton productions and shipments a common currency evolved, bank notes. They were traded for goods and services just like minted coins or bullion. Bank notes from Columbus could be traded for goods or services in Apalachicola and vice versa, but the final payment filtered back to gold, in bullion or in minted gold coins, and also in silver.

The primary success of the South as cotton producers and other farm products was directly related to one thing, free labor, slavery. The North had, for years, opposed slavery, and though these issues had existed for decades, they exploded in 1860 following the election of Abraham Lincoln. As a result of his election, South Carolina, Alabama, Georgia, Louisiana, and Texas seceded from the Union.

On April 12, 1861, the war began when Brig. General Beauregard opened fire on Fort Sumter in Charleston harbor forcing its surrender. Lincoln called for volunteers to suppress the rebellion, but Virginia, North Carolina, Tennessee and Arkansas refused and joined the Confederacy.

Union forces were defeated at the battle of Bull Run, and again at Manassas. This saw the rise of Robert E. Lee. He defeated General Hooker at the battle of Chancellorsville, Va. In February 1862, forces under General Ulysses S. Grant captured Forts Henry and Donelson. Two months later he defeated Confederate troops at Shiloh, Tennessee. By December Grant focused on capturing Vicksburg and opening the Mississippi River. By June 1863, Lee began a move north to Pennsylvania, on July 1st he and his army clashed with Union troops at Gettysburg; after three days of fighting Lee was defeated and forced to retreat. This was the beginning of the end for the Confederacy. In the summer of 1863 Union forces advanced into Georgia, and the following Spring General Sherman took Atlanta, then marched to Savannah. In March 1864 Grant was given command of all Union forces. By the end of 1864 it was becoming obvious that the Union was out-manning the Confederacy.

Columbus, Georgia, had been an industrial center for the South before and remained so during the Civil War. It had a foundry there which made guns, tools, ship parts, and other metal utensils; it also minted gold and silver.

During the Civil War many products, including cotton, were sent to Apalachicola to be shipped overseas. The Union army tried for most of the war to blockade the Apalachicola Bay; their ships were too big to sail the bay, so they stayed off shore near the passes into the bay. Blockade running was limited to several excellent sailors who possessed fast schooners which could also sail in shallower waters. When Union forces were able to reach Apalachicola, locals would put a barrel on one of the widow walks on the larger houses that could be seen from the river, alerting the Confederate soldiers that the Union forces were in town.

One such sailor, known for his skill in avoiding Union forces, also transported the majority of the cotton sent to Apalachicola to Cuba for the benefit of Spanish forces; that sailor's name was Frederick Buck. In 1862 millions of dollars in gold was transported to the Iron Bank of Columbus from New Orleans because the Confederacy expected Union troops to over-run the City. That money was used to support the Confederacy for the next two plus years. Toward the end of 1864 Jefferson Davis knew that for the Confederacy to succeed it may require help from a foreign nation; on or about November of 1864 he sent a message to the leaders in Columbus to pursue help from Spain.

The lady who oversaw shipping from the foundry knew the sailors capable of negotiating such request, she chose Frederick Buck. Mr. Buck sailed to Cuba, negotiated an agreement, and sent the information to Ms. McKenzie, head of shipping. Jefferson Davis gave the go-ahead. On February 15, 1865, Ms. McKenzie sent a message to her sister S. McKenzie in Apalachicola stating that her shipment would be sent on March 5, 1865. She confirmed that her order of 364 pieces would be delivered. On March 5, 1865, the shipment left Columbus by boat headed to Apalachicola. On March 7, 1865, Ms. McKenzie sent a confirmation letter to her sister that the shipment went out on schedule.

From my research, meeting with descendants from the foundry's employees, I saw notes written in a ledger book dated February 15, 1865, March 5, 1865, and March 7, 1865, stating that $300,000 in gold bullion, $40,000 in American gold coins, and $24,000 of Spanish gold coins were shipped to Frederick Buck by ship on March 5, 1865. Further notes stated: Shipment interrupted by Union forces near Fort Gadsden, ship severely damaged, twelve of fifteen man crew found dead, no survivors found, ship ran aground down river. Union forces thought to be a patrol including free black men, sixteen found dead, no one remained. Gold missing from ship.

I had almost finished my report, but I still hadn't spoken to Mrs. McKenzie who lives in Apalachicola. I decided to approach Miss Mac the next morning first thing, maybe call Mrs. McKenzie during lunch and hopefully see her Monday afternoon. I called Tess and read over everything I had written, so far I figured I should have probably six pages typed. She said she thought it sounded really good and was excited about helping with the typing. I told her I would call her tomorrow night and let her know how it went. I felt really tired, it seemed I'd been working on this project for days. It must be getting late, I went into the kitchen to get a snack before going to bed, it was only 2:30! Mom asked if I was feeling alright, she felt my head to make sure I wasn't running a fever, then told me to go watch TV, she'd fix me something good.

Dad was in the living room, I tried to tell him all about my report, but he really wasn't interested, but he did say he wanted to see the finished product. I told him it would be next week after Tess typed it for me, at that he suggested that I needed to take a typing class. Gun Smoke came on shortly after that and that ended our conversation. It was barely dark when I went to bed. I don't know if I even took off my clothes.

Monday morning I was up before Mom or Dad, it was the most sleep I'd had in a long time. Mom fixed breakfast, Dad had coffee with me, and I rode to school with him. I usually didn't like doing that because I'd have to stand around for half an hour waiting on school to begin. Today, I was waiting on Miss Mac when she arrived at her room, she looked surprised but asked what I was up to? "Miss Mac, I'm almost finished with my report on the Civil War, but I need your help." She just looked at me surprised like, so I continued, "From my research I found that there is someone in Apalachicola that I think can provide some important information, and I need you for an introduction."

Miss Mac just stood there looking at me like I had lost my mind, she shifted her weigh from one foot to the next, finally put her books down on her desk, turned back to address me and said, "Who is it?"

"Patricia McKenzie!"

"Well, at least you want to meet someone that appreciates history. Why do you want to talk to her?"

"Well, I've been told that she may have some information, articles, or correspondence that her grandmother may have saved….regarding the Civil War."

"I'll assure you that if her grandmother saved it, she'll have it. That woman doesn't throw anything away. I don't understand how anybody can live in a house like that. She's got stuff that was made before the Civil War, and she thinks they're all really valuable. I wouldn't give you ten cents for the whole lot. But you do what you must."

"How should I approach her?"

"Just tell her I sent you, she'll help."

"Okay, Miss Mac, thanks a lot. I hope to turn in my report next week."

"You had better! That's when it's due!"

During the lunch break I went into Dad's office and asked if I could use the phone. The assistant said sure, so I looked up Patricia McKenzie's phone number and dialed it. On the third ring she answered. "Mrs. McKenzie, my name is Matthew Drugar, James Drugar is my Dad, and Miss Mac, I mean Miss MacFadden, is my history teacher. She has us writing reports about the Civil War and she suggested to me that you may be able to help me."

"I'm sorry young man, what did you say your name was?"

"Matthew Drugar."

"And who is your Dad?"

"James Drugar, he's the principal at the school."

"Oh yes, I know James, fine young man. So, what is it you need?"

"I need some help with a history report I'm writing and Miss MacFadden suggested I talk to you."

"Well, you must be one of her pet students? She only refers students to me when they are her favorites."

"I sure hope so. Could I come talk with you this afternoon after school?"

"Sure you can, it just can't be before three o'clock, I have a hair appointment from one o'clock until three."

"That's fine, would three-thirty be okay with you?"

"Three-thirty? Yes, just not before three."

"Okay, and thank you Mrs. McKenzie, I really appreciate it, and I'll see you at three-thirty." As I hung up the phone, I had visions of walking into a haunted house, an old ghost sliding down her stair banister, big black cats starring out the windows. I got to thinking that if this doesn't turn out well, then all of my great efforts would be taken as make-believe. One source reporting doesn't get much credit. At sixth period I went over to the library and reviewed my report, at least what I had, with Miss Whithers. She acted really please and said she thought I had done an excellent job. I told her where I was going after school, even told her about the haunted house, the ghost sliding down the stair banister, and big black cats. She got a kick out of that.

At three-thirty I knocked on Patricia McKenzie's front door. She didn't come to the door, so I knocked again; about the fourth knock she opened the door. "Mrs. McKenzie, I'm Matthew Drugar. We spoke earlier." She was a small woman, looked to be in her late seventies, her hair was gray, but it was pulled into a bun in the back, she wore a bright blue day dress, and had on dark blue shoes that had thick but high heels. A pair of glasses hung on her nose, she looked at me above the glasses, not through them.

"Why yes, young man. Come right in." She had a two story house, very old, the house had big and tall windows, but each window was covered with what looked like quilts, almost no light shown in. There were only a few lights, at least there were only a few on. The floors were solid pine, the walls were painted but they appeared to be pine or cypress, the ceilings looked to be over 10 feet high. There was a large room on the right and she directed me to have a seat in there. There was a big couch, a couple of cloth covered chairs, and a rather large chandelier hanging in the middle of the room. I sat on one of the chairs, she sat on the other. "Now young man, what is it you're looking for?"

"Mrs. McKenzie, I'm writing a report on the Civil War, more particularly I'm writing my report about the relationship Columbus, Georgia had with Apalachicola during the Civil War. I was told that your Grandmother may have had a sister who worked at the foundry in Columbus during the Civil War? I was wondering if you had any old documents, maybe letters or other correspondence that were saved from that time?"

"Well let me see, I'm sure I must have something. Grandmama never threw anything away, neither did my Mama, and if they didn't throw it away, I felt I shouldn't either. Come on in here with me." And she got up and led me to the room across from the one we were sitting in. The door was closed but as the door opened I noticed that it was about the same size and shape as the other one.

She turned on a ceiling light, it was not a chandelier, but a single light bulb hanging from a long brass rod attached to the ceiling. It did not light up the room very well. She made some statement about the room not being very light, then turned on a couple of lamps that sat on dark end tables. There were book shelves that covered one solid wall, completely filled with books, a long dark table butted up against another wall. On that table boxes were stacked at least three boxes high, underneath the table boxes were stacked two deep and two high. Against another wall boxes were stacked two deep and at least five boxes high. I could feel the dust dancing toward my nose. Mrs. McKenzie turned to me and asked, "Now what year was it you wanted to explore?"

"I think it should be the last part of 1864 and the beginning of 1865." She got a serious look on her face, then started walking back and forth in front of boxes, first the ones on the floor, then the ones on the table. Once she opened one, gave it a glance, then closed it back up, and moved to another box. She stopped and looked at each box, for what I don't know, I couldn't see any writing or dating on the boxes, most just had dust on them. Finally she got down on her knees and started starring at the boxes under the table.

She turned to me and said I needed to help her, so I knelt down with her and she started pointing to different boxes and said, "Pull those out to where we can inspect them." I started pulling them out one at a time, she would open the box, look in, pick out a couple of folders, then put them back and say, "Pull out another one." That went on for at least six or seven boxes until she held a folder in her hands and said, "Now, let's see if this might be what you are looking for." She handed the file to me, I spread it on the floor and flipped through several sheets of notes, a couple of letters, but nothing seemed to make any sense. I told her not that one so she pulled out another one. We repeated the process probably five or six times until she handed me a folder that read "Columbus Foundry". I told her this may be the one, so she said for me to bring the box into the other room so we could get some light enough to read. We settled back into the chairs from before and I started going through the file.

There were letters to her grandmother, there were list of items ordered or sent, and notes about local happenings. I was on my third folder when I first saw Columbus Foundry letter head, the letter was dated February 15, 1865, and addressed to Sissy, it read, "I do trust that you are doing well. This war is wearing on all of us, certainly it will be over soon and we can get back to our lives again. I just wanted to confirm that your order will go out on March 5, 1865. All 364 pieces will be shipped. I will keep you informed if I receive any further information regarding your event. I am so looking forward to getting down there to see all of you or maybe getting you up here for a visit with us. God speed. Love, Lori"

I got excited thinking I might have solved my mystery! This was the proof I was looking for. I told Mrs. McKenzie that this was it, but she said that I should look some more, there was lots of correspondence in there. I put the letter aside and went back to reviewing the contents in the file. The very next letter was dated March 7, 1865, addressed to Sissy, it read, "Sissy, this will confirm that your order was shipped as planned on March 5, 1865. I hope all goes well. Please keep me informed as to how well you're holding up down there. I think of you often. Much love, Lori." I asked Mrs. McKenzie if I could take these letters with me, but she said she could not allow that, but I could copy them word for word, which I did. It took less than 20 minutes to copy everything I wanted. I thanked Mrs. McKenzie over and over again and told her I would let her know how well I did on my report. I practically ran all the way home. I had all I needed, now I just needed to finish with a good and solid closing. At the bottom of my report I wrote

Conclusion: I've been told that much of what happened in the past never made it into history books. Substantiated claims are often hard to come by, but I present to you correspondence which substantiates the ledger claims from Columbus, Georgia. I received the following letters from Patricia McKenzie, granddaughter of S. McKenzie, both dated in 1865.

February 15, 1865: Sissy: I do trust that you are doing well. This war is wearing on all of us, certainly it will be over soon and we can get back to our lives again. I just wanted to confirm that your order will go out on March 5, 1865. All 364 pieces will be shipped. I will keep you informed if I received any further information regarding your event. I am so looking forward to getting down there to see all of you or maybe getting you up here for a visit with us. God speed, Lori.

March 7, 1865: Sissy, this will confirm that your order was shipped as planned on March 5,1865. I hope all goes well. Please keep me informed as to how well you're holding up down there. I think of you often. Much love, Lori.

The 364 pieces represents the $364,000 worth of gold sent to Apalachicola. It never made it. What might have been the outcome of the Civil War had the shipment arrived in Apalachicola and later to Cuba? History books don't explore this event, but the big question is, "What happened to the gold?"

There are four possible outcomes:
1. The surviving Confederate troops on the ship took the gold and disappeared into the swamps.
2. The Union forces found the gold on the grounded ship and they took it.
3. The gold sank to the bottom of the river and was never found.
4. The Apalachicola Indians who remained in the swamp found the gold and hid it in the swamps.

From my point of view and opinion, based on the weight of the gold I doubt that the Confederate or the Union soldiers could have carried off the gold. It makes sense that the gold is lying on the river bottom somewhere. But Indian legend says that the Indians found the gold and hid it in the swamps. Maybe it's a just reward for the cruelty shown to them by the white man.

I took my finished report and read it to Mom. She said she really liked it. I read it to Dad when he got home, he said he really liked it too. I called Tess and read it to her, she said to bring it on, she was ready to type it. I asked if she could type it this week if I was able to get it up to her maybe tomorrow, she said certainly, so I told her I'd call her back after talking to Dad about borrowing his car after school tomorrow. At supper I asked Dad if I could use his car to take the report to Tess tomorrow so she could type it this week and he agreed. I called Tess after supper and told her I'd be there by 4:30 the next day. Today was Monday, December 1st, my report was due by Wednesday next week, December 10th, and school got out for Christmas on Friday December 19th. We wouldn't go back until January 5th, 1959.

I was ready for Christmas! Wait! I needed to get Tess something very nice for Christmas. That thought hit me like a brick. What in the world could I get Tess? It's a good thing I finished the report, I have lots to worry about. The next day when the last bell rang I went to Dad's office to pick up the keys to his car, he gave me five dollars and told me to fill it up. I said I'd be home by dark. At 4:15 I drove into Tess's back yard. She met me out back, gave me a hug and a kiss, then we went to the back porch to review my report. She made a few grammatical suggestions, I told her to correct everything she could. She said she'd have Cloud review it after she typed it. I asked her if she would type a couple of copies for me just so I'd have an extra one, a back-up plan. She laughed and said she would. I told her I'd be back Friday afternoon for the weekend. She was walking me to the car when Elzie drove into Cloud's yard, of course we went to visit with him.

He had a big smile on his face as we approached, "What are you doing up here in the school week?" I told him that Tess was going to type a report for me this week and I brought it up to her. "That's good, get the work done during the week, 'cause we have something special this weekend." That got both me and Tess fired up,

"What?" we both said at the same time.

"Saturday morning we have a dove hunt planned, and Tess is invited." Well, that did it, Elzie was now King of entertainment. I was excited, Tess was excited, I think we probably acted like little kids on Christmas morning. Tess asked if Cloud was going to join us, Elzie said that would depend on Cloud. The planning, it's almost as much fun as the actual event. I finally calmed down and said I hated to leave but I had to get home, Tess made me promise I'd call her as soon as I got home, and I left them standing in the back yard, waving good bye.

The drive home was a little sad as well as exciting, another dove hunt, a special hunt, with Tess. I called her as soon as I walked into the house. Mom and Dad sensed my excitement, asked me what's going on, I practically blurred out, "Tess is getting to go on a dove hunt with Elzie and me this Saturday." I think they were as pleased as I was. The Christmas season had begun. Happiness and excitement hung in the air like a thick fog; a new year was soon upon us. That evening I thought about all the things that had happened to me just since May, and I thought about all the things I wanted to happen during 1959. I was as happy as I'd ever been, and I was excited about what lay ahead. I never could have seen what was in store, and not all of it was for the best.

Chapter 14: The Knowing

The week moved along like a slow current, without football or baseball practice to go to in the afternoons, boredom followed me home after school each day and it slipped under the door when I tried closing it out. I kept thinking about what I should get Tess for Christmas. I knew better than to give her clothes, or books, or just about any girl-thing, because if I picked it out she'd probably have to exchange it for something else. And, I knew better than to ask my Mom to help pick anything out, Tess would know as soon as she opened the present that Mom had helped. It needs to be something from me, by me, for her, and only her. At least I had something to worry about all week, maybe a lot longer. I never thought of myself as a worrier, but I think I had the curse, it seemed I was always worrying about something. This year I also needed to get Mom and Dad something special, and that was something I could talk to Tess about. I'd do it this weekend.

Dad agreed to let me use his car for the weekend so when Friday's classes came to an end I went to his office to get the keys. My bags were already packed, my gun and shells ready. I'd also packed the 20 gauge and some shells for Tess, so it didn't take but a few minutes before I was headed out the door. I gave Mom a kiss, something I hardly ever did, but she seemed pleased, she gave me a strange look, then said for me to be careful. I told her I would and if she needed me just call Cloud or Tess, either of them would know where I was.

I drove into Cloud's back yard just about the time Tess arrived home from school. Sage was with her so I told her I'd be over to her house as soon as I unpacked. They were waiting on me on the back porch. Tess had made a pitcher of ice tea and had some snacks spread on a table. Sage was munching on something and didn't even look up as I entered the room. Tess handed me a folder titled "The lost treasure of the Confederacy". Before I even opened the folder Tess said that Cloud gave me an A! My heart soared. I started reading the report but I didn't notice any corrections from what I had given Tess earlier in the week. I asked about any corrections, she said there were few and mostly were only commas and quotation marks. She also said that Cloud had reviewed it before she typed it, and felt it justified an A. There were three copies in the folder and she had added the title to each. After we put the report away we stayed on the porch waiting on everyone else to come home. We talk about the hunt for the next morning, Tess acted like I should know all about it, but I had to tell her that this would be the first morning dove hunt I'd ever been on. My only dove hunts had been on Little St. George, at least where we actually kill some birds, the outings at the airport had never produced any birds.

At some point we got around to talking about Christmas and I asked Tess for help with presents for my Mom and Dad. She asked what they liked, I said I didn't really know, so she started with questions, first about Dad. "What's his favorite hobby?" I don't know. "What's his favorite sport?" I don't know. "What's his favorite clothing?" I don't know. "Does he wear hats?" Not that I recall. "Then why don't you buy him a really cool hat, something he can wear to ball games as well as a hunt?" I thought that sounded like a good idea, wow, that was easy!

"Yea, and you know what I could do?" I said. Tess looked surprised, when I went from not knowing anything to having a great idea.

"What?" she asked.

"It's a big deal when you kill your first green head mallard, they have a tail feather that curls, so we always stick one on our hunting caps, or any other cap we wear, to show off our first green head. I could get Dad a really nice hat and stick one of my curl feathers in it for him." I don't really know if Tess thought that was a good idea, but she did smile and said good, now what about your

Mom? I started with Mom by saying that I really wanted to do something special for her. She's always supportive of my activities, with the exception of pulling jokes on judges.

Again Tess started with the questions, clothes first, I nixed that pretty quickly, I certainly didn't want the responsibility of picking out women's clothes for Mom. She asked about jewelry, I told her I knew nothing about jewelry, so she asked what Mom wears to church or to an event. I told her I didn't know. She asked if Mom likes to wear a necklace? I told her I didn't know. She started looking concerned, I guess she thought that I never noticed anything about my parents. But she didn't change subjects, she asked if she had any necklaces? I said I guess so. Then she asked me to describe one that Mom wears. I said I couldn't, but I asked if she thought a necklace with a mallard curl feather would be cool? She slapped me on the shoulder with that one. She went on to say that women generally like jewelry, and that they couldn't have too much. I kept saying that I wanted it to be something special, something from me that represents me. She started talking about gemstones, suggesting maybe a diamond, rubies, sapphires, or even pearls. Pearls! That did it, I told her about the big oyster pearl I found, or it found me, on Little St. George when we went dove hunting. She thought that sounded perfect, and said Cloud has a friend that makes jewelry and could possibly mount the pearl where it could hang from a nice chain necklace. I told her I'd bring it up next week. I was getting in to this Christmas gift idea, but I couldn't figure out how to get her to tell me what she wanted without me actually coming out and asking her, and I decided that would not be cool.

Thank goodness Cloud and Elzie showed up about that time, and before they could get out of their car, Alida drove up. They joined us on Tess's back porch and of course, the first thing I had to do was read aloud my report. When I finished Elzie suggested we skip the dove shoot the next morning and go drag the river for gold. Tess said that wasn't going to happen, she was going dove hunting and we'd better take her. Well, that was settled! Elzie said we'd have to be poor dove hunters instead of rich gold hunters. Cloud suggested we were getting kind of rich, but not in a good way. Elzie then suggested that he and I go build a fire in the fire pit. So, we took off and the girls went to start supper. It was just about dark when Tess came to retrieve us for supper, Mama Sol was to join us. We gathered on Cloud's back porch, everyone seemed happy, the Christmas spirit was settling in at Owl Creek just like it was in Apalachicola.

The next morning Elzie woke me at five o'clock, coffee was already made. I had gotten dressed and was pouring myself a cup of coffee when Tess walked in, "Pour me one too!" I poured hers and added honey just like mine. Cloud joined us on the porch but said she wasn't going hunting. She needed to start Christmas planning and preparations, and hoped to have some lights hung by the time we got home.

It was still dark when we left for the hunt. Elzie drove us until we were about five miles from Bristol, then turned down a clay road. He drove another half mile or so, then pulled up next to a white Chevy truck where a man and his son were waiting on us. When we got out Elzie introduced us to Don Freeman and his thirteen year old son, Luke. Don explained that the birds would be flying early, and they would be flying low, so we had to pay attention as to where everyone was so not to shoot in anyone's direction. The site was a recently harvested peanut field, a little over a hundred acres, and he told us that there was a drainage ditch in the middle of the field, it still held some water and the birds would be working around the drainage area all morning, moving from feeding in the field to water. He instructed that we would spread out along the drainage ditch, and we were not to shoot up and down the ditch because we'd be shooting at each other.

The plan was to shoot away from the ditch toward the field, and don't shoot any bird that was low enough to be shooting at each other. The sky was just beginning to lighten in the east when we started into the field. He placed Elzie at the first stand, then proceeded another fifty to seventy-five yards, where he placed Tess and me. He and his son went on another hundred yards or more and set up there. It was a really chilly morning, Tess and I both had on heavy coats, mine was camouflage, hers was dark brown. We both had hats with pull down ear muffs. We stood there talking and looking, but it still wasn't light enough to see birds flying.

We had been there for maybe 20 minutes or more before it lightened up enough to see birds flying. At first there wasn't any activity, but well before the sun hit the horizon the birds started flying. Tess and I loaded our guns, she was shooting my single shot 20 gauge, I had my 12 gauge Browning. I tried to give Tess some last minute instructions, reminded her to lead the birds if flying side-ways to us, but stay directly on the bird if coming toward us. The first bunch to come our way was headed directly toward us, Tess killed one on her first shot, I shot another one. While she reloaded I picked up the birds. The activity picked up immediately. Elzie started shooting and we could hear Mr. Freeman and his son banging away down the field.

For the next two hours birds were in and out of the field, we got lots of shots. Every so often you could hear Mr. Freeman holler "good shot" to his son. Elzie would holler every so often just to make us look his way. He was having a great morning.

After about an hour I counted Tess's and my birds, we had 20 between us. I told her that she had better be good to me or when the game warden showed up I was going to tell him that she had killed them all. She asked why that mattered, I explained that the limit was 12 each, and if she shot over the limit she would get a fine, plus the game warden would take her license away. At that she said, "I didn't know I was supposed to buy a license!"

"What? You don't have a license?"

"No one told me I had to have one!"

"You just wait until we get home and I tell everyone that I fell in love with an outlaw!" She suggested we leave the field, but another bunch of birds flew by about that time and I downed two. She was afraid to shoot. So I made up a song right then, "Tess the outlaw gal!" It didn't go over very well. But when I told Elzie he really got a laugh out of it, then he told her he didn't have a license either. I could just imagine what Judge Olsen would do to me if I showed up in his court because I broke the law shooting too many doves. Maybe I'd better listen to Bud and make friends with the football players from Chattahoochee.

We were out of the field before 10 o'clock. Everyone had just a few birds over their limit, but we all had a great time, and Mr. Freeman was happy that we joined him. Elzie told him he'd bring him some alligator tail next time he was coming this way. As best we could tell Tess killed 14 birds, I was impressed, but I'm always impressed with Tess. Even Cloud was impressed when we told her about Tess's shooting. When we drove into the yard at Cloud's, she was on a ladder putting up Christmas lights. Elzie said we got home too early, now he would be expected to hang lights. I suggested he give Cloud a choice, hang lights or clean birds; he thought that was an excellent idea. Cloud didn't think so! But she did like my song, Tess the Outlaw Gal. Tess said I led her astray! I told her to be nice, or she'd get switches for Christmas. She gave me "that look", so I changed my tune.

After Elzie and I cleaned the birds we helped decorate all afternoon. By supper time, Christmas lights were shining. Cloud gave Elzie and me a job for the next weekend: we had to go cut a Christmas tree. I decided I needed to cut one for my folks. But Tess and I decided we also needed to go Christmas shopping, and we needed to work out the details. Sunday morning Tess pulled out her note pad and we started making a list for each of us. We were two and a half weeks until Christmas, we thought maybe we should do our shopping before we cut down the Christmas trees. She said she would find a store that sold men's hats, and Cloud said for me to bring the oyster pearl next weekend. I realized right then that I needed to plan for more than just my folks and Tess, the rest of the family was very important to me as well. Maybe I could talk to my Mom about that when I got home this evening.

Before I headed home Elzie called me to him and said that we needed a pick-up truck for the Christmas trees. He said he'd call Mr. Siglio and ask if it was all right to use his truck, then he'd let me know during the week. I suggested we get a tree for Mr. Siglio as well. The ride home was lonely but exciting. This was going to be the best Christmas ever.

After supper that evening I asked Mom and Dad if they would help me with some planning, that caused a concerned look from both of them until I clarified that it was Christmas planning. I needed to buy Tess, Cloud, Alida, and Sage, and Mama Sol a Christmas present. Then it dawned on me that I needed to get Walter, Elzie, and even Mr. Siglio something as well. Mom went through the same process as Tess did, and by the time we got through we decided that Mom would help me pick out something Cloud and Alida could use at their homes, Mom would also help with Sage and Mama Sol, but Dad intervened and said he wanted a say in Mama Sol's present. Dad suggested that for Walter, Elzie, and Mr. Siglio I should give each of them a team baseball cap, he even offered to ask Coach about getting three extras.

As for Tess, Mom asked what I had in mind; I told her I didn't know but it had to be from me, represents me, and just for her. At that Mom got up and went into the dining room and returned with a small box, she said it came in yesterday's mail. I opened the box to find my All Conference football. If you are selected to All Conference in any sport you receive a small gold plated ball representing the sport, and All Conference and the year is printed on the ball. I already had two more from football and baseball from my sophomore year. Mom said it would be perfect to present Tess with a gold charm bracelet with the three All Conference balls on it, plus if everything worked out as it should I should have three more by graduation. It's from me, represents me, and it's for her; it's perfect.

The next day after school I went downtown to our only jewelry store and picked out a gold bracelet and asked them to connect the All Conference balls to it and also explained that they needed to be spaced so three more could be attached in the future. On Wednesday the 10th I turned in my report to Miss Mac. By Wednesday evening Mom had picked out a beautiful oyster plate with gold trim for Cloud, and for Alida she found a shellacked driftwood platter for her dining room. Sage would get a monogrammed book bag. Dad picked out a very large box of Fanny Farmer Chocolates for Mama Sol.

On Thursday night Elzie called and told me to get the pick-up from Mr. Siglio on Friday after school and drive it to Owl Creek for the weekend. He also said he promised Mr. Siglio a tree as well. Friday afternoon after school I picked up the truck from Mr. Siglio, he had filled the gas tank for me and told me to bring him a beautiful Christmas tree not over six feet tall. I told him I'd do my best, then headed to Apalachicola State Bank and withdrew $100 from my savings account; it was one third of my total balance I had saved over the years, but it would pay for the best Christmas ever! At home I packed my bags, wrapped the oyster pearl in a handkerchief and stuffed it in my pocket. Mom was in the kitchen. As I headed out the door, I gave her a kiss and said I'd see her Sunday afternoon with a tree. She said that she and Dad would have the decorations waiting. As I drove across the bridge the bay was calm, the marsh had all turned brown, and I realized that duck season was still open. I needed to start planning more time to be in the marsh. But this weekend was set aside for shopping and tree cutting! And Owl Creek was waiting on me!

Tess and Sage were in the yard when I arrived, they helped me unpack and we were on Tess's back porch when Cloud arrived. Cloud hollered to come help and the three of us helped haul wrapped packages into her house for several minutes. "Whose are these?" from Sage.

"I think one might be for you," Cloud teased. That got Sage excited. We piled the packages on Cloud's back porch and she instructed where the tree would go when we got around to cutting one. At that point I don't know who was more excited, Sage or me? This would be my first Christmas with other family kids and I was feeling like family.

Minutes later Elzie and Mark drove into the yard. Elzie got out and retrieved a very large cloth bag from the back of Mark's truck. We were all eyes when he came into the back porch, but he didn't say anything except for me to follow him. He went straight to my bedroom, placed the bag in my closet, then turned to me and said, "Don't let anyone near that bag, and you stay out of it as well. If I catch you or anyone digging in there, I'll take out my disappointment on you! Understand?" I couldn't help but smile, and I assured him I'd protect it with my life. He muttered something about that not being much and we joined the others on the back porch.

I remembered the pearl in my pocket and gave it to Cloud. "Wow, that is a nice pearl," Cloud exclaimed. At that Tess had to have a look, she was impressed as well. Cloud said she would take it to her friend in the morning. Tess turned her attention to me and said that she found a men's store in Marianna and when she called them they said that they do sell men's hats. Tomorrow morning we would drive to Marianna. Elzie stated that he was making tree stands for the Christmas trees on Saturday and if we could get our shopping done pretty early we might have time to cut trees Saturday afternoon. Tess spoke up and told Elzie that good shopping takes time. Elzie looked at me and without even a smile said, "How should we know that?" Cloud said something about men and walked into the kitchen; Tess and Sage, as if by instinct, followed her.

Elzie looked at me, shrugged his shoulders, and told me to follow him. At the barn he started picking through lumber and pieces he could use for the tree stands. "We'll need three stands," he began, then stopped for a second and said, "no, with Mr. Siglio we'll need four." I had to think for a minute, but after counting Cloud's, Alida's, Mr. Siglio's, and mine at home, I agreed. "I should have these in good shape by the time you and Tess get back, and even if we have to cut the trees on Sunday morning we'll have stands on them when you head home."

"Mr. Siglio told me he wanted a tree not over six feet tall," I told Elzie.

"We better buy him a ladder if it's that tall." I could tell Elzie was even getting excited about Christmas, so I figured now would be a good time to talk to him about something no one had spoken of.

"Elzie, will there be any sort of get together for Christmas like it was for the Fourth of July?" At that he turned to me and said,

"I would think so, but we'd better talk to the boss about that." And we went to see Cloud. Cloud and the girls were in the kitchen chattering about something when we entered the back porch. Hearing us, they got quiet. "Not a good sign!" Elzie whispered.

"Why?" I asked.

"Because when women go quiet, they're planning something, and if they are planning something, it means we have to work."

"Work at what?" I asked.

"It doesn't matter, it's still work." He replied. Cloud appeared about that time and asked what we wanted for supper. Elzie was quick, "to be rich!" he replied.

Cloud was just as quick, "Well, for tonight would you rather be rich or hungry?"

"That depends on what you're going to feed us!"

"I think that was my question to begin with! And I might add, if you're naughty Santa won't come see you."

"How about Matt and I grilling some ribs?"

"That's more like it, now you two go start your fire or something. We've got things to talk about."

As we walked over to the fire pit next to the big screened-in room Elzie put his hand on my shoulder and said, "Son, there has never been a man that understood a woman. Let me give you an example, once there was a man walking on a beach in California and he found this bottle, so he picked it up and being a man he automatically rubbed it, and out jumps this genie.

And the genie said that he would give the man a wish. The man says, I thought I'd get three wishes, but the genie said no, I'm a one wish genie; so what's your wish? The guy thinks for a bit, then turns to the genie and says, I'm afraid of flying and I really want to go to Hawaii, so build me a bridge to Hawaii. The genie steps back, looks out over the ocean, and said, do you realize what you're asking? Why to build a bridge to Hawaii it would require engineering greater than anything humans have ever accomplished. Why don't you think of something else you would like? Well, the man scratches his head, thinks for just a minute, then says, I'd like to understand the mind of a woman. The genie steps back, rubs his head for just a minute, then asked the man, do you want that bridge to be two lane or four lane!"

Yep, Elzie could draw you in to most anything. After I stopped laughing he instructed me to start building a fire. It was getting dark by the time we had a nice bed of coals, Cloud brought over two racks of ribs, a basting sauce with a brush, and a beer for Elzie. During supper Cloud said that we need to start making plans for a Christmas get-to-gather. Elzie gave me a wink, then said we were thinking along the same lines.

The next morning Tess and I headed to Marianna, we left Owl Creek about eight o'clock. It took just under an hour and a half to get there, but the time changes at the Apalachicola River so it was 8:30 when we arrived in Marianna. The City was decorated for Christmas. The old Court House on Main Street had the largest wreath I'd ever seen, it covered most of the double doors leading inside. It must have taken most of a pine tree to make the large oval, an exceptionally large red bow was tied to the top, with three smaller bows on the bottom, all of it surrounded by blinking Christmas lights. On each street corner lamp post images of Santa Clauses hung like shopping bags at the toy stores, and strings of flashing Christmas lights stretched across the streets in every block in the commercial area.

Basford's Men's Store was located downtown at the corner of Main and First Street. It was two story, old red brick, with large plate glass windows across the front. The door, like the Court House, displayed a large wreath, and blinking Christmas lights encased the double door entrance. Displayed in the windows were men's suits, khaki pants, different types of boots and shoes, all setting behind a miniature Nativity scene. As we entered the store we noticed that the dressier clothes were against the right wall and to the back of the store, but to the left side ranch style clothing was displayed. There were several racks of boots, belts of all sizes, and to the rear were hats of all types.

As we headed back toward the hats a man appeared, he was tall, very thin, balding, but he had the largest handle bar mustache I'd ever seen. He was wearing boots and khaki pants. His shirt was right out of a western movie scene. "May I help you find something?" He asked. I told him I didn't really know, but we were looking for a hat for my Dad, a Christmas present. He pointed us in the direction of the hats and said to holler if we needed anything. It didn't take but a few minutes to pick out a hat for Dad, it was a wool fedora by Stetson, medium gray, with a dark gray band. I tried it on, it fit me perfectly so I assumed it would fit Dad as well. The man who waited on us told me that if it did not fit Dad perfectly just bring it back and he'd get one that did. The gentleman rang up my purchase, it was $28.50. He placed the hat in a nice, decorative hat box, and we headed back to Owl Creek.

It was 11:30 when we drove into Cloud's yard. Elzie was sipping iced tea when we entered the back porch, and Cloud was bringing out a tray of sandwiches. Within half an hour Elzie and I were off to cut Christmas trees. We drove south, back toward the bay, until we reached an area where the soil is more sandy; it's where the short leaf pines grow and when young they make great Christmas trees.

We found a nice ridge and pulled the truck off the road and slightly into the woods. Elzie grabbed his axe and said for me to follow him. We started sizing up trees, deciding which would be best for each house, and then Elzie started cutting them off at the base of the tree. He cut, I hauled, and within an hour or so we had four nice trees in the truck bed. Back at Owl Creek I helped Elzie with the tree bases; I say I helped because while he built the bases I retrieved beers for him. It only took two beers and the bases were constructed and attached to the trees. We stood them up in Cloud's yard, then requested the women folk to come take a look.

Cloud and Alida walked around each tree at least four times, then they talked to each other in low voices, making sure we were not part of the conversation. Elzie smiled at me, then went for another beer. Minutes later Cloud instructed me to take that one, she pointed, and put it in the designated spot on her back porch. After I completed that task, Alida did the same. After those two were delivered we left the remaining two for me to take home on Sunday.

The rest of the day went by quickly. Tess and I took a walk along the high ridge overlooking Owl Creek, and during supper Cloud, Tess and Alida made the plans for Christmas afternoon. It would be similar to Fourth of July, but Cloud insisted we have Christmas oysters along with whatever Elzie was going to cook. Elzie said he's making the arrangements and everyone agreed we should all gather around two o'clock on Christmas afternoon. Alida said she would put everyone on notice.

They made sure that I knew that I was to be certain Mom and Dad joined us. I told them we would all come in one car. The excitement hung in the air like the smoke from Elzie's bar-b-q. It was twelve days before Christmas, I don't think I'd ever been this excited about Christmas! I think my smile gave me away because Elzie told me that my smiling all the time made him nervous. "Boy, you need to stop that smiling all the time or you'll get bugs in your teeth!" I think he was getting excited too. The next morning I was on the road home by ten o'clock, two Christmas trees in the truck bed, me singing Christmas songs. I drove directly home, put our tree in the living room, then drove to Mr. Siglio's fish house.

"Paisan!" Was the first thing I heard as I stepped out of the truck. "Help me take it to my house!" and we were off to deliver his tree. Once it was unloaded he drove me home, thanking me every bit of the way. I told him to plan on a trip to Owl Creek Christmas afternoon. He said he would love it.

The next Friday, the nineteenth, we would be getting out of school at lunch for the Christmas break. It was a fast week! Miss Mac gave us our history reports on Wednesday, I got an A+! The first A+ I'd ever gotten, and she made me read my report to the class. When I finished Bud and Bob started with "Droo! Gar! Droo! Gar!" until Miss Mac made them stop. That was Christmas enough. By Friday at noon we were wild as could be, I think the teachers were glad to see us go.

I had made arrangements to go to the houseboat and spend Friday and Saturday nights there with Elzie, then go to Owl Creek for a night, then home on Monday. I was ready to get back to the marsh, and Elzie said he thought we could get in a good shoot Saturday morning. I met him at the houseboat around two-thirty Friday afternoon. He thought we should have a go at the ducks that afternoon so we headed to Sam's Bight by three. He hunted with me in my boat, we stooled out all eighteen decoys. It was close to four-thirty when the first bunch of teal pitched into our decoys. We picked up five from that bunch. Before dark we picked up two more teal, one pintail, and two mallards. I classified that afternoon as "perfect". Later that evening before going to bed I heard Elzie talking to Cloud on the short wave radio, after the conversation Elzie said that he needed to pick up Cloud in the morning and bring her back to the houseboat, she wanted to measure for something. He suggested that I hunt in the swamps the next morning.

It was dark when Elzie woke me, I could smell the coffee. I got dressed quickly and had some coffee with him, then some cereal. He said he'd be back in a few hours and we'd decide what we were going to do for the next day or so based on what chores Cloud dreams up. I loaded my shotgun with buckshot and went ashore while it was still dark. Within minutes it was beginning to get some light in the east so I started easing out toward the old road bed, my plan was to slip hunt down to the Indian mounds, then sit there a while, maybe see those turkeys Elzie had told me about.

Once away from the bank it was still dark in the swamps, so I let my eyes adjust, then very slowly eased on toward the road bed. By the time I reached the trail I could see well into the trees but the ground was still dark. I decided to wait. I sat down by a large oak and listened. It always amazes me how the woods sound especially when waking up; at first some birds, crickets, cicadas, and as the morning warms gently, the sound of dew falling on the leaves. It was cold but with clear skies and I was excited to be back in the swamps. After a few more minutes I began to make out trees, bushes, trails, and then colors. The sun was still below the horizon when I stood up, I stayed there a while longer, listening, letting my eyes cover the area without moving my head. Slowly I began to move toward the Indian mounds, they were maybe 100 yards further down the trail.

I had gone maybe 20 or 30 yards, moving only a few steps at a time, when I felt it. It startled me at first, I had never felt it before, but I knew I felt it. Something was watching me! I froze, leaned against a tree and started scanning with my eyes. I knew not to move my head in any quick motion, so slowly I rotated my head, searching with my eyes every bush, tree, open area. I stood there frozen for what seemed like a long time, though it was probably for just minutes. Nothing. I felt it, but saw nothing. I didn't want to move for fear I'd startle it, whatever it was. I slowly slid down against the tree, being as quiet and slow as possible. It seemed to take forever just to sit down. I settled against the tree and continued to scan with my eyes; I continued to feel it as well. I knew something was watching me, but nothing moved. The cold was beginning to numb my toes and fingers, and my eyes were beginning to water. I kept waiting on something to move so I might see it or hear it. Nothing. The feeling didn't go away, but after a while I slowly eased up and was about to move along when crash! Off to my right something hit a branch or palm frond. Looking quickly I saw the white flag of a deer as it darted from sight. The old boy had been watching me! I no longer had the feeling, now I had the knowledge.

My senses were humming, for the first time in my life I felt another animal, he sensing me, me sensing him. I stayed put for a while longer. Just when I was about to continue on toward the Indian mounds I heard Elzie crank his motor and head up river. I slowly continued toward the mounds, and as I approached I picked out the trail that led to the other side, just as Elzie, Cloud, Tess and I had traveled before. I slipped along to the other side to where I could look out over the lower swamps. I picked out a tree and slid down next to it. There was a small palmetto bush next to the tree so I pulled out my pocket knife and cut four palm fronds and stuck them in the ground around me, making a blind. The moving to the mound had warmed me a bit, but as I settled in again the cold bit my fingers and toes, my eyes again began to water.

I had been there less than an hour, the sun was beginning to show through the trees, lighting up the tree trunks and palmetto bushes, when a fog appeared right at ground level. It looked like small clouds floating just above the ground, spread throughout the swamps in front of me. I sat there staring at this phenomenon, thinking how I would describe it to Elzie and Cloud and Tess. Thinking they would believe I made it up, but it was there, clouds floating along the ground. There was no breeze, only the warming air from the rising sun. I had been watching this scene for several minutes when I noticed some motion off to the left front.

I stared through the mist, watching, waiting, thinking that I might have a deer coming my way. But instead, a man appeared out about 40 or 50 yards, coming from what I guessed was the mouth of Thank-You-Ma'am creek and headed parallel to me, moving toward the northeast. He wore all dark brown clothing, dark boots, and instead of a hat he wore a handkerchief around his head, pulled to the back of his head. I did not recognize the gun he carried cradled in his left arm. He looked directly at me, I nodded, but I doubt he saw me because of the palm fronds I had around me, he moved along, slip hunting fashion, moving slowly but steadily. He was almost directly in front of me, about 40 or more yards out front, when I noticed more movement behind him. I turned my attention from the man to the figure following him. It was a woman, dressed very similarly to the man, except she had a pack on her back. As she moved further into view I glanced again at the man in front of her, it was then I noticed that the man's hair was long and in braided pigtails, and he had a feather woven into each pigtail. I've seen strange things in the swamp before, but that was the strangest. I glanced back at the woman and realized that the pack on her back was actually a baby carrier, and in it was a baby. None of them, baby included, made a sound. They slipped along in the mist like a dream. I blinked my eyes a few times, they were still there, not a dream. As they moved further away from me I glanced back in the direction from where they came, nothing else followed. I glanced back at them but they were gone. I stood up to see if I might still be able to see them moving away from me, but saw no movement. I stood there a few more minutes then decided to sit back down. It was strange. I had never seen hunters like that before. Certainly Elzie would know who they were.

    I stayed there for a long time. A coon came by at one time, squirrels began barking in the trees, the sun was well up in the sky and the mist had disappeared when I decided to work back along the old road bed hoping to see the deer again. I moved very slowly, stopping every few feet to look and listen, then moving slowly again. I was past the spot where I started on the old road bed earlier when I heard Elzie's boat again. I assumed he was bringing Cloud back to measure whatever it was she was concerned about. I decided to continue further along the trail for a while, then work over to the river bank and then back to the houseboat. Squirrels were working the acorn trees, jumping from one tree to the next, barking at everything that moved. I moved along slowly, stopping regularly, scanning for any movement; after a while I worked my way over to the river bank, then walked back to the houseboat.

    I unloaded my shotgun and as I entered the houseboat, Elzie was sitting at the kitchen table. I stood my gun in the corner then sat on the couch. Cloud came out from the bedroom and said good morning. We chatted a bit, then Cloud started washing up some dishes in the sink. I turned to Elzie and said "Elzie, I felt him this morning!" He turned to me and said go on. "Well, I was making my way slowly toward the mounds just at light enough to see when I got this strange feeling, like something was watching me. I could feel him. I didn't know what it was but I knew something was watching me. So I sat down by a tree and went to looking and listening." By the time I got this far Cloud stopped washing dishes and turned to listen to me. Elzie had that almost smile on his face, anticipating my next descriptions. It was as if he was watching a movie he had made. I think he knew exactly what I was about to say. "I sat there for a long time, just listening and scanning with my eyes. I saw nothing. After a while I decided to move on to the mounds. As I got up and began to move, crash! Off to my right I saw his white flag as he broke into the brush."

    Elzie got as excited as I had. "So you saw him? I've had that happen to me a hundred times. Feeling him but couldn't see him. You'll get him one day soon. Just like what happened to me, one day you'll feel him without him feeling you, and then you'll get your shot." Just listening to Elzie talk about the deer got me excited. I felt I had just crossed a big barrier. One day soon I would get my first big buck.

    Cloud had been quiet, but as Elzie and I calmed down a bit she turned to me and said, "Didn't I tell you, you have the gift?"

    I sat there for a few minutes before saying anything, Cloud turned back to the dishes. "It was a strange morning. I saw something I have never seen before." Elzie looked at me oddly and asked what it was. "When I got to the mounds I eased over to the other side where you told me you had seen turkeys before, I thought I might get a shot at one. I found me a tree to lean against, cut me some palms to make me a ground blind, and started waiting. As the sun got up enough to put rays in the swamps, a mist, a fog, formed just above the ground. It was really beautiful, but strange looking.

Anyway, I had sat there for a while when I saw motion out front and to my left. A man came slipping through, hunting. He wore dark brown boots and clothing, and instead of a hat, he wore a scarf or handkerchief around his head." At that, Cloud turned from the dishes and started listening to me. Elzie's expression changed, becoming much more focused. I continued, "He was almost straight out in front of me when I noticed movement from the direction he had come, I turned and there came a woman, dressed just like him, except she had a baby on her back. I turned back toward the man and saw that his hair was long and in pigtails and he had a feather woven in to each pigtail." Cloud dropped a dish she was holding. I turned toward her, her face was bright but had turned almost white.

"That was my great grandfather, Chief Two Feathers!" She said it so quickly I didn't even realize what she had said for a minute. "And that woman was my great grandmother, and the baby was my grandfather." I didn't know what to say, I thought they were just people, not someone from past history.

I was trying to say something back to her when Elzie spoke up and said, "Load your gun. Wait right here." He was gone for just a minute and when he returned from the bedroom he had his 30-30 rifle. "Come on and follow me." We were out the door in a flash, Elzie led the way. He didn't go to the road bed, he just started up the river bank toward Thank-You-Ma'am Creek, then cut over toward the mounds. When we reached the end of the mounds closest to the river he went to the left side, walking on the lower swamp side up until I pointed to the spot I had been sitting. "You stand right there, and when I get out to where they walked by you motion for me to stop." I stood in front of my palmetto blind, Elzie walked out to where the man and woman had walked in front of me, I waved for him to stop, and then he motion for me to join him. When I got to him he said, "And you think this is the spot they crossed?"

"Yes sir."

"Ok, then start making zig zag movement in that direction, and I'll do the same in this direction. Look for tracks. If they were here there will be tracks in this swamp." For the next 45 minutes we zig zagged like hound dogs, we never found a track. When we got back to the houseboat Cloud was drinking tea on the front porch,

"Elzie, when are you going to believe? I've told you before, people do have visions. Those were my great grandparents." As Elzie and I took a seat on the porch Cloud turned her attention to me, "Matthew, remember the invisible sand? Well you just experienced it. You are a fortunate person. Not many people are blessed with the gift. Your insights will grow. Learn to trust them. Two Feathers was a chief of a small tribe, he was killed by white settlers. My grandfather helped our tribe assimilate with the white man. We are here today because of him. I'm so excited for you, you have connected with our family in ways many of us have not. I believe you will have more visions. The next time you do, just enjoy it, and pay attention, there may be lessons to learn or clues offered to you."

I didn't know what to say or think for that matter. Evidently Elzie didn't either, as he just sat there a few minutes, then said he thought he'd have a beer. At that moment I wished I could have a beer too. The three of us sat there in silence for a long time, Cloud turned her attention back to the dishes and the sink, I stared out the window toward the river, and Elzie just stared, at what I don't know. After a bit he got up and went out onto the front porch and went back to staring.

Cloud worked back and forth between the kitchen and the bedroom, measuring windows, cleaning up after Elzie for a while, but finally she rejoined me in the living area. She sat quietly for a few minutes then addressed me, "Matthew, when you saw Two Feathers what did you think?" I felt like I should have some deep feeling about the moments, but they were just moments, nothing special. I needed to say something and not sound like a kid. I had acted stupid enough around her in the past.

I gave it a try, it was only a try, "Honestly, the man looked like most hunters except for not wearing a hat. He was slip hunting, moving faster than I usually do, but intense. He was a hunter, that's all I thought until he was passed me enough for me to see his hair. I thought the pigtails were strange, but around here there's always someone strange. But, I have never seen a woman in the swamps, especially carrying a baby. That was strange." That didn't seem to satisfy Cloud, she persisted,

"Did you have any strange feelings, like with the deer?" I didn't know what else to say so I just shook my head no. "When you saw the woman was she hunting? Or just following? Did she look distressed?" Again I shook my head no, but said I thought she was just following. After a bit Cloud asked if I was going to hunt again this afternoon. At that point I didn't know what was going to happen, I just told her I didn't know.

About that time Elzie came back into the living area and said he thought we should load up and head to Owl Creek. Cloud said to give her a few minutes and she would be ready to go. I wasn't sure if he meant for me to go as well, or if he was coming back, but before I asked him to clarify for me, he turned to me and said we both needed to go to Owl Creek. In less time than it took me to tell my morning story we were packed and I was following them in my boat. I really didn't understand but down deep I felt that Elzie was uncomfortable with my story. I started wishing that he could see Two Feathers and his wife just like I did. I decided I needed to keep that wish to myself. Entering Owl Creek I felt like it was as mystical as anything I had ever seen or experienced in my life. I was looking forward to telling Tess about my morning.

When we got to the landing no one was there. I don't think anyone was expecting us. We grabbed our gear and headed up the hill. By the time we reached Cloud's back yard someone yelled that Cloud was back and like magic folks started coming out of their houses. Tess was soon by my side, "We didn't know you were coming back today!"

"I didn't either, but I'll tell you about it when we can be alone." That startled her, she got a strange look on her face and she whispered if everything was okay. I nodded that it was, but I knew that she knew something wasn't quite right. I took my gun and bag to my bedroom, then joined the others on Cloud's back porch. Elzie had settled in with a beer, Cloud went directly to the kitchen and put on a pot of tea. Alida, Sage, and Tess pulled up chairs as if we were going to entertain them with stories. The quiet stung me like a bee, I got the feeling like everyone knew something was wrong, but no one would ask or start a conversation. Finally Cloud came out with a pitcher of ice tea, everyone took a glass.

No one spoke for some time, but finally Sage turned to Alida and asked in a loud voice, "Mama, is something wrong?" Alida said she didn't think so, then turned to Cloud as if to ask.

Cloud put her tea down, looked everyone in the eyes and said, "We just decided that we wanted to be here with you. Christmas is next week and we didn't need to be down in the swamps. We have plans to make." That did it, the girls started talking about the "event" for Christmas afternoon, Elzie looked like he was dozing off for a nap, and I just smiled at Tess and nodded, at what I have no idea. About an hour later I woke from a nap, Elzie was still snoring slightly. The girls had taken the "event" into the kitchen, they were laughing, and singing, mostly Christmas carols, and something in there really smelled good. I went in to see what smelled so good, Cloud was just bringing a tray of cookies out of the oven. Tess poured me a glass of milk and I helped myself to a half dozen cookies. Alida was making a list, people's names, the dishes to bring, who would make cakes, who would provide the vegetable, what meat we would prepare, and who would be in charge of contacting all members of the tribe. That struck me as odd, it was 1958, yet these people, as ordinary as anyone, still referred to themselves as a tribe. Why not family? That's something Tess and I needed to talk about.

It was around four o'clock when Tess and I went for a walk along the high ridge overlooking the creek. We stopped at the bench, and as soon as we sat down she turned to me and said, "Okay, now tell me what happened!" I thought for a minute, trying to figure out how to put it all together, then started in.

"Elzie told me last night that Cloud wanted to come to the houseboat to measure something, so we decided I'd hunt in the swamps this morning while he ran up here to pick up Cloud. I was in the woods before daylight, I had planned to hunt at the mounds. I had to wait until light enough to see but I eased out to the old road bed while it was still dark, and as it started getting light I began moving toward the mounds. I hadn't gone very far when I got this really strange, but strong, feeling that something was watching me. I sat down by a tree and started scanning for any motion I might see. I sat there for a while, the feeling never left me. Finally I eased up and started to move toward the mounds, then crash, I turned toward the noise and saw the white flag of a deer. He had been watching me the entire time. I felt him."

At that Tess smiled at me, then said, "Cloud said you had the gift!"

I continued, "But that wasn't the strange part." She sat back and looked at me, I continued, "After the buck jumped I went on to the mounds, I crossed the mounds on the same trail we used before, and found me a site where I could look out over the swamps. I sat down by a tree, cut some palm fronds for a blind and settled in. When the sun got up high enough to put rays in the swamp a mist formed, like a fog, right at ground level. I'd never seen anything like that before. I had been watching it for a little while when I saw some movement out front and to my left; I thought it might be a deer and I got ready just in case, but a man appeared through the mist.

He was hunting, he had a gun cradled in his left arm, he wore dark brown boots, had dark brown clothes, but instead of a hat, he was wearing a scarf or handkerchief around his head. He was moving parallel to me from my left to right. He was almost directly in front of me when I saw more movement behind him, it was a woman. She was dressed like the man, but she had a pack on her back and she was carrying a baby in the pack. When I glanced back at the man, he had moved further to my right, and I could see that he had long hair and it was braided into pigtails, and in each pigtail there was a feather woven into the pigtail. I watched them for a few minutes, I even blinked a couple of times to make sure I wasn't dreaming. They moved off to my right, I glanced back in the direction they came from to see if anyone else was with them, there wasn't, but when I turned back to them they were gone. I stood up to see if I could see them further up the swamps, but I didn't see anything else.

When I got back to the houseboat and told Elzie and Cloud about what I had seen Cloud almost fainted. She said I saw her great grandfather, great grandmother, and the baby was her grandfather. At that Elzie told me to get my gun and follow him. We went back to the mounds, I showed him where they crossed, then we looked for tracks for most of an hour. There weren't any tracks."

Tess was staring at me like children stare at clowns, almost mesmerized by what she was hearing. I leaned back away from her and asked if she thought I was nuts. She blinked, sat back and said, "That's big medicine! Cloud saw it in you. I've never had a vision like that. How did it feel?" That startled me, it was exactly what Cloud wanted to know, I told her I didn't feel anything. I just saw them. We sat there in silence for a few minutes, then Tess asked if that was the reason we came back early.

"I don't know, but after I told my story, and Cloud said it was her great grandparents and grandfather, and Elzie and I went to look for tracks, when we got back to the houseboat Elzie said we needed to go. And here we are." Tess retreated into her thoughts; she stared out over the creek for what seemed like a long time.

After a bit she turned back to me and said "You have a gift. There's deep meaning here, I hope we can figure it out together." It made me feel really weird, I had never thought of myself as "big medicine" but if Tess thought it was big, then I was willing to find out.

"As long as you don't send me to the looney house, we'll tackle it together!" At that she said she loved me! She kissed me, then said we needed to go help the common folk get ready for Christmas.

Elzie was awake when we returned and he seemed to be back in his normal good mood. He made no comments about the morning activities. Every time Cloud looked at me for the evening and the next day she just smiled. Once when I was sitting on the porch and she walked pass me she patted me on the head. Now I know what dogs feel like!

The next day, Sunday, Tess and I got to go to Wright Lake. It was an early Christmas. Plans were made, we would all celebrate Christmas Thursday afternoon, beginning at two o'clock. Sunday afternoon late Cloud presented me with the pearl necklace her friend made for my Mom. It was beautiful, the oyster pearl was mounted in an oyster shaped gold shell and hung on a gold chain. Even Tess looked envious. I couldn't wait to see Mom's face on Christmas morning.

Monday morning after breakfast Tess walked me to my boat, I told her I'd see her Christmas afternoon, maybe I could stay over for a couple of days. She said she liked that idea. Then she asked, "Do you think you could take me back to the mounds during the holidays?" I told her I would work on it, maybe Elzie and Cloud would help make it happen. The river was calm, the skies clear, and the swamps were turning winter gray as I headed down river to Christmas in Apalachicola.

Chapter 15: The Best Christmas Ever

Monday, Tuesday, and Wednesday went by like a cold front blowing through, Mom cooked everything, baked all kinds of cookies and candies, and together we wrapped packages for everyone on our list. Mom and Dad, every year, bought presents for the underprivileged kids in our community. I had watched them year after year, never understanding why they did it, but this year they had me deliver the presents to the National Guard Armory on Christmas Eve. I got there about 5:45. There was to be a gift giving at 6:00, and kids were already lining up outside the Armory. Many didn't even have on coats, and it was getting cold, some without socks, some without parents. I retrieved the large bag of wrapped presents from the car and was headed into the Armory to deliver the presents to the Philaco Women's Club when a small, young boy, standing in line with other young boys saw me and said, "Mister, are you Santa Claus?"

It stunned me for a moment, I didn't know what to say, so I said, "No, I'm just one of his helpers!" The little guy then said for me to tell Santa thanks! When unloading the presents inside, I noticed that Mom had put on the presents, Boy-age 7-9, Girl-age 6-8, and more. By the time I got back home I could hardly talk, I was all choked up, tears in my eyes, I told my parents that I had never understood until today why they did what they did. That evening Dad built a fire in the fireplace, and we sat around watching TV. I kept thinking about the kids at the Armory, and for another first in my life, I felt guilty about having so much, to be a kid of privilege. We weren't rich, but compared to the kids I saw today, we were rich. My past attitude embarrassed me. I swore I would become a better person, and share more.

When I was much younger I would be up before daylight on Christmas morning. I remember one Christmas morning, I think I was five or six, I woke Christmas morning before five in the morning, I slipped out to the living room and there next to the lighted tree was my request from Santa, a bicycle! It was red, had a light, and tassels hanging from the handle bars. I went over and climbed up on it, I was small enough to sit on the seat with just the kickstand holding me up. I was so excited, but I knew that I wasn't supposed to be up that early, so I went back to bed. Mom woke me around 7:30 and told me that Santa had come, I told her I knew. She asked how I knew and when I told her I had been up at 5:00 and had sat on my bike so she just left me in bed. Dad thought it was funny.

The next morning, Christmas morning, Dad was up early. I woke around seven and could smell the coffee. I joined Dad in the kitchen, even had a cup of coffee with him. Mom finally got up around eight. Funny how when you're much younger all you want to do is open presents, but at sixteen and you're an only child, all you want to do is give presents. The three of us took our coffee and moved to the living room. I had to play Santa and hand out presents. I started with Mom's. As I handed her the gift I got for her I told her that I wanted this gift to represent me and it was only for her. When she opened the present and saw the gold oyster shell with a mounted pearl, hanging from a gold chain, her eyes lit up and then welled with tears, and she had to excuse herself and left the room. Dad looked over at me and said I did a very special thing, he was proud of me.

The next gift I gave to him, there was a small box and a bigger box. I instructed that he open the small box first. As he opened the small box he reached in and pulled out a Green Head Mallard Curl Feather! He looked really confused, so I told him to open the large box. As the lid came off a big smile spread across his face, he retrieved the Stetson from the box and placed the curl feather in the band. This was the best Christmas I think I had ever had at home, Mom and Dad were both surprised, excited, and happy. They gave me some shirts, socks, a couple of boxes of shotgun shells (which I really appreciated) and I thought the gift giving was over until Dad reached behind the chair he was sitting in and handed me another box. I couldn't imagine what it must be, but as the lid came off the box my excitement soared, it was a professional Rawlings Lew Burdette Baseball Glove. It slid on my hand like silk. Dad spoke up and said he thought I might need a new glove for the upcoming season. It was a fine morning. Merry Christmas!

By 12:30 we were packed into the car and headed for Owl Creek, Mom had baked a cake, and she had wrapped all the presents for me to deliver. I realized it was the first time Mom had ever been to Owl Creek, I really wanted her to enjoy herself. I told her that when we got there I would take her around and introduce her to all the family. She gave me a funny look, but she didn't say anything. We drove into Cloud's back yard before 1:30, you could hear kids playing even before getting out of the car. Tess saw us arrive and came to greet us. I unloaded the gifts and asked Tess to help me.

Our first stop was Cloud's back porch, we dropped all the gifts there, then we went to Tess's house to speak to Alida and Sage. I spoke to Alida and said that Tess and I would be at Cloud's and my parents were with us, she didn't seem concerned, she was cooking away at something in the kitchen. Back at Cloud's Mom and Dad were visiting with Cloud, we plopped down next to them and I asked where Elzie was. Cloud said he was over at the fire pit cooking as were several other men. She also said that Walter and Mr. Siglio would be along in a little while. My parents looked very comfortable, which surprised me, I thought Mom would be nervous since she wasn't in her normal surroundings. I told Cloud that we had brought presents and asked when we should give them. Cloud suggested we take care of that before we gather with all of the guests, then told Tess to ask her Mom when she and Sage would be able to come over. Tess excused herself. Dad asked about Mama Sol. Cloud said she would be over shortly.

Mom and Cloud started talking about the afternoon activities, who all would be there, what Mom could do to help, and everything else women talk about. Dad and I sat there like stumps. After what seemed like hours Tess returned with her Mom and Sage. Mama Sol showed up just a few minutes later. I asked if I should go get Elzie but Cloud said it was probably best not to disturb him, she didn't think Elzie had enough confidence with his help to leave them unsupervised. Dad got a chuckle out of that. Cloud suggested I proceed so I presented a present to Alida, Sage, and Cloud, and told them it was from our family. Tess seemed surprised I didn't give her a present.

At that time Dad took over and presented a present to Mama Sol. It was actually the largest box of candy I had ever seen and Dad had it packed in even a much larger box. Mama Sol's eyes were shining. They all opened their presents, each making comments you would expect them to make. When Mama Sol saw the box of candy I thought she was going to jump and holler. She immediately made everyone have a piece. After everyone sort of settled down I brought out Tess's gift, handing it to her I said that I wanted her to have something that represents me, and only for her. Big smiles. When she opened the box her eyes widened, then the big smile, she knew exactly what the All Conference charms were. She jumped up and gave me a big hug then told me to help put it on her wrist. I think I impressed everyone! Everyone seemed happy, I felt really good, but the thought struck me that Tess hadn't gotten me anything. I didn't know if they didn't give gifts or what the situation might be, but it was a happy occasion and I wasn't going to spoil it.

It wasn't long before Walter and Mr. Siglio drove into the yard, so everyone automatically started moving toward the big screened in room. Tess and I helped take dishes over, as did the others, but when everyone was at the big room, Tess and I were with Cloud to finish the last of the chores at Cloud's. I was ready to head back over when Cloud said for me to wait just a minute. I was expecting Cloud to hand me something else to take over but she and Tess cornered me in the kitchen and said "We have something for you. It's from us, represents us, but only for you." Then they handed me a box, not a big box, but it was wrapped with Christmas paper. I opened the box, unwrapped the object from the paper, and in my hand was an Indian medicine bag about the size of my hand. It was soft leather, had a drawstring top plus a sewn in strap which could completely secure the contents inside. It had a leather strap which allowed me to hang the bag around my neck. The strap was actually three long narrow straps woven together, then rolled to make the combined strap strong and smooth. On the bag my initials were stamped. At the bottom of the bag small leather fringe was sewn across the entire bottom. I knew what a medicine bag was but had no clue why I should have one or what I should do with it.

Cloud sensed my confusion, she began, "Matthew, most Native American men had medicine bags, each was customized for the individual. For some it was for spiritual quest, some for supernatural powers especially if you were the designated medicine man or shaman, and for others it was to maintain personal harmony with the physical, spiritual, and supernatural being. As you go through your life quest you will add items to the bag while at other times you will remove items from the bag. Only you will know when each item meets your personal goals and desires. Tess and I have given lots of thought for what should go into this bag at this time of your journey, but only as a beginning, what you remove and replace will depend on your journey. Most bags contain items from the Plant Kingdom, Animal Kingdom, Mineral Kingdom, and the Man's World.

To begin your journey we have placed the following in your bag: from the Plant Kingdom you have Sage and Rosemary, both fragrant and represents your connection to our area and your spice of life. From the Animal Kingdom we have placed the tip of a buck's antler, plus skin from an alligator, and the scale of a redfish. And for extra strength we added locks of hair from Tess. All connect you to our environment and your love of the natural world. From the Mineral Kingdom we have given you sand from our seashores, plus the pearl of an oyster. Your strength is tied to the sea and the Islands that adjoin it. From the Man's World we have placed a silver dollar to represent your future success, and a locket with yours and Tess's picture. Success and happiness stem from love. May yours grow eternally.

Now Matthew, this is not a toy or an item to show your friends, or a conversation piece. This bag represents you and gives you strength; it connects you to your spiritual world as well as the physical world, and maybe even the supernatural world. I have told you that you have been given a special gift. Honor it, trust it, and encourage it through your dreams and desires. The invisible sands will show you the way." I reached over and hugged Tess, then hugged Cloud. I wasn't able to speak, I was afraid to try for fear I'd break down and cry. I unbuttoned the top button on my shirt, hung the bag around my neck, then tucked in under my shirt. At that, Cloud told us to come on and we went to join the others. As we headed out the door I grabbed the three baseball caps I brought for Elzie, Walter, and Mr. Siglio, I had not wrapped them thinking that they probably wouldn't like the Christmas gift idea anyway.

Tess held my hand as we crossed the field. There were more people there than had been at the 4th of July party, many I'd never seen or heard of. Tess said she would introduce me but I needed to see Elzie, Walter and Mr. Siglio. We went directly to the fire pit, Elzie had lots of help around him, but I don't think he was letting anybody do much. He had split the fire pit into two parts, one for the pig which was completely covered under the sheet of tin, and the other part he was cooking duck poppers. Walter was shucking oysters to eat raw, and more to grill over the open fire. Mr. Siglio was right there with him, but not working, just smiling and talking to anyone that would listen. As I approached each one of them I wished them a Merry Christmas and presented them with a team baseball cap, then added, "This is more than just a Christmas gift, I'm also trying to drum up some support for the upcoming baseball season!" That seemed to satisfy them, even Walter took off his straw hat he wore everywhere and put on the baseball cap. Elzie, of course, put his on backward in catcher fashion.

In the screened-in room there was more food than you could imagine. Cloud, Alida, and Tess had decorated the room for the occasion, and almost every square inch of the serving counters were filled with food, cakes, cookies, and several homemade loaves of breads. Mom was right in the middle of everything, helping to set plates, arrange items, and running her mouth like she was one of the family. It really made me feel good that she was a part of this. Children were playing and hollering, and singing Christmas songs. It was unlike any Christmas I'd ever known, and I loved it.

When we finally all gathered in the big room to eat, Cloud rose and asked everyone to give thanks. She raised her arms, hands pointed upward, and gave a blessing, "Great Spirit, today we celebrate life, we celebrate joy, and we celebrate love. We give you thanks for all you share with us. Keep our people well and safe, and help us to give back all the love and blessings you have shared with us. Help us to help others, to show love, to celebrate life. Our life is joy, and our joy is life. Give us strength, and show us the way. We raise our voices and hearts to you. Amen!" I was sitting next to Mom and Dad, Tess next to me; when Cloud said Amen Mom said Amen! I never had imagined having such a large family. To this day I believe Christmas at Owl Creek changed my life; it made me a better person.

It was dark when the party ended, as like the Fourth of July party, everyone leaving had a platter full of food to take with them. The children were still singing, happiness hung in the air like the songs. I had brought my bag and was going to stay for a couple of days. Mom and Dad, Cloud and Elzie, Tess and I, plus Alida, Sage, Walter and Mr. Siglio gathered on Cloud's back porch, Cloud made some coffee and we all sat around for most of an hour just enjoying the company, celebrating a Christmas like no other. I told Mom and Dad that I'd call them and let them know when I would be home, they just said to have fun. They left about the same time as Walter and Mr. Siglio. Alida and Sage went home, Tess and I went back to the fire pit to sit with it until the fire was completely out.

The dark sky was filled with stars, a chill had set in, no breeze interrupted the smoke vanishing into the night. It was past eleven when I walked Tess home, then went back to Cloud's back porch. Elzie was still awake, sitting by himself, as I walked in he said to join him for a few minutes. I pulled up a chair and he directed his attention to me, "Matt, this was a great day! I've been part of this family for many, many years, and I've had many Christmases with them, but this by far was the best. You're the main reason it happened. I'm proud of you and I thank you."

I just couldn't help myself, "So, you don't mind hanging out with a jail bird?" That got him laughing,

"If you don't behave I'll tell the whole truth about your gator gigging, and over-limit shooting of doves and ducks, and you'll be back before the judge!" We both got to laughing so loud that Cloud came out to the porch and wanted to know what was going on. Elzie told her he was just hanging out with a jail bird.

She gave a little laugh then said, "Birds of a feather!" She took him to bed and I turned in. Lying there before going to sleep, I thought back about the past six or seven months, it had been much of a journey. I took my medicine bag from around my neck, placed it on the night stand, and said a prayer, "Great Spirit, guide me along my journey, allow me to make great medicine, achieve great things, enjoy eternal love. Prepare me for my trials!"

Friday morning, December 26th, Tess came over to Cloud's at eight o'clock in the morning. I was sitting with Elzie on the back porch, having coffee. "Fix me one too," was the first thing Tess said. As I handed her the coffee she made her pitch, "I've been thinking and I think we, meaning me, Matt, and Elzie and Cloud, should go spend the night at the houseboat. And I want Matt to take me back to the Indian Mounds."

Cloud responded, "When?"

"Today!" Cloud looked at Elzie, Elzie shrugged his shoulders, gave a nod, and Cloud said we would be ready to go within an hour. And in less than an hour we were on our way. Elzie had the forethought to pack some leftovers from the day before. It was a nippy ride, but the river was calm, skies clear, and we bundled up for the trip. As soon as we arrived at the houseboat Elzie said we needed some firewood, so Tess and I gathered wood while Elzie and Cloud heated up the houseboat and put food away. We had been there less than an hour when Tess said she was ready to go to the mounds. Elzie and Cloud said they would remain at the houseboat, so Tess and I put on our coats, Elzie loaned me his 30-30 Winchester, and we headed out into the swamps.

I decided to go to the old road bed first, then follow the same path I took to the mounds when I felt the deer. We weren't far from the houseboat when I stopped and asked Tess what she wanted? She asked what I meant, so I asked if she wanted to hunt? Or just walk to the mounds? Or what? She thought for a minute then said, "Why don't we slip along like you usually do when you hunt. If you feel something or see something I want you to tell me and explain what or how it is." I nodded, then told her to stay close behind me, but walk quietly. I told her to stop when I stop, and don't speak or make any noise, and if I sit down, do the same. She nodded, and we started toward the old road bed, once there I stopped and listened for a while, giving the swamps time to quiet down, adjust to us being there.

After a bit I started toward the mounds, moving slowly, only a few feet at a time, then stopping and listening again, then moving on again. When we got to the area where I felt the buck and saw his flag I stopped, motioned her to me and told her where I'd been when I felt the buck and where I saw his flag. She nodded, and seemed excited to be here. After a few minutes we moved on toward the mounds. Reaching the mounds we crossed over on the same trail we had traveled before, and when we reached the other side we moved to the tree where I had sat before. We sat down, I adjusted the palm fronds around us, making a blind. Tess sat on my left, snuggled up to me, and we waited and listened. We had been there the better part of an hour when I saw some movement out in front of us, I squeeze Tess's hand and with my finger, keeping my hand down low, pointed in the direction I saw the movement. Within a few seconds we saw the turkeys, it was three hens and they were moving toward us. I thought Tess was going to giggle out loud she got so excited. I kept squeezing her hand and motioning for her to be still.

The turkeys kept coming toward us moving to our right but also toward the mounds and ridge behind us. For maybe ten minutes we watched them, they pecked along, stopping every few moments to look and listen, then moving on. Tess calmed down, but held my hand tight. She had never seen a wild turkey, I had never had some coming directly toward me. She very slowly motioned if I was going to shoot one, I barely moved my head no. I think she was relieved I wasn't going to kill one. We watched them until they fed past us to our right and then moved toward the ridge behind the mounds. When they were gone she leaned over to me and whispered "That was magic!"

I had to show off, so I leaned over to her and whispered, "Big medicine!" She almost laughed out loud.

We stayed there maybe another half an hour, then she whispered that she was ready to go, so we got up and headed directly toward the river, then back down the bank to the houseboat. When we got to the houseboat I thought she'd never hush about the turkeys, Cloud and Elzie were actually laughing at us, mostly Tess, for being so excited. Of course Elzie had to ask if there were any gobblers with the bunch. I told him no, just three hens, but he added that in the Spring we'll call up ole Tom, and have us some smoked turkey.

After the left-overs for supper we sat around the fire until late, listening to the owls holler up and down the river, then we all went into the houseboat; Elzie and Cloud went directly back to their bedroom leaving Tess and me alone in the living area. Tess looked at me, I shrugged my shoulders, then told her it was too cold for me to sleep on the front porch. The couch was too narrow for two to sleep, so we took the back pillows and laid them on the floor alongside the couch. Tess took the couch, I took the floor. As we were about to go to sleep Tess leaned over the side of the couch and whispered she loved me, I told her the same, and then she reached down and pinched my nose. I said I wasn't a dog, then she patted my head. I told her that if we ever got a houseboat it had better be two bedrooms.

    The next morning way before daylight Cloud came in and put on coffee. She didn't turn on any lights and she was trying to be quiet, I heard her as soon as she came in the room but decided to act like I was asleep. In just seconds Tess said, in an extra sexy voice, "Oh Matt!" And the lights came on. Once Cloud saw that Tess was just funning with her she said we were lucky she wasn't carrying her gun! Tess giggled, then told Cloud that I was such a gentleman, then she patted me on the head again. I decided it was time to get up.

    While coffee was brewing I went back to the fire pit and stirred up the coals, put on some fresh wood and the fire sprung to life. Tess brought me a cup of coffee and joined me at the fire. Elzie and Cloud were soon there. Being on the river, before daylight, sitting around a fire, stirs you. You start hearing the river sounds, the fish strike, the occasional owl, dew beginning to fall on leaves, and then seeing the mist above the river as daylight comes on slowly. We sat there quietly, drinking our coffee, listening, and feeling the chill. Elzie always had a stick, and he constantly put on new wood, then poked at the fire with his stick. He wasn't much of a talker early mornings. We sat there until the sun's rays were just about to hit the horizon, then Cloud said she would scare us up some breakfast.

    After some grilled toast with cheese Cloud asked what were the plans. No one had a plan, but I knew that I needed to get home. I stated, "I really need to get home for a day or two, then I'd like to come back and spend most of a week. I want to do some more duck hunting, and I'd like to have another shot at that buck." The look on Tess's face shocked me, she actually looked hurt, Cloud made no comments, but Elzie said he thought that was a good idea, as long as we were at Owl Creek for New Year's Eve. That satisfied Tess and Cloud, both smiled, and Elzie gave me a wink. I realized I still had lots to learn, especially about women.

    By mid-morning we were headed back to Owl Creek. We unloaded and cleaned the boat, then went to Cloud's. Tess agreed to take me home, first I said I needed a bath, I smelled like campfire smoke. We visited with all the family, the kids were having fun playing with all of their new Christmas toys, I kept feeling like I needed to be home, but I was ready to spend a week or more hunting. Around four o'clock Tess and I left for Apalachicola, we made a detour to Wrights Lake first.

    By five o'clock we were on Highway 65 headed South. We drove into my driveway at 5:40. Mom and Dad looked shocked when Tess and I walked in the back door. "We didn't expect you so soon," Mom began. Dad asked if something was wrong, but I told them that I needed to be home a couple of days, but then I wanted to take my boat and go back. Elzie and I were planning several days hunting, and I needed my boat and gun. That satisfied them, Tess not so much. I walked her back to her car, told her I loved her, and said I'd be back to Owl Creek in just a couple of days. She got in her car, but before she could start the engine I got in on the passenger's side and said, "Let's talk!"

    "About what?" Her look didn't seem right. I needed her to understand.

    "Tess, I'm never happier than when I'm with you, but I need my folks to know I'm not abandoning them. We just had the best Christmas together in my life. For the first time ever I think my folks felt appreciated. You helped make that happen. They love you, they know I love you, but I want them to feel that I appreciate them. I'll be back in a couple of days. Just trust me on this. We'll have fun, but I want them feeling good too." She got it!

    "I know, it's just that I want to be with you all the time, and I know that's not possible now. But I'll still miss you like crazy."

"You'd better! Call me as soon as you get home. What is today, Saturday? Yep, I'll see you Tuesday morning. Maybe we can have a duck hunt together." She liked that idea, I liked that idea. The sun was setting when she drove out of the driveway. When I went back inside Mom was cooking Hamburgers and fries, mine and Dad's favorite meal! That evening Dad and I watched TV until eleven o'clock. As I lay in my bed I gave thanks for my folks. It surprised me that they gave me so much freedom. I was about asleep but I remember thinking, maybe praying, that I hoped they were as happy as I was.

Sunday morning I actually went to church with Mom and Dad, and it wasn't bad, afterwards I didn't feel like a sinner going to hell; maybe I wasn't paying attention. Sunday afternoon I did what you are supposed to do on Sunday afternoons, I took a nap. Monday was a whirlwind, I filled up both of my gas cans, checked all of my hunting gear, counted shot gun shells, made sure I had my hunting boots for the swamp and my waders for duck hunting, and cleaned my gun. That evening I packed my larger duffle, after-all I was leaving for a week or more. I also made sure I had my long underwear, and my heavy hunting pants and coat, plus a wool scarf Mom had given me. By bedtime I was so excited it was hard to get to sleep. I was up the next morning before Mom or Dad. I was drinking coffee when Dad came into the kitchen, "Son, how long will you be staying?" I hadn't actually counted days so I started thinking out loud.

"Today is Tuesday the thirtieth, Thursday is New Year, we don't start back to school until Monday, January twelfth; I'll probably be home around the tenth. You know you could come join Elzie and me on a duck hunt?"

"Well, we'll see. If I can manage that I'll call Cloud and she can contact Elzie and one of you can come fetch me up."

"That would be great Dad, please try to do it."

Dad launched my boat at eight o'clock that morning. I called Tess just before leaving the house and told her I'd be there in about an hour. She was waiting on me at the landing site. When she saw all my gear she asked if I was moving in. I told her that was the plan, but I figured Cloud would kick me out by the time school started again. Elzie and Cloud were on the back porch when Tess and I hauled all my gear to my room. Elzie laughed, Cloud whistled, then asked if my folks ran me off? I told them that my folks had locked me in my room and I had to slip off under the cover of darkness just to come see them. Hearing that Cloud turned to Elzie and said, "My God, he's one of you!" Elzie responded,

"Yes, and I'm mighty proud of him!" Home again, home again!

It was Tuesday, New Year's Eve was the next day, I wasn't for sure but I doubted that Elzie would want to leave on New Year's day. My doubts were correct, we stayed until Friday, January second, 1959! 1959, wow, I sat day dreaming on Cloud's back porch about 1958, much had happened, I became a jail bird, I fell in love, I became part of a tribe, sorta, at least I had a whole other family. It seemed that from the end of May until now everything that happened was just one adventure after another. I had seen a turtle lay her eggs, and later seen the eggs hatch and followed the babies to the gulf. I had improved my baseball and football abilities, I had learned to throw a castnet, gig frogs and gators, and learned how to use a fly rod. I received a new boat and a new shotgun, killed my first ducks, had a couple of great dove hunts, and most importantly, I had come to realize that there was a part of me that I was just beginning to explore. Having feelings of things I could not see, but felt, and seeing things that were not actually there, it all existed. It wasn't just my thinking that made them be there, it was more of an existence, an acceptance, maybe just the acceptance of the existence. It was still very confusing, but I was willing and ready for the experience.

I was in a dream-like state, relaxed on a chaise lounge, when Tess walked in, I felt an urge to surprise, "Is this heaven? Are you an angel?" I thought I'd get the best of her, but she replied,

"No, I'm the devil and you're in trouble!"

"Well, that's disappointing!" She laughed, came over and sat down by me and asked what I was doing.

"Just dreaming and remembering all the great things that happened this year. There was this angel that I met and she tricked me into falling in love with her."

"That's strange, the exact same thing happened to me!" I gave up, it's hard trying to get the best of a woman, especially a smart woman. "And anyway, it's New Year's Eve, what shall we do to bring in the new year?" I gave that some thought, maybe three seconds of thought, then replied that we should go to Wrights Lake and make plans. She thought that was an excellent idea, and a few minutes later we were in her Mom's car headed to our favorite spot.

We were back well before dark, as we walked into Cloud's house I asked Cloud if there was anything planned for the New Year's celebration. She said the only fireworks we'd see would be around the fire pit, Elzie was cooking. We were all long asleep when the New Year rolled in.

New Year's day was like a Sunday, nothing going on, everyone seemed lazy. Right after lunch Tess came over and said we should take a walk. We headed back to the ridge and the bench, once there Tess asked how long would I be at the houseboat. I told her that the only date I promised my folks was that I'd be home on the 10th. She asked if I was serious about us having a duck hunt, I said most definitely. "I'm trying to get my Dad to come for a hunt as well. I'll make some plans with Elzie, maybe you and Cloud can come back for a day or two and you and I can duck hunt then." She smiled, then changed the conversation.

"Matt, what do you want to study in college?" I sure didn't see that one coming, I was having a hard time just imagining being a senior in high school.

"Tess, I don't have a clue, what I want most is to play college baseball."

"I assumed that, but I've been thinking about college a lot lately, and I think I want to be a doctor."

"A doctor! Tess, that would be great, I'm sure Elzie and I both will need a good doctor in the future."

"Matt, I'm serious. I really think that I want to be a doctor, a general practice doctor, maybe in a small town like Bristol or Blountstown, even Apalachicola." I just wasn't in the mood to be real serious, but I knew I needed to be supportive.

"Tess, I believe you can be anything you want to be, and if I'm still alive and kicking, I'll help anyway I can. You know I do know how to gig frogs and gators!" I think, at that, she gave up talking about the future. She just said,

"Men!" and we headed back to the house.

Tess had supper with us, we were on Cloud's back porch when I asked Elzie if we had a plan. Before he answered I also told him that my Dad might come for a duck hunt, and I wanted to take Tess for a duck hunt, and could Cloud and Tess come for a couple of days? He just nodded okay, didn't say a thing for a bit, but turned to Cloud and asked if she could get him a calendar and time schedule. "It's getting to the point that I'm running a resort instead of a hunting camp!"

Cloud, never one to be out gunned, said, "Well, I don't think there is any way that you could keep up with a time schedule or a calendar, and you're a long way from being a resort." She then turned to me and said that she and Tess would love to come for a couple of days, just pick out which days works best and let her know. Elzie got up and went for a beer!

Chapter 16: Celebration

Friday was January 2nd and we were up early. Elzie had a good size cardboard box in the kitchen and he was taking supplies out of the cupboard; Cloud walked in, "What are you doing?"

"I'm getting some supplies for the houseboat!"

"Well, thanks for asking. What am I supposed to do if you take all the food?"

"You could go shopping!" Cloud wasn't surprised or upset, she just liked getting after Elzie, kind of a reminder that he needed to act mannerly occasionally. Elzie went on packing supplies and within a few minutes he called his trusted right hand man for help, I went to get the box of supplies and took them to the boat. After that I got all of my stuff together and hauled it to the boat as well, his boat was bigger so it all went into his boat. As I went back inside to gather more supplies I noticed Elzie had his wallet opened and was handing Cloud money, it appeared to be a routine thing. Within minutes we were packed, had our guns, and were headed out the door when Tess came over.

"Were you going to leave without saying goodbye?"

"Of course not, we're just packing the boat. I was coming to see you in just a few minutes." Maybe I was getting a bit like Elzie. We stood there, a bit uncomfortable, for a few minutes, then finally said we had to go, I kissed Tess goodbye, told her I'd be in touch this evening, then Elzie and I headed to the boats. As we got in the boats he looked over at me and said,

"Boy, don't you get us in trouble with the lady folks!" As much as I tried, I couldn't come up with a good come back. We headed down river.

At the houseboat we reversed the previous process, I got on the houseboat walk way and Elzie handed me supplies to haul inside. It was getting close to lunch when Elzie said he needed a beer, it sounded like a good idea to me, but he didn't include me. While having a sandwich we made a plan, duck hunt this afternoon. While Elzie took a little nap I loaded the decoys, our guns and shells, and a few snacks in my boat. He got up around 2:30, made himself a cup of coffee, put on some camo and said let's go. As we got in my boat I asked where we were going to hunt. "I don't know, you're the guide."

"Ok, let's go take a look!" See, I was learning.

At the mouth of East River I took the left prong, ran just a little past the cutoff to East River Pocket, and cut off the engine. We could see well back into Sam's Bight, plus some of the Pocket, and the outside marsh island we had hunted on before. I dropped an anchor, got comfortable and we waited. We had been there maybe 30 minutes or so before we saw birds beginning to move. They were coming out of the bay toward the marsh, but they weren't going to Sam's Bight, or the Pocket. They flew in over the marsh island then turned to the west and pitched into the water on the other side of the marsh bank on the west side East River. Elzie was watching, "Ok, let's go. Trim your motor, we've got to jump a flat at the end of the marsh and into Austin's Hole." I had not hunted Austin's Hole, though I knew what and where it was, but in just a few minutes we were across the flat and headed toward the back of Austin's Hole. Birds started getting off the water, they were spread out all across the back of the Hole. There were a few blinds in the back, Elzie pointed at one and said to go there. We stopped in front of the blind, tossed out our decoys, then slid into the palm blind.

"Who's blind is this?" I asked.

"Don't know, but this afternoon it's ours!"

"Won't the owner be mad if he shows up and we're in his blind?"

"Probably, but the marsh rule is: opening weekend each person owns his own blind, everyone respects that, but after opening weekend all blinds are first come first serve."

"I didn't know that! So if I ran into Sam's Bight to hunt one morning and someone was in our blind I just leave it to them?"

"I would suppose unless you want someone shooting at you!" That was good enough for me, we arranged the palms a bit, then settled in to wait on the ducks to return.

It didn't take long, the first bunch of teal must have had 20 or more birds, we picked up six. Over the next couple of hours we picked up eight more birds, three mallards, two gadwalls, and three wigeons, they were all nice and fat. Back at the houseboat Elzie told to me to breast a couple of mallards, we were having duck for supper. Duck breast smothered in onions and gravy, over toast, with a side of greens. It was fine! Along about 9:30 Elzie called Cloud on the radio, told her we were doing fine, had a nice duck shoot, and that he would check in with her tomorrow. We were both asleep by 10:30.

Saturday morning Elzie was up well before daylight, I smelled the coffee and joined him. While having coffee he asked what I wanted to do today. I gave it a little thought and decided I'd like to try again for that buck. He said he had plenty to do around the houseboat and my hunting for a buck was fine, then he suggested I take his 30-30 Winchester.

It was just beginning to lighten in the east when I loaded the 30-30 and stepped onto the bank. The morning was calm, and cold, but I felt excited. I stood there for a few minutes getting my thoughts together, putting a plan together. As it lightened just a little I started up river along the bank, I decided to go directly to the Mounds like Elzie and I had done when looking for tracks, hunt there for a while, then slip hunt back along the old road bed and explore a couple of the ridges that ran cross-wise from the old road. I found my blind at the Mounds, re-staked my palms and leaned back to wait on full daylight. Daylight came silently, no breeze, no birds singing, no dew dropping on leaves, just stillness. The sun rays were just beginning to show through the trees when I got this strange feeling, it wasn't like the feeling I had when the buck was watching me, it was sort of a presence, like I was sharing the Mounds with somebody else. It didn't alarm me, I didn't start looking around, and I didn't hear anything, but I had a sense that I wasn't alone.

I sat there maybe 15 more minutes when I saw some movement coming from the same direction that Two Feathers and his wife had come from, then from behind a large cypress tree out walked Two Feathers. He was dressed the same as before, same scarf over his head, but no gun. Instead he was carrying a large bag, a strap over his left shoulder attached to the bag. It appeared heavy. I blinked just to make sure, yep, he was still coming my way.

At first I was fearful, then excited, then telling myself to just stop. Cloud had said I would have more visions, that I should watch and listen, there may be a sign or clue I was being offered. So, I sat there, watching Two Feathers walk again along the same trail he walked before, but this time after he passed me for a short distance he stopped at a large cypress tree. The tree's trunk split at the bottom, at ground level, creating an opening at the base. He lowered the bag and started taking items out of the bag and burying them in the tree trunk. It took only a few minutes until he was finished, he then took out his knife and cut some palm fronds and piled them around the tree trunk, hiding the items. When finished he stood, looked around, then continued in the direction he disappeared last time. He was gone! I stood up to again look to see if I might see him moving away in the woods. Nothing! I sat back down. What was this about? I realized that I had seen another vision, what was he telling me? What could it have meant? My mind was running crazy, was I dreaming? I pinched myself on the arm, yep, I was awake.

I decided to go look at the tree, maybe the items were still there. I slowly got up, stepped away from my palm blind, then eased over toward the tree where he had placed the items. As I moved in that direction I realized there wasn't a large tree split at the bottom. There were plenty of cypress trees, but none real large, there were no tracks. I returned to my blind and sat down. I needed to think. I sat there for quite a while trying to figure out what seeing Two Feathers could have meant, what could have been in the bag, why was I seeing these visions? I decided that I had better not tell Elzie about this, I would wait and tell Cloud, she could decide if I should tell Elzie about this event.

The swamps began waking up, a light breeze in the tree tops, squirrels were beginning to bark, and I could see some occasionally in the tree tops. I decide to go look for my buck. I started back down the old road bed, it was really grown up, but a trail was easily seen, and I slowly made my way toward the south. About where I usually hit the trail coming from the houseboat a slough drops off on the left, it's very shallow water and most like the regular swamp, it runs for maybe 50 or 60 yards, then elbows back to the left. At that elbow there is an oak ridge that runs back to the east, I worked in that direction. I hadn't hunted this ridge but I was amazed how beautiful it was; the oaks were old growth live oaks with hickory and white oak among them. The ridge was wide and not a lot of undergrowth, just a sprinkling of palms and small bushes.

The squirrels were everywhere. I paused every few feet, slowly scanning in every direction, maybe 30 or 40 yards down that ridge I got that feeling again, not like something was watching me, but something was near. My senses increased, I could smell the swamps, as well as the growth on the ridge, I moved slowly. After another 40 or 50 yards the ridge cuts back to the left again, I moved in that direction. I hadn't gone 20 yards when I felt that I should sit down, like an invisible hand reached out and touched my shoulder and gently pushed me to the ground. I slid down next to a hickory tree, kept my knees up and braced the 30-30 on my knees. In less than a minute out steps a nice buck, maybe 40 or 50 yards down the ridge. I had a bullet in the chamber, I slowly pulled the hammer back, and as the buck turned to where I had a broad side shot I settled the sights on the base of his neck and squeezed the trigger.

The recoil and the sound shook me, I was back against the tree, automatically working the lever, ejecting the spent bullet, re-chambering a new round. I looked for the deer, I couldn't see him, I stood up and there he was, lying on the ground right where he was when I pulled the trigger. The gun was cocked, I moved slowly toward him thinking that he might jump up and try to run, I was ready to shoot. As I approached the buck I could see the blood on his neck where I was aiming, I touched him with the barrel of the rifle, he didn't move. I had broken his neck. He was dead. I put the rifle back on safety, then stood there for a minute just staring at the buck, he was a nice eight point with a wide beam. A sadness came over me, I wasn't prepared to face a dead animal, one so beautiful, one whose life I had just taken. Birds didn't affect me, this did. I laid the gun across his body, knelt beside him and prayed, "Great spirit, I give thanks for this animal whose life has been sacrificed, I will share it with all of our people. May it benefit all who worship you. Please guide me in my quest." I pulled out my knife and cut some hair from his tail, I unbuttoned my shirt, retrieved my medicine bag and put the buck's hair in with the other items. "This represents Animal Kingdom, it gives me strength, ties me to the earth."

I was up and pulling the buck to a clear spot where I was going to gut him before dragging him back to the houseboat when I heard Elzie holler, "Matt! Matt!"

"Over here Elzie!" he couldn't have been more than 50 or 60 yards from where I was. In just a minute he was rounding the ridge at the elbow, I waved and he spotted me. As he approached he said,

"I heard you shoot, heard the bullet hit, knew you had a big one." He stood there with me, both of us just staring at the buck, both smiling. "Well, the work starts now! Let's gut him back at the houseboat. If we pull together it won't take us long to get back there, and I've got a water hose so we'll clean him up real good."

We started off at a good pace, by the time we got back to the houseboat we were both wet from sweat, both of us swearing that the buck weighed at least 200 pounds or more. As we dragged the deer up close to where we would gut him Elzie said, "That's good, leave him right there a minute, I'm going to have a beer." When he returned he handed me a beer too. "Anyone that kills a nice buck like that ought to have a beer!" We sat there next to the deer, each of us drinking a beer, him making me swear that I'd tell no one that he gave me a beer. I swore!

There was a big hickory tree close to the fire pit with a large limb stretching toward the river, we threw a rope over the limb, attached it to the buck's horns, then lifted him up high enough that the hind legs barely touched the ground. Elzie became the professor again, first showing me how to cut through the chest bone, then showing me how to gut the deer, how to avoid hitting the urinary tubes, how to cut the genitals away from the animal, and lastly how to save the heart and the liver. We washed the deer's insides first, then the whole deer. Elzie said we should let it dry, it was certainly cold enough. Then he turned to me and said, "I guess we're going back to Owl Creek! A friend of mine has a cold storage in back of his store in Sumatra, he'll let us age it there. We'll skin it when we get there. I'd better go call Cloud."

About that time I was thinking I should have another beer! Elzie returned, said we needed to lock up the houseboat, take enough stuff for overnight, we'd be back the next morning. We loaded the deer in Elzie's boat with a little gear, locked up the houseboat, left my boat there, and headed to Owl Creek. Cloud and Tess were at the landing when we arrived. Elzie borrowed Mike's truck and we took the deer to Elzie's friend's store. Behind the store was a beam for hanging deer and hogs, we strung up the deer there and Elzie instructed how to skin a deer. After the skinning we washed the deer again, then took it into the cold storage unit and hung it. Elzie put a large bucket under the deer to catch the blood and fluids that drain from the buck while aging. Back at the house Elzie explained to me that Robert, the store owner, also had a butcher shop inside and he would process the deer for us in ten to fifteen days. He explained that the aging process helps tender the deer, and Robert would wrap the meat for freezing. I asked him that we share the deer with all the family. He said, "We always do!"

I went and changed my clothes and washed up a bit, then returned to the porch, Elzie had gone to bathe and Cloud said he was going to take a nap; that left me with Cloud and Tess. After a few minutes, when I knew that Elzie would not be back to the porch, I turned to Cloud and Tess and said, "I have to tell you something." Cloud moved her chair closer to me and said to go on. "I hunted alone this morning. I saw Two Feathers again." Cloud and Tess both moved closer to me, they said nothing, but they were both focused on me completely. I continued, "I didn't tell Elzie because of last time, you have to tell me whether I should tell him about it or not. But I started at the mounds early this morning. I got there before good light, back at the same blind, as the sun rays finally shown through the trees I got this sense of someone being there. It wasn't like what I felt with the buck, it was just a feeling of sharing, someone close by.

Within a few minutes Two Feathers stepped out from behind a large cypress tree, from the same direction he came last time. This time he was alone. He walked almost in the same path as last time, except this time he didn't have a gun, he was carrying a bag with a strap over his shoulder, it appeared heavy. Anyway, he walked past me, then stops next to a very large cypress tree. The tree split at the bottom creating a hollow spot at ground level, he knelt down and put the contents of the bag into the hole. He then cut several palm fronds and stacked them around the tree, hiding the hole and the contents. Then he got up and walked off just like he did the time before. I stood up to see if I could see him moving away. I couldn't. I waited a while trying to figure out what I should do, then decided to take a look at the tree, maybe see what might have been put there. As I moved toward where the tree was I realized that there was no large cypress tree, split at the bottom, only smaller trees. And, there were no tracks."

By the time I finished Cloud was smiling, Tess just sat there looking at me like I was some sort of shaman. Cloud began, "Matthew, there's some strong medicine going on with you. So this time you felt something?" I nodded yes. "I believe that there is a message here, I also believe that you need to be open to receiving signs as to what the message is. It will come to you, no one else can tell you what the messages are, only you will know when they are delivered."

"What about Elzie?"

"I think we need to leave Elzie out of this for now. We can talk about it later."

"Do you want to hear about the deer?"

"Certainly!" From both of them.

"Well, after Two Feathers came for a visit, I sat there for a while, then decided to go hunt for my buck. I was back on a ridge I hadn't hunted before when I got that feeling again, not like something was watching me, but like something was close. As I was easing along I got a strange feeling, like a giant invisible hand reached out and touched my shoulder and pushed me to the ground. I sat down by a tree and within a minute my buck steps out in front of me not 40 or 50 yards away. He turned sideways to me and I broke his neck. I want to tell you something else, when I got to him I felt really bad, killing that animal was the saddest thing I've ever done. I gave thanks for his life, swore I'd share it with all the family. I also put some of his hair in my medicine bag." At that Cloud got up and came to me and hugged me. Tess reached over and took my hand, squeezed it.

Cloud said, "Matthew, you already are and will continue to be a great warrior!"

Elzie got up an hour or so later, Cloud fixed an early supper and while the four of us ate together Elzie suggested that Cloud and Tess join us tomorrow at the houseboat for a couple of days. They both said they would be ready by eight the next morning.

Sunday morning we were back at the houseboat, all four of us, it felt like a celebration, everyone was happy. I had forgotten to bring the single shot 20 gauge for Tess, but Elzie said he had a light weight double barrel 20 gauge and some shells, Tess could use it. He retrieved it from his bedroom, with a box of shells, so Tess and I got out on the bank and she shot it a few times. She felt comfortable with it so we planned an afternoon hunt for just the two of us. We gathered wood for a fire for the evening, had some lunch, and about 2:30 we headed down river in my boat, I took all 18 decoys. When we got to the mouth of East River, I did the same as Elzie and I had done a couple of days before, I anchored the boat in the east prong near the Pocket.

We watched for most of an hour before birds started getting up out on the bay and heading to the marsh, quite a few pitched down back in Sam's Bight so I decided to hunt there. I went straight to the blind Elzie and I had made, spread the decoys in a semi-circle fashion leaving an opening right in front of the blind, then pulled the boat into the blind and rearranged the palms. I gave Tess instructions like I did when we dove hunted, she said she knew the routine. I cautioned her that ducks, especially teal, fly faster than doves, but when they are coming directly to us, just hold on and fire; but, if they are flying cross wise she needed to add more of a lead than with doves. Within a little while a small bunch of teal came by, I whispered to lead them, she shot both barrels, didn't cut a feather. She ejected the two spent shells, reloaded, sat down and said, "Damn! They do fly fast!" I couldn't help but smile, then told her I did the same thing, and still do sometimes. Shortly another bunch pitched in over the decoys, we both got one. Her spirits soared! By dark we had seven birds, five teal, one mallard, and one wigeon, Tess killed three teal. She was excited.

Back at the houseboat Tess and Cloud fixed supper while I cleaned the ducks. Elzie tended to the fire and had a beer. It's a shame one can't have a beer with ducks like they can with a deer! The evening was beautiful, stars could be seen in all directions, a really cold chill settled in during the night.

197

When we woke the next morning Elzie already had a fire going and was drinking coffee. We all fixed a cup and joined him around the fire. It was just getting light in the east when Tess said she wanted to hunt at the Mounds this morning. We waited until light enough to see in the woods before she and I headed up river along the bank. We went directly to the Mounds from the river bank like I had a two mornings before, rearranged the blind and sat down against the tree. The cold stung our feet and hands within minutes, Tess leaned over closer to me and whispered, "I don't know if hunting is worth this or not." I told her to snuggle up, it would warm up as soon as the sun gets up. We huddled together, our faces almost touching, watching the woods come to life.

It was getting good light, but the sun's rays weren't in swamps yet when I saw some movement off to my right. I squeezed Tess's hand, then pointed to my right with my finger, I leaned back a little, giving her better vision, and out steps a big doe, followed by a yearling. They were leaving the ridge, headed toward Thank You Ma'am Creek. We watched them until they vanished into the swamps. That warmed her up. We readjusted a little, but still snuggled, our faces close so we could whisper. It was maybe 20 minutes later, the sun's rays were beginning to be seen higher in the trees, but not at ground level yet, when I saw movement out where Two Feathers had appeared. I squeezed Tess's hand again, keeping my hand down I pointed in the direction of the movement; we stared and waited.

It seemed to take forever, but I'm sure it was just seconds, when three turkey hens moved into the open to where we could see them well. I turned my head slightly to where I could whisper in her ear, "I think that's the three hens we saw before, they must be roosting by the creek." The turkeys were not feeding, just moving along at a steady pace, headed toward the east end of the Mounds, where the ridge runs back to the south and east. It's where the oak trees are, acorns for the turkeys. As they passed in front of us I noticed more movement back in the direction that they came from. I squeezed Tess's hand again, and again pointed with my finger. Within seconds a big gobbler stepped into view. I waited until he was behind some trees and brush to lean to Tess and whispered, "A big gobbler, you kill him, when he goes behind a tree where he can't see us move I want you to raise your gun, slip the safety off, and when he reappears from behind the tree shoot him in the head. I'll tell you when." She nodded very slowly.

The gobbler was still a good 60 yards or so out from us, we had to wait. He wasn't moving as fast as the hens, but he was following their trail. I picked out the spot I thought he would be the closest, if he stayed on the hen's trail, then placed my hand on Tess's arm. We waited. As the gobbler moved closer I kept trying to find the biggest tree he may go behind so Tess could get in position to shoot. He plodded along, finally he was probably 35 to 40 yards when he went behind a large cypress tree, I squeezed her arm, she raised her gun, slipped the safely off, and when the old Tom walked into view she pulled the trigger. The kick knocked her back briefly, I jumped up ready to finish the Tom off if he started to run, he lay kicking and flopping his wings, face down. He was dead before we even got to him. I think I was more excited than Tess, she kept stroking his feathers, I kept trying to show her the length of his spurs, she got tears in her eyes, then told me that she now understood how I felt when I shot the buck. I gave her a hug, told her I was proud of her, then picked up the bird and we headed back to the houseboat.

Elzie and Cloud were sitting around the fire waiting on us. When Elzie saw me carrying the Tom he jumped up and came to get him. Lifting the bird he said, "Wow, this old Tom must weigh 20 pounds. Nice job Matt."

"I didn't kill him, Tess did."

Elzie's eyes got wide, that almost smile appeared, he said, "By God, that girl's got potential." At that moment I thought Cloud might actually throw something at him. We laughed, Cloud gave Tess a hug, Elzie patted me on the back, said I did a good thing. I cleaned the gobbler, Elzie iced it down in one of his ice chests. The rest of the day and evening we mostly sat around the fire, Elzie entertained us with stories. I had a few I couldn't tell Elzie.

Tuesday morning we headed back to Owl Creek. Tuesday afternoon Elzie had me packing duck and turkey for freezing. That evening I called Dad, I told him about our duck hunts, my deer and Tess's turkey. I think he was impressed. I insisted that he come for a duck hunt with me, he stalled a bit, said he needed to talk to Mom, I told him I'd hold on. It didn't take long, he told me Mom thought that was a good idea, I told him I'd come get him Thursday morning, we could hunt Thursday afternoon and all day Friday. He said a couple of hunts would be great, I told him I would be at the boat basin at noon on Thursday. He gave the ok, said he'd be waiting.

Wednesday was our day of rest, Cloud washed some clothes for me and Elzie, I re-cleaned the guns, and Elzie and I ran in to Sumatra to fill our gas cans with gas for our boats. By evening we were sitting around the fire pit, Alida and Sage joined us so of course we had to entertain them with Tess's great hunting abilities. Mama Sol even walked over and visited for a while.

Chapter 17: Remarkable Coincidences

Thursday morning Elzie had me up early. By nine o'clock we were headed back to the houseboat, I had to pick up Dad at noon in Apalachicola. I dropped off my bags and gun, then headed to Apalachicola. I told Elzie Dad and I would be back before one, I also asked if he would like to hunt with Dad and me this afternoon, but he declined and said I needed to appreciate the opportunity of hunting with my Dad, old river rats didn't need to interfere with such an occasion. Dad was at the boat basin when I arrived, we threw his gear into my boat, then we headed back to the houseboat. Elzie had fixed some sandwiches when we arrived, I wondered if Cloud had fixed them and sent them with Elzie, but of course I knew he'd never admit to it.

We sat around until almost three, I told Elzie that I thought Dad and I might try Austin's Hole again, he reminded me about the flat we had to jump to get in there. By three thirty we were putting out decoys. We sat in the blind watching for birds, I told Dad about every hunt Elzie and I had, and how many birds we'd killed. He said that he and Elzie had had a few hunts together when he was growing up, but did say he'd never killed a deer or a turkey. I wanted to tell him about my visions and the feelings I had when hunting, I just didn't know how he would respond, and I didn't want him thinking that I was going to the far side of cuckoo. So, I didn't go there!

It was a little after four when the first birds pitched into our decoys, they were wigeons and must have been eight or ten in the bunch. Dad killed two his first shot, and a third with his last shot. I killed two. Dad acted really excited as we picked up the birds, "That's the first ducks I've shot in twenty years."

It made me feel good, I responded, "Well maybe we should do this more often!" He smiled at me and said that sounded good. We had less than an hour and a half before shooting time was over, but we picked up five more birds during that time. Back at the houseboat Elzie had a fire going, something cooking on the stove.

He handed Dad a beer as we unloaded, I went to clean the ducks. Elzie said we needed three widgeons breasted and prepared for cooking. I guess the hired helped didn't get to have a beer. It didn't take long to clean the ducks, and after I washed up we gathered in the kitchen to eat. More smothered duck breast in onions and gravy over toast, with collard greens and sliced tomatoes. My belly was happy. "Where y'all planning on hunting in the morning?" Elzie asked. I was planning on hunting in Sam's Bight and as soon as I said that Elzie decided he'd hunt East River Pocket. "If you would loan me six decoys in the morning, I might be able to add some meat to the pot." How was I to disagree, they were his decoys.

"Sounds good to me!" After supper I cleaned up the kitchen, checked the ice over the ducks, then joined Elzie and Dad around the fire. It was a great evening, good and cold, dark skies with lots of stars, no wind, and owls hollering up and down the river. Dad and Elzie had another beer and began talking some of their past duck hunts.

"The hunts I remember the most were the ones when Walter joined us down on Little St. George," Dad began. "Remember the red heads we got into in Pot Cove?" Elzie got to laughing, then started telling about how Walter thought he'd outsmart Dad and Elzie and put them back in the cove and he'd get out on the point where he was sure he'd get most all of the shots. Turns out Walter didn't get any shots, the birds flew wide of the point and pitched into Dad and Elzie's decoys. They picked up 20 birds that morning, Walter didn't fire a shot. Dad was actually having fun, it's the first hunting stories I'd ever heard him tell. They carried on until well past ten, then Elzie said we should turn in, we needed to be in the blind before daylight.

Friday morning was still and cold, Dad had brought a thermos so he filled it with coffee before we left for the blind. After setting out the decoys we both poured a cup and sat in the blind, drinking coffee, listening to the bay, not saying much. It was still dark when the first bunch of birds dropped into our decoys. Dad whispered, "That must be mallards." Even in the dark you could see their size and they looked big. They moved around in the decoys for a bit, but got a little nervous and swam over closer to the marsh. As it got light enough to shoot the birds flushed and we both picked a pair. Four mallards, fat and beautiful.

For the next hour and a half we had birds working the back end of Sam's Bight, we killed a few teal, one pintail, and four more widgeons. We left with our limits, Elzie was waiting in the prong outside the Pocket. He had his limit too. Back at the houseboat we all jumped in and cleaned the birds in just a little while, had a light lunch, and then Dad said he needed to get back. I tried to get him to stay another day, but he decided not to, so I took him back to town. I said goodbye and headed back to the houseboat, when I got there Elzie said we should go to Owl Creek. He also said that I needed to take my boat because he promised my Dad I'd be home tomorrow and I needed to see Tess some before I had to go back to school. SCHOOL! Why did he have to bring that up?

By four o'clock we were back at Owl Creek. The next day was Saturday, the tenth. Tess stayed with me all day on Saturday until I had to leave, we talked about the coming year, what we would be doing, how we could run back and forth to see each other, and of course, there was still more hunting season left. I left Owl Creek around four, Dad picked me up at the boat basin at five. Mom had supper ready at six-thirty, it was the first meal we had had together in eleven days. At supper Dad talked about how much fun he had on the hunts, he also said he had forgotten how entertaining Elzie was. Mom said we should do that more often.

Sunday was a day of rest, this time I did not go to church with Mom and Dad, but I did spend a lot of time thinking about life, the future, and the visions I had. They had to mean something, I wouldn't think that you would have a vision and it not mean anything. The first vision was just about Two Feathers and his family moving through the swamps, the second he was hiding something. Cloud had said that many Indians remained in the swamp, did not move with most of the Indians to the reservations, maybe that's what the first vision represented? It was about the only thing that made any sense to me. The second vision was hiding something, what could he be hiding? Maybe the gold? But the missing gold came later, long after the Indian Removal Act. Was Two Feathers even alive then? Was the vision just to let me know that the Indians really did get the gold? How would I ever know? This all seemed way too complicated to me; maybe I should talk to Cloud about it the next time we got together, maybe next weekend. But going back to school changed my thinking!

We all gathered outside the school early Monday morning, waiting on the bell to ring. Most of the guys had stories to tell about the holidays, who hunted, what they killed, and even things they got for Christmas. I think I impressed them all with my buck story. I did not tell them about Two Feathers. The bell rang, Mr. Blaylock welcomed us back from never, never land. He first asked number 7, Bud Carlson, if he received any bank stock in his stocking, Bud just nodded no, so he then turned to number six, Billy Fields, and asked him if he got a shot at Rudolph. Of course Billy said yes that he did, had blood on his roof to prove it, but evidently the shot wasn't lethal, he'd try harder next year. We were back in the routine, Chapman High's road to greatness!

Miss Mac's class was as usual, Billy and Wayne kept plinking hair clips against the metal chairs making a sound that was just loud enough for Miss Mac to hear, as she would move in the direction of one plink that Billy made, Wayne would make another on the other side of the room. That went on the whole class, I don't think we ever got to history. However, the next class, Government with Mr. Lawson, piqued my interest. We began the study of ownership as it relates to assets and how they are taxed by the government. We started with individual ownership and talked some about tax rates, then we talked about partnerships, how they function and how they are taxed. I thought all of that was pretty interesting, but next we talked about corporations, Mr. Lawson called them C-corporations, and how they were taxed differently. He explained that Corporations have a special tax rate, different from individuals. He also explained how corporations can pay taxes and then distribute tax free dividends to the share holders, or if they don't pay the taxes and pay out dividends to the individual stock holder that they would pay taxes at their individual tax rates.

Mr. Lawson also told us about a new form of corporations that had been created just this past year, they're called Sub-S corporations and they are taxed either as a normal C-corporation or as a partnership which is taxed individually to owner's interest. At some point I asked Mr. Lawson why did people create Corporation to begin with? His answer hit me like a thrown ball, "Corporations can have many stock holders but they are not publicized, so the stock holders can remain anonymous. The Chairman and Secretary's names are published , but corporations use Corporate Contacts for most transactions, the board members and the contact person don't even have to be stockholders. Even other corporations could be the contact person." I remembered looking up the ownership and taxes for Little St. George Island, it was owned by a corporation. I didn't pay attention to the contact person, but I thought I should have a look.

We were most of the way through class when Bud asked Mr. Lawson about Trusts and how they work for owning property. Mr. Lawson explained that Trusts function a lot like a corporation, the trust can have only one or many beneficiaries for the trust's assets. The trust can also pay taxes or it can distribute assets and the beneficiaries can pay taxes similarly to corporations, but Trusts can have broader flexibilities, they can control the assets, distribute assets on a non-equal basis to the beneficiaries, and if constructed properly the trust can shelter assets from beneficiaries' estate taxes. It's one of the more private legal instruments in use. I decided that I needed to spend some time back in the Property Appraiser's office.

When school was out I walked downtown to the Court House and into the Property Appraiser's office. Hilda gave me a big smile and said that if I needed her help to just ask. I first looked at the tax records for Little St. George Island, it was owned by a Delaware Corporation, the Contact Person was Hendley, Gore, and Hurts, Inc. of Atlanta, Georgia. Hilda told me they were a law firm. I wrote the information down and was about to leave when I thought about Owl Creek. I asked Hilda to look up Cloud's property. She pulled up a site map of the area, it showed individual lots within the site plan, but when she pulled up the ownership it was all owned by a Trust, the Taylor Family Trust created in 1927. The records showed the name of the Trustee as Hendley, Gore, and Hurts, Inc. My mind started racing, how could that law firm represent Little St. George Island and the Owl Creek properties. And, who should I ask? Rather, should I ask?

I left the Court House and walked back home. I went directly to my room without speaking to Mom, she came in shortly after and asked if something was wrong. I told her I didn't know, I was just working on some homework, everything was fine.

The next morning I went to Mr. Lawson's room before school started and asked him if it was normal for a law firm to represent a corporation and a trust at the same time. He said certainly, that some law firms specialize in corporations and trusts, and it's not uncommon to find them as Contact Persons or Trustees for several corporations and trusts in an area. That eased my mind a little, but I still thought it was strange. What would a law firm have in common with Little St. George Island and Owl Creek? A couple of brothers was the only answer I could come up with. That thought sat on me for a couple of days, I couldn't get it off my mind, but I sure didn't want to go asking questions about things that were none of my business.

By Wednesday afternoon I had expanded my train of thought, I got to thinking how all of the houses at Owl Creek looked so similar, and then remembered that the houses in Columbus, especially Yellow Bird's house looked just like Mama Sol's. Most of the houses in that neighborhood were similar to Owl Creek's. When I got home from school I asked Mom if it would be alright to make a long distance call. She asked what it was about, I told her some homework. She gave the go-ahead.

It was four o'clock our time, that would make it three o'clock in Columbus. I asked the operator to connect me with the Property Appraiser's office in Columbus, Georgia. I also told her I didn't know what county Columbus was in. It didn't take her long to figure it out, and in just a minute or so I was talking with the Property Appraiser's office in Muscogee County. I told him I was interested in some property located on River Road, house number 224, and asked that he tell me who owned the property. It didn't take him long and he was back on the phone to me, it was in a trust, The Robertson Family Trust created in 1927, the Trustee was Hendley, Gore and Hurts, Inc. I wrote the information down and was about to hang up, then decided to ask about other property on that street. I told the Property Appraiser that I thought there were about a dozen houses in that neighborhood, could he check? Again, it didn't take him long and he was back on the phone with me, "There's actually 14 parcels in that neighborhood, they are all under one plat, and each lot and house are owned by the same trust, with the same Trustee." I thanked him and hung up. Wow, two trusts, one corporation, and all three had the same law firm representing them. What are the chances? The Indians? Two tribes? Or maybe one Tribe living in two locations? And the construction of the houses seemed to all be alike. Who would build these house alike, at different locations, different times? How about some timber people?

Dad had said that he thought Elzie still did some timber work, at least contracts. Should I ask Cloud? Maybe I'll just talk to Tess about it, she's probably the only one I can talk to about it. I would see her this weekend. Thursday night Dad got a call around 7:30, I heard him say, "That sounds like a lot of fun. Yes, I think we can make it. Sure, we'll be there at four o'clock." He then called me to him and said that was Elzie. Walter called him, said the redheads are stacked in Pot Cove. He'll pick us up at Mr. Siglio's Friday afternoon at four o'clock, we're going on a duck hunt. I called Tess, she answered on the third ring,

"Hello"

"Tess, I've got something really important to tell you, it has to be in person, but Dad just had a call from Elzie, he said Walter had called and said redheads are stacked in Pot Cove and we're going on a duck hunt starting tomorrow afternoon, we won't be home until late Saturday afternoon."

"Could you come up for most of the day Sunday?"

"I think so, I'll ask. I'll let you know." And I went to talk to Dad. He said it would be fine, so I called Tess back, I'd see her Sunday morning. Dad said to pack and get everything ready tonight, right after school tomorrow we needed to get our stuff and be at Mr. Siglio's by four o'clock.

I packed my waders, camo, warm clothes, and my hunting hat with the pull down ear muffs. Dad had extra shotgun shells, we both had automatics. A redhead hunt, I'd heard all the old stories, never got to go on one, this should be exciting, especially if Dad was excited about going.
We were at Mr. Siglio's by 3:45, of course Elzie was already there drinking coffee with Mr. Siglio. "Paisan!" as we entered the fish house. The wind was out of the North-Northwest and getting colder, Mr. Siglio had all the doors closed, he had a potbelly stove in the middle of the fish house, it was filled with oak and burning, the string of lights down the middle of the room, over the fish tables were on. It felt like a big adventure. "Bring me four!" as we started out the door. We waved goodbye to Mr. Siglio and piled into Elzie's boat. The bay was choppy, but we were headed downwind, it kept the cold, salt spray from hitting us.

When we got to Walter's we unloaded at his boat house, then Elzie had me put my waders on and we anchored the boat into the wind, using a double anchor. We tied the stern to Walter's house boat pilings. "Those two anchors have saved my butt several times," Elzie, as always, giving me instructions. "If that wind picks up tonight we need to check it several times."

Walter had a fire in the fireplace, the house was warm, and something smelled really good on the stove. We all found a place to sit and Walter started telling us about the redheads, "There's at least a couple thousand birds using Pot Cove; I even saw a small bunch of geese yesterday when I went down to check on them. We should have a great hunt in the morning. The tide will be low so we can move really close to the water and still have the marsh for cover. We need to be there before daylight." A few minutes later Walter asked me to come help him, we went out to the pole barn and hooked up his trailer to the jeep, I then followed him into the tin barn and he retrieved four bags of duck decoys from the back of the barn, he took two and I took two to the trailer. He had four dozen redhead decoys, all decoys strings had heavy anchors. He said we might need the heavy anchors tomorrow if the wind picks up. I asked if we could drive pretty close to the backend of Pot Cove, he replied, "Close enough!" I knew that meant we had to haul decoys and crates to sit on for more distance than what would be easy. Putting decoys out when you're in your boat is a snap, hauling decoys a few hundred yards and then putting them out makes you appreciate your boat.

We had a duck and sausage gumbo for supper, it was outstanding. The men had a couple of drinks of bourbon while we sat around the fire, I just listened to the stories. Walter had a couple of mattress and sleeping bags for Dad and me, we stretched them out in front of the fireplace and everyone was asleep by ten o'clock. Four-thirty came fast, Walter had coffee going even before waking us, we had coffee, some cereal, and by 5:30 we were headed to Pot Cove. Daylight wasn't until about 6:45, I thought that would give us lots of time, we'd have to sit in the marsh and wait on daylight. I was wrong.

Walter stopped the jeep about 100 yards from the back end of Pot Cove, I was instructed to put on my waders, Walter and Elzie had theirs as well. Dad didn't have waders, just some tall rubber boots, I think he'd done this before, he knew what was coming. We first hauled the decoys, each with a bag, to the edge of the Cove. Elzie and I started putting out the decoys, spreading them as we did at the mouth of the river, we left the large opening in front of where we would be sitting, but placed the forty-eight decoys all along the marsh and out into the Cove water. After that was complete we left the decoy bags at the water's edge and went to get out crates to sit on and our guns and shells. Dad and I had a metal, military box, with a cover that we carried our shells in, I got to carry that back to the bay along with my shotgun. Then back to get my crate.

Once we got everything there Walter instructed us to place our crates about eight or ten feet apart so we wouldn't be too close for shooting, and place the crates on top of the decoy bags. He later explained that the marsh often softens up and the decoy bags keep the crates from burying in the mud. Walter then went to move the jeep further away from the Cove so as not to flare the birds. By the time Walter got back to the Cove there was redness in the eastern sky.

Minutes later, still pretty dark, the first bunch of redheads strafed the decoys, there must have been a hundred birds in the bunch. It sounded like a fighter jet flying overhead. They didn't land, but Walter said they would be back. As the skies continued to lighten you could see bunches of birds flying up and down the bay, some staying out over the bay, others making passes over the Cove. It was just getting shooting time when the first bunch pitched into our decoys, there must have been a hundred birds, we all came up shooting. Dad dropped a couple, Walter and Elzie both dropped a couple, I don't think I cut a feather. I couldn't believe it, there were birds all over the sky and I didn't kill a single bird. After I helped Elzie pick up the birds, he saw my disgust, then gave me instructions, "Matt, remember, never shoot at the bunch, pick a single bird at a time."

The next bunch of birds that pitched in I dropped three. For over two hours birds came and went, some pitched into the decoys, others stayed just outside of range, but there must have been thousands of birds flying around Pot Cove that morning.

It was close to ten o'clock when Walter said, "Get down, hear them? To the east, don't move." I sat there motionless, trying to figure out what he was talking about, then I heard them, Geese! And then, Walter started playing magic on a goose call, I didn't even know he had a goose call, but he gave a couple of loud cluck and moan calls, then started a series of clucks, he went quiet as the birds approached. They were coming from the east, just out over the decoys. Walter was calling shots, he waited until the birds were directly out in front of us, so we all had a shot, then called, "Take'em!" We all picked a bird and stayed with him all the way to the water. Walter picked up two, the rest of us picked up one. My first Canadian Honker!

After we picked up the geese Walter went to get the jeep, this time he actually drove to about fifty yards from where we were. We hauled birds and guns, then crates and shells, then we bagged the decoys and hauled them to the jeep. Back at the house we counted the total, five geese, thirty-four redheads. I didn't asked what the limit was. We cleaned birds for over two hours, then had lunch, and then cleaned our guns and washed off the decoys and the trailer we used to haul the gear. It was fast and furious, but it was the best duck hunt I'd ever had, and I had it with my Dad, and my two adopted dads.

Elzie dropped us back at Mr. Siglio's at five o'clock, Dad delivered four fat and cleaned redheads to Mr. Siglio, he was all smiles. We took a few home with us. Elzie promised he'd smoke some ducks and geese in the coming week. Mom said from the look on our faces we must have had quite a time! Dad assured her we did. That evening I called Tess to tell her about the hunt, she said Elzie was already entertaining everyone with all of the details. I told her I'd see her tomorrow. I was asleep well before ten o'clock.

The next morning I had breakfast with Mom and Dad, then took off for Owl Creek, I promised my folks I'd be home around dark. Tess was waiting on me when I drove into her yard, she came out to greet me and asked what was so important. I said we'd talk in a little bit, but I first have to see Cloud and Elzie, she went with me, they were on the back porch having coffee. As we entered the room Elzie started, "Well, the great hunter returns!" Smiles all around. Elzie and I had to again tell them all about the hunt, especially how I didn't kill a single bird when the first huge bunch came in, but it was fun, Cloud and Tess humored us.

Within an hour Tess and I were headed to the big ridge and the bench. As we sat down she started, "Ok, what's so important you couldn't tell me on the phone?" I knew I had to be careful how I told her what I had found. Tess was very protective of her family, I respected that, and did not want her thinking that I was butting into something that was none of my business.

I began, "Tess, one of the classes I'm taking this year is Government, I know I told you that before, but this past week Mr. Lawson started teaching us about different forms of ownership, as in corporations, partnerships, and even trusts. His intention, I believe, was to show how property taxes and income taxes affect these different types of ownership. Remember earlier when I had to go to the Property Appraiser's office and look up property taxes on our family's properties? Well, I also looked up the ownership and taxes for Little St. George Island, not just Walter's property, but the rest of the Island. It's owned by a Delaware Corporation. That didn't mean anything until Mr. Lawson told us about corporations and how individuals can remain anonymous through the corporate structure. He also said that corporations use contact people to deal with the public, it keeps the public from contacting the corporate leadership and owners from complaints and such. Anyway, the contact person for Little St. George is a law firm in Atlanta, Georgia, named, Hendley, Gore, and Hurts, Inc."

By now Tess's eyes were beginning to roll around in their sockets. I continued, "I know this sounds boring, but there's lots more. During our class Bud asked Mr. Lawson about Trusts, I think his father must have a Trust, anyway Mr. Lawson explains that Trusts are a lot like Corporations in that the owners or beneficiaries can remain anonymous. Through all of this I kept thinking about my report and the lost gold, I know that sounds ridiculous, but I started thinking about the houses here and how they were like the houses in Columbus." Tess's eyes narrowed, she tensed up, I realized I was on shaky ground. I continued, "So I called the Property Appraiser's office in Columbus and asked about the ownership of Yellow Bird's house, I didn't call her Yellow Bird, but he says that her house in owned by a Trust. So, I asked about the other houses in the neighborhood, he checks those and they are also in the same Trust, and the Trustee for the Trust is Hendley, Gore, and Hurts, Inc." Tess's interest picked up, she became less tense. I continued, "Now I wasn't trying to be nosy, but because the houses are so much alike I decided to look up Cloud's house, thinking that Elzie might be included, but Cloud's house is owned by a Trust. Every house in this development is owned by a Trust, the Taylor Family Trust, and the Trustee is Hendley, Gore, and Hurts, Inc."

At that Tess sat back, I could feel her confusion, she remained quiet for a while, I knew her mind was running wild just as mine had. Finally, she turned back to me and said, "What difference does it make Matt?" That one hit me between the eyes! I had to make sense, I couldn't upset Tess because I was overly curious.

"It's not about the ownership, that doesn't make a difference, it's about the reason. Now I know it's none of my business, I'm just really curious. I've been thinking since we went to Columbus why the houses there are like the houses here, and then I got to thinking who would build similar houses and I kept coming back to 'a couple of guys in the timber business.'" At that all the dots lined up with Tess, and she started laughing,

"You think that Walter and Elzie built all these houses?" Well, the thought had crossed my mind, but listening to Tess say that made me feel like I was nuts. But I had to finish, I hope she doesn't think I've completely lost my mind,

"Tess, it's not about the ownership, it's not about who built the houses, it's about the money. Maybe the gold was found by the Indians and maybe they hid the gold. Maybe it's the gold that's made all of this happen." Tess sat back again, smiled at me like I was a child, then, very adult like, and trying to reason with me, she said,

"Matt, if I remember correctly, there was $364,000 worth of gold that went missing?" I nodded. "In today's dollars what would that amount to? Maybe a few million dollars?" I nodded. "Do we look like we live the millionaire life style?" It was time for me to shut my mouth, I had overstretched my thinking. Just listening to Tess made me feel like I was trying to be a big time detective with a flawed case.

Elzie lives on a houseboat, Walter lives in a small cabin on an island without running water or electricity, and everyone I know here at Owl Creek doesn't have a lot to show. They all live a pretty simple life. For that matter, my folks, and me, live a higher life style than they do. I felt like an idiot! Well, it wasn't the first time! Maybe I just needed to learn how to keep my mouth shut! We sat there a little longer, silently I might add, and after some self-analyzing I turned to Tess and said, "Maybe I've been hit in the head one to many times playing football!" She laughed some more at me, then said we needed to get back, maybe have some lunch. I don't remember much about the rest of the day, but by dark I was home. As I lay in bed that night thinking, I still couldn't get the idea out of my head that there was some remarkable coincidences in all of this. What if the Indians did find the gold? What if Walter and Elzie were somehow tied to all of this? I guess Tess was right, what difference does it make?

Chapter 18: The Glue

There were only two more weeks of duck season, then the dreary month of February. Nothing good happens in February, unless you play basketball, which I didn't. But baseball practice begins by middle March, I got excited just thinking about it. Maybe the next two weekends I could stay with Elzie on the houseboat on Friday nights, hunt Friday afternoon late, then again on Saturday morning, then be at Owl Creek for Saturday night and most of Sunday. The week went fast. Thursday night I packed my gear and started putting some things in my boat. I loaded my waders, my slicker suit, my rod and reel and a small tackle box. I checked my gas and life vest. The rest of my clothing, gun and shells I'd put in the boat when ready to leave. Friday by 3:45 I was on my way, going directly to my duck blind. I decided to hunt East River Pocket but when I pulled into the small channel that leads into the Pocket I realized that someone was already in my blind. I stopped just short of pulling into the pocket, cut my motor, and stood up. Two guys stood up in the boat located in my blind. One was big and I recognized him immediately, "Shuler, you're a long way from home."

Shuler recognized me, "Drugar, is this your blind?"

"Evidently it's yours this afternoon."

"I didn't know this was your blind, but it makes it even sweeter!"

"No worry, I've got other blinds." And I headed to Sam's Bight. The tide was falling fast and I had to pole over the flat at the mouth of the Bight. My decoys were out and I was settled into my blind before 4:30. I heard Shuler and his buddy start shooting over in the Pocket within minutes. Before five I had picked up three teal, but the tide was really pouring out and I surely didn't want to get stuck back there this late in the day. I decided I would head on up to the house boat. I picked up my decoys, idled to the mouth of the Bight, but the tide was too low for me to pole across. I put on my wades and drug my boat across the flats. Finally I got to deeper water and cranked up.

As I eased by the Pocket, Shuler and his buddy were out of their blind, but they weren't going anywhere. The Pocket had turned to soup. Shuler immediately started hollering for me, "Drugar, Drugar, come help us!"

I pulled into the entrance channel and got as close to the Pocket as I could without reaching the shallow area. The two of them were just standing there in their boat waving at me. They were out of the blind, not even trying to pick up their decoys, but stuck in the mud.

"Shuler, you're going to have to pry your way over to this channel." He held up a paddle, a broken paddle and pleaded

"Drugar, we tried but our paddle broke."

"Don't you have an oar?"

"No, just this paddle."

"Then it looks like you're going to be sitting there until mid-night. The tide will be back up then."

"Come on Drugar, help us. I've got a date tonight in Apalachicola."

"Not tonight you don't."

"Please Drugar! Throw us a rope and drag us out of here."

"Shuler, I know I've got a good arm, but even I can't throw a rope 60 yards."

"What are we going to do Drugar?"

"The tide will be back up around mid-night, you can run out of there then."

"Come on Drugar, throw us an oar."

"Shuler, I can't throw an oar 60 yards either. And even if I could you couldn't catch it."

"Come on Drugar, can't you help us?"

"I can get someone to call your date and tell them not to expect you."

"Come on Drugar, I'd help you."

"Like you did our first game? You hit me in the back three straight plays."

"Come on Drugar, you got me back for that."

"Well, maybe I did." I sat there for a moment trying to figure out a way to get him my oar. Then it hit me. "Okay Shuler, I'm going to try to get you my oar." I pulled out my rod and reel and the small tackle box. I didn't have any heave weights but I tied two smaller weights together and then tied them to the end of my line. "Shuler, I'm going to cast my line over your boat. Once you get it I'll tie my end to the oat and you can pull it to you." And that's what I did. I cast over his boat, then cut my line from my rod, and tied it to my oar in a fashion that it would not pull loose. When the oar was tied and ready I called to Shuler, "Okay, now you can't snatch this line. It's only 12 pound test and if you snatch it it'll break. So stand on the bow of your boat, raise your arms as high as you can so the oar's handle will stay out of the mud, and pull slowly."

I eased the oar into the soup with the handle aimed at Shuler, keeping the handle out of the mud. As Shuler started pulling slowly I fed the rest of the oar out toward him, the paddle end lying flat against the surface. It took a little time but Shuler got the oar to him. He let out a yell and started thanking me. "Don't get too excited Shuler, you've still got to pry your way out of there. Kick up your motor and place the oar against the back of the stern and pull." It didn't take him but a few tries to figure out the process. He headed toward me, a foot or two at a time. By the time he was within a few yards of the channel I decided I'd head on to the house boat.

"Shuler, are you planning on hunting here in the morning?"

"Hell no! I'm not ever going to hunt over here again."

"I tell you what, I'll pick up your decoys tomorrow when the tide gets up, and Sunday afternoon around five o'clock you bring me my oar and I'll give you your decoys."

"Where do you live Drugar?"

"At the corner of 12th street and Ave C. One story house, half brick, lapboard siding the rest, painted green."

"I'll see you Sunday at five, and Drugar, thanks."

It was only a little after dark when I got to the houseboat. Elzie had a fire going plus I could smell something cooking on the stove. He was happy, beer in hand, even agreed to hunt with me on Saturday morning. We hunted in the Pocket and used Shuler's decoys. We killed four teal, picked up Shuler's decoys, and laughed our way back to the house boat. By 1:30 that afternoon we were back at Owl Creek. Tess was happy to see me, and I acted like I had good sense, I didn't even mention the conversation from the past weekend.

For Saturday night Elzie prepared duck poppers, plus duck breast smothered with onions, with gravy, over toast, and Cloud made a remarkable salad that contained lots of greens, tomatoes, peppers, and shrimp. The sauce for the salad was by far the best salad dressing I'd ever had. She would not tell me what was in it. I bribed Tess with the charge of finding out the ingredients. Sunday was the 25th of January, the year was already passing so rapidly I couldn't keep up. It seemed that Christmas was just a week or so ago, but that was several duck hunts ago.

School was going well, my grades were good, and I was already beginning to look forward to Spring. Before heading home I told Tess that next weekend was the last weekend of duck season, I asked if she would like to join me, she declined, said that it was too cold, and she thought Elzie needed to hunt with me the last weekend. I was in great hopes that the last weekend would be really special, Elzie and I had had several really good hunts, it had been a wonderful season, lots had happened to me, and the houseboat seemed more like home to me that my actual home.

During the week I checked in with Elzie and told him I expected to be at the houseboat Friday afternoon late just like the past weekend, he said he'd be ready. I called Tess and told her I'd be there Saturday evening. Everything was set, or so I thought. Thursday afternoon during the last class, I was at the library, someone delivered a note to me from Dad, he said to drop by his office after school. When I got there he told me that a recruiter from the University of Florida would be at the gym after school on Friday, he represented the football and baseball teams for recruiting, he would be meeting with Coach Waller, and Coach requested I be there. There goes my afternoon duck hunt. That evening I called Elzie and Tess, told them what happened, but told Elzie I'd be over early Saturday morning and would meet him at the houseboat. I told Tess I'd be to Owl Creek late on Saturday.

Friday's afternoon meeting with the recruiter didn't start until almost five o'clock, he met with some other guys earlier, but my meeting was pushed to the last one. It went well, he asked about my grades, what position I played in baseball, and asked if I intended to go to college. Of course I told him I did, and hoped to go to UF. He said he'd set up a meeting with the baseball coach for late spring and suggested I come watch a game in Gainesville. I told him that would be great. It was past six o'clock by the time I got home, I didn't even have time to get my boat ready for an early start tomorrow. I called Elzie and told him I'd be after daylight getting there. He said he understood, we'd make a plan after I met him at the houseboat. The next morning I put my stuff in the boat, took Dad's car to the filling station and filled one of my gas cans that had gotten low, and Dad launched me and my boat around eight o'clock.

The morning was calm and cool, the river and bay looked like glass, as I idled out of the boat basin I noticed that the tide was high so I decided to jump the flat across the river on the south end of Little Towhead Island. The flat wasn't very wide, once beyond that I could parallel the bridge to the small hump, then cut under the bridge and from there it was a straight shot to the mouth of East River. It was a short run to East River, I was running almost wide open the whole way. From the mouth of East River it's only a few miles up to the houseboat. Elzie's boat was tied up to the stern of the houseboat next to the back porch, his usual spot. As I got close I idled back and eased up to a cleat next to the door into the front porch. I tied my boat, then went inside the porch and looked to see if Elzie was out by the fire pit, he wasn't so I went inside.

Elzie was slumped over on the couch. I thought he was asleep but that wasn't normal for Elzie. I spoke his name loud enough that he would hear me if he was asleep, no response, so I reached over and shook him lightly and again spoke his name, he moaned just a bit but hardly moved. I shook him harder and spoke his name louder, he moved his head some but didn't lift his head. I got scared in a hurry, I shook him again and raised my voice even louder, he finally responded and lifted his head. His look shook me, his face was flushed, his eyes red and watery, he was having trouble breathing. I got in his face and spoke his name again, he tried to focus on me, but acted like he couldn't see me. Finally he recognized me and tried to speak, he was weak, but he did say something I could hear, "Matt, get me to a doctor." Then he slumped over again. My mind was racing like crazy, I had to get him in my boat, but I'd better call someone, I had only one choice. I ran into his bedroom, turned on the short wave radio, picked up the receiver and start yelling,

"Cloud! Cloud! Pick up Cloud! Cloud are you there? Cloud please pick up. Cloud, Cloud, Cloud." Finally I heard her voice, "Matthew, is that you?"

"Yes Cloud, it's me, I'm at the houseboat, Elzie's real sick, I've got to get him to a doctor. Call my Dad and tell him to meet me at the boat basin in 20 minutes, tell him to have an ambulance there."

"Ok, I'll call him right now and I'll be on my way there."

"Cloud, bring Tess, I'm going to need her help."

"Will do." And I turned the radio off and ran to Elzie.

The adrenaline had me pumped, I reached down and grabbed Elzie and pulled him in to an upright position, put my arm under his and around to his back, all the while telling him he had to get up. He started coming around but was weak and hardly awake. I literally drug him outside and sat him down on the walk way next to my boat. I jumped into my boat, pulled the stern up close to the houseboat and reached for Elzie, he was about to slump over again. I yelled at him to wake up, you have to get in my boat. I pulled him to me knowing that I probably had to break his fall into my boat, and fall he did, right on top of me. I rolled him off me, he laid flat on my floor boards, I grabbed a life jacket and forced in under his head, untied my boat, cranked it, then pegged the throttle. I thought my boat was fast, if I could have had 30 or 40 more horse power I'd have pegged it too. Back down East River, wide open, out the channel at the mouth, to the bridge, under the hump, and to Apalachicola. As I passed Little Towhead Island I made a slight curve out, then back into the entrance of the basin. You're supposed to idle in the boat basin, I ran wide open until I had to make the right turn toward the ramps.

As I rounded the curve I could see Dad on the left launching dock, he was waving, an ambulance was sitting on the ramp close to him. The concrete ramps are a single slab that runs almost the length of the width of the basin, but on each end there is about 12 to 15 feet unpaved before the bulk heads start, I directed my bow to the grassy part on my left hand side. Dad saw what I was doing and came running. One of the medics grabbed a stretcher and followed, the other medic jumped behind the wheel, made a swing to the right, then backed the ambulance back toward the spot I was headed. As my bow hit the grassy area I accelerated, pushing most of my boat up onto the grass. As I cut the power Dad and the medic were already in my boat and rolling Elzie onto the stretcher, it took just a few seconds and they had him loaded into the ambulance. They headed out Bay Avenue, at 12th street they would turn right, run past our house on the next block, and be at the hospital within a minute, the hospital is only 7 blocks from Bay Avenue.

We watched the ambulance speed away, when they were almost out of sight Dad turned to me and said, "It's a good thing you were there, you did a fine job son."

"What do you think could be the matter Dad?"

"I don't know but it sounds a lot like he might have had a heart attack."

"Do you think he'll be ok?"

"I don't know son, but doctors can do a lot these days. It will depend on how much damage is done if it's the heart."

"Cloud is on the way."

"I know, I told her we'd wait here at the basin for her."

"Dad, I asked her to bring Tess, I will need some help. I left the houseboat opened, didn't even close the door. I've got to go back and secure the houseboat, I'm going to take Elzie's boats back to Owl Creek, Tess can drive my boat. I will call you when we get there and then I can either come home with my boat or if we need to do something for Elzie or Cloud I'll work from there."

"That sounds good son, Cloud and Tess will be here shortly, if the police don't stop her for speeding. As soon as she's here I'll go to the hospital with her."

We stood there, not saying much more, just hoping Elzie was okay, and waiting on Cloud and Tess. I thought about Walter and asked Dad if someone could contact him. Dad said he had already called Mr. Siglio and asked him to contact Walter by radio. He would let me know more when I called him from Owl Creek. I had been there less than 10 minutes when Cloud came flying off the bridge and turned toward the boat basin. I was ready to run for cover when she slammed on breaks in front of us. She and Tess jumped out of the car, asked where Elzie was, and what had happened. Dad said he'd fill her in on everything when they got to the hospital. Dad told Cloud to follow him to the hospital, and off they went, leaving me and Tess standing there watching the two cars speed away down Bay Avenue.

When they were out of sight Tess turned to me and asked what happened. I gave her all the details, then told her we had to go back to the houseboat and secure it. "We need to take Elzie's boats back to Owl Creek, I need you to drive my boat." That's all that was said until we reached the houseboat. I tied up again to the cleat nearest the door to the front porch. We immediately went to work, I first checked on the generator, it was too heavy for Tess and me to move it into the houseboat, but Elzie had it chained and locked on the pad he built for it, so I pulled out the canvas cover for it and tied it down tight to weather-proof it. Tess was inside taking refrigerated things and placing them in an ice chest. I decided I should take Elzie's guns back to Cloud's so I went into the bedroom to drag out the gun box from under the bed.

I'd been running on adrenaline since I found Elzie, my mind racing like the wind, but when I walked into Elzie's bedroom it all came tumbling down. A knot filled my throat, my eyes turned to tears, my strength poured out of me like water from a pitcher. I sat on the edge of the bed, I could not hold back my tears, I could not hold back crying. I sobbed like a child! Tess heard me and appeared like an angel, she immediately jumped on the bed, snuggled up behind me and held me. She kept whispering "It'll be okay, it'll be okay." It took me a long time before I could even speak, I finally quit sobbing, but I couldn't stop the tears. My throat cleared of the knot and I said to Tess, "What if he dies?" She just kept telling me that everything would be okay, but I kept saying what if he dies? She kept whispering,

"It'll be okay." When I could finally sit up, I turned to Tess and said,

"No Tess, it won't! Elzie is the glue that binds us all together!" And then the tears flooded my face again. Tess took me in her arms again and kept whispering that it would be okay, to have faith, Elzie was strong, it'll be okay. At some point I must have collapsed, my mind shut down, Tess evidently put a pillow under my head. It was past 11 AM when I woke, Tess was cleaning the kitchen, I felt ashamed, humiliated from crying like a child, I hated to face her, but she didn't give me much choice. As I sat up she appeared, it looked like she had been crying also.

"Are you feeling alright?" She asked. I shrugged my shoulders and nodded. She sat down beside me, took my hand, and said again that everything would be all right. I only nodded. She wrapped her arms around me, said she loved me, then said that it was a good thing that I was there for Elzie. My eyes were burning but I wasn't crying, I knew I had to get up and moving, we still had lots to do, but I needed to say something so Tess would know how much I cared about her, and how much I appreciated her.

I cleared my throat and said, "It's a good thing you're going to become a doctor, Elzie and I will need your help for a long time." She giggled, then gave me a long hug, then said she had boxes that needed to be put in Elzie's big boat.

We got back to work. I pulled out the gun box, removed the guns and put them in the big boat. We cleaned as best we could, closed all the windows and pulled the curtains tight. I shuttled Elzie's small boat around from behind the houseboat to the river and tied the bowline to the stern of the big boat, I figured I could tow the little boat at a pretty good speed if I had enough bowline. There wasn't enough on the little boat, but Elzie had extra lines in his big boat, so I tied the two together and that gave me plenty for towing. Once we had everything packed in the big boat we made a final inspection to make sure we didn't overlook anything, then I locked up the main rooms, and hid the key in Elzie's special spot. Elzie had a plaque over the door that read, "If this boat's a-rockin, don't come a-knockin", and on the back side he had a hole with a sliding cover, that's where the key went.

Tess got in my boat, cranked the engine, and then I untied the bowline and pushed her out toward the middle of the river, she put the motor in gear and eased away from the houseboat to wait on me. I untied Elzie's big boat, cranked it and moved into the river, slowly feeding the towline out for the little boat. I slowly brought the big boat to plane, the small boat followed without any problem, Tess followed behind. As we approached East River Cut-off I slowed down and pulled the smaller boat closer, I knew that with the sharp curves I needed to go slower but also have the smaller boat close enough to control how it towed around the curves. We made it through the Cut-off without any problems, brought the boats back to plane and we headed to Owl Creek. Tess did a great job handling my boat. At Owl Creek we slowed to an idle, I brought up the smaller boat close to the big boat, and we idled all the way to the landing.

We secured the boats, unloaded all the gear, and stashed it on Cloud's screen porch until she could tell us where to put everything. Cold stuff went into the refrigerator. I then called Dad to find out what was happening. Mom answered the phone, told me to hold for Dad, he said the hospital stabilized Elzie, then sent him on to Tallahassee Memorial by ambulance. He said Cloud should be at her house very soon, he said she would be going to Tallahassee this afternoon and possibly staying overnight. He said he was waiting on Walter and they would be going to Tallahassee later today. He told me to stay here until he gets more information which would probably be tomorrow. I asked that he keep me informed and let me know if there was anything I could do. He said he would and hung up.

Cloud drove into the yard 15 minutes later. Tess and I went to meet her, Cloud's face looked pale, she had been crying, but she moved like she was on a mission. She said she had to get a few things together and that she would be going to Tallahassee and spending the night. Tess asked if she wanted her to go with her, Cloud smiled and said no, but she appreciated her offering. Cloud told us both to stay here, stay close to the phone, and she would keep us informed as she founded out information. She also asked Tess to go get Alida. Tess went, leaving me and Cloud alone, Cloud turned to me and said, "Thank goodness you were there, if not Elzie would be gone by now." I asked if he would be alright, she said no one could be sure right now, it was his heart, but he would get good care in Tallahassee.

Alida walked in and Cloud turned her attention to her. "Alida, I've got to go to Tallahassee, I'll be staying overnight, I'll call you as I find out any information. Matthew will be staying here, please take care of him. I may have to stay longer than a day or two so you might have to call the school for me, but we'll make that decision tomorrow." Alida said for her not to worry about anything here, she would take care of anything and everything. Cloud went to pack, 15 minutes later she drove out of the yard, headed to Tallahassee Memorial to be with Elzie.

A cloud of worry formed over Owl Creek, the family came together, each helping the other, all evening and into the next day someone would be checking on me, asking if I had heard from Cloud yet. Tess stayed with me constantly. Alida brought me food for each meal so I could stay at Cloud's by the phone. Mama Sol came over and stayed for a couple of hours with me, she didn't say much, but her presence made me feel better, as if she possessed healing power. Cloud called about ten o'clock that night, she said that the doctors told her that Elzie had what they called a garden variety type heart attack, there was some damage but with lots of rest and medication he should recover. They said he probably won't be running as hard as he used to, but he should live many years, if he follows the rules and does as he's instructed. Cloud then laughed and said based on what the doctors said about following the rules she'd give him a week. At least he was out of danger for now, Cloud's humor put us all at ease.

Tess stayed with me until 11:30, I walked her home. When I returned to the back porch I just wasn't tired, I'd been wired all day, it hadn't worn off so I dropped down on one of the chaise lounges and leaned back to think. The last couple of months had been great, the best Christmas ever, the best duck hunts and the big buck, I felt so proud and blessed to have such friends and family that made it all possible. The thought of Elzie not making it scared me to death. What would it all mean without him? It's like I told Tess, he's the glue that binds us all together. Without the glue we drift apart. He just can't die, at least not anytime soon, we'll all die in time, but his time needs to be way out in the future. What would happen to Cloud? Elzie is part of Cloud, Cloud part of Elzie. In spite of all of Cloud's teachings, the connection to life and after life, the thread of love that ties us together, the thought of Elzie dying chilled me to my bones. There is so much more he needs to teach me, more fish to catch together, more ducks to shoot, more stories to tell, and more festive cooking events to share. He just can't die! He just can't die! He just can't die! Several hours later I woke, I was cold, the sadness hung on me like a wet shirt, I made my way back to my bedroom and passed out on my bed.

Chapter 19: Ashwanna

Tess woke me the next morning, it was already past eight, I still had my clothes on from the night before. She told me to get up and take a shower, it would make me feel better and she would be back shortly with my breakfast. She was already setting my plate when I appeared in the kitchen, she handed me a cup of coffee, with tupelo honey, and directed me to eat. She sounded more like a mom than a girlfriend. As I sipped my coffee and started on the eggs she said that Cloud had called her Mom, she said that Dad and Walter would be coming back through Owl Creek just after lunch, they said for me to have my bags packed. I asked about Elzie, she said he's still stable. Cloud is staying with him.

After breakfast I started going through the gear we piled on Cloud's back porch, trying to figure out what items should go out in the barn, which items should stay inside, after just a few minutes of frustration Tess said that I should stop and let her and Cloud deal with it when she got back and things normalized. I felt I should at least do something and told Tess that. She suggested I take a walk with her. "But shouldn't we stay by the phone? What if something happens?" Tess took me by the hand and led me outside, once there she said that there was nothing we could do if something happens, Cloud was there, and I needed to relax. We walked to the high ridge, then on to the bench, there we sat and stared at the creek, not saying anything. After a while Tess said that when I get home, tonight, she wanted me to visualize us together, there at the creek, feeling loved and then share that love with all of the family. Then she said, while looking directly into my eyes "Then send love and strength to Elzie and Cloud, make them as one, together in strength." I really didn't think I could do that, I usually had a hard time visualizing, but I promised her I'd try.

Dad and Walter arrived just after lunch. I put my bag in Dad's car while he went to visit with Alida. When he returned Walter said that he wanted to take a ride down the river and he'd like to go with me in my boat. Dad said he would pick me up at the boat basin. I thanked Alida for taking care of me, then kissed Tess goodbye then Walter and I headed to my boat. Dad left in the car.

The ride home was sad but still a beautiful afternoon, the river was slick, the swamps gray, the sky was clear. We saw no one the whole trip home. Walter's boat was tied up at Mr. Siglio's dock, I idled to his boat, he stepped into his boat, turned and told me not to worry, Elzie was strong, he'd be okay. I told him I hoped so. He said he would check in with me during the week and waved goodbye, Dad was waiting at the boat basin. Mom had supper waiting on us, no one even spoke during supper, I don't even remember what we had. I called Tess before going to bed, she just said to be strong. As I lay in bed that night I tried to pray, all that came out of me was "Great Spirit"! Nothing more, I tried to visualize Tess and me at the ridge overlooking the creek. I saw nothing. The next morning Mom woke me and said, it's time to go back to school.

It was February 2nd, it felt like it had been an eternity since last Friday afternoon. I went to school, I attended classes, I don't remember anything about school. All I could think of was Elzie lying up in bed in the hospital in Tallahassee with tubes running in and around him, Cloud helping him to be strong, to focus on strength, to rest, to believe. I called Tess every evening to check on Elzie, to see if Cloud had called, to make sure she was still okay, and each evening when I got Tess on the phone I could hardly talk. I kept choking up, tears filling my eyes, she felt my pain and did most of the talking. By Thursday I had decided that I wanted to go to the hospital to see Elzie, I asked Dad if I could have the car for the weekend, I wanted to go get Tess and we wanted to go see Elzie. He said I could go. I called Tess and told her I'd be at Owl Creek Friday evening and I wanted the two of us to go visit Elzie, she thought that was a good idea.

I left Apalachicola at four o'clock Friday afternoon, met Tess just getting home from school at 4:45, she had Sage with her. While Sage went to play in her room we sat on the porch and talked. She had almost no news, Cloud said she would call if there was news, if not she was just going to stay with Elzie. Tess told me that Alida had called the Bristol High School and reported that there was a severe illness in the family and Cloud had to take emergency leave. Alida arrived home around 5:30, we sat around and talked but she really didn't have any additional news other than what Tess had told me. As she went to start supper around six the phone rang, it was Cloud. Alida talked to her first, told Cloud I was there, so after Alida and Cloud talked a bit she handed me the phone. Cloud sounded tired, but she didn't sound down, her spirits were strong, she said that Elzie was doing better, "He's beginning to complain, so I know he's getting better." I told her that Tess and I would be over there in the morning. She said Elzie was in room number 314, and that I should tell the receptionist that we were family.

Tess and I stayed on Cloud's back porch well into the night, she promised she would get me up early and we would get an early start for Tallahassee. It was 9:30 when we walked into Elzie's room, Cloud was leaned over in a chair, dozing off. Elzie was wide awake, he took one look at me and waved me to him. I moved over to him, trying not to wake Cloud, and leaned over, he whispered in my ear, "They won't let me have any beer in here! You've got to get me out of this place!" I stepped back and looked him in the eyes, he had that almost smile on his face, but he was still bloated, his eyes weren't clear, and he had an IV in his left arm.

I had to respond in kind, "Maybe I can slip you some in here before I leave." He smiled, and grabbed my hand and squeezed it.

"It's good to see you Matt." I didn't know what to say, but I needed to say something, he had to know how I felt,

"I'm here and I'll stay here as long as you need me."

"Well hell son, you can't do that, you have to get back to school, and I imagine I'll need you for 20 or 25 more years."

That was good enough for me, I smiled back at him, then said, "Well, I need you to get better, there's not a pond or creek anywhere around here we could fly fish in."

Cloud heard us getting louder, got up and hugged me, then Tess. Tess came over and gave Elzie a hug, told him we had missed him, then Elzie asked her if I had been behaving myself. She replied, "About as much as you do!" Our life's order was restored, smiles replaced the stress lines, our combined strength began to grow. We spent most of the day there with Elzie, the doctors came by a few times, even tried to run us off once, but Elzie wouldn't have any of it, he made it completely clear that if we left, he was leaving too. Doctors don't smile much, but that doctor did when Elzie said he was going to leave with us. As he left the room he smiled at us and asked that we not try to slip Elzie out, Cloud assured him that Elzie wasn't going anywhere.

Tess and I left late that afternoon, headed back to Owl Creek, our attitudes were greatly improved. Back at Owl Creek everyone came by to ask how Elzie was doing, Tess entertained them with the stories from the hospital, I went back over to Cloud's and called Dad, he was happy to hear of Elzie's spunk, "Sounds like he's in recovery mode!" I asked that he call Mr. Siglio and inform him and ask him to call Walter, he said he'd take care of it. I told him I would be home before dark tomorrow. Later that evening I asked Tess if she would like to go with me to check on the houseboat tomorrow morning, she said that would be a great idea.

Sunday morning early we were headed down river in Elzie's big boat. When we walked into the houseboat the first thing Tess said was, "It smells like Elzie!" I had never noticed before, but it did, almost like the swamp. I made an attempt to check on all the equipment, but Tess suggested we take advantage of the timing and shortly we were holding each other, wrapped up in our love. It was late in the afternoon when we got back to Owl Creek, we decided that we needed to check on the houseboat every weekend. I headed home shortly afterwards, feeling positive that Elzie was recovering, happy that despair had been fought back, praying that tomorrow would even be better. At home Mom and Dad had me give them updates on Elzie, and they told me how proud they were of me. I didn't tell them about the trip to the houseboat.

  The next week was a repeat of the week before, we went to see Elzie again. His color was greatly improved, his attitude improving, Cloud had decided to go home on Sunday and back to work on Monday. Elzie promised he'd behave without us there, and we promised we'd be back the next weekend. Sunday morning early Tess and I returned to the houseboat. At some point I told her I thought we should move into the houseboat, just the two of us, we could live off the land. She thought that was a good idea but she didn't think that the University of Florida would move their College of Medicine to East River. I made the argument that I could appeal to them to do so based on the quality of their future student. She told me I'd better stick to baseball. But she did think that we should come to the houseboat as often as we could.

  We were back at Owl Creek when Cloud arrived. She looked real tired, but she was smiling. We all gathered on Cloud's back porch, including Alida and Sage, and listened to her report on Elzie. She said that the doctor told her again that what Elzie needed most was to rest and take his medicine. He also said that his diet had to change, at that Cloud said it might be easier just to shoot him, there was no way he was going on a diet. She didn't even mention beer, so I didn't either. We made plans to go back to Tallahassee the next Saturday, February 21st, but on Thursday night, the 19th, Cloud called me to say that the doctors had just called her and said that they were discharging Elzie on Saturday morning. She was to pick him up at 8:30 that morning, he was confined to the house for some time, but he would be home. I asked if it would be alright for me to be there for the weekend, she said I'd better be there!

  When I got to Cloud's on Friday afternoon late she was preparing to go to Tallahassee, she decided to go spend the night with Elzie so she would be there to talk to the doctors when they made their final rounds. She said she expected to be home by nine-thirty or ten o'clock on Saturday morning. On Saturday morning when they drove into the yard we were all on Cloud's back porch, Alida and Tess had balloons and ribbons tacked all over the porch, a big welcome home sign strung across the door. Elzie was moving pretty slow, but he had a big smile on his face, and Cloud had a good grip on his arm. All the neighborhood was there, they all made a big fuss over Elzie. He stretched out on one of the chaise lounges and reveled in all the attention he was getting. Cloud put up with the festivities for almost an hour then she ran everybody out and said Elzie had to rest.

  Tess and I were headed out the door when Elzie called us to him. He was still smiling but had a request, "Will the two of you take my boat and run down to East River and check on my houseboat? Check the gas, you may need to get some before you go." Tess and I said we'd be glad to do that for him. We didn't mention that we had checked it the last two weekends. We went and filled the gas cans, then headed to East River. The run was wonderful, Tess standing next to me, Elzie doing much better, I felt hope returning and the shroud of worry that had covered me since I had found Elzie slumped over finally felt like it was lifting.

  We spent a little over an hour at the houseboat, then Tess decided we needed to take the bedcovers and sheets and she would wash and dry them during the week. We could bring them back next weekend. I figured Elzie would be pleased; they wouldn't smell like the swamp. While Tess stripped the bed I sat in the living area just smiling, feeling happy as I could ever imagine. I was sorta daydreaming, not paying too much attention to anything, just waiting on Tess, when I noticed the picture of Walter, Elzie, and their sister. It was always there, I just didn't pay much attention to it, but when I did I kept getting the feeling that the sister looked so familiar. I told that to Tess, she said it was because she looked, or at least Walter and Elzie looked, a lot alike. I guess she was right, but the first time I saw her on the Island I got the same feeling, now I was getting it again. Maybe the last couple of months had me thinking in strange ways. I put it out of my head, we locked up the houseboat and headed home. Elzie was surprised to see us bringing in the sheets and bedcovers, but Tess told him she needed to fresh them up or he wouldn't be able to stand sleeping there, then she accused him of not washing them on purpose to ward off visitors. That got him to smiling, he winked at me, then said women take all the fun out of "river rat living."

    Cloud sent me over to visit with Tess in the evening. She said she didn't want Elzie up and talking a lot, he needed rest. I agreed and went to help Tess and Alida. It was almost 11 when I slipped back in and went to bed. Sunday morning I had coffee with Cloud. She seemed happy, but still very concerned, she told me that it was really important for Elzie to rest a lot. She was afraid that he'd want to take off down river or something like that and put himself in a bad situation. I assured her that as long as I was around I wouldn't let him do so, she only smiled at that. Later in the morning Tess and I went for a walk, we didn't talk much, just held hands, and smiled at each other a lot. I headed home before four in the afternoon. Elzie told me to tell my Dad that he was okay. I told him I already had.

    Driving home I realized that there were only six days left in February, Elzie had been in the hospital for just over three weeks, hunting season was over, but March was the beginning of baseball season, that raised my spirits somewhat. I started thinking about how much my life had changed, not just from last year, but even from just the last three months. Hunting was in my blood, I loved every minute of it, and from hunting I had experienced and realized that there was so much more I had to learn, to understand, to help me on my journey.

    Journey! That's what this had become, a growing, a desire for something I didn't even understand, but I wanted to get to that place where I was confident, and understood what was actually happening to me. The visions I had did not scare me, but I couldn't figure out what they meant. Why did I have them, why me instead of someone like Cloud? I wanted all this to start making sense. I couldn't talk about any of this with anyone except Tess, and Cloud to some extent; I surely couldn't talk about my experiences with the guys in my class at school, they would laugh me out of school, and lord only knows what names they would give me. No, best I keep this part of my life to me. But I also realized that I had grown apart from my friends at school, the things that they enjoyed doing didn't mean much to me any longer, I wasn't interested in chasing other girls, I surely wasn't going to slip off and drink with some of them, and with the exception of playing sports I really didn't have much in common with them anymore.

    The thought of pulling another joke like we did last year on the judge would never get my attention now. Even just showing up at the Canteen didn't interest me unless Tess was with me. Even if we had the option to go there together, neither of us would get excited about doing so. School, for me, was changing, for the first time in my life learning was important, not just making good grades, but learning. Learning became preparation, I was going somewhere, my journey, and the learning would prepare me for that journey. This all made sense to me, but what that destination was remained a mystery.

    I decided that the next time I had a chance to visit with Cloud we should discuss this mystery; maybe she could give me clues, or direction. As I pulled into our driveway at home I decided that I think too much. Certainly it couldn't be good for me. Instead of Cloud, maybe it was Elzie I needed to talk to, he didn't appear to let life interfere with his desires. I didn't bring any of these thoughts up during supper with Mom and Dad. I figured they were concerned enough already with my being gone so much, throwing life's journey at them during supper would probably be too much. Before going to sleep that night I prayed to the Great Spirit to help me find my way, to understand this journey, to comprehend the visions, to be strong during my quest. I requested Ashwanna!

The last week of February was cold and wet, the kind of cold that hurts you down to your bones. I remember walking to school with ice on the ground for two days. I needed my cold weather hunting clothes to handle that cold, but pride over-rode warmth, so I bundled up best I could with school clothes and suffered. But the cold is not what I remember the most about the last week of February 1959. It was when the dreams began. The first dream I remember was Monday night, February 23rd, Yellow Bird was in it. She kept trying to get me to come to Columbus. She kept telling me that it was there, what I was looking for, it was there. I woke during the night sweating like I was playing in a football game, totally confused about what had happened.

When I finally got back to sleep Yellow Bird appeared again. She kept telling me to come stay with her, I'd find it there. I kept asking what was there? She just kept telling me to come to Columbus, I'd find it there. The next morning before going to school I called Tess and told her about my dreams, she was as confused as I was, but she said she'd talk to Cloud about it when they got home and she'd call me that night. Tuesday evening Tess called, said she had talked to Cloud. Cloud said that often times stress brings on dreams, don't worry about them, just listen when you have a dream, often there would be clues.

Tuesday night Yellow Bird appeared in my dreams again, this time she said only one thing, "The car wasn't broken." That's it. She repeated it three times. That's all I remembered the next morning. I didn't call Tess again that morning. Wednesday night was different, Yellow Bird wasn't in the dream, instead there were three, sometimes four, Indian men sitting on a river bank, some fishing, some just looking and listening. That's all, just men fishing. That certainly didn't make any sense, so I figured it had no meaning.

Thursday night the Indian men appeared again, fishing along the river bank, except this time there was a sheriff there asking them questions. I could not hear what the sheriff said in my dream, I don't even know why I thought he was asking them questions but I knew in my dream he was asking them questions. It was all really confusing. I decided I should talk to Cloud about it. Friday afternoon Dad let me use his car again to go to Owl Creek to see Elzie and stay until Sunday. Elzie was looking better but he was still very weak, he sat on the porch with me for an hour or so when I got there, then went back to bed.

After supper Cloud joined Tess and me on the back porch. I told Cloud that I was experiencing some strange things through dreams and I couldn't make any sense out of them. She first started by asking me if I usually dreamed a lot. I told her not much, but occasionally I would wake in the morning and remember some dream from the night before. She wanted to know how these dreams were different. I had to think about that for a few minutes, but finally began, "In dreams I've had before I never got the feeling that my dream was trying to tell me something, it was just a dream about an event or something funny. I'd forget it within minutes. These dreams this week woke me up at night, they were so real, and in each dream I felt like the dream was trying to tell me something. It was very strange. I told Tess about the first dream with Yellow Bird in it, she kept saying 'Come to Columbus, you'll find it here.' The second dream Yellow Bird was in it again, but this time all she said was 'The car wasn't broken.' That's all she said. The third night in my dream there were three and sometimes four Indian men fishing along a river bank, some fishing, others just looking and listening. Last night the Indian men were fishing again except this time there was a sheriff there asking them questions. Now I couldn't hear the sheriff but when I woke I knew that he was asking the Indians questions. None of this makes any sense to me. I feel like I'm going nuts, if I keep this up I might not want to go to sleep at night."

Cloud had listened to me intently, she didn't immediately respond. After a bit she said, "Matthew, I've told you this before but you do have a special gift. The visions will give you clues just as dreams will give you clues. Don't let them bother you, they will not hurt you. You just have to relax and listen or observe. In time they will make more sense. I believe in time you will find your answers. Maybe in time you will need to go to Columbus, that trip helped you with your report, maybe there's another story. Only time will tell. Just enjoy the ride."

"Cloud, it's hard to enjoy the ride when you think you're going nuts."

"I'll assure you, you're not going nuts, but I do believe you've been chosen for something special."

"Like what?"

"I don't know, but in time you will. And when you do, I only ask that you share it with me." Tess moved over next to me and put her arms around me, Cloud smiled, then excused herself saying she needed to check on Elzie.

Once she was gone Tess turned to me and said, "I told you, you are special!"

"Yeah, a special nut job!"

"You stop that, it's true, you are special and together we'll figure this out. And, if we have to go to Columbus again, we know the way." I put my arm around her, pulled her close to me and said,

"I wish we could go to the houseboat right now!"

"Me too!"

Saturday morning Tess said she had the bed clothes washed and dried. When Elzie was up and moving around a little I asked if Tess and I could use his boat again to check on the houseboat and take the bedclothes back. He said of course we could, that he appreciated us checking on it for him. He also said that I needed to run the generator every week, that letting it set up was the worst thing we could do to it. I promised I'd run it for a while today.

We were getting our things together to make the run to East River when Cloud asked me if I dreamed last night? I told her I didn't remember if I did dream. She said that I probably didn't. I could only think, thank goodness.

The weather had warmed quite a bid by Saturday morning, but we still needed coats, the wind was calm, and the river was as beautiful as ever. I told Tess on the way that within the next couple of weeks the spring leaves would appear and the swamps would turn from gray to exquisite green. We both agreed we were ready for that. At the houseboat I got the generator running and Tess went to make up the bed, I was just headed into the houseboat when Tess appeared on the front screened porch. "I have a question," I stopped to listen, "should we wait to make up the bed until after?" I didn't reply, I just followed her back inside.

Before heading back to Owl Creek I ran the refrigerator some, we checked the gas for the stove, ran it enough to heat the living area, then shut everything off again, then tied the cover for the generator down tight. We laughed at Elzie's sign when locking up and hiding the key, I told Tess we needed a sign that said "this boat's a-rockin'!" The next morning was March 1st, spring would be blooming soon, baseball practice starts within a couple of weeks. I had coffee on the porch with Elzie, we talked baseball, spring fishing, and the tupelo bloom. He made me promise I'd take him to Bristol when the honey was ready and buy some from one of his friends. He also promised to come to some of my games this spring. Before heading home Cloud sat with me and Tess for a little while. She reaffirmed to me that my dreams had meaning, listen to them, don't rush anything. I told her I was in hopes they would just quit! She smiled at me and said "What's the fun in that?"

"It's not your head the dreams are screwing with!" At that she told me to be careful going home. When she got up to go check on Elzie she patted me on the head again. I told Tess that she makes me feel like a dog. Tess just barked at me. I headed home shortly after that.

Basketball season was coming to an end, I hadn't seen a game all season. Some of the guys who played said they were ready for baseball season. Spring baseball, the smell of fresh cut grass, good ole red clay on your hands, it was about here. School had become routine. Billy and Wayne got in trouble almost every week, I think they actually enjoyed it! The teachers weren't pushing too hard, and the anticipation of spring was escalating. The official start of baseball practice was Monday,

March 16th. Seven of us decided we'd start getting in shape and taking batting practice on Monday, March 9th.

I planned to go back to Owl Creek on Friday afternoon. I think Dad had decided I would only live with them during the week. Thursday night I received a call from Tess, she said that Cloud told her to tell me that Walter and Mr. Siglio were coming up to see Elzie on Saturday. As soon as I hung up the phone I told Dad the plan and asked him to join them. He said he would see. Cloud and I drove into her yard within seconds of each other on Friday afternoon. She acted excited to see me, however, she didn't pat me on the head. We gathered on the back porch immediately. Elzie was in good spirits, but he said he had been having some minor angina pain and Cloud had set him another appointment to see his heart doctor for Tuesday the coming week. Cloud put on some coffee while Elzie had me give him all the news, the only news I had was that Walter and Mr. Siglio were coming to see him on Saturday, and hopefully Dad. He got excited about that, and was telling me how he wanted to make a run to the houseboat with me when Cloud walked in. "You aren't going anywhere until the doctor tells you that you can!"

He winked at me and said, "She loves me!"

"Yes, but love requires co-operation, and if I don't get some co-operation you're not going to get love!"

Elzie's eye brows both shot up, he looked at me again, then winked, "I think she's serious!"

A short time later Cloud sent Elzie back to bed. Tess arrived home a few minutes later and joined Cloud and me on the porch. She had barely sat down when Cloud turns to me and asked if I had any dreams this past week. I told her only one, she wanted to know what it was. "I dreamed Yellow Bird was sitting in her rocking chair on her back porch, waiting on me!"

"Did she speak to you?" I shook my head no. "How do you know she was waiting on you?"

"I don't know, but when I woke up and realized I had dreamed about her I knew she was waiting on me." Cloud's expression changed, like she was amused. I decided this was a good time to talk, I had Tess there if I needed help, so I began, "Cloud, I've been wanting to ask you some things, about my dreams, my visions." She looked straight at me and said

"Yes?"

"I realize that lots of people have dreams, but I've never heard of people having visions. Why am I having these visions and you're not?" She sat back, I felt she was trying to organize her thoughts before answering me,

"Matthew, what's the difference between a dream and a vision?"

Now how am I supposed to know that? I thought for a few seconds, then said, "Your eyes are opened with a vision!"

"You are exactly right! And that one item makes you special, most everyone dreams, it's all in our mind, visions in dreams. But when you dream with your eyes open, it's a vision. Few people can do that."

"But why me? Why aren't you having these? It seems to me that you having these visions would mean so much more than me having them."

"Why do some ball players play better than others?"

"Because they have more ability."

"That's what you have, more ability!"

"But Cloud, you are so connected to whatever it is out there! You understand feelings, life, death, history, future, everything. I'm just a kid that plays football and baseball."

"No young man, you are not! You've been blessed with a great gift, you don't need to depress it, you need to embellish it. It will grow if you do, it will give you insight, guidance, faith, and love and joy. Don't depress your gift."

I really knew before I opened my mouth and started this discussion I should not have asked those questions, I knew she would do this to me. Every time I need her help, helping me understand what was going on with me, she challenged me, almost daring me to jump in further. I figured either I was nuts for listening to her, or she was nuts for suggesting I plunge ahead. I turned to Tess, almost begging her to take me somewhere, she understood the look in my eyes, and she said, "Matt, don't doubt, listen to Cloud, there's so much more out there. I will be there with you and for you. Just let it happen." Lots of help she was!

I decided I needed to take a walk. I got up and said I needed to walk some, I asked Tess if she wanted to go, she said she needed to take some things to her house but she would join me in a little bit. I walked out the door, the sun was still up, though evening was coming on fast. Where should I go? Where would Elzie go? I headed to the fire pit. It didn't take me long before I had a good fire going, the evening was beginning to chill a bit, the fire felt good. I sat there staring at the fire, allowing all of my frustrations to go up with the smoke. Before Tess showed up I was already feeling better, I knew that Elzie's teachings were paying off.

Tess pulled up a chair close to me, then reached over and held my hand, smiled at me, told me not to worry, no one could push me in any direction I didn't want to go. "How in the hell do I know where I want to go regarding these things? I know I want to play baseball and football. I don't want to have visions of old Indians hiding things in the swamp. I don't want Yellow Bird or any other Indian waiting on me for god only knows what. I just want to be a normal guy doing normal things!"

"What about your feelings, your knowing, when the buck was there? Do you want to give that up?"

"Of course not! That was one of the greatest moments in my life."

"Why is that so different from visions? Or dreams? Understanding the dreams without anyone talking?"

"Because those aren't normal!"

"Okay, what's normal?" She did it to me, just like Cloud, made me talk myself into my own corner. I puffed up like an old tom cat and stared into the fire. She let me pout for a few minutes, then reached over and kissed me and told me she loved me. We were quiet for a while, then Tess said that she would be right back, Cloud was preparing some ribs for me to cook. I needed to clean off the grill.

Elzie and I were on the back porch the next morning having coffee, it wasn't quite nine o'clock, when Walter and Mr. Siglio drove into the yard, as the two got out of the car the back door opened and out stepped Dad, the king's court had arrived. Cloud heard the commotion, took one look, then went to put on more coffee. Elzie's face lit up like the light house! The men sat around, telling stories, laughing at each other, making fun of Elzie, and harassing him for not having cooked something for their arrival. Elzie looked them straight in the eyes and said, "I was going to but Cloud wouldn't let me!" They laughed so hard tears were in their eyes. I sat there watching, knowing that I was fortunate to be a part of this friendship, this family. Inside they were all worried about Elzie, but they sure weren't going to show it in front of him. Elzie really was the glue that bound us to each other. We stayed on the porch for more than an hour talking and laughing, finally Cloud came out and insisted that Elzie rest some. The others told him they would be around for a while, and as soon as Elzie was off to bed, they turned to me and said they wanted to take a ride to the houseboat. I was the captain!

I ran over and told Tess the plans had changed, I was made captain and had to take the men to the houseboat for a visit, she said she understood and she was glad I was going to do it. The weather was still a little cool so we bundled up and headed down river. We saw no one on the river, the gray swamps didn't hinder our spirits, the sky was clear, the river calm, and we skimmed along the surface of our river leading us into spring. At the houseboat we opened the windows to air out the rooms, I fired up the generator as instructed, we ran the refrigerator, and lit the stove. We were all acting busy until Walter said that Elzie should be here, it was almost time for lunch. Everyone got a laugh out of that, but I checked the cabinet and found some pork-n-beans and sardines, asked if that would do, and of course they all said yes, so we had a river lunch, but no beer to wash it down.

    We stayed for a couple of hours, then headed back to Owl Creek. Back at the house they bragged on Elzie for teaching me how to prepare excellent river lunches. Elzie said he wished he'd been there. It was almost dark when they left, Elzie was happy for the visit, I was really happy Dad had come, and after they left Elzie and I stayed on the porch alone, he told me that he'd be ready in a few weeks, and we'd better take that same trip for the two of us. I agreed!

    I headed home around lunch on Sunday, I had coffee with Elzie that morning and told him that some of us on the baseball team were starting practice on Monday, I think he was as excited about it as I was. I told him I'd be back on Friday, then went to see Tess before leaving. She was busy helping Alida so I didn't stay long, I told her I'd see her Friday, she walked me to my car and kissed me goodbye, as I was getting in the car she leaned in close to me and whispered, "I missed our trip to the houseboat today, but I'm really glad you got to take the men. Matt, just know that I love you, I believe in you, and you need to trust, not just me but yourself. Remember, it's only the beginning." As I pulled out of the yard I had that knowing feeling, it was all good, and I felt loved.

    Monday, sixth period, I went to see Coach, he gave me two large bags of baseballs and a dozen bats, that afternoon after school I began breaking in my new glove, and I wore a blister on my hand from swinging the bat. Spring baseball was here, it was time to hit, run, and holler! Six of us worked out each afternoon, we warmed up our arms, then threw batting practice to each other in the cages, and ended up running bases instead of sprints. We all wanted to be ready for next week when baseball practiced officially. At supper one night that week Dad told me that Coach had ordered all new bats, and new base bags. Beginning of baseball season, it's a lot like waiting on Christmas.

    Friday afternoon Dad let me take the car to Owl Creek, I wanted to spend some time with Elzie, he had gone to the doctor this past week and I wanted an update. He was sitting on the back porch when I arrived, Cloud wasn't even home yet. As soon as I walked in the door he wanted to know if I started practice, I told him "un-officially", then sat down to visit with him. Evidently Cloud had given him a haircut, his hair was really short, and he must have been sitting in the sun some because his face looked tanned. His almost smile was constant, and his attitude was really improving. He told me the doctor changed his medicines, but basically said that it was time for him to start some light exercises. I asked like what, he said some walking, maybe even working around the fire pit a bit, and, "You know, cooking up some of those low fat ribs and chickens and such!" Yep, he was on the rebound. We were in the middle of spring fishing when Cloud and Tess walked in, their smiles lit up the room, and they even said nice things about Elzie and me, we figured they must want something. They did, they insisted on a boat ride to the houseboat tomorrow, if the weather was good!

    We took off around ten o'clock, the weather was beautiful but still a little cool, Elzie was all smiles. At the mouth of the Brothers River Elzie had me idle back and requested we ease along close to the west bank. I asked what he was looking for, he said gold! That got the girls to giggling, I was beginning to think he was making fun of me, but I went along with it, but after forty or fifty yards along the bank Elzie told me to make note of this area, there were a series of channels coming out of the swamps, old pull boat roads that dated back to the timber days, he said that it made for really good fishing. He said that below each of the old road trails the river bottom had holes that held bass. I took note! After a couple of hundred yards he gave the go-ahead, and we went back to plane and to the houseboat.

Watching him walk onto the houseboat was like watching a kid at a circus, he was all smiles, he had to touch everything, but he wouldn't sit on the couch, he said the last time he did that he had a heart attack. Cloud told him the couch didn't have anything to do with his heart attack, but he insisted that she sit on the couch, he was taking a chair. He had me crank up the generator, turn on the refrigerator, light the stove, and after all that he suggested I go build a fire in the fire pit. Shortly we were sitting around the fire, listening to the birds, not saying much, just enjoying life. By 2:30 Cloud had me closing up the houseboat, made Elzie agree to go home, and we headed back to Owl Creek.

That evening Tess and I had supper with Alida and Sage, I went back to Cloud's just before eleven. She was sitting on the porch when I walked in, it startled me, I said, "I didn't expect you to be up!"

"I stayed up just to thank you, it was a great day, and we all really enjoyed it. Also, Elzie is doing much better. His doctor told him that he needed to start doing some light exercising. Today was a good start." That night as I lay in bed I thanked the Great Spirit for the glue!

Chapter 20: The Big Leaguer

The first week of official baseball practice was joyful! Unlike football, baseball practice is always a fun time. I've never walked onto a baseball diamond and thought about anything else but baseball. Taking ground balls, turning double plays, taking batting practice, it's all just fun. Even running bases is fun, much more fun than running wind sprints. The first week was good, we were already shaping up to be a good team this year, but the second week changed the perspective, as Coach presented us with a gift.

It was Monday afternoon, we had already warmed up and starting batting practice when a man walked onto the field and over to Coach. He had gray hair but he didn't look old. He appeared to be just under six feet tall, but had a thick chest, and arms you would expect on a football player. He was as light on his feet as any man I'd ever seen, and a presence that commanded attention. He had a big smile and a chew of tobacco packed in his right jaw. Coach blew his whistle and waved us all over to him. As we gathered he began, "Boys, I don't know how many of you know Jimmy Bloodworth, but Jimmy is a friend of mine. He grew up here in Apalachicola, he lives back here in Apalachicola now, but he's spent the last 22 years in professional baseball. He's played for the Washington Senators, Detroit Tigers, Pittsburgh Pirates, Cincinnati Reds, and the Philadelphia Phillies. I asked him to come take a look at you and possibly help us take our play to the next level."

I had that knowing in my gut, he was going to teach me some things. He didn't say much at first, just that he was glad to be back home, and that he had started right here on this field just like we were. He also said he hoped some of us would get the same breaks as he had, he said the big show was all it was made out to be. He said he wanted to watch us take batting practice, so he backed up and we went back to our regular routine. Every so often he would stop the pitcher and direct his attention to the batter, making suggestions about his stance, his stride, and any other thing he saw. We were still on the first batter when he called us all back to him again. As we gathered in front of him he asked Bud to get a bat, then asked me to step in front of him, then directed, "Bud, take your bat and put it out in front of you just like you were swinging, but stop your bat about three quarters way through your normal swing." Bud followed the instructions, once there, Mr. Bloodworth told me to hold Bud's bat out toward the end of the bat, I did as I was told, and then he told Bud to continue his swing with his wrist. I could hold Bud's bat without much resistance. He then showed us how to grip the bat, first putting your hands together, then twisting your hands to where you line up your middle knuckles on your fingers. It felt strange, but when he told Bud to again stretch his arms like a swing, and for me to hold his bat, it was a struggle to hold the bat, Bud had much more power with his knuckles lined up.

He went on to explain that golfers do the same thing, and once you get used to holding the bat in this fashion we would be able to tell the difference in the power we had when hitting. We all took our turns at the plate, then coach had us take infield. Mr. Bloodworth watched for a while, then asked Coach to give him a few minutes. He first started with Bud at first base, he showed him some footwork that would give him better balance, and stretch when needed. Then he worked with me and Bob Riley at second base, starting with how to position yourself if it's a forced out at second base, telling us how we position ourselves like a first baseman does. He showed us how to switch weight from one foot to the next, how to stretch like a first baseman does to receive the ball, and how to position ourselves to the bag in those conditions. He then turned his attention to me, "Drugar, when turning the double play, if a right hand hitter is at the plate, what's the first thing you do?"

"Cheat a little, move in closer to the infield and closer to the bag."

"That's exactly right, now show me how you and Riley turn a double play." We got close to the bag, he backed up then rolled the ball to Bob, I came across the bag, took the toss and acted like I was throwing to first. "OK, it's obvious that you two have been doing this before, but I want to show you a few tricks that will help you along." He then directed his attention to me first, he walked to the second baseman side of the bag, then drew a line in the dirt about three feet from the bag, running parallel to the bag. "Now, Drugar, with a right hand hitter you're going to cheat a little, in some, closer to the bag, but I want you to start practicing this, first by drawing the line, and then after you're comfortable with it, the line will be in your head. When the ball is hit your first move is to get to this line, as the ball is thrown, move to the bag based on where the ball is thrown. Let me show you." And he tossed the ball to Bob and told him to toss the ball to the first baseman's side of the bag, Bob did and he made the traditional pivot move to first base. He then had Bob toss the ball directly over the bag, this time he move directly to the bag, stepping over the bag with his right foot, dragging his left foot on top of the bag, planting his right foot and throwing to first base.

He went on to explain that a runner expects the second baseman to move down the line toward first when turning the double play and it's his intention to cut you down. If the play is fast and the runner is a ways off you turn the traditional pivot. However, if the play is slow and you're standing on the right hand side of the bag, the runner is coming after you, so when the ball is thrown you want to move across the bag, drag the left foot, planting the right foot, your weight is there, and it's your throwing strength.

Next, if the ball is thrown to the outside of the bag and you're already moving, you'll never make the play. But if you move to the ball thrown to the outside you do the same thing, you slide outside, drag your left foot to the edge of the outside bag, planting your right foot, your strength, and throw. All of these moves he did with such fluid motion it appeared effortless. He had Bob and I try this for several minutes, he made a few suggestions as we went through the motions, but said we had it, and to practice it every day.

He then turned his attention to Bob and went through the same procedure, except from the other side of the bag. He showed Bob how his line should line up with the bag, and how to make his pivot depending on where the ball is thrown to him. We went to practicing in slow motion while he went to work with Billy Smith at third base. We then went back to batting practice and he told us that any ball hit on the ground should be played as a double play.

"Anytime you are on the field during batting practice, make every ground ball a double play ball. Do this every day until its automatic. When I was in high school we'd practice turning double plays 15 to 20 times a day. When I was in the pros we'd turn double plays two or three hundred times a day. It's what makes a double play combination a great combination."

After batting practice we went through regular infield and outfield routines, first with the outfield throwing to different bases. Mr. Bloodworth worked with each of us on how to position ourselves for the throws and how to move for the tags. By the end of the day I felt I had learned more in a couple hours than I had in all my years of little league and high school. When I got home that evening I talked my Dad's ear off, he seemed pleased.

The next day Mr. Bloodworth showed up again, this time he gave us instructions on running bases and types of slides. He said we needed a sliding pit, and he and Coach would put one in within the next few days. "Boys," he began, "many games are won from knowing how to run the bases and how to slide. I promise you, by the end of this week you will have the knowledge and ability to win ball games with your base running and sliding." By Thursday that week we had a sliding pit and he personally ordered a pair of sliding pads for each of us. He taught us how to bounce slide, how to hook slide, and how to hook and roll slide when you need to slide away from the bag and hook your body back to reach the bag.

For base running he taught us that when stealing a base to always hold a couple of handfuls of dirt to keep from hurting our fingers when sliding, he also added that lots of flying dirt made it hard for an umpire to see, same was true for the player trying to put you out.

The one thing he told us I remembered, when trying to score from third when a slow hit ball is to the third baseman, the catcher will move to the front of the plate to protect it, always remember when the catcher moves to the front of the plate, move in on the grass from the baseline so the third baseman has to throw over you or around you, it gives you a better chance when sliding. It was a great week of practice, we all learned a lot, and each day we improved. I could feel the strength in my hitting just by changing how I held the bat, and one day while taking batting practice Mr. Bloodworth told me I had a good eye, I told him I used to hit a lot of rocks. He got to laughing and asked if I was the kid Walter worked with last summer. I admitted that I was, he said, "I was wondering what or who Walter was working with, Walter couldn't hit a cow in the ass with a baseball bat." I laughed with him, but then he admitted, "Son, I've hit a lot of rocks in my day too."

By the time I got to Owl Creek on Friday night I was wound tight. I entertained Elzie first, then Cloud and Tess for the whole evening. I think they probably had an overdose of me and baseball that evening. The next week was the last full week of March, the following week we would start games. Mr. Bloodworth came out a couple of times during that week, mostly just to see how we were progressing, but he did make a few corrections on player's hitting and some fielding. He asked if we had been practicing in the sliding pit, we all showed him our strawberries on our hips, even with the sliding pads, your body still pays a toll. He told us he'd be at most home games and wished us good luck.

I was back at Owl Creek for the weekend, Elzie asked more about baseball, I kept him occupied. We all seemed to be in a routine, for me it was school, baseball, Owl Creek, for Tess it was school and me. For Cloud it was school and Elzie, but Tess and I had the responsibility of walking Elzie every day. Of course I was only there during the weekends, but Tess went for a walk with Elzie every day. Things were rolling along good, at least until the dreams came back. The first week of April, which was only a partial week, I dreamed about Yellow Bird again, it was the same dream, her sitting on the back porch rocking and waiting on me. Every morning when waking up I got the same gut feeling, she was waiting on me, for what I had no idea.

Friday, April 3rd was our first ballgame, we were playing St. Joe, it was the fifth inning, and neither team had scored. Lefty had turned out to be a really good pitcher, he had a good fast ball, but he also threw a mean slider. I led off with a single to left field, moved to second on a pass ball, and then to third with a ball hit to St. Joe's second baseman. Billy Smith hit a slow roller to the third baseman, I broke for home. The catcher moved to the front of the plate, and Mr. Bloodworth's coaching took over. I moved onto the grass to block the throw from the third baseman. The catcher was reaching high for the ball as I slid to the inside of the plate, well out of line with the plate, but as I passed the catcher I rolled back to my right and drug my fingers over the edge of the plate. The umpire yelled safe, and the crowd cheered. The catcher turned toward the umpire as if to complain, and with the commotion Billy broke to second and made a perfect bounce slide, he was standing when the second baseman tagged him. Safe! We ended up winning that game 2-0, all because of base running and sliding. Good coaching pays off!

It was almost eight o'clock when I got to Owl Creek that evening, Elzie was waiting on my report, I entertained him with play by play, Cloud and Tess just smiled at me, at least Cloud didn't pat me on the head. The next morning I told Cloud about the dreams, she just said that it appears to her that I have something to do, and she said it would come to me in time.

April flew by, we played games every Tuesday and Friday, of the eight games we played that month we won seven of them. My hitting was solid, and I hit one homerun during the month; Bob and I continued to strengthen our double play combination, we had five double plays during the month. And people were beginning to talk about us! What player doesn't like having people say good things about them? Of course every weekend I went to Owl Creek, on Saturday the 18th I told Tess about the Junior-Senior Prom, our class had to put it on for the seniors, prom night would be Saturday, May 23rd. She seemed excited to go. It was hard to believe, we moved into the last month of the school year, soon Tess and I were going to be seniors, it was time I started thinking about college.

    I always knew that I needed to go to college, I always expected to go to college, and since Mom and Dad went to the University of Florida, I figured I'd go there too, but I also wanted to play college ball. If I could not make it at Florida, I wanted to play somewhere. It was the second week of May, I think it was the 12th, when I received a letter from Coach Blankenship, baseball coach at UF, he invited me to a game. UF was playing Florida State on Saturday, May 16th, at five pm in Tallahassee. He said he would have four tickets waiting on me at the gate, and for me to come introduce myself to him when I got there. It was four in the afternoon when Elzie, Cloud, Tess and I showed up at the gate, I really wanted to watch the teams take batting practice and infield. We found our seats behind the Gator dugout and during the batting practice I spotted Coach Blankenship talking to some reporters by the fence just outside the dugout. I told the others I'd be right back and went to introduce myself to Coach Blankenship, when he broke off the conversation with the reporters I called his name, he turned, and I walked up to him and introduced myself to him, "Coach Blankenship, my name's Matt Drugar, I appreciate you getting tickets for us to see the game."

    "Drugar? From Apalachicola?"

    "Yes sir."

    "I've heard a lot about you the last couple of years, what position do you play?"

    "Second base, sir."

    "How's your season coming this year?"

    "Good, we're 11 and 3."

    "How's your hitting?"

    "I'm hitting about 450 right now, with three homeruns."

    "Excellent! How are your grades?

    "I expect to finish the year with about a 3.4 gpa."

    "Good, y'all enjoy the game, and I'll follow up with you soon. We want you to come visit us in Gainesville. And good luck." I think I floated back to my seat, when I sat down Tess asked how did it go. I told her we were going to visit Gainesville sometime in the future. She giggled. The Gators won that game 4-2. It set me on fire, I was more convinced than ever that I wanted to play for the Gators.

    The next weekend was the Junior-Senior Prom, earlier in the month some of the moms in our class arranged for Austin's Clothing store, downtown, to measure all the guys for tuxedos, Mom picked up mine Friday afternoon while I was playing ball. I was to pick up Tess Saturday morning at Owl Creek, she was to stay with us Saturday night, and I would take her home on Sunday. Saturday morning Mom got me up early and told me to get Tess back to Apalachicola before 11, she had a hair appointment. She also instructed me to pick up Tess's corsage at the flower shop downtown. I didn't even know that Mom had called Tess a week before and got the color of her dress, and her preference for a wrist corsage or a regular corsage. Thank goodness for Moms, if it hadn't been for mine I'd probably shown up in blue jeans.

    As soon as we arrived back at our house Mom whisked Tess away to the hair dresser, that was something else I didn't know, Mom had asked Tess if she would like to have her hair professionally done, it would be Mom's treat, Tess said it was wonderful. I hadn't done much work on getting the Armory prepared for the Prom because of the baseball schedule, but the girls in the class did a great job, it was decorated in a Roman decor, all of the tables had flowers, and a professional band was hired for the music. Since 7th grade car washes, cake sales, and Seafood Festival booths, our class had accumulated $2500. I think we spend $2000 of it that night. The seniors never even said thank you! But we had fun. Tess wore a light blue evening gown with a wrist corsage. It was an orchid trimmed with rose buds, I don't know who picked it out, but it sure made Tess happy. She was more beautiful than I'd ever seen her, she smiled all evening. And we got lots of attention, I don't think it was because of me.

Our final ball game was Friday, May 29th, again it was for the Conference playoff, and again it was against Port St. Joe, and Shuler was their first baseman. We mouthed off at each other for most of the game, but in the 8th inning Shuler hit a single to right field, and we had a double play situation. Lefty was pitching to a right handed batter, he hit a shot to Bob Riley and when I came across the bag for my throw to first I didn't see Shuler in the baseline as I threw to first, he'd moved out of the baseline toward the outfield. As he trotted off the field he told me, "Drugar, I wasn't going to give you another shot at me, I'm going to play college ball and I wasn't going to let you interfere with that!" I told him good luck! We won that one 3-1. Including the playoff games we ended the season 15-3.

That evening I drove to Owl Creek, the whole way there I kept thinking about what happened this time last year. I didn't miss the canteen, and I surely didn't miss the judge. Five days later we began summer vacation. For the previous couple of weeks I'd been thinking about summer vacation, what had happened last year, my time on the Island with Walter, and the time up the river with Elzie. I had decided that I wanted to go back to stay with Walter for a little while, to help him with whatever he needed, and especially to run the turtle patrol. I had talked to Tess about it and she wanted to join me there, so I contacted Walter and Elzie, both thought it would be a good idea. Mom and Dad also agreed.

Friday night after the game I drove to Owl Creek, Tess and I made a plan, I was to finish school on Wednesday, June 3rd, I'd have Walter meet me at Mr. Siglio's at four o'clock, spend Wednesday, Thursday, and Friday with Walter, and then Saturday Tess, Cloud, and Elzie would join us on Little St. George for three or four days. I got excited, then I got Tess excited, we talked about watching a mama turtle lay her eggs, making the turtle run each morning, maybe visiting our big sand dune overlooking West Pass. I felt it was what I was supposed to do. And it worked out just that way, with one exception.

While I was there with Walter before the others showed up I kept looking at the picture of Walter and Elzie with their sister. I had often thought about the picture from the first time I saw it, but I had dismissed the feelings, after all she was their sister, her looks were similar to their looks, but on Sunday afternoon, June seventh, while Cloud and Tess had gone for a walk, I was sitting in the living room with Walter and Elzie, I kept looking at the picture, and I asked the two of them, "What was your sister's name?"

Walter looked at Elzie, then at me, and said, "Tess."

It didn't register at once, but then it hit me, "Tess? As in my Tess?"

"Yes, just like your Tess. Our sister was named Tess."

"When did she die?"

"In 1917."

My mind went blank, I don't even know why I asked those questions, but something inside me snapped, my mind started running, what was significant about 1917? I'd have to sleep on it.

Later that day I told Tess that Walter and Elzie's sister had been named Tess, it didn't seem to bother her, why was it bothering me? The next couple of days were golden, it wasn't too hot, the moon had been full, we hunted for turtle crawls each night, and on Tuesday night we found an old girl at about the same place as last year and we watched her dig her nest, lay her eggs, and Tess saw the turtle tears. She cried right along with the turtle, and we walked the old girl back to the gulf, patted her goodbye and promised we'd look after her babies.

Each morning we made the turtle run, looking for nests from the night before, staking those we found, later covering them with the heavy wire, staking them down to prevent the hogs from digging up the eggs. Each morning we made a stop on our high sand dune, and we played in the gulf waters before heading back to the house. Walter gave me lessons on throwing a short-brail castnet, and he fished alongside me, giving me instructions, and pointing out how to determine which way a mullet was moving based on the swirl he made at the surface. I caught enough mullet to feed us for a couple of nights, we put out the crab traps, and we grilled oysters over the open fire in the fire pit. The vacation was everything I had hoped it would be, I really didn't want to go home, I hadn't even hit any rocks or thrown the football at the swing, but Thursday morning we loaded up and left Little St. George Island and Walter. I think Walter was ready for a break anyway, being alone on the Island satisfied his need for solitude, the light house was his beacon.

I would be back soon, after all summer had just begun. I stayed home Thursday afternoon and all day on Friday and Friday night. I would go to Owl Creek on Saturday and spend the night. I didn't dream at all on the Island, but Thursday night the dreams returned, Yellow Bird was still waiting on me. Friday afternoon I joined Mom and Dad at the breakfast room table, they were having a serious discussion, so I didn't butt in, I just listened. Dad was telling Mom about some school administration problem, some of the employees weren't doing something right, it all seemed silly to me, grown people doing whatever Dad said they were doing, but what I did recognize was the look on Dad's face. I knew he was concerned but his eyes were tight, stress lines formed at the edges, and his intensity was striking. Mom was trying to console him, but he was fixated on one subject, determined to solve the problem. It made me feel uneasy so I left the table and returned to my room.

I flopped down on my bed and decided I'd try to visualize a calm place, maybe project a happy moment. I fell asleep, but strangely I knew I was asleep, and I began dreaming. I knew I was dreaming, and I realized that I was asleep, this was something I had not experienced before. All images became crystal clear, if I focused on something I could increase my visualization of it right down to its basic structure, as if I looked at a rock, then focused on it closer, I could see into its molecular structure. What surprised me was that this did not scare me, it was as if I was a spectator of my own dreams. I don't know how long I was out, but when I woke I remembered the dream, it just seemed really weird. I lay in bed for a while longer then went back in to talk to Mom and Dad.

Mom was beginning to work on supper, Dad was at the dining room table in the next room making notes about school stuff. I tried to start a conversation with Dad, but he told me he was real busy and needed to stay with his notes. I went back in to talk to Mom, I wanted to tell her about my dream, but she said she was busy and couldn't stop right then. So, I decided to take a walk down to Lafayette Park. It was getting later in the afternoon, the sun was soon to set, the colors stretched across the bay like a rainbow, St. George Island was a strip of gray ribbon separating the bay from the sky. I sat there for a while feeling a little lost, my dreams were really beginning to bother me. I felt I should understand them, certainly there was a meaning to some of them, but they were all so strange, and this last one where I could look into anything I stared at, what could that be? I decided that I would talk to Cloud about these dreams, but this time it wasn't going to be about some special gift I had, I needed to figure out how to assess them, and if she couldn't help me then I needed to talk to a doctor somewhere. Coming to that conclusion made me feel better, at least I had a plan to do something. By the time I got home Mom was putting supper on the table, guess what? It was Friday night, hamburgers and French fries. They were as good as always!

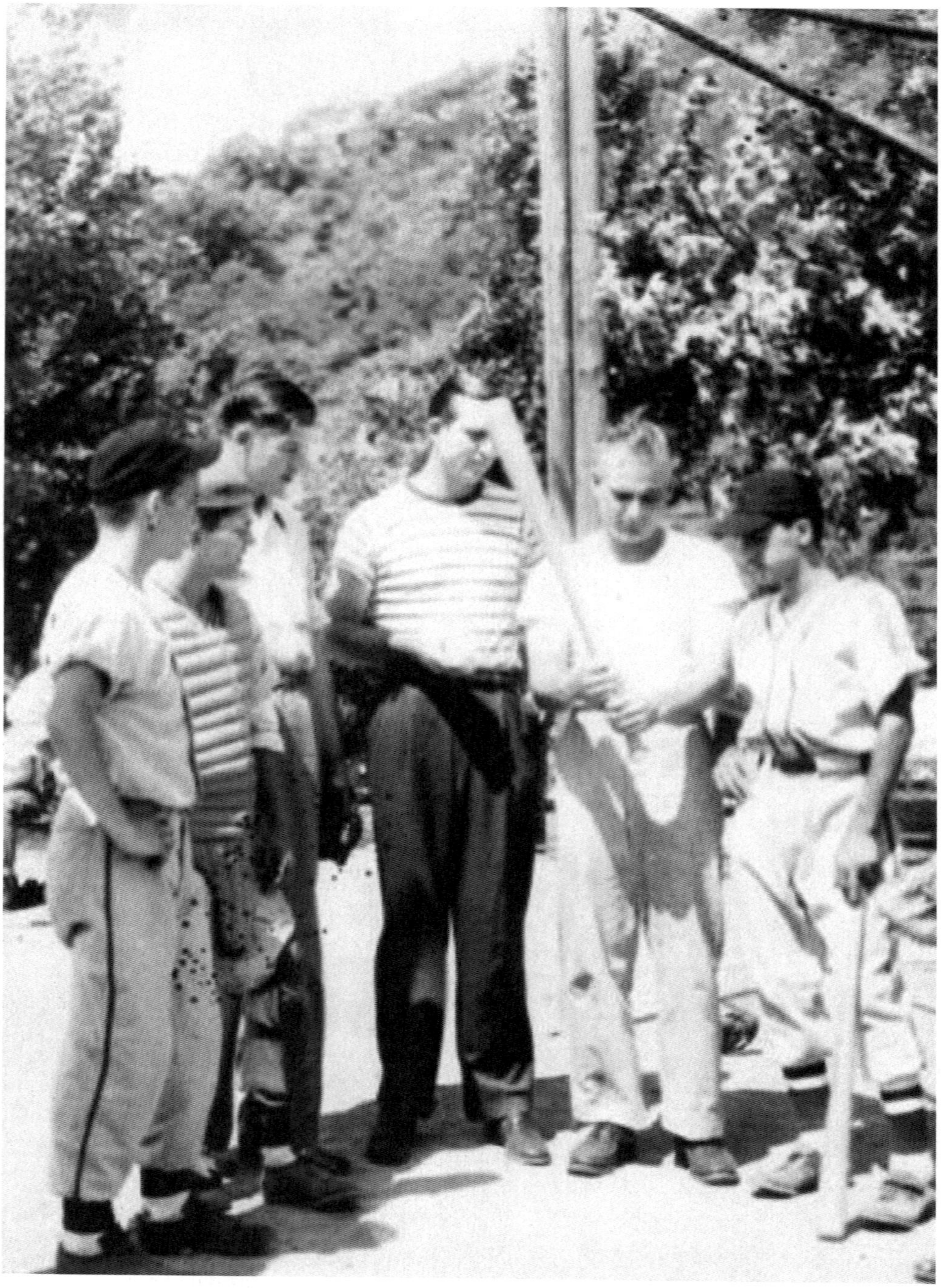

Chapter 21: Yellow Bird

Saturday morning I left Apalachicola before 8:30, by 9:30 I was having coffee with Elzie on Cloud's back porch. Around ten o'clock Tess came over, I had received my All Conference baseball a couple of days before, I presented it to Tess, she grinned with excitement. Elzie went to rest, and Cloud came to sit with us. When I felt the timing was right I started, "Cloud, I need your help! Now please let me explain, I'm not looking for encouragement, I need some serious guidance."

She looked sideways at me, sat up straight in her chair, and said, "OK, let's hear it."

"My dreams are back, Yellow Bird continues to appear, just rocking and waiting on me. I feel I understand that dream, but I can't figure out why she's waiting on me. But yesterday I took a little nap, and I dreamed. The strange thing is that I knew I was dreaming while I was asleep. I realized I was asleep, and I realized I was dreaming while asleep. Then each time I looked at something, if I concentrated on the object, it would begin to grow, well maybe not grow, but my focus allowed me to look into the object, like you would examine something with a microscope, and adjust the power making the smallest objects become bigger and bigger. I finally woke up, was totally confused about that dream, and I began to think I might need some professional help."

At that last statement Cloud sat back, I knew she was trying to decide how to approach me, "Matthew, I certainly don't have the ability to psychoanalyze anyone, but I don't think you need professional help. I think that your brain is trying to tell you something, trying to make you focus on something, to take you out of your comfort zone. If you knew you were dreaming, and if you knew you were asleep, then maybe you should approach your dreams like you would analyze a project. Try asking questions during your dreams, see if the dreams will offer answers."

"Like what kind of questions?"

"Well, start by asking why Yellow Bird is waiting on you. I think that's where I would start. She seems to be the most stable dream you're having." I decided that made sense, I'd try to engage my dreams. After a while I asked Cloud if she knew that Walter and Elzie's sister was named Tess? She said she did, but she didn't have anything else to say about it. I didn't have any dreams while at Owl Creek, at least I don't remember if I did.

Late Sunday afternoon I headed home, Summer baseball was to start first of the week, I wish I was more excited about it, but there was a lot going on in my head, maybe baseball would help me redirect.

Sunday night Yellow Bird appeared for another visit, but she was far away, I could see her but I couldn't engage her. The next morning I was awake long before Mom and Dad, I decided to research dreams to see if anything I read would make any sense, I pulled out Mom's encyclopedia and turned to dreams. After half an hour reading about types of dreams, what they mean, who can have them, are they in color, I finally read something about lucid dreams and how with lucid dreams you can solve problems. That sounded like something I wanted to do, I just had no idea, and the book didn't say, how to have lucid dreams. I was determined to concentrate on my dreams and try to have a lucid dream. The more I thought about it the more confused I became. I didn't even want to dream, now I was trying to dictate the type of dream I was having, and I didn't even understand what that type of dream would be. Maybe I should go to baseball practice very early today!

At breakfast Mom asked if something was wrong, I told her no, but shortly after that I asked Mom if she dreamed. She looked at me funny and asked if I had a bad dream, I told her no, but that I was dreaming a lot and some of them were upsetting. She said everybody has bad dreams occasionally, not to worry about them. Easy for her to say, she didn't have an Indian woman visiting her every night or so, and waiting on her!

I was at the baseball field an hour earlier than planned. I sat on the bleachers until some of the other guys showed up, once we started warming up everything was fine again, like I said before, I've never gone onto a baseball diamond and thought about anything else but baseball. Practice went well, we fell right back into our normal routines, and Coach said he was still working on scheduling games, we'd probably start games next week.

Monday night Yellow Bird came to see me again, this time she seemed closer, like I was standing near to her. She was rocking in her rocking chair, but she was staring right at me. I watched for a few minutes, then asked, "Why are you waiting on me?" She stopped rocking, looked me right in the eyes and said,

"To help you find the truth!" That threw me! I was talking to an Indian woman in my dreams!

"What truth?" She began rocking again, but slowly,

"The truth of who you are!"

"But I know who I am!"

"You think as a child, there's more!"

"How do I find the truth?"

"Come see me!" I woke up, I sat up in bed thinking that it must be getting daylight, it was three in the morning. I didn't want to go back to sleep, this was really getting too weird! I tossed and turned for more than an hour, but finally dozed off.

I woke again shortly, but went back to sleep. This time the picture of Walter, Elzie, and their sister appeared, I was standing in front of it, staring at the picture, I didn't know why, but I kept staring at the picture for a long time. Finally, I moved up very close to the picture and stared at the sister's image, her eyes were tight, stress lines appeared at the corner of her eyes, her intensity was striking. I kept staring at the picture, it was so familiar, those eyes, those eyes were what? I got closer, again I recognized the eyes, those eyes, and it hit, those are Dad's eyes. I backed away from the picture and the sister was there, I moved up closer and Dad's eyes appeared. I realized I was dreaming, but this was really strange, it scared me, I woke in a sweat, my heart was pounding, I wanted to call for Dad, but what would I tell him?

I got up and went to the bathroom, I washed my face, I paced back and forth in the bathroom, finally I went out and sat in the living room, I checked the clock, it was 4:30. I decided I needed a cup of coffee and went into the kitchen. When Dad got up at 6:00 I was sitting at the breakfast room table drinking my third cup of coffee. The coffee had me wired, Dad asked if everything was alright, I said I just couldn't sleep. He poured a cup for himself and joined me at the table, "Something bothering you, son?"

"No sir, just couldn't sleep, I've been dreaming a lot, makes it hard to rest well."

"Yea, I've had times like that myself. Don't worry, it'll pass." It didn't! For the next few days Yellow Bird came back, but we didn't talk anymore. The eyes appeared a few times as well.

I called Tess each day and told her about my dreams, by the third day she started acting like she was really getting concerned for me and at one point she asked what we needed to do about the dreams. I was very deliberate, I spoke very slowly, and I told her, "Tess, we've got to go back to Columbus, I've got to go see Yellow Bird."

There was no hesitation in her voice, very matter of fact she said, "When do we leave?" I told her I'd let her know shortly, I had to talk to Dad.

That afternoon, it was Thursday, I went to the school to see Dad, he was working on paper work, when I walked in he looked up, acted surprised and asked what was wrong. I told him that Cloud asked if I could take Tess to Columbus to do some things for her, she asked if I could go tomorrow, maybe stay with Ms. Robertson overnight and be back to Owl Creek on Saturday. Dad acted as if my request was a little strange, but he said if Cloud wanted us to do something, then he figured it was alright. I asked if I could go to Owl Creek this evening so we could get an early start tomorrow. He agreed. I went home and called Tess, I told her I'd be up there tonight and we would go to Columbus tomorrow morning early. She said she'd talk to Cloud and square things with her Mom.

I arrived at Cloud's at 7:30 that evening. Tess and I met with Cloud right after I got there, I explained that I needed to go and if Dad asked about the reason I requested that she tell him we were helping her. She agreed. Tess and I were about to go over to her house when Cloud asked me if she should call Yellow Bird and tell her we were coming to see her tomorrow, I looked her in the eyes and said, "No need, she knows I'm coming." Cloud understood.

Tess and I left Owl Creek the next morning, June 19th, at 6:30, we arrived at Yellow Bird's house at 10:30, which was 9:30 Columbus time, Yellow Bird answered the door almost immediately. "Welcome young Drugar, I've been expecting you."

"Yes Ma'am, I know!"

We followed her back to the back porch and took a seat, she faced me and asked, "Why did it take you so long?"

"It's new to me, I really didn't know what to do. But I'm here and I want to know."

Tess sat there watching me and Yellow Bird, she had no idea what we were talking about but she knew that I was where I was supposed to be. Yellow Bird said that I should begin with my Grandparents, I needed to go to the police department and research the accident report, they died on October 21, 1926. She gave me directions to the police department, Tess stayed with Yellow Bird, and 15 minutes later I walked into the Columbus Police Department.

The entrance was a small room, a door leading to the main office was directly in front of the door I entered, there was a short wall on the right hand side of the entrance door to the main office, a counter ran the entire length, with an opening to see into the main office. As I approached the counter a lady stood up from a desk and walked toward me, she appeared to be in her early 40s, heavy set with dark hair but a big smile, "Yes sir, what can I do for you?"

"My name is Matt Drugar, I am researching information on the death of my Grandparents, McDonald and Teresa Drugar, they were killed in an accident on October 21, 1926."
The lady's expression changed, but she acted like she wanted to help, she turned to another lady at another desk and asked her to assist me with the accident report.

She introduced the lady as Melanie, she appeared to be in her late 20s, had a big smile, and said, "Come on honey, I'll hep you find the report." I followed her down a hall, then into another room filled with filing cabinets, once there she asked, "Now honey, what date was that accident?"

"October 21, 1926." She shuffled through lots of files until she settled on one, then asked the name again, I said Drugar, and she pulled the file from the cabinet. She spread the file on a table and told me to have a seat. She scanned the file, then spread the official accident report in front of me, we read it together.

"My, my, a train wreck!" and she moved the file directly in front of me. I began reading. The report stated that the accident happened at 10:15 at night, the car the passengers were in was stopped on a train track, immediately past a bend in the track, two passengers. The train hit the car broadside, the train was not going fast since it was approaching the residential area of the city limits, but the car was crushed and thrown from the tracks. The passengers were DOA at the hospital. "I'm really sorry honey about your grandparents, that's just awful."

"Thanks, is this all there is?" She took the file, flipped through a couple of pages, then said,

"That's about it except for the train's conductor's statement." She passed the file to me again and pointed to the statement. It stated that the conductor said that the passengers had time to get out of their car before the train hit it. It also said that the conductor stated that he could see the passengers, they looked like they were asleep. The train lights were very bright, he blew the whistle several times, he didn't understand why they didn't move. He said he tried to stop the train, but he was towing too great a load to stop quickly.

There was also a statement from the hospital, it simply stated that the bodies were too mangled to assess any other possibilities except accident by train crash. I thanked the lady and she showed me out of the police station.

Back at Yellow Bird's I told her and Tess what the report had said. Neither had much to say, but Yellow Bird had something else on her mind, "How much do you know about your Grandfather, Matthew?"

"Very little, just what Dad has told me. He was only 9 when they were killed, so he said he didn't know much. He did tell me that his Dad was in the timber business and timbered the swamps."

"He was a powerful man, he had many workers, and had great influence in Columbus at that time."

"Where did he and my grandmother live?"

"They lived in a rental home, his work kept him moving every couple of years as the timber was thinned. To my knowledge they never bought a house here."

"What do you know about my grandmother?"

"I know very little, she was a handsome woman, but very private, she kept to herself."

"Yellow Bird, what should I do now?"

"I suggest you go to the hospital and check out your Dad's birth."

She gave me more directions, and 15 minutes later I walked into Muscogee County Memorial Hospital, I followed the same routine as with the Police Department, and shortly found myself with another young woman, Phillis, in the records department. I told her I wanted to see the birth records of my Dad, James Matthew Drugar, his date of birth was October 1, 1917. After a short search she produced the birth records, it showed the mother as Teresa M. Drugar, and the father as McDonald James Drugar. It did not show time of birth, and to Phyllis's surprise, it did not show the hospital stay or billing. "Now that doesn't make any sense, all records show hospital stays and billings. I wonder why not. Let's just check." And she started researching patients at the hospital for September 30 and October 1, 1917. "No, I don't see any records of Teresa M. Drugar having been in the hospital on either of those days. Matter of fact, for those days I only see one woman in the hospital for having a birth, and she died in child birth. That's strange."

I don't know why I asked, but I said, "What was her name?"

"Tess Ann Taylor." I felt my heart stop, my mind shut down, I couldn't move. It hit me like someone swinging a baseball bat at me. All those visions, the eyes, the strange connection I felt just looking at the picture, Walter and Elzie, and Dad. Why hadn't they told me?

"Sweetie, are you okay?" The records lady asked. I told her I was and thanked her for her time.

When I got back to Yellow Bird's Tess knew something was wrong by looking at my face. I followed her to the back porch and sat down close to Yellow Bird. Yellow Bird knew, and now she knew that I knew. I didn't know what to say, and I really didn't feel like talking. I kept wondering why someone had never told me, why hadn't Dad told me the truth? We sat in silence for a long time, Yellow Bird fixed some ice tea and we drank tea in silence, at some point Yellow Bird addressed Tess and asked if we were staying with her tonight, Tess looked to me, I shook my head no, and started getting ready to leave, it was only 2:30 in the afternoon, 3:30 Owl Creek time, we could be home early evening.

I was about to get up when Yellow Bird reached over and took my hand, "Matthew, you have strong medicine in you, Cloud says that you are and always will be a great warrior. But know this, you cannot appreciate your future unless you know where you came from. You come from good blood, be proud, and be honorable. Please come see me again." She stood up as I stood up, I reached over and gave her a hug, and told her I appreciated her. I then whispered in her ear, "When you need me call me in my dreams!" At that she smiled, reached up and patted my face, and said, "Ashwanna!"

Tess and I headed home to Owl Creek, we didn't talk at all until we were well out of town, I figured I would wait a bit before telling her what I found, but she started first, "Matt, Yellow Bird told me what you would find, but she also told me some things you would not find, she wants you to know the truth." I glanced over at her, she was as solemn as I'd ever seen her. "Your grandfather was, as Yellow Bird said, a very powerful man, and very persuasive. When he met Walter and Elzie's sister he became obsessed with her, he called on her, he gave her gifts, he pursued her constantly. He kept Walter and Elzie busy in the swamps, and anytime they weren't around, he chased after her. In time she succumbed to his desires, they had an affair that lasted only a couple of months, it ended when she became pregnant.

She didn't tell Walter or Elzie until she really started showing, and for a while she wouldn't say who the father was. It was only just before she was to deliver that she told them, she was suffering from sepsis. When she went into labor she was already in bad shape. When Walter and Elzie got to the hospital the doctor told them that she might not make it. They called Captain Mac. He and his wife wanted a child, she couldn't have any. The doctors were able to save the child, but not her. Walter and Elzie weren't in any position to raise a child, they stayed in the swamps cutting timber most of the time.

Captain Mac said that they would take the child, Walter and Elzie agreed. They knew the child needed a birthright! Yellow bird said that an illegitimate child born in Columbus at that time didn't stand much of a chance. Captain Mac convinced the hospital to show his wife as the mother and him as the father, it completely bypassed adoption. No one in Columbus cared, and the hospital recognized that it was best for the child." I drove along trying to wrap my head around this, not understanding why Walter and Elzie had never told me about this. Tess continued, "Your Dad doesn't know any of this!"

"What? Why not?"

"Because they didn't want him to know that he was illegitimate." That shut me up, my mind continued to race, after all these years why hadn't anyone told him? We had gone another few miles when Tess started again, "Matt, there's more!" Damn, how can there be more? I waited on her to begin, "Your grandparents didn't die from an accident!" I had felt that, but hearing it slammed my brain. My gut knotted up, my mouth became dry, I could hardly swallow. Tess continued, "Somehow Captain Mac heard the rumors about the gold, he became obsessed about the gold just like he had with Walter and Elzie's sister. He worked quite a few Indians cutting timber in the swamps, he convinced himself that they knew where the gold was buried, so every few weeks he'd pick out one or two Indians, buy them some liquor, and after they got to drinking he'd start asking them questions. When he couldn't get any answers he'd start beating them. He beat quite a few and the word got around to the other Indians, they decided he wasn't going to beat them. One night Captain Mac and his wife got a sitter for your Dad and they went to a play. After the play when they walked back to their car, a couple of Indians crept up behind them and cut their throats, shoved them into their car and drove it to the rail road tracks. You know what happened after that."

How I continued to drive is beyond me, but I did, in a daze, but I drove on. Sometime later Tess continued, "The next morning Walter and Elzie were contacted, they knew that the boy, your Dad, shouldn't have to deal with such an awful thing, they left Columbus with him within a few days. They moved to Apalachicola. They knew Captain Mac had a house there so they contacted a judge they knew in Marianna and with the help of an attorney that the judge knew they created a trust for your Dad, they were the Trustees.

For several years they took turns running the timber operation Captain Mac left behind, while the other one looked after your Dad. I guess you know the rest." I guess I did and it hurt. We drove on in silence for well over an hour. Finally Tess said something that changed my thought processes, "Matt, what came out of this is you, and now you have an extended family. And Matt, you are very much loved!" Tears welled up in my eyes, my mouth again went dry, and a knot filled my throat. I couldn't talk, so I drove on.

It was dark when we arrived at Owl Creek, Tess went to report in with her Mom, Cloud was waiting on me on the back porch, Elzie was in the bedroom. She knew the minute that she saw my face that I had not taken the news very well, she stood and came to me and hugged me. I broke down in tears, I couldn't speak. I felt embarrassed, but I could not control my tears, she left me briefly and went to get me a wet and dry towel. By the time Tess came back I had stopped my crying but I was still having a hard time speaking. We all sat there in silence until I could finally speak, I turned toward Cloud and said, "If you knew these things why didn't you tell me? Why did you send me up there?" I felt mad, I felt embarrassed, I felt betrayed, and for a brief period I felt alone!

"Because it was not my place!"

"But I trusted you!"

"And you still can!" Tess came over and sat down by me, took my hand, and squeezed it.

"Why didn't Walter or Elzie tell me?"

"Because it's not their place. They haven't even told your Dad."

"Why not?"

"That's something you have to talk to them about, but not now, Elzie doesn't need the drama, and neither do you."

I sat there staring out into the darkness, not being able to manage my thoughts, everything was hitting me at once. I couldn't look at Tess or Cloud for fear I might break down again, so I excused myself and went to the bathroom next to my bedroom up front. I washed my face a couple of times, then went into my room and flopped down on my bed. My eyes felt like they had sand in them, I closed them, and the next thing I remembered was waking up. Tess had come to check on me, she was already sitting on the side of my bed, embarrassment returned.

"Matt, Cloud made us some supper." I sat up, I was hungry, I hadn't eaten anything since six o'clock that morning. We joined Cloud on the back porch again, she had fixed me a couple of sandwiches and some chips, I washed them down with a coke. She told me that Elzie was tired and needed lots of rest, evidently he had tried to be too active and it caught up with him. Silence wrapped itself around us, we sat there not talking for what seemed like a long time, finally Cloud excused herself and went into the bedroom with Elzie, leaving me and Tess alone. Neither of us said anything for a long while, I didn't know what to say or do, I was even thinking about going home, but it seemed too late for that now. I decided to wait until tomorrow. Tess stayed a while longer then said she needed to go, I nodded, and she got up and walked home alone. I went back to bed. That night Yellow Bird returned, she was in her rocking chair, I was sitting in front of her in another rocking chair, she smiled at me and said that everything would be alright. Then she said it was not my place to judge, my place was to celebrate family. I would know when it was right to discuss these things with my family. I awoke the next morning feeling appreciative. My first act that morning was to apologize to Cloud and Tess, it was time I manned up!

Cloud didn't even let me finish when I tried to tell her that I was sorry, she said she loved me, that she knew, but I needed to go see Tess. Tess was on her back porch when I walked in, I went directly to her, I knelt down in front of her and asked that she forgive my stupidness, that she was the love of my life and I was very sorrow for my actions yesterday. She gave me a big smile and said, "You had your right, it was a tough day even for a great warrior!"

I stayed until after lunch, but I felt I should be home, I needed to spend some time with Dad. Cloud understood, and Tess understood. As I drove home, I hoped that I would understand. Mom and Dad were at the breakfast room table when I walked in, both were surprised to see me, Dad began, "What are you doing home, I thought you wouldn't be back to Owl Creek until late today?"

"We got it all done yesterday. We got back to Owl Creek last night around 7:30 or 8."

"Well, what brings you home today?"

"I just decided I wanted to be with y'all." At that both of their jaws dropped opened like a puppy after a bone!

"Are you alright son?"

"Dad, I couldn't be better!"

Mom then asked if she could fix me something to eat. I told her not now, but I sure would like to have hamburgers and fries for supper. She thought that was a good idea.

Later in the afternoon I called Tess, I told her that everything was alright, and that I loved her. She said she knew.

Chapter 22: The Ties that Bind Us

The next week we played a couple of ball games, I don't even remember who we played, I don't even remember if I got any hits or if we turned any double plays, but I do remember going back to Owl Creek on Friday evening and staying until Monday morning. While there Cloud, Tess, and I had some serious discussions, we decided that the next weekend, Fourth of July, Independence Day, would be a good time to make a trip to Little St. George Island. We decided to make it a single day, not stay overnight, just a visit with Walter.

I stayed home on Friday night with Mom and Dad, I told them that Elzie, Cloud, and Tess would be picking me up at Mr. Siglio's on Saturday morning and we were going to go to Little St. George just for the day, that Cloud thought Elzie needed a day in the sun and of course, a boat ride. Mom and Dad said it sounded like a fun day.

They picked me up at eight o'clock the next morning at Mr. Siglio's, Cloud had radioed Walter and told him we were coming just for the day. He said it would be good to see everyone. Walter was waiting on us when we arrived. Elzie had to give me instructions on how to secure the boat, like I hadn't learned from several past trips, and within minutes Walter had us sitting on the porch drinking ice tea. We visited for most of an hour and then Cloud and Tess said they wanted to walk down to the Light House, Walter offered to take them in the jeep but they declined, said they really wanted to walk.

They hadn't been gone long before I told Walter and Elzie I had something to discuss with them. They acted interested, like I had some plan to spend lots of time on the Island, fishing and chasing sea turtles and such, but I told them this was different. I began, "First I want both of you to know that this past year has been the best in my life, you have treated me like family, and I appreciate it." They seemed a little uneasy with my personal feelings, but I continued, "For the last few months I've been having some strange dreams, and I've been feeling like I was being lead to do something, but I had no idea what. Now I won't bother you with all of the details, but I wanted to know more about my grandparents, so a couple of weeks back Tess and I made a trip to Columbus. We met with Alice Robertson."

When I mentioned her name Elzie looked over at Walter and said, "Yellow Bird."

I continued, "I got to asking her questions but instead of answering them she sent me to the Sheriff's Office, and to the Hospital. What I found while there was that my grandmother was not the birth mother of my Dad." Their faces went pale, their looks changed from being interested to looking guilty. I continued, "It seems that we are related after all. At first I was hurt that no one had told me anything about this situation, but I later found out that my Dad doesn't know either. There are a couple of things that I've learned from this experience, one is that I should not judge anyone for actions I don't understand. And second, I've learned that family is the strongest bond there is. I'm here today to tell you that I think it's time we come together as family, and my Dad needs to know that he's not an orphan and never was, even though he lost the only mother and father he knew. My Dad loves you and he trusts you, after all, he did turn me over to you when he needed help, and I especially needed help. I want him to know how special and strong the ties that bind us are."

They both sat there, like little boys who've misbehaved, not wanting to look at me, not wanting to say anything, but finally Walter looked me straight in the eyes and said, "Matthew, we didn't have the heart to tell him he was illegitimate. We made sure he had a birthright! We did what we considered was the noble thing to do, we certainly didn't have the ability, especially at that time of our lives, to raise a child. Your grandfather and grandmother did. If we had to do it again, we'd do the same thing."

Elzie then spoke up, "Your Dad knows that we love him! We tried to make his life as good as we could."

"I know that, but I think it's time he knows the truth. It's time he knows we're all family."

They both stood up and hugged me. Tears filled my eyes, but their eyes got watery too. After a couple of minutes I asked Walter if I could borrow the jeep to go pick up the girls. He said of course. When I returned with the girls, they were on the porch drinking a beer. I guessed things were okay. The next few hours were full of fun, Walter pulled out a gumbo he had made the day before, so we feasted and laughed, and promised we'd be back soon to enjoy the Island.

Two weeks later on Saturday, July 18th, at ten a.m. I asked Dad if he would go with me for just a little bit, I had something I wanted to share with him. He agreed and we got in the car, I drove, and we headed downtown. I drove to Bay Avenue, turned left toward the boat basin, at the boat basin I turned right and followed the road around the curve, under the bridge and then up Water Street for a couple hundred yards. I pulled in to Mr. Siglio's fish house. "What are we doing here?" Dad asked.

"I want to introduce you to some folks." We got out and walked into the fish house.

"Paisan!" We were greeted. "Come, come, have a seat, I'll fix you some coffee!"

Walter and Elzie were sitting at the table with Mr. Siglio, they rose, shook Dad's hand, and while Mr. Siglio put on some coffee, I turned to Dad and said, "Dad, I'd like to introduce you to your uncles." Dad looked baffled,

"What are you talking about?"

Walter spoke up, "James, have a seat, we've got something to tell you!"

For the next two hours we laughed, we cried, we hugged, and we drank coffee! Mr. Siglio sat there with us, he actually cried more than we did. Every so often he would get up, go splash some water on his face, say "Mama Mia! Mama Mia!" then rejoin us. I don't know how many cups of coffee we drank, but it was a joyous occasion. When Dad and I got home that afternoon Mom asked if everything was okay?

Dad said, "It couldn't be better!"

We played baseball a couple more weeks, then took a week off before starting early football practice. I spent every weekend at Owl Creek, Elzie and I made a few trips to the houseboat, and of course, Tess and I made a few trips there alone.

My birthday was August 28th, it was a Friday, I went to Owl Creek, there was no party, no cake, and it was later in the evening before I even realized it was my birthday. Tess felt bad that she hadn't made me a cake, but I told her that being there with her was present enough. Anyway, at 17 who needs a birthday party?

Labor Day was Monday, September 7th, my senior year officially started Tuesday, September 8th, as we gathered out in front of the school before classes started we talked about football, we talked about being seniors, but we didn't talk about how I now had a larger family. Classes had become more important, I needed to concentrate more, I needed to prepare for next year when I start college. We had the same teachers, our class remained the same, and for two and a half months football was everything.

We didn't go undefeated that year, we lost one to Blountstown, they beat us 14 to 13; we missed an extra point. Their big time quarterback had gone on to play college football at FSU, but they did have two running backs that could scoot. We did a pretty good job on defense but we couldn't keep those two out of the end zone. I threw two touchdowns that game, but we missed an extra point, and ran out of time. Blountstown finished 8 and 2, we finished 9 and 1, and were conference champs.

That fall we had another dove hunt on Little St. George, I got to invite two friends and their fathers, Bud Carlson and his dad, and Rob Riley and his dad joined us, the hunt was as good as the year before, everyone had a great time. Elzie was there and again he waited with the jeep while Walter caught some mullet. At the end of the hunt the fathers allowed us boys to have a beer, with the promise we wouldn't tell our mothers.

In October Tess and I submitted our applications to the University of Florida, she continued to say she wanted to be a doctor, I continued to say I wanted to play baseball for the Gators. Thanksgiving was really special, Elzie joined me for opening day of duck season, and we actually spent the night at the houseboat. Elzie had gotten stronger, he was learning to pace himself, which meant that I had to pick up some slack. That didn't bother me! I also got to do some deer hunting. It was extra special because once again I got that feeling, the knowing that game was close, and a young buck stepped out in front of me, much like the one the year before, but he was young and I watched him for several minutes and let him walk off. That alone was enough to excite Elzie when I told him the story, he said, "Thank goodness, I don't think I could help you drag another one out like we did last year. And, there's always next year."

Christmas was sad this year, Mama Sol passed away the week before Christmas, she was 82. Tribe members from all over came to her funeral. I had never noticed, but back on the far corner of the Owl Creek property there were burial plots, Tess's dad was buried there, Mama Sol joined him. Her dying really affected my Dad, the day we buried her he wept. For years he would teach other children things that she had taught him, things that Cloud now teaches children.

Baseball season was our best ever, as seniors most of us had played together for at least six years, some even further back than that. We were strong, our skills were great for high school athletes, and we only lost one game that season, it was to Crawfordville. One of our pitchers was sick, Lefty was really off that day, and in the fourth inning Coach moved Lefty to left field and brought me on to pitch. I had a good arm and I often pitched batting practice, but that day, throwing as hard as I was able, the Crawfordville team hit me like I was throwing batting practice. Matter of fact one of their team members hit one so far that I think it still might be going. I didn't make it through that inning, after them scoring three runs, with no outs, and two men on base, I called Coach to the mound. He acted like I was crazy, but I begged him to bring Lefty back in, which he did, and he shut down their rally. They still beat us 5 to 1.

That Spring Tess and I got our acceptance letters to the University of Florida and in early March Coach Blankenship sent me a letter of invitation to attend a game in Gainesville. Mom and Dad took Tess and me there for a weekend. Aside from watching the Gators play, we got a tour of the campus, checked out dorms, and, based on encouragement from the administration and Coach Blankenship, we decided to begin college immediately after school was over. The administration and Coach Blankenship said it would give us time for the adjustment to college life before the craziness of fall. Coach Blankenship also said that he wanted me to play summer baseball with a team there in Gainesville, evidently there was a league similar to our summer league, but with more competition. He said it would help me make the leap to college ball.

Our senior prom was Saturday, May 21st, 1960, Tess came to Apalachicola for the weekend. As like the year before she was the most beautiful girl there, and I say that without prejudice. The junior class did a bang up job in decorating and providing a great band, they had an Aquatic theme, and before the night was over Tess and I cornered the junior class president and told him what a great job they had done and we appreciated it. Some senior classes have to have a little class! Tess's graduation was Thursday night, June third, I went to Bristol for the event and then back to Owl

Creek. My graduation was Friday night, June fourth, of course Tess was there and stayed with us overnight.

    The next morning while having breakfast Walter and Elzie drove into our yard in a Willis-Overland jeep wagon, it was dark green, three years old, but it only had ten thousand miles, and it looked like it just came off the show room floor. We heard them when they blew the horn, so we went out to see what the racket was. They handed me the keys and said I needed to take good care of it. I'm sure you can imagine my excitement! Mom and Dad didn't even know about this gift, but Dad agreed to keep it insured, and Walter and Elzie made me promise that Tess and I would come home often.

    They had a cup of coffee with Mom and Dad while Tess and I took the car for a spin. When we got back Mr. Siglio was there, it was like a party all over again. After a while Walter left with Mr. Siglio and I took Elzie and Tess back to Owl Creek. I returned home later that day, I had to pack on Sunday, and I left for Gainesville on Monday morning. Coach wanted me to come early, I had to take a physical, get checked into my door room, and meet the coaches from the local summer league team. I would return on Friday evening to pick up Tess and we would go back to Gainesville on Sunday morning.

    My trip to Gainesville took just under four hours, I met up with Coach Blankenship at the athletic department, he had one of his assistants take me to my dorm, he said that for the summer I'd have the room to myself, but in the fall I'd have a roommate. He showed me where I could have my meals, then we returned to Coach Blankenship's office. Coach told me not to eat any breakfast the next morning and report to his office at 8 am for my physical, he had a doctor waiting on me when I got there. They took some blood, schedule me for some ex-rays, checked my eyesight, hearing, and reflexes, then Coach took me to Gainesville High School to meet the summer league coach. He was young, but seemed well organized, and he said he was glad to have me aboard. He gave me a schedule for the games and said that we'd have practice the following week.

    Wednesday and Thursday Coach had me sign-up and scheduled my classes for the summer, meet the trainers at the field house, and he watched me hit some in the cages. Friday morning I headed to Owl Creek to get Tess. It was exciting, it was a new adventure, and it was one Tess and I would do together. Everyone was excited to see me, it felt like a party on Friday night when I got there, Elzie was actually at the fire pit cooking and within a few minutes Cloud had me delivering things to him. He seemed as excited as I was.

    Sunday morning got there in a hurry, we packed Tess's bags in my car, gave everyone a hug goodbye, and loaded up. There was a small envelope on the passenger's side seat, Tess picked it up and we drove out of the yard. As I turned onto the dirt road that leads to the highway Tess opened the envelope and read the note, it said "There's a little something in the glove box for you", it was not signed. Tess opened the glove box and retrieved two small white boxes, as I came to a stop at the highway, she opened the boxes and lifted out two gold chains with a gold object on each. My mind exploded, realizing what I was looking at I practically yelled, "Escudos! Pieces of eight, they're doubloons Tess! They're doubloons! It's all true! The legends, the gold, it's true!" She laughed, she giggled, and she reached over and hugged me. She hung hers around her neck, I leaned over and she hung mine around my neck, I tucked in under my shirt, it lay against my medicine bag. We sat there for a few minutes trying to comprehend what just happened, realizing that our life's journey had just opened a new chapter. With anticipation we pulled onto the high way and headed to the University of Florida.

EPILOGUE

It was Thanksgiving before I got a chance to go home for a visit, the summer ball games last right up until we began fall classes. Tess got to go home once during the summer, I let her take my jeep, but Wednesday before Thanksgiving I dropped her off at Owl Creek, and headed home.
It was past ten p.m. when I arrived home, Dad had my boat hooked up to his car, my camo and waders were packed, the boat was gassed up, and my shotgun and shells were ready. He told me that Elzie was waiting on me at the houseboat on East River. He launched me and my boat about eleven o'clock, I ran under the bridge, took crooked channel around to East Bay and headed to East River. The night was dark, the bay like glass, I had just gotten past Towhead Island, the lights of town were no longer affecting my eyesight, when I noticed the spray behind the boat. The phosphorus was in the water and the spray behind my boat looked like fire. The bay water was mirror-like and I could see all the stars being reflected in the water, it was like running between two heavens, leaving a string of fire behind me. Elzie was as happy to see me as I was him.

The next morning the tide was real low, we couldn't even make it to our blind, so we pulled the boat into the marsh on the little island outside East River Pocket, and took a couple of oyster crates and a dozen decoys and moved around toward the bay. There was a small pool of water surrounded by flats, but near the marsh, we stooled out there, sat on our crates and had one of the best shoots ever. It was truly a Thanksgiving treat. We only hunted that morning, by late afternoon he was ready to head back to Owl Creek, so I spent Thursday night and Friday there, going home early Saturday morning to spend with Mom and Dad.

Tess did in fact decide she wanted to be a doctor, and after graduation she began medical school at the University of Florida. I played four years of baseball at Florida, and was the Captain of the team my senior year. After graduation Coach Blankenship hired me as an assistant coach, and while Tess attended medical school, I tried to impart the tricks of the trade to the new recruits that arrived each year, telling them the stories about Jimmy Bloodworth and how you win games from base running and sliding. Tess was fortunate to be able to do her residency at Shand's Hospital there in Gainesville, she was there two years, I continued to coach.

From there we returned to Apalachicola, Tess set up her practice there, and I began writing my stories. And that house at the corner of 7th street and Avenue B that was sold so Dad could go to college, well as it turned out, it wasn't sold, only rented, and the Trustees, Walter and Elzie, deeded it to us when we returned home. We're expecting our first child soon, a boy, and we've decided to name him Walter Elzie Drugar, it only seemed fitting. Tess will teach him the Indian ways, I'll teach him the Island ways, and the knowing of the swamps. Certainly a part of him will always be a little River Rat, and a Salty Dog.

And to you, the reader, please allow me to thank you for sharing this story with you. And I'd like to tell you that if you've never stood on an island beach and looked as far east and as far west as you can see, and not see another human being, you should, it will change your life.
And if you've never experienced watching a sea turtle drag her heavy body from the surf and make her way to the base of a sand dune, dig her nest and lay her eggs, see her tears, and follow her back to the sea, you should, and it will change your life.
And if you are exceptionally lucky, you can watch baby sea turtles bubble up from the sand and make their dash to the gulf. You should, and this too will change your life.
If you have never made love to your true love high upon a sand dune, while the sea gulls cry, and the waves crash upon the sand, you should, and it will change your life. (Here I would suggest you use a bit more discretion than we did in 1958.)

If you have never tied your boat to a tree along the river bank, then eased into the swamps and let the environment engulf you, smell the sweetness that permeates the swamps, maybe sit on an Indian mound and share the knowing passed on from thousands of years, you should, and it will change your life.

We all travel our on roads, and as you travel yours on your life's journey, I bid you Ashwanna!